THE BINDING SAGA

ROB DILAURO

FEAR FRONT
PUBLISHING

Cover Design by Dennis Preston
Edited by Majanka Verstraete

This is a work of fiction. Names, characters, places, brands, media, and incidents are either the product of the author's imagination or are used fictitiously. Any resemblance to similarly named places or to persons living or deceased is unintentional.

PRINT ISBN 978-1-946082-50-3

THE BINDING BOOK ONE

ROB DILAURO

FEAR FRONT
PUBLISHING

Chapter One

Origins Of Love And The End Of The World

Jason Cain and Elizabeth Rinehart
Philadelphia, PA
October 15th, 2002

Jason Cain walked through the busy streets of the city with a chill in his bones and an idea burning in his mind.

He had just turned twenty-three in October, and was a senior psychology major at the prestigious School Of

Behavioral Medicine, which was a wing of the city's main hospital, St. Augustine located downtown.

He was a solitary prisoner of his own mind, and a genius inside of a young man who felt he was nothing but a

goof, Jason truly had a difficult time interacting with society, especially the opposite sex. There were only a few times he had an actual sexual encounter, only to fail in pulling the veil of his virginity with a clumsy and insecure display resembling the antics of a teen comedy. This was all about to change however, on this exact night, and his heart would melt the ice he had inside of his soul.

Jason stepped into Books and Beans on Davis St., a late night bookstore which catered mainly to students looking for research, hipsters and punks popping in between smoking cigarettes and being cynical, and other city types that lurked the night.

Books And Beans was two floors high. One floor was literature for every taste, and the top floor contained music from every culture and genre, video games, and a massive catalogue of DVD'S.

The walls were a bright blue which resembled the clean waters of a tropical isle. The first floor of the gargantuan super store also housed a cappuccino bar located near the front doors with every caffeinated drink someone's tastes could handle.

Jason was searching in the Special Interests section where he rifled through books about the Occult, books on Wiccan religion, dark magick, and the history of witches; mainly the incidences in Europe, and of course the infamous trials in Salem and other parts of the United States. This was not a hobby, nor an interest. In fact, Jason was utterly disgusted by the entire notion. His skeptic mind would not allow him to believe in haunted homes, spell casting, the supernatural, or any type of witchcraft in general, and the young student also had a personal thought, that anyone who practiced or believed dealt with a severe bout of mental illness.

Jason picked up the massive collection of what he called ridiculous trash, and headed towards the registers in the front of the store. All the while, his eyes could not see his oncoming fate due to the sudden image of a young black-haired woman in his head, screaming like a banshee. The shouting in his mind did not allow him to hear the light footsteps of an angel which were slow, certain, and careful, but in this case even angels can fall.

They both crashed hard to the floor, the books falling everywhere like a heavy rainfall, Jason shook his pain, stared ahead, and saw her. His fate flashed in her incredible eyes without a word. "Oh my god", he muttered to himself silently. "You are lucky you didn't shatter my arm", she said with a venomous albeit charming tone, "Are you all right? I could have sworn I was going away for attempted murder", Jason said.

He stood up and reached out his hand to help her, and a tiny smile slid across her face, she actually found his humor interesting, although mixed with a dry sarcasm.

As Jason lifted her petite hand in his, he felt as if he had been hit by lightning. His heart raced, and his pulse was quick, "I am so sorry, I should have looked where I was going."

He examined every feature: her raven black hair cut short, her mesmerizing blue eyes hidden under cat eye glasses, and he was so entranced he felt like he had ingested his tongue, no words could escape him.

The mystery woman heard him give a timid goodbye as he began walking toward the front doors, so embarrassed that he left the pile of books on the floor. She suddenly felt desperate words creep into her throat, and she had no idea why. This young woman was not a firm believer in love at first sight, in fact, romance was not something she knew too much about, nor did she care to. She felt sappy films like *Sleepless In Seattle* and Love Actually were laughable at best, and that kind of film love never happened in her own world.

Nonetheless, she released her words like she was fighting off a tight grip, "Hey!"

Jason turned around, and she felt a huge smile once again, and said with absolute courage, "I'm Elizabeth. I really couldn't let you go without buying you a coffee. After all, it seems like you're not really having a good day."

That's what you think, Jason thought in the back of his mind, and smiled.

"I don't drink coffee," he said out loud. Luckily for Jason, his goddess was persistent, "Well, how about a muffin, or at least a sugar packet? Just sit with me, please?"

He smiled as he shook her hand in agreement, "Hi, I'm Jason."

His rushing mind said what he could not, "I'm all yours."

Jason still thought of the strange image of the woman in his brain as they both walked side by side to the refreshment area.

Chapter Two

The Rogers Family Portrait Of Pain

Susan and Helen Rogers
Fort Wayne, IN
May 11th-June 12th, 1982

Susan Rogers was just out of high school when she met Bill Johnson. She had attended Curtis High School, an extremely by-the-book-establishment on the outskirts of Fort Wayne, Indiana, which was not far from her home.

The students were taught regular study, as well as Bible study in the afternoons, but there was always something about these teachings that never agreed with young Susan. She always believed in something greater, something mystical. Susan could never describe it, but it was in her blood.

She lived with her mother in a dilapidated two bedroom single-home approximately one mile away from her school. Her mother, Helen, never left the family home, but had apparently lived off of an insurance policy left behind by her late husband which was in no way a fortune, but had gotten her by for many years.

The house was built by Susan's grandfather a great amount of time before, a wedding gift for Helen and her husband, Samuel who had passed away from what was described as a mysterious illness when Susan was just a baby. She never knew her father, but his photos hung everywhere in the house to at least remind her that at one time a patriarch did exist.

The house was a white-wash color, and there was extreme chipping on the outer surface. Outside, was a wooden fence painted baby blue to show signs of a normal, content family. The inner walls were covered in ripped flower pattern paper, signs of the home rarely being managed, and ironically, the true metaphor for the family dynamic.

Susan's bedroom was a tiny single person area with a wooden bed, one authentic oak dresser, and the room was adorned with the items of a simple innocent girl, including teddy bears, as well as a few posters depicting musicians and movies that enticed her, and a bookshelf filled with books, where stuffed behind them were texts on the art of witchcraft, as well as black and white magick: her hidden passion that she seemed to always feel inside of her soul.

Susan's mother was solitary and quiet, and the bedroom door which belonged to her was always sealed shut. Susan had never seen the inside, and was always instructed by her mother that it was nothing but forbidden.

One time, Susan had felt adventurous, and she paid a very high price for her actions.

One summer afternoon, she had attempted to open her mother's secret, not realizing that Helen was looming behind her, and as she quietly attempted to turn the brass knob of the door, her angry mother's voice shook the room, "Susan Michelle, what the hell do you think you're doing, you little demon, I told you, it is not your time, and you will pay. Oh yes, little girl, you will pay."

Helen grabbed Susan's little wrist so hard that her nails dug deep into the skin. Susan winced as she was pulled into the kitchen and flung against the sink with a massive thud as her mother hissed, "I'll teach you what happens when you pry with mangy hands."

Helen grabbed her wrist once again, turning on the hot, rusty faucet until steam rose from the tap, she exclaimed once again, "You will learn."

Susan's hand was pulled into the water, and it began to feel like her flesh was being burned on a hot stove, and as her skin blistered and turned a very bright fluorescent red, she screamed in the worst agony she had ever known, and that was when her mother cupped her mouth with her other hand.

"When it is time, you will learn all. Do you understand?"

Susan had been treated in this manner her entire life. She was never taught anything about normal life, or puberty as she had reached a certain age, and even with her flowing blonde locks and her piercing hazel eyes that seemed to always have a shimmer even though her life was unbearable, she had never known about the opposite sex. Susan was not accustomed to the knowledge of physical pleasure, but one spring evening, Helen had caught her daughter discovering herself, and she had viciously beaten her daughter with a leather strap across her undiscovered area, until her pubic bone swelled like a helium balloon.

Susan never had a boyfriend, mainly because of the fear her mother constantly built in her, but that was all about to change.

One night after graduating from Curtis, Susan and her two friends, Kelly and Lauren, drove out of town to a local bar called The Wild Pony, and there she laid eyes on the one man that would break into her fear of her mother, only to instill his own.

The Wild Pony was a tiny establishment with one long bar, seats filled with run of the mill locals, fake cowboys, and women who piled on make-up, doing everything they could to bait their next gentleman.

There was also a tiny dance floor with a jukebox to the right filled with nothing but honky tonk, rockabilly, Elvis, and a plethora of classic rock.

The girls sat down at a table near the front door, fearful that their ages would be discovered. In this part of town, it seemed okay to sleep with an under-age girl, but getting one drunk would definitely cost you.

Bill stared at young Susan from his stool next to the bar, his leathery face peering directly into her soul as he took a swig of his bourbon. Bill was a twenty-nine year old truck mechanic who lived not too far from the town, he was older looking even as a man in his late twenties, with a lean and muscular physique. He had a farmer's tan from working in the mid-western sun through the summer months, and was dressed in a graying white muscle shirt, dirt-covered jeans, and a camouflage cap, looking like the work of the day had coated him in dirt and grease. But there was something about this strange man that made Susan's heart flutter, and she noticed his sudden gaze, as did her small crew. Bill proceeded to saunter towards the giggling table, and Susan felt like her already rapid heart was going to beat right out of her chest.

Chapter Three

Pain Is Pleasure

Jason Cain
Philadelphia, PA
September 19th, 2014

Pure darkness, only one solitary lamp cut into the blackness of the room, the bed was unkempt, and there were empty liquor bottles strewn across one end of the room to the other. Tears rolled down Jason's face as he lifted a fifth of whiskey to his dry lips. The liquid felt like gasoline shooting down his throat as he stared obsessively at the dresser by the far wall. Covering the entire glass of the mirror were photos, faded memories; Elizabeth looking absolutely breathtaking in every shot, he saw her face smiling back to him in his mind.

Jason spoke silently as if someone was in the quiet room with him, "I love you, Liz. Why don't you love me anymore? I have nothing if I do not have you, nothing."

He once again stared at the mirror, looking at his lost Queen smiling back at him.

Suddenly, one photograph in particular caught his eye; Elizabeth in all of her beauty adorned in a two piece bikini on one of their many exciting vacations. She looked glorious. He wiped away the tears, took a deep breath, and proceeded to undo his jeans.

Jason ripped the photo from the glass, and began speaking with a breathy tone, "Oh Liz, you are beautiful. It haunts me, Liz, it haunts me." He began to stroke himself slowly, speaking through the moans escaping his lips, as if he was mounted on top of her soft flesh, thrusting. He heard her screams of passion in his thoughts, " I love you, and I would do anything to get you back. Come back to me, baby", he said, right before he cried out in ecstasy, falling back hard on the bed.

As Jason rested his head on the mattress, he heard a shrill scream and jumped. As he got up to his feet, he walked slowly towards the mirror only to see the woman in his mind what seemed to be years ago, screaming as her skin burned and blackened in the mirror before him.

Jason began to shout and the image before him quickly disappeared as he shook.

Chapter Four

Innocence Lost In Torn Material and Shattered Dreams

Susan Rogers and Bill Thompson
"The Wild Pony" Bar Outside Fort Wayne, IN
June 12th, 1982

The seedy bar had closed, and the more than tipsy girls were ready to head back for home, but even though they had all been there the entire night, it was Susan, through Bill's coaxing, who had drank the most of the trio.

The girls were laughing, and still having the best time, when Kelly finally exclaimed with a sudden burst of authority, "Susan, we should probably get you home now. We all know how your mother Helen gets, that fucking bitch. If I had my way,...anyhow, come on, Susie."

Bill cut her off quickly, "You know, I'll take her back. I mean, we were having such a good time it'd be a real shame to waste it now. I'll just let her sober up, and I will shoot her right back, all right?"

Kelly looked as if she was in deep thought when she finally muttered, "But I'm telling you, Bill, don't do anything stupid. She doesn't really know about, you know, that stuff." Bill flashed a grin like a snake getting prepared to strike. "Don't you worry any", he said. "She is in good hands."

With that, Kelly nodded, and the girls got into the station wagon and drove away, tires spitting rocks into the air.

Bill drunkenly shambled over to Susan who was tipsily swaying, her back against a tree as she finished her almost empty bottle of cheap beer.

Bill's shadow seemed to reflect his monster in the overhead

outdoor light as he approached. "So, you feeling okay? Not too drunk, are you?" She replied with a no, but as she stood up, and fell right back on her behind. "My butt," she laughed as Bill attempted once again to pull her up.

"Hey, you like me, don't you?" he asked with a look of concern as he continued, "And no matter what happens between us, you wouldn't tell anyone anything, right? You're a sweet girl, I have a feeling you wouldn't. Please, come here."

Bill pulled a wobbly Susan to his chest, and she giggled as he placed his tongue directly into her mouth. She pulled back gently and stated, "I don't do this. Please, let's just sit back and enjoy each other."

Bill's eyes flashed with a tinge of rage. "Oh, I do want to enjoy you", he snarled as he attempted to kiss her neck, and with his rough hands ripped the dress fabric covering her chest, revealing nothing but a white bra. "Look, Bill, take me home. Okay? We are not doing this", she whispered in commanding tone, with tears forming in her eyes, "Take…me…home."

Bill growled, "Fucking bitch!"

He wildly swung at Susan, hitting her directly on the top of her right eye, splitting the skin instantly. She cried out, and in a daze, attempted to run. Bill felt like his hunt was only beginning and he toyed with her, "Okay, you want to play like that? I'll give you a head start, you dumb bitch!"

Susan ran until her body ached, and she did not look back for one second, but her unawareness cost her dearly when all of a sudden a broken piece of tree branch smacked her directly across the back of the head.

She fell hard, witnessed stars circling her eyes, while crimson coated the ground in a speckled spatter as Susan, with her one open eye saw Bill pull down his filth covered jeans as she whimpered groggily.

"No one can hear you out here, little girl. There was never anywhere to run." He proceeded to crouch over his captive, his hard but short member swinging above her beaten form, he began to spit his venom yet again, "I know what you country whores are like, have a young one, you have a husband, isn't that right, darling?"

Susan cried for her attacker to reconsider, sticky blood

flowing into her eye and down the side of her bruised, dirty face. He then leaned over her beaten face, spitting as he spoke, "And if you don't, I am going beat the dog shit out of you."

Susan closed her eyes, and tears mixed with the red, sticky blood as Bill's horrific ranting continued.

He threw his body on top of her limp twitching stomach, ripped the snap from her bra, picked up her Head, wrapped it around Susan's neck, forming a violent homemade gag.

His manhood finally penetrated her, tearing tight muscle as he gyrated drunkenly.

Moments later, Bill whispered in her almost inaudible ear, "You're going to be the mother to my child, and no one will convict me, because I will murder you if you tell."

He shot inside of her rawness, and fell limp on top of her, and Susan sobbed silently, not realizing the worst had only begun.

Chapter Five

Those Were The Days

Philadelphia, PA
September 19th, 2014

Jason woke from his drunken coma, knocking the empty bottle off of his stomach, causing it to clatter onto the carpet. He rubbed his swollen eyes, and proceeded to head toward the bathroom.

The bathroom area was a good size, but was evidently occupied by a single, broken man. There were dirty towels on the wet, dingy floor, and one solitary clean towel hung above the rod holding the shower curtain. The sink had traces of facial hair that had never been washed off of the surface, and there was a large medicine cabinet above the sink, with two sliding glass panels, but the glass was not visible. Just like the dresser mirror, the outside of one of the mirrors was covered in pictures of her.

His personal torment did not have a retreat. He placed her everywhere; she was omnipotent, a god. She saw all, because to Jason she was all.

Jason vigorously rinsed out the stale alcohol with mouthwash as he looked up to one particular picture: he and Elizabeth sitting at a table with family and friends, a cake showing the words Congrats, Our Famous Writers. The memory rolled in Jason's head like a sudden motion picture. He began to dwell on one of his finer moments he and his lady had encountered, together.

Chapter Six

The Rose of Love Still Red

Jason and Elizabeth had lived together in a small one bedroom apartment for a little over two years. The night at Books and Beans had changed the mindset of both parties, forever. Jason began to believe in himself, and Elizabeth began to realize at a rapid pace that romance wasn't such an imaginary thing after all. Jason still attended school, and Elizabeth had begun to intern for a major publishing company, Lion Heart Press.

They spent every waking moment that they had together. They went to dinner, movies, art galleries, and other events a loving, fun couple frequents. If someone saw Jason, more cases than not she would be right by his side.

The apartment was small, with plain white paint on the walls, a tiny bathroom, and an even tinier kitchen area.

The bedroom was bigger than the living room, but that did not bother them since they spent most of their time in that room. They were struggling financially, but officially a couple. They were inseparable, but also a force.

Jason began a manuscript about his theories on the occult. He began to jot down a piece of a chapter every other day, Elizabeth read a lot of books and always gave her feedback, as well as jotting down notes and ideas.

She was always Jason's biggest fan, and it was certain she would always be in his corner. They both had a mutual plan and that was to light the literary world on fire with their ideas.

Little did the couple know that dream would soon become real.

Chapter 7

A Mother's Declaration

May 15th, 1980

A little over six months had passed when young Susan noticed she had new feelings inside of her body, and when she finally discovered that she was pregnant she had attempted to end her life over a dozen times. Helen was on a rampage. When her daughter was nearly ready to give birth, she ranted, "I know that you coaxed that man into reaping your innocence. You begged him to put himself inside you, with your devilish trickery!"

On the day Susan was forced to leave, Helen stared right into Susan's puffy, drenched eyes, and began to speak in a low, informative tone. "Susan Rogers, you must leave this house, you must be a woman, and be strong like I have conditioned you to be." She turned her back to a weeping daughter and continued, "For I know the road that lies ahead of you is rough and rocky, it is in no way easy."

She turned to her daughter once again, with signs of tears forming, "What you are about to go through will be terrible. Bill Thompson is a horrible man. But the fact does remain that you made this bed, and you must go to him."

Helen placed her fingers under Susan's drenched chin, and lifted her eyes to her own, "I have many secrets to share with you, but now is not the time, you are in no way ready." Susan, pain shooting from head to toe, pondered on what her mother was saying, but could not respond.

Helen took her hands from her daughter's face and continued, "That man will probably rape you, strike you every day of your lives together. I know this. The fact remains, Susan," Helen began to have a snarl curl into every one of her words; "You are still...weak. You are a timid little girl, the strength of the Rogers women does not envelop your soul." Helen stood up, stared down at her daughter, with an almost devilish smile,

"But it will, my girl, and once it does...I'll be ready for you."

Helen began to wrap her arms around herself in an almost sensual joy. "And, you will never have to look upon that man's hard face ever again." Susan sunk lower to the floor, confusion tattooed on her face, as Helen turned to her daughter, and slowly lifted her, "Now go. Go be with him; you will find your way."

Susan's mother leaned in close, and Susan flinched as if her confusing mother would knock her down again, Instead, for the first time ever since she was a baby, Helen gently kissed her aching forehead.

Susan was stunned, and attempted to wrap her arms around her mother, the monster, the unloving.

Helen gently pushed her arms away, and said, "Be a mother, be a wife, do what you are told, do not expect what I speak of to happen overnight."

Susan retreated to the door, picked up her bags weakly, and turned to face her mother once again when she said, "I will tell you this, my little girl, once you witness the change...you will know immediately."

Another sly smile slid across her face.

Before Susan opened the creaky door, she said lovingly but confused, "Goodbye, mother." She stepped out into the open air, took one more look at the decrepit state of the house she had grown up in and drove off in Bill Thompson's rusted red truck, never looking back.

Helen sighed and approached her secret room when suddenly darkness enveloped her, almost dancing on the walls in front of her eyes. She began to cry out, "What do you want, demon? I did what you asked, what more do want from me?"

A ghostly voice echoed off of the walls into Helen's ear, speaking her name, "Helen."

Helen balled up her fists as her heart raced under her clothing, the whisper continued, "Helen."

At that moment, a dark-haired woman with eyes ablaze stood in front of her bulging eyes, screaming, "HELEN!!"

Chapter Eight

The Rose Of Love In Bloom

Philadelphia, PA
September 23rd, 2002

The book was almost complete. Jason and Elizabeth's dreams were very quickly becoming realized. Lion Heart Press perused many transcripts, and slowly but surely warmed greatly to the idea.

Jason continued to do last minute research and work vigorously, typing and jotting like a man possessed, and Jason and Elizabeth's love was beginning to blossom even more.

Elizabeth became an extremely important piece of Jason's family, they were both steady friends with Jason's older brother, Scott, and his wife of three years, Cara. Scott was a bit taller than Jason, and some women would say more pleasing to the eye; he had a great solid build, a crop of short brown hair, and eyes that his wife would call 'the springs' because they were so piercingly blue, she could not help but always be mesmerized.

Scott served many years as an Army Ranger, and also did more than a few combat tours. He was what some would consider a true warrior, and if he ever spoke about his tours of duty, he had harrowing tales to tell for the rest of his existence.

Scott was home after a highly honorable discharge, but you could never strip the soldier from the man, he was strong, he was polite, and a rock of a human being. His other half Cara was a combat nurse that he had met overseas when he was in intensive care for a gunshot wound to the abdomen he had received in the field, for this he received a Purple Heart. Cara was shorter than Scott, and she had a petite strong frame, and the face of a supermodel. She had emerald eyes, sandy brown hair cut short in a pixie hairstyle, and a take-no-prisoners attitude just like her husband.

The couples met at a swanky bistro called Dario's. The place was top shelf, and the food was five-star, and the only reason Jason would ever consider something so pricey would be to celebrate his amazing news, Lion Heart had given both Elizabeth and himself a three thousand dollar advance to acquire the rights to their hard work, and this did not include the other potential payments in the deal. Needless to say, soon the hard working, always ambitious couple would be living a life each of them had never known.

The entire party sat at a glass table with a striking arrangement set in the middle with roses, both midnight black and an almost bright burgundy red. The curtains were made of the finest silk, and the molding around the doors was gold-plated. "What can I say, Cara and I are just so damn proud of the both of you. And it is so great to see your words soon reaching the masses", Scott said with major enthusiasm, champagne glass raised in the air.

Jason was flattered, but felt flushed with embarrassment when he and Elizabeth's family walked in.

"Congratulations my boy," yelled Jason's father, Eric, as he patted him lovingly on the back with one hand.

Jason's mother, Jennifer, also congratulated the couple with big embraces. Elizabeth's family was much smaller. Her mother and father had passed a few years before, and she was the only female left in her entire family.

Elizabeth's party consisted of her uncle Pat and two of her male cousins, Robin and Tim. The excited table ate their meals, talked and laughed for hours, and lived every moment to the fullest.

Just then, Jason, with a throat clearing showing he was about to speak, stood up from the chair, and all eyes were directly on him. This was truly his moment to fulfill his then ultimate dream.

"Everyone, thank you, thank you so much for dropping by this evening, and we both love you all so very much." Jason began to sweat a little as he continued to speak. "I have a few announcements to make. Elizabeth and I are moving out of the dingy pig pen we have come to love so much. We will be moving into our first new house, together." Everyone gasped, and the room cascaded with excitement and congratulatory comments. Jason, with a nervous grin continued, "And number two," Jason's palms began to get with worry about what he was about to do, and continued, "Nothing I do in this world would be anything without my muse by my side." He squeezed his eyes shut and cleared his frog once more, turning to his beautiful partner, "Elizabeth, please, may I have your hand for what I am about to do?"

Elizabeth placed her hand gently into his sweaty palm, and felt like it was the greatest sensation in the world when he happily stared into her wet eyes.

"Elizabeth, you have been with me through it all: the good, the bad, and the ugly, so to speak. You are my world, you are the heart that beats steadily within me, you are everything."

Jason and Elizabeth began to both tear heavily when he said, "I thank God every day I crashed into you that night."

Elizabeth giggled with breathy and tearful glee when she looked at Jason, "I'm so glad you had the muffin."

Everyone at the table laughed, and held each other close as they continued to gaze upon this glorious moment in both families.

"Elizabeth Mary Rinehart, I am not complete without you, and I cannot move on my journey without my light to guide me", Jason confessed lovingly, as his body began to vibrate slightly.

He knelt down on one knee, looking up at Elizabeth's sparkling eyes, and said with nothing but absolute truth and conviction in his words, "Will you be my wife?"

Elizabeth began to scratch her temple and scrunch her face as if she was thinking hard on her answer, obviously her own humorous ice breaker, and this motion worried Jason. She said softly, " It would be nothing but an honor, to be your loving wife forever."

Jason stood and kissed his new fiancé deeper than they ever have before. Elizabeth turned to whisper in his ear, with a fire that hung on every word, "You are mine forever, and nothing will ever change that...nothing."

Chapter Nine

Her Bloody Valentine

February 14th, 1984

It had been over a year since Susan had given birth to William Thompson. He was a beautiful angel-faced child who looked more like her, and she always thanked God he did not inherit too many characteristics of her animal husband.

Every single day that Susan left her mother was more terrifying than anything she had ever faced with her abusive mother. Bill not only attempted to assault her when he came home drunk, but he called her every single word that could tear someone's soul to shreds.

He ripped her of her self-esteem, and smashed her face at least twenty times a week. Any less would be a true miracle.

Susan was only twenty-three, although you could never tell from her outer exterior. She was bruised and marked on her face, arms, back, and legs, her once youthful body was now limp and achy. Her locks had turned gray in certain spots from the sheer stress of life, and the constant wish for a release from death itself. The fire that had always burned in her retinas had died out, and the only thing that actually made her happy was the smile on her child's face. But, her only reason on this earth, it seemed, was to make sure her horrifying husband was content and happy, which he never was. She cooked his meals, which on several occasions she thought of lacing with rat poison, the idea of Bill's steak making him bleed from the mouth, his gurgles as he asphyxiated on his own vomit made her giddy inside, possibly even a little wet. For some reason, she never acted on it, but she did feel the pure hatred boiling inside of her, even though she was afraid of what he would do if she did not finish the task, and worst of all, what he would do to their son.

Susan was taking Bill's special dinner out of the stove, when she heard the door slam shut, the sound made her sick inside. She was taking the spiced ham to the table when Bill stepped into the kitchen, Susan sighed, and muttered under her breath, "Fuck."

The young wife turned to face him, and realized he was holding a bouquet of red roses, she was bowled over, especially when it came to the fact that she never received anything from him, unless it was a slap, a punch, or a swift kick.

Instead of chocolates, she got bruises. In the place of a heart filled with candy, Bill filled her real one with piles of excrement. Bill, stinking of booze, looked at her and said calmly, "Happy Valentine's Day, baby. Didn't think I forgot this special day, did you?"

She looked into his kind but bloodshot eyes, and for the first time she felt a very tiny shred of hope. She spoke. "Bill, I can't believe you." In the blink of an eye, he threw his hard fist into her nose.

Susan fell back, and her baby screamed and wailed in his high chair. Bill turned to their screaming baby, when Susan yelled, "No, Bill! Not our little boy!" He turned around as she was on the tile, blood weeping heavily from the tear in her nose, coating the front of her shirt, and spattering the tile.

"Shut the fuck up, you ugly bitch." Bill roared into her face as he pulled her from the ground, and threw her against the kitchen table, hard. Susan was doubled over the table top, the wind knocked completely from her lungs as Bill rushed behind her, unfastening his belt at the same time. He pulled the belt completely from the loops, wrapping it tightly around his wounded wife's throat. The leather tightened around her neck, causing veins to protrude. They were quickly very visible, all pumping furiously.

Susan could not hold onto a grasp of air, and felt her eyeballs begin to sink. Bill turned his stinking breath to her ear, spitting as he growled lowly, "You thought I wouldn't figure it all out, didn't you?"

Susan's head went towards his chest with a snap, the belt tightening, "I know you tried...to...poison me. You're going to respect my love for you, and you are going to pay."

Bill, still holding the belt tight with one hand, scooped a handful of rose petals from the table, and held them in front of Susan's bulging, red eyes as he spoke with murderous intent, "These flowers are for your coffin. How do you like that?"

She made a noise through her strangulation, and she was struggling very hard to utter something. Bill, arms flexed tight, released the belt but only a little, "You got something to say? Let's hear it."

Susan, belt still around her throat, attempted to crane her neck so at least one of her sore, wet eyes met his. She gasped only a few raspy, gravelly words, but he heard her very clearly, "Do it. Please...do it."

He stared at her with shock on his face. Susan had never stood up to him in all of their years together. Bill chuckled as he released the belt, dropping her to the table, gasping and spitting, "You're not going to get that lucky...but I am."

He stepped behind Susan and pulled her dress upward, moved her underwear aside, and entered her, violently, the "Bill Special." He pumped with an animal ferocity, until he felt himself about to burst. As he came, he tossed Susan's limp and exhausted body back towards the table, semen dripping down her legs as she sobbed and did everything to fight for the air that had left her.

"You are a lot of fun, you know that? I think I'm going to keep you around." Bill buttoned his jeans, and slapped his beaten wife on her backside, before he stepped out of the kitchen.

Susan heard Bill's truck pull away, and she wobbled to her screeching baby's side. She picked him up from the chair, placed him to her burning chest, and suddenly released a banshee scream, "MOTHERFUCKER!!" She was finally at the end of her rope, and she began to realize the change her mother was speaking of, and was almost certain it involved murdering her abusive albatross.

Chapter 10

Black Magic Woman, Black Magic Man

Jason Cain and Will Thompson
Philadelphia, PA
September 22nd, 2014

Jason planned to meet his friend, Will Thompson. At three p.m. on a Tuesday afternoon, he walked into Mickey's which was located about two blocks from his apartment.

Mickey's was darkly lit, with five tables next to the bar, a television hung on a mount connected to the wall, and a jukebox against the wall played "Babe, I'm Gonna Leave You ."

The song reverberated through the room, and headed directly to Jason's broken soul causing one single tear to roll from his eye. He wiped it quickly with the back of his hand.

"Jimmy, two shots of whiskey and one Bud, please?" The bartender knew Jason from his recent drunken theatrics, and hesitated for a second before he handed him anything at all.

Jason stared at the jukebox, and then said, "Could you turn that fucking song off? Please?"

The bartender walked toward the box, and angrily but agreeably pulled the plug from the wall, and as he was about to turn toward the bar, Jason's new friend, Will, walked through the door.

He cried out to an already tipsy Jason, "Are you buying or what?" Will was a dark-haired man, and much older but he was the type who always looked a younger. He wore a black dress shirt, midnight black boot-cut jeans, and a scuffed pair of fashionable combat boots. Will could have been the missing member of a death metal group. Around his neck was a pendant containing a woman's photograph, and he had once told Jason it was his mother who passed on years before.

Will stood to Jason's left, "I see you're off to the races early?"

He sat down on the stool as Jason stated sarcastically, "Just trying to forget, and this is the best way to kill memory."

Will nodded, ordered a beer, and lit a cigarette. "Still killing yourself over the divorce?"

Will asked, expelling smoke from his nostrils, Jason stared down at the bar, "Come on, leave me alone about this shit, will you? "

His new friend blew smoke again as he continued to instruct his Jason, "Hey Jason, I know that you miss her and all, but you have to get over this, man."

Jason knocked back another shot, slammed the glass on the bar top, as Will dabbed out the remnant of his burning cigarette in the ashtray, "I'm surprised Jimmy lets you drink here after that shit last week."

Jason clenched his jaw, and addressed the incident, "All I did was cry. I had too many shots, my mind became a blur, I fell off the stool, and as some patrons were helping me up I might have yelled out Elizabeth's name in the moment, but that's all that happened."

Will chuckled, "Yeah, from a mountain top, my friend, it was quite a sight."

He touched Jason's shoulder, "You are killing yourself with this, and I hate seeing it."

Will suddenly stared down at the counter top, "Maybe, if you cast a spell, or something, you know?"

Jason rubbed his face with both hands, sighing, "Listen, you know I don't believe in that shit. I know you think it really works for you, but it's not my thing, you know that."

Will sighed deep, and ordered another beer. He cleared his throat as he tried to explain, "Sometimes, when you do not have any other plans, when you have exhausted all your options, you have to believe in things that do not seem like they could be real. I mean, people go to a man revealing their deepest darkest secrets, and they plan their lives around a being they have never seen, every day. They behave a certain way because a book told them to do so. How are my beliefs any different from that?" Jason bent his head, feeling the alcohol now.

Will ordered his friend two more shots, and continued, "Also, like I told you before, regardless of what your book says I have never been to a psychiatrist. Just because I am sworn to witchcraft, it does not mean there is something wrong with my psyche."

He turned toward Jason, "Also, I make sure to get rid of the bodies after my sacrifices." Jason and Will chuckled slightly, and Will lightly punched his arm.

Jason pleaded once again, "Why do you really think that shit works? I mean...how do you know?"

Will's face began to look serious, almost stone as he spoke, "You want to know why? Because I saw it with my own two eyes. It changed the whole dynamic of my family...for the better. If you truly believe, I mean really believe it on the inside, in your guts, magick can truly give your heart desires, wealth, health, happiness, even love."

He laughed with a sinister tone, to break the tension of the subject, and Jason peered at the wall in front of him. Jason could not face Will when he asked, "You really truly believe that magick can bring love?"

He turned to face Will again, with a sarcastic expression across his face, "Well, tell me genius, if witchcraft could do that, then how come the Wicked Witch in *The Wizard Of Oz* couldn't get laid? She was wrapped up tight, she needed some cock!" Jason began to laugh, head swaying lightly from the alcohol and his buzz becoming heavier.

Will knocked down the rest of his beer and began to look at Jason, angrily. "Listen, asshole, just because you did some research, and had some fame with your own bullshit ideas on the subject does not mean you know anything. First of all, your theories are not psychologically proven, at all. Secondly, you are now poking fun at my heritage. I know it's not Christianity, not science, but that's what we were about, what I was taught, all right?"

He began poking himself in the chest, "My mother was my inspiration. She didn't have a pointy hat, or a fucking wart on her nose. She was beautiful, inside and out. And she was not mentally deficient, okay?"

Suddenly, Jason felt shame, and moments later turned with a

look of pure apology. "Jesus. I'm sorry, I wasn't trying to call you a psycho." Jason clicked his teeth, "I just don't have the faith, don't believe in the unexplained, I believe in what I see, and I just don't see this stuff helping anyone."

Just then, Jason swallowed hard. "So, about what you said. You said that magick can bring love. What exactly did you mean, bring...love?"

Will smiled a tiny smile. "What I meant was you can recite words, and if you believe them...it can allow you the opportunity for someone to love you, or love you again."

Jason furrowed his brow." You mean, mentally force someone to fall in love with you even if they are not attracted to you? That's kind of mean-spirited, isn't it?"

Jason began rubbing his head, "I mean...a person should have a right to choose who they desire, right? If that was not the case, we should live in some third world country, where the fate of who you're with is sealed."

Will lit a cigarette, exhaling, "It is not forcing someone to want you, it's more like...they realize fully in their head that the person who calls out for them in their minds is right for them. Earthly powers forbid a person to cast such a spell, but I have a solution." Will took a long drag from the cigarette, expelling smoke from his nostrils. This time with the way the interior lights hit him, he looked similar to a dragon breathing fire.

"I have a book, it is extremely old, and it belonged to my mother, and her mother before her. Enclosed is a spell. It is the only one that allows you to bend this rule. In witchcraft, if you recite words to hurt someone...or force them to do anything they would not do freely, that can come back to you...threefold, like bad luck."

He seemed to peer into Jason's soul now, causing him to feel a sick excitement about the idea. Will continued, "It's like a romance get out jail free card, nothing can touch you. With this spell, you can fix the past. What I am trying to say is you can have her once again."

Jason's jaw dropped a little, and he picked up the last of his shots, the jukebox began to play Santana's *Black Magic Woman*.

Will smiled and tapped the bar, when Jason yelled, "Jimmy, what the fuck! You turned it off, didn't you?" Jimmy ran over to the blaring box, and checked the outlet. The cord was still on the floor. The bartender grabbed the plug still on the carpet in confusion, and looked bewildered. Will dabbed out his second cigarette, "Wow, That's strange. What do you think?" Jason and Jimmy the bartender stared at each other in disbelief.

Chapter 11

"The Cauldron" Begins To Boil

May 7th, 2005

Jason and Elizabeth's many years of work were finally unleashed, and everyone caught the buzz, *Cauldron Of Lies* was released to critical acclaim. It reached number one on almost every top ten list, and it received an excellent review in almost every publication imaginable, and for a non-fiction title, the reception was quite astonishing.

Jason and Elizabeth were both famous in their own right, especially Jason.

They both attended signing after signing, where fans were always snaked around the block, and on one such occasion, Jason had been scrawled his name on the inside jackets of Cauldron for hours.

Jason, through his travels on the book circuit, always received a very warm reception from fans, but always had a security guard posted in whatever store he appeared in, just to be safe.

He never had an altercation with someone whom he felt he was a threat, except for a few bits of hate mail stating their true feelings on this man, he was a monster, a piece of garbage, and that Elizabeth was the true bride of the devil of lies and deceit.

The situation was going to become a little more personal on this exhausting day where five eager fans left in the line, including a young woman who could only be described as Goth. She stared directly at Jason, and the sneer plastered on her face struck a chord of fear in him every time he looked at her.

The woman was apparently in her late twenties, had long, black hair pulled into a bun, kept in place by what looked like a pair of dark styling chopsticks, and on her face was so much black makeup she looked like something from hell itself.

As she approached the table, his heart sunk.

The woman looked down at him with murderous eyes as she licked her blackened lips, and began to speak, "Jason Cain, the famed author." She snickered before she continued. "My name is Wendy Collins, my earth name cannot be repeated. I have been a witch, as you call it, for many, many years. In this day and age, practitioners could be comfortable, although secretive about their beliefs, but now, because of YOU and your ridiculous tome, it is impossible to be taken seriously...or accepted."

A portly security guard stood nearby, his body poised to attack, but Jason waved him off. He allowed the young, angry woman to continue, and Wendy did just that. "I don't know who you THINK you are...what you THINK you know...but you have brought only shame to line your dirty pockets. You are an awful MAN."

She then reached for something in a bag on her shoulder. The officer behind her stepped closer. Jason began to sweat inside of his shirt as if he had run a marathon. She licked her lips as she spoke in a low tone, "Yes, an awful man. It's funny, I had a very vivid dream about you, men. Not only the work of your book, but the poison you have spread on this planet ever since you stepped forth on her soil, knuckles dragging into her soft earth, you all have angered her."

Wendy stared at Jason again, her glare underneath the midnight-colored make-up made it look like her eyes had burned, and turned to hot ash. "I come here to tell you that you will pay for your crimes...all of you. And I welcome her, and she welcomes you. You are the maker of your end, Mr. Cain...YOU!"

With that, the woman rushed toward the table attempting to attack Jason who at that moment fell off his chair. Wendy cackled as the heavyset guard grabbed her around the waist and began to roughly drag her to the front door.

The crazed woman continued to laugh and yell, "I mark you, Jason Cain! You king of lies! She's coming, for all of you!"

Jason looked straight ahead in terror, the altercation with the woman was all it took for him to change his mind about the existence of witchcraft in the world. All it took was a cosmic kick to change a person's ideals, instantly.

Chapter 12

The Change Of Susan Thompson

June 25th, 1984

Susan was sitting quietly in an old chair in the living room, her baby boy laid across her lap staring up at her lovingly. Susan smiled back at him, wincing from a cut on her lip, another recent gift from her generous husband. Her baby was the only light in the true darkness of the room, as well as her life.

William tugged on a tiny piece of jewelry around her neck, and in this moment of complete peace, she took a deep breath and peered out of the open window. The living room she sat in had old furniture, nothing fancy, but nothing trashy. It had a white couch adorned with a flower pattern, vines interconnecting every which way attached to blossoming roses.

Susan always used to look at the pattern and think that this was symbolic to her own life, and once she felt the change in herself, the pain would stop. Her life was the jagged, green pointy vines; the roses, her future blossoming again. It truly resembled her new life, finally free from Bill. Also, in the room were two brown end tables and a medium-size television set atop on an oak stand. The walls were a pure white, almost like that of a hospital.

They were very plain, very antiseptic, and pictures of deer and elk adorned the walls, with a stuffed deer head above the opening which lead to the hallway containing the other rooms in the house. Her horror had been gone for a few days working out of town, and she knew the nirvana she was feeling would end very soon.

She stared at her child again, when she heard a truck door slam hard. Susan rose from her chair, holding her child tight, and looked out the window facing the cement driveway.

Her peace was diminished instantaneously when she saw Bill

stumbling toward the front door, half-empty beer grasped in his paw-like hand, and his body covered in oil and dirt.

Susan swallowed hard, and she went to the door to wait for it to open. The door opened in what seemed to be slow motion, and in the horror movie playing in Susan's head, a snarling beast stood on the other side.

She placed a fake smile on her face, the gash on her lip still giving her trouble.

Bill closed the door behind him, and smiled at her. He kissed her on the cheek sloppily, and began to slur as he spoke, "Did you miss me?"

Susan's responses were as false as her painful smile, "Of course, Bill."

He headed toward the kitchen, and while finishing the bottle in his hand, he opened the refrigerator to retrieve another.

Bill walked back to the living room, and stared down at Susan who was once again sitting in her chair, "So…how's the boy, and how are you?"

Susan looked up, continuing her deception, "We're both fine. How did the job go?"

Bill sipped his beer, and began to explain, "Well, everything went well."

He sniffed, and continued, "The company cut down on their budget, so there's definitely going to be a shortage of work now. You know what that means? No repairs, and I'll be home, a lot more often. What do you say to that?"

He bent over Susan, and kissed her on the mouth with his breath reeking of barley and hops.

When he walked away, she quickly wiped a tear from her eye. Bill's news put a huge knife directly into any spirit she had left. Bill stumbled back into the living room, and plopped down hard on the couch next to a shaking Susan. He looked at her with what he would call passion in his eyes. Bill began to woo her, and it made sick swirl in her stomach. "I really missed you; I thought about you all the time. Your sexy little body glistening on top of me, riding, grinding, screaming out my name."

With that, he quickly sprung to his feet, the bulge in his jeans visible to Susan's eyes. He glared down at her as he commanded, "Why don't you put the boy in his room, and let's get a little, crazy."

Susan looked back, with nothing but disgust. Bill began to chuckle, and spilled some of his beer onto the floor when he shook his head in disbelief, and stared down at the floor.

Susan began to feel her body shutter, when Bill knelt down, and growled, "Listen to me, bitch. I don't give a shit whether you want to or not. I don't give a fuck about your needs. I want to fuck, and I'm going to do it. So, take the damn kid in his damn room and meet me in the bedroom in five minutes, snap to it."

Susan sighed when Bill got up and made a beeline to the hallway. She stood, and walked toward the baby's room.

The room was adorned with a lot of blue, a typical color for a baby boy, Susan placed him gently in bed, and smiled down at her son.

She allowed only one word to escape her lips, as her smile widened, "Soon." She knew what she had to do. If her husband wanted her, he was going to get all of her: her seething pain, and her revenge. She walked into the kitchen, as if in a cat-like stroll and opened the utensil drawer. She sifted through the egg beaters, and other miscellaneous items until she found her prize, a small but sharp knife. Susan heard Bill's booming voice echoing through the hallway, "Why don't you put on that lacy number of yours."

Susan headed toward the bedroom, and continued to smile, because she knew who was going to do the actual tearing. She opened the wooden closet, grabbed the silky lingerie, and headed toward the bathroom, not looking at Bill sprawled out on the bed. Susan quickly slipped off her cotton house dress, and placed the blade into the lining of her underwear. She stared at herself in the mirror of the medicine cabinet, and grinned at the image smiling back. Susan was now an assassin, and it was time for her to receive her payback.

She walked back into the bedroom, and looked at her husband with false seduction, he was lying on his back, with filthy socks and a pair of brief underwear, his erect member lifting the fabric. Susan sounded proud and sure as she spoke. "I know you want to play, so let's play a game, okay?"

Bill took a sip of beer, giggling like a schoolboy as she

continued, "I want you to let me do, everything. Take care of YOU for once."

Bill sat up, "Come over here, mama,", Susan crawled onto his grimy chest like liquid sex, staring into his eyes, " You have to allow me to lead."

He nodded in agreement as she stuck her tongue in his foul mouth. Susan's mind raced with nausea, but her outer exterior displayed another story. She appeared like a vixen, waiting to cater to her husband's every desire.

Bill did as he was instructed, until suddenly he grabbed her by the waist, flipping her onto her back. Susan yelled, "Bill! Don't!" He crawled over her, kissing her stomach and chest, sloppily.

He looked her in the eyes, and she knew the game was over when he said, "Shut up. I will do whatever I want."

He began to place his warm, sweaty hand under her lingerie, as Susan begged, "Goddamn it, Bill. Please...don't."

Bill cupped her behind, and ran his other hand up the lining of her underwear. She closed her eyes tight. Susan knew Bill would find her surprise, and then the game would truly be over, because he would kill her in cold blood.

Bill, still kissing her with eyes closed, ran his finger across something sharp, and he winced, and stopped his mouth raping. He looked at the cut on his finger, and complained, "Shit!"

Just then, Susan pulled the knife from the side of her hip, and rammed it into Bill's watering eye. He screamed in pain, and Susan could hear the baby in the other room screaming loud, even over his cries.

Susan then lunged in as if to kiss him and bit his lip. Bill bellowed even louder, falling to the other side of the bed, the knife still in his socket, and blood pouring out of his face.

Susan flipped him over to face her. His gums were completely exposed, and the blood was quite a sight. She had bit off his bottom lip along with the muscle and tendon, and spat the fatty mess onto the floor, she hopped on his chest, Bill was in way too much agony to fight her off. He screamed like a wounded girl as she looked at him venomously and pulled her arm back, swinging it forward, slapping her balling beast.

Susan spoke with pure hate and authority, "Shut up. Shut up and listen to me, or I'm going to cut out your tongue." The fear in Bill's eyes was intense, but his cries changed to a whimper when Susan pulled his briefs off of his sweaty legs, shoved them into his throat and began to speak. "Bill, I have no pity for you, so listen."

He continued to peer into her blood-streaked face as she began to explain her feelings for the man shivering underneath her, "I hate...you. I could not hate a person more. You killed me, mind, body, and soul, and I am going to enjoy every single moment of what is about to happen to you."

She began to tear a little as she bent directly over Bill's ghost-white face, "You never let me talk...you never listened to me." She turned his head, pulled the blade from his gushy socket, and took it to his earlobe. The knife began to slice down, slow and precise. Susan raised her head, resembling a hungry, rabid animal; she was loving it. She placed the bloody piece of the ear to her lips as she grinned like a Cheshire cat, "You hear me now, don't you, you fuck?"

Bill's bloodcurdling screams were blocked by the bloody gag of fabric, and Susan dropped the ear and continued, "You were never a man. Real men do not put their hands on defenseless girls."

Susan placed the already bloody blade against the tip of one of Bill's fingers as she held his arm tight, "You used these horrible, disgusting hands and you struck me again and again." She grit her teeth with animosity as she cut at two stubby fingers. The blade went straight through to the bone and blood flowed more and more as the two fingers fell clumsily onto Bill's chest. His eyes grew wide as he witnessed the bloody digits. He whimpered, the sound drowned out. Susan looked at her prey again, this time with tears flowing down her face, mixing with the blood as she spoke in a low tone, "You raped...me. You raped me and forced me into a life with you!" She shimmied downward, sitting on Bill's quaking ankles and squeezed his limp cock hard in her fist. "All of the time, you forcefully put this...disgusting thing in me."

Her voice rose, "This dirty fucking cock of yours ripped through me; it destroyed me. It's who you are."

Bill whimpered as she placed the knife against his sweaty sack. As she stared back into the terror in his eyes, Susan smiled once again, and felt a bit of wetness coat her vaginal walls as she slowly sliced into his flaccid penis, the blood soaking her working hands. Bill screamed louder than he had when his fingers and ear were being cut, and Susan once again leaned over her husband. "I'm leaving you. The baby and I …we are gone. You will never see me again," she smiled, "but you will always remember me."

She grabbed his cheek, nails digging deep into the fatty skin. "I will always haunt you."

Susan threw the bloody head to the carpet, stood her feet on the floor and hovered over his crying face, placing the knife to his throat, "I'm leaving now. Do not move until I'm gone, do you understand me?"

Susan grabbed clothes from the dresser, took off the bloody lingerie and threw it to Bill who was crying on the bed, cupping the bloody mess between his legs.

She turned to him once more, "You better get something on that, before you bleed to death."

Susan picked up her crying child from his bed, and headed for the door, leaving everything behind.

She stepped out of the door, walked to the truck and smiled big as she heard Bill yelling obscenities from inside.

Susan placed William in his seat, and turned the key in the ignition. She drove far away from the house. Finally, she knew exactly what her mother had attempted to say, the change she spoke of.

It was not just a change in thought, it was total empowerment, her utter vengeance. It was all clear to her. She began to shed tears of joy as the truck headed in the direction of her true home. She spoke silently to herself, "Mother, I'm coming home."

Bill was now on the floor, screaming and cursing Susan who was already on her way home, "Fucking bitch! I will kill you…you fucking whore!" He placed his hands over his face when the room suddenly grew black, a mist circling before him, slowly changing form.

With tears in his eyes and still cupping his lack of manhood, Bill looked up and sneered, "What the fuck are you doing in my house, you old hag?" The image approached him, and his screams could be heard echoing through the house.

Chapter 13

The Life Of The "King Of Lies"

January 12th, 2006

Cauldron's popularity was still in full swing. Jason had appeared on every morning show, as well as every late night talk show.

The book had just acquired a massive hardback deal, and Jason and Elizabeth had received a small fortune on sales. Everywhere Jason had gone, people stopped him and asked for his autograph. Elizabeth sunk more and more into the background as Jason Cain became the true star.

Although the altercation with Wendy had planted dread, he continued to ride the wave of success. There were already talks for Jason to write another book, and things were going great for Jason Cain.

On the day he found out about the deal for the second book, he drove back to his beautiful home, and parked his brand new Lexus in the massive garage located to the left of the front of the house.

The outside was garnished with flowers which spread across the entire length of the yard, and there was one single giant tree, where hanging from the thick trunk was a wooden swing for two. The back of the house had giant bay windows where they had a beautiful view of a rippling lake about ten yards from their home.

Jason opened the front door to see Elizabeth working furiously at the computer. When Cauldron was
in talks, Lion Heart had made her a literary talent scout.

The living room she worked in was incredible by anyone's standards, there was a huge sectional sofa, three matching love seats, a glass table containing a stack of coffee table books, a monstrous big screen television. A chandelier made of pure crystal hung above all of the clean, state-of-the-art pieces. The rugs were snow white and soft to the touch, Elizabeth absolutely adored making love on them when her and Jason had some quiet time. The walls were ocean blue, which Elizabeth had requested to always commemorate their meeting at *Books And Beans* years before.

Jason strolled over to Elizabeth. Her hair was pulled back, her magnificent eyes staring through a pair of designer glasses. He kissed her on the top of the head, smelling her shampoo and shuddered. He smiled when she turned around, and she jumped up from her black leather chair, and embraced her husband.

They locked lips passionately for many minutes. The love she felt for this man was still nothing but electric.

Elizabeth began to speak when they fell to the long, comfortable couch together, "You received a call from the publisher, apparently after you left the offices, they have decided that they want the new book idea, sooner than later."

As she said this, there was a huge grin on her face. Jason on the other hand, did not look so pleased.

He looked down to the carpet as he spoke, "Fuck, this is not good. I have absolutely no clue what to write about."

His insecurity took over as he continued, "I am a fraud...I'm not a true writer." Elizabeth comforted him by climbing behind him, and rubbing his shoulder lightly. She bent down to his ear, "Jason, you can do absolutely anything you put your mind to. You are the most brilliant man I have ever laid eyes on."

In reality, she always knew she had just as much to do with the success of the first book, but she never dared steal the limelight from her soul mate. Elizabeth slunk back to Jason's lap, and stared lovingly into his sullen eyes, "I love you, and I know you can do this."

She placed her soft tongue gently into his mouth, and proceeded to wrap her arms around him. Jason's body was in the mood to ravage her, but his mind was not. His ideas had changed after his encounter with Wendy, and he truly wanted no part of the world of witchcraft. He knew if he was going to write another book, it would be a different subject altogether, but he had absolutely no idea what it would be.

As Jason laid Elizabeth on the couch, and hovered on top of

her, he attempted to shake the thought of Wendy Collins, the woman who inadvertently destroyed his love of writing, as well as his life of lies.

Chapter 14

When Jason Met Will

September 20th, 2014

There seemed to be nothing mystical about Jason's encounter with his new friend, Will Thompson, it always felt like it was just the right place at the right time situation.

It was night when Jason stepped into the Blackbird Brew House, a hip coffee bar located a few blocks from his lonely apartment. He had never frequented the place before, but he desperately craved a cup of hot coffee after the pounding headache he acquired from ingesting a fifth of bourbon.

Jason opened the glass door, and searched for a table in the back. About five feet away was another table, and sitting in the chair facing him was a young looking dark haired man sipping a coffee cup, and intently turning the pages of a book.

The waitress walked up to Jason's table, and took his order. She looked to be in her mid-twenties, had neon purple hair, and a hoop earring hanging from one nostril. Her earlobes were lined with earrings, and both arms were covered in intricate tattoos. She was surprisingly polite, and smiled when he made his order, she fit right in at this place, where everyone seemed to be what Jason would call eccentric.

One of the tables had three people, one guy had a huge Mohawk, and the man and woman sitting next to him would have been great pincushions. The coffee bar itself had dark lighting, and the chairs were black oak with crimson colored seat cushions, the floor was checkered and the walls were painted pitch black, and covered in concert and club flyers. Heavy techno pumped from the sub-woofers mounted in the corners of the ceiling. The attractive, young tattooed woman came back to Jason's table, holding a solitary coffee cup,

"Well, here you go, Mr. Plain, one black coffee, one cream." She smiled when she asked her next question, "You really aren't creative when it comes to your drinks, are you?"

Jason shook his head no, said thank you, and she stepped away. To anyone else, it would have been obvious that she was flirting, but someone as broken as Jason would never figure this out, nor would he have cared.

Jason blew on his plain coffee, and attempted to take a sip of the hot liquid when suddenly, the man at the other table said something aloud and Jason replied, "I'm sorry, did you say something?" The man picked his head up and looked at Jason with a massive grin. He was wearing a black Misfits t-shirt, and his eyes were a very deep blue. He opened his mouth, still smiling big, "You're him, man!" He held up the book he was reading, a copy of Cauldron, as he continued, "You're Jason Cain, holy shit."

Jason's mouth formed into an uncomfortable expression, "Yeah, I guess I am."

The man began to stroke his ego again, "That's cool." The man, book in hand, walked over to Jason's table, opened the inside cover and asked, "If it's not too much trouble, you think maybe you can sign this for me?"

Jason reluctantly nodded in and stated, "You know what? I don't have a pen, I feel so bad. Maybe you can get one from the waitress over there."

The man closed the book with a black-nailed hand, and with no disappointment in his words he began to speak, "Nah, that's cool, I'm not one of those fan boys anyway."

He put out his hand to shake Jason's and said courteously, "It was real cool to meet you, a real treat."

Jason nodded and the mystery man turned to walk away. For some reason, he suddenly had a deep feeling creep through, as if planted there.

Jason did not want to be alone, and this man looked interesting enough to have a conversation with, he called out, "Hey, sir?"

The man turned to face him, and Jason resembled a young teenager asking someone on a date, nervous and embarrassed, "How would you like to have a seat with me? Maybe hang out?" The man cracked another smile and replied jokingly, "Hey, I'm a fan all, and I'm sure you noticed the nail polish. But I gotta tell you, I don't swing that way. Sorry."

Jason looked confused when the man laughed, "I'm just fucking with you, chief. I would love to chat."

The fan sat down, placing the book on the table in front of him. He reached out his hand as he introduced himself, "The name's Will, Will Thompson. So, what brings you to this place?"

Jason answered, "Guess I couldn't sleep....had a lot on my mind lately."

Will replied quickly, "Lost love, huh?" Jason looked amazed, "How...how did you guess that?" Will gave him his explanation, "Well, it was either career issues, money problems, or love issues, but you have the look of a broken man. So, what I did, I peered into your very soul, and was able to feel the pain you feel. I'm what you would call a witch."

Jason's face became stone, and his pulse quickened. "Jesus Christ, you're not going to kill me, are you?"

He threw his hands in the air, "I'm sorry, the book was written a long time ago. It is old news and I am surprised you're still reading it. I meant no harm, really." He placed his arms back on the table, and his voice sounded threatened, "So if you're trying to harm me in any way, back the fuck off, okay?"

Will snickered, looking confused, "No, I don't want to hurt you, I'm a fan; I meant every word. I'm honored to 'meet you." He played with his hair, and crossed his legs when he continued, "Everyone's entitled to their opinion, even if yours is, bullshit."

Will's grin was once again plastered on his face and Jason responded angrily, "You know, I could really be offended by that little comment of yours, but I'm not." He took a sip of his now cooler coffee and he began to confess, "You know why? Because you're right, I fucked up." He began to tell Will about the day Wendy Collins attacked him, and how the altercation caused him to change his thoughts, he then went on about how he could not write another book, how his fame had fizzled out quickly. He spoke in length about his problems with Elizabeth, how he thought about her constantly, and how he could not let her go. Will did nothing but listen intently as he continued to unload all of his pain and suffering.

Finally, after talking non-stop, Jason became silent, looking as if he had lifted a huge boulder from his chest.

Will smiled and said with pity in his words, "That's some crazy stuff. I'm sorry for you man."

He stood up from his chair, and looked down at Jason, "You want to go smoke a joint with me?"

Jason just smiled and nodded. The two walked from the coffee bar, and headed to the back alley. It was dark and gritty, and lit by one solitary bulb on top of the back kitchen door.

They sat on a low wall of brick and Will lit a perfectly rolled joint. He took the first long puff and passed it to Jason. He puffed and asked Will, "Can I ask what got you into witchcraft?"

Will grabbed the joint from his hand and answered, "My mother." He took another puff, and continued, "She taught me when I was old enough, she really believed in it. In fact, it changed her life for the better." He blew out smoke, and looked toward the ground, "I miss her every day." He then pulled a piece of jewelry from underneath his shirt. It contained a tiny photograph, he asked Jason, "Would you like to see her?"

Jason nodded and Will unsnapped the chain, placing it in his open hand.

The pendant was shaped like a frame, and it was made of pure silver. The picture inside the snap was of a young woman. She had blonde hair, angelic features similar to his new friend, and a look of sheer happiness.

It was a look that showed her life experience, a look that reflected that she had been through something, and came out of it, free and clear.

Jason could see all of this because he knew no one truly smiled like that in photos, this was a real smile. Jason was hypnotized by the picture. "She's beautiful", he said to Will, still staring when suddenly he heard a voice in his ear, a woman's voice. It echoed loudly in his brain, "You are the one."

Jason sealed his eyes, shook his head, and passed the chain back to Will. Will looked concerned, "You cool, man? You look like something's up."

Jason continued to stare downward and answered, "No, I'm all right. I guess this is just some real good shit."

"Yeah, I guess it is.", Will laughed and continued to smoke.

Jason asked another question, "So where are you from, I mean...originally?"

Will looked wildly at Jason, "What do you mean?"

Jason quickly answered, "Well, I can tell you have a bit of a drawl, that's all. It's not thick, but you can tell, if you listen hard."

Will took a puff of the dwindling joint paper, "I'm originally from Indiana, from the Mid-West. But I've been around, Kentucky, North Carolina, California, pretty much everywhere. But now, I have business here." Will then quickly changed the subject, "Have you seen this wife of yours lately?"

Jason looked straight ahead of him, his expression completely left his face, "Well, I did see her on the street." Jason paused and continued, "She was holding our son's hand."

Will grinned. "The plot thickens, you have a son."

Jason exhaled the air deeply, "Yes, I do. God, I miss them both so much."

Will began his investigation, "Why don't you see him? Did something happen?"

Jason exhaled again, pain began to form on his face, "I grabbed him. I didn't mean to, I just had so much shit going on in my mind. Elizabeth made sure to throw it in my face, and she received full custody."

Will put his hand on Jason's shoulder, and sighed as he spoke. "You lost control. It was an accident, right? You can tell when fathers are abusive monsters, you can see it in their eyes." He stared down at the concrete, his voice became deeper, "Believe me...I know." He asked another question, and took his hand off of Jason, "So what happened with your wife?"

Jason answered him, even though he did not care to. "Look, I don't talk about her much. I don't feel comfortable talking about her." Jason felt a tear form in his eye, "I will tell you this, I would do anything to get it all back, do anything to get her back."

They both fell silent, Will stood from the wall and turned to

Jason, "It's been real, I should get going, but I have to ask, you still don't think I'm a mental case, do you?"

Jason smirked and shook his head, "No, but you are something else though. You really helped me out, you have no idea." Will did not say a word for a while. Then he finally said, "It's nice to help a good guy like you." He pulled a cigarette pack from his pocket, ripped off a piece of paper, and then fished in his other pocket, inside was a pen.

He laughed, "Well, what do you know, had one after all." Jason did not think anything of this.

Will jotted down his number, and handed the small piece of paper to Jason. They shook hands, and Will said, "It's been real."

Then he walked back to the front of the coffee shop, leaving Jason sitting on the wall.

As Jason stood up, he heard the woman's voice once again, "You are the one."

He walked fast, attempting to shake the woman's words, but the detached voice would haunt him further as the night drew on.

Chapter 15

To Grandmother's House We Go

June 26th, 1984

A groggy Susan opened her eyes to darkness, and she realized she had passed out in the truck on the trip to her mother's. She yawned and looked down at William, sleeping soundly, then she shuddered when she saw an image peering back at her through the driver's side window.

Susan shrieked when she saw his mangled mouth, rotten teeth and gums exposed, his bottom lip missing. Her shrieks turned into screams.

Her deformed husband's words were simple, "Run all you want, you cannot hide from yourself."

Susan awoke, screaming so hard she could taste a little bit of blood. William instantly began to cry and look around, realizing she and the baby were safe and sound.

She unbuckled her son's car seat and held him close to her chest to calm him. She whispered, "It's okay, mommy's here. It's okay. Daddy will not hurt you anymore, I promise."

After a few moments, Will calmed down and closed his eyes, Susan placed the baby back in his seat and turned the key in the ignition. In mere hours, she would be home after all of these many years. "Let's go see your grandmother", she said. As she began to turn back onto the dark road, Susan had many thoughts swimming through her head. What would her mother show her? What would she teach her? Soon the sun was up and Susan turned the truck onto the gravel driveway, looking directly at her past. She stared at the dirty front windows and began to feel tears stream down her cheeks. She could not believe she was there, and gently shook her son awake.

He rubbed his little eyes.

She smiled down at him with a sense of hope, "We're here, baby. We are truly home." Susan took the baby out of the seat, and closed the passenger side door.

Her mother's house had looked more beat-up than ever, the fence that Susan remembered had chipped, and half of it had collapsed. As she saw the state of her childhood home, she felt her nerves jangle. She noticed the wood panels of the house had fallen apart, and pieces had fallen to the browning grass. The windows were caked in grime, and she could not see anything inside as she stepped onto the porch, clutching Will tight.

Susan stood by the splintering door and took a huge breath, "Okay, here we go." She knocked lightly on the door, but no one answered. She knocked again, when suddenly the door swung open, as if an invisible force had wrenched it open.

Susan slowly stepped into the darkened room; the flowers on the wallpaper had decayed and ripped, pieces hung like vines, and as she stopped dead, she heard a voice, "Susan, is that you?" Susan clutched Will hard and responded, "Yes mother, it's me. I came back to see you. I realize now what you wanted me to do; I felt the change you spoke of."

Susan began to step in the darkness, toward her mother's voice, and continued, "I felt the thrill of it, the thrill of hurting a man, a man who destroyed me."

The voice in the darkness called out, "ALL men, my dear, silly child. ALL men are bad, ALL men destroy."

Susan felt as if she was going to swallow her tongue as she heard her mother's final sentences, "You have not finished. Your bastard husband is still alive." Susan's heart dropped when she heard footsteps coming toward her, and she saw her mother's eyes.

Her mother looked horrible, old, and beaten, Helen's skin was pale and appeared to be cracking, her eyes were sunken, and her hair appeared silver in certain parts, charcoal gray in others. She had appeared to have aged hundreds of years. Helen placed her bony, gray-skinned finger on little Will's forehead and looked at her daughter, who felt like she was going to urinate on herself.

Her sickly, dead-looking mother spoke again with hatred in

her words, "You did not finish. Bill is still alive, and then you bring this…this thing…this BOY into my home. He will grow to hurt, to destroy, to feed off of misery!"

Susan began to plead with the former shell of her mother, "This little boy is an angel, he is not like Bill, he never will be. I could not kill his father; I guess I just didn't have it in me. But, I hurt him, Mother, I hurt him." Helen raised her paper hand to a crying Susan's face, and spoke as her daughter shuddered, "Child, I told you to return when you felt the change. You were supposed to KILL your husband, not maim him. He was supposed to die. This child was supposed to die!"

Susan strongly interrupted her mother, "What did you just say to me?"

Helen stared at the baby once again, her voice slithering like snakes, "The child…must…DIE!!!"

With that, the shriveled monster slashed Susan's face with jagged fingernails, snatching the baby from her Hands, Helen ran to her closed bedroom door, Susan still wincing in pain. She placed her hand on her cheek and placed her fingers in front of her face, now coated in blood.

Susan shook the dizziness, and realized her mother had taken her sweet, innocent child. Susan screamed out his name, "Will! William!"

Then she noticed where her mother had taken him, the forbidden bedroom of her childhood. She rushed toward the door, and pulled on the knob; it was locked, Susan slammed on the wood of the door, screaming and crying, "No! Mother! Don't kill my baby! Please!"

The distressed mother ran around the trying to find something heavy enough to smash the door open. She lifted an old rocking chair, and swung it full force into the closed door. The furniture shattered like a broken glass bottle, and she began to feel dizzy as she spoke to herself, "How come this door won't break?" She began to yell again, "Goddamn you, mother!" The door was made of regular material but it was strong as steel, almost as if there was some kind of force field surrounding the secrets inside. Susan attempted to calm down, and made one last attempt to get

Helen to open her secret room, she pleaded with a fake pride, "I am ready, I am ready to fully understand." She began caressing the wood of the door like a kitten begging to be let inside of the house, "Please, let me do it. Let me feel the power of the Rogers women, I'm ready!"

Susan made no noise, waiting for an answer. The room was silent, when suddenly she heard the click of the knob. She breathed a sigh of relief, and entered the bedroom, slowly.

Helen was nowhere to be seen. In fact, there was nothing strange about the room at all; a bed, pillows fluffed, sheets clean and pressed, and there was a dresser with a circular mirror attached, makeup and jewelry boxes lined an end table. There was one window showing the view of the backyard, no books, no candles, nothing out of the ordinary, and worst of all, no William.

Susan began to hyperventilate and she yelled again, "Where the fuck is my baby, you old bitch?!" She threw the makeup dresser to the ground. The mirror shattered into pieces onto the floor, Susan became an enraged animal.

She began to throw objects in the room out of the window, and snarled and screamed, "Where's my baby? Where is my baby, you bitch?"

She walked towards the bed and flung off the mattress as hard as she could. Susan noticed something odd when she flipped the bed with all of her might sideways, the legs of the bed snapping as it was pushed. She attempted to slow her breathing, looked down, and noticed there was a heavy wooden hatch with a brass handle.

Susan smiled, even though she felt sick, "She must be down there, she must be." As Susan knelt down and opened the hatch, she noticed there were concrete stairs leading into darkness. She swallowed, and began speaking to herself again, quietly, "This is her secret, this is what she had been protecting."

She placed her foot on the first step and took a very deep breath as she mustered strength, "Well, it's time

o reveal them all." Susan headed downward. This could have been her descent into hell itself, or it could be her destiny. She had no idea what lay ahead for her. All she knew was she would do anything to feel the love of her baby again.

Chapter 16

She's So Lovely, She's So Deadly

September 22nd, 2014

Jason was tied to a wooden chair. He saw visions of a young blond girl, her piercing blue pools had become blood red. Her beautiful teeth became cracked and jagged, razor sharp. She laughed and moved towards his crying eyes.

He yelled to her, "Who are you? What the do you want from me?" She rubbed her hands across his face.

She smiled and licked her lips. "You are perfect...you are mine", she hissed as she ran her hands down his chest, and continued to slink downward.

Jason pleaded for her to stop, as she repeated her cryptic message, "You are perfect, you are the one."

He began to sweat buckets as the creature's hands slid down his stomach, nails digging into his thighs, Jason began to heave and sick crept up his throat.

The clawed hand ran down to his exposed member, and the evil woman's eyes met his closely. Her face then became distorted, beginning to change.

Jason was suddenly peering at Elizabeth's perfect face, her raven hair flowing. She began to stroke him, and he looked directly into her eyes, moaning.

Elizabeth slid down on her knees, and began to place her sweet lips on him, Jason rolled his head back in pure ecstasy. She sucked lightly and moaned as her ex-husband looked down at her, she stared back up him, lovingly She began to speak, "Oh, my Jason." Jason replied, "Yes?"

She smiled. Just then, her face once again became the monster from before. She placed her hand on his manhood and tugged. He winced, as she spoke, "You will die, you will all die."

Jason pleaded as the woman, staring at his sweat covered face with burning red eyes, ripped her hand back. Jason woke up, howling. His sheets were soaked in sweat, and his hand fumbled for the whiskey on the end Table. He could not see anything in the dark, but he continued to attempt to reach the bottle. Just then, he felt something, a lighter. Jason flicked the tiny flame, and he noticed a severed member laying on his stomach, and he screamed, violently.

And then, he truly woke up. Jason screamed as he clicked on the lighter. There were no monsters, and no detached appendages. He placed his head in his hands, and began to speak to himself, "What the fuck is happening to me?"

Jason jumped out of bed and headed toward the bathroom. He clicked on the light, and peered into the mirror on the medicine cabinet. He looked at himself, and gave the image staring back at him a pep talk, attempting to calm down, "Get yourself together, man. You are strong. There is nothing wrong with you."

His moment of calm was suddenly disrupted when he saw the woman in his nightmare glaring back at him.

Jason yelled out, grabbed a glass off of the sink he used to rinse his mouth and threw it straight into the glass. The shards flew all over the bathroom, and a few of the tiny pieces hit Jason's forehead.

"Fuck!", he yelled from the pain, and rushed out of the room, flecks of blood ran down his head and he quickly grabbed a towel. Jason plopped onto the disheveled bed, and looked at the clock. It was only four a.m. The alarm suddenly went off, and Santana's *Black Magic Woman* played through the static.

Jason slammed the off button with a closed fist, "Fucking Santana, why do you haunt me?" he muttered under his breath.

He picked up his cell phone, and dialed his new friend. Will answered, right away. He did not sound groggy, or surprised, in fact, he seemed like he was waiting on Jason's call. "Hey, it's Jason Cain. Listen, I have to speak to you. Can you get together this morning, maybe?"

Will responded quickly, "Sure, is something wrong, man?"

Jason did not want to speak about his dreams, but they both agreed to meet at the place of their first meeting at ten a.m. "Thank you for this, Will."

He told Jason not to worry and hung up. Jason began to think hard about what Will had told him about bringing love back. He started to think that maybe the dreams were a sign, and that something needed to be done.

And maybe, for the first time ever, he needed to believe in the unexplained.

Chapter 17

The Rose Begins To Wilt

January 20th, 2006

Jason was at his computer, his mind was blank, and he seemed to be writing nothing but nonsense. The screen in front of him read, *the theory of the mind fuck fucking shit fuck damn cannot think damn it.*

He groaned, and threw a stack of paper into the waste basket beside him. Jason's fame was beginning to fizzle, and Cauldron had dropped from everyone's lists, as well as their lips. He was no longer attending talk shows, and he was no longer doing signings. No one cared about the great Jason Cain anymore. Jason had attempted many times to come up with a new idea, but nothing ever came to mind. His behavior became erratic, he became angrier, more volatile. There were times that Elizabeth and Jason's arguments became so tense, it was as if he would actually put his hands on her. Elizabeth was never scared, she just figured it might be a passing phase caused by stress. She knew her husband was seriously upset about the new book, and was always able to forgive anything he had done for the sake of the relationship.

Jason was still at the computer, typing nothing of importance, when she walked into the living area. Elizabeth dropped her car keys on the end table by the front door and walked over to him, Her preoccupied husband did not even realize she was in the room.

Elizabeth kissed him on top of the head and wrapped her arms around his chest from behind, Jason smiled when he felt her warm skin. He finally acknowledged her presence, "How was the appointment?"

She thought of an answer and cryptically replied, "Fine", and then she changed the subject altogether, "How is the new book going?"

Jason just rolled his eyes, "Don't ask me about that, Liz, you already know the answer."

She bit her bottom lip, "Not good, huh?" She began to put her soft hands under Jason's shirt. She pulled at the hairs on his chest, "Listen baby, you will think of something."

Jason suddenly frowned and stared blankly into the computer screen in front of him, "You have to understand something. If I don't write something soon, we're screwed." He stood up from the chair and continued to complain, "The gravy train is gone. It has derailed, the talk shows, and all of the money."

Jason waved his hands into the air, and faced his now sullen wife, "All that we have left is your salary, and the remaining money from the book, it's pathetic." Elizabeth waltzed over to Jason, and placed her hands on both sides of his face. She stared at him with her loving eyes, and spoke to him softly, "Listen baby, none of this means anything to me. Only YOU are important to me." She wrapped her arms around his waist, "This could all be gone, but if I didn't have you, I would feel dead." She embraced Jason's quivering lip tenderly, and looked him in his wet eyes, "Look. I have something to talk to you about. We should go sit on the couch. So please, come over here with me."

Jason could not get his mind off of his work and began to walk back to the computer chair, "Can this wait, please? I really do have to get to work." Elizabeth just smiled, "Look, you have to take a break sometime, okay? If I wanted you to go crazy from your writing, I would ask you to also become caretaker for a hotel."

Elizabeth was attempting to get her shaken husband to laugh, but it didn't work, Jason rose from the chair, and followed Elizabeth to the comfortable sectional.

She sat him down next to her, and turned his head to face her, placing her hands tightly she took a deep breath, "I have something to say to you, and I think it's really great. I'm just going to come out with it." Jason's face looked puzzled as she continued, with a sly, albeit loving smile. "Remember I told you I was feeling a little woozy at certain times, and I felt like I had the flu for a few weeks?"

He nodded, and she continued her explanation, "Well, I went to get an opinion, and I received one."

Her grip tightened, and her smile became bigger, "Hold on to your seat…we are going to be parents. I'm pregnant."

Jason remained silent, looking as if he was going to crack a smile, but instead his eyes widened, and he began to shake as he spoke, "You're…pregnant?"

He pulled his hands from Elizabeth's, and she began to look confused, "You're not happy about this? I mean, I thought you would be happy about this." Jason sprung up from the couch, "I would be happy? No, Liz, I am not fucking happy."

Jason stopped his furious dance to face her, "We cannot do this, we are about to lose everything."

Elizabeth's eyes began to well up, and she had no clue what to say about his reaction, Jason continued to rant, "I cannot find my new subject, and we're not making big bucks anymore. I am…nobody again!" He walked over and knelt in front of his wife, her face awash in a sea of runny mascara and tears.

Jason looked at his broken wife and said, "We can't keep this baby, we have to rethink this, Liz. I cannot bring a child into this world knowing I'm not bringing in any money."

Elizabeth sat still and she was visibly shaken. Her hands pulled away from his hands, and began to curl into a ball. She jumped up, screaming, "Fuck your book. Oh my god, that is ALL you give a shit about." Elizabeth turned to face him, still kneeling but looking up at him, "I just told you we were going to be parents, and you spring this shit on me?" Elizabeth stared at her husband, almost looking through to his soul when she said, "I am not getting rid of this baby, not for you, not for anyone." In a rage, Jason hopped up and threw a vase on the glass table facing the sofa. Pieces of the flying glass flew every which way, also cutting into his wife's forehead, she fell to the ground, crying.

Jason quickly came to and ran to her aid. Elizabeth curled up on the floor covering her face with both hands.

Her husband had a look of disgust on his face, and he attempted to comfort her, "Are you okay?"

Elizabeth pulled away and stood up. Blood slowly dripped from her wounds as she grit her teeth, "Fuck you, Jason. You pig."

His features contorted as he rose to meet her at eye level, and suddenly he swung his hand back.

Elizabeth continued to look at him and said proudly, "Go ahead, you worthless motherfucker...HIT ME." Jason's face turned to normal, and his hand dropped to his side. He looked petrified.

She plopped down hard on the couch, placing her hands over her face, and Jason quickly rushed out of the front door, slamming it so hard everything in the house rattled. As he walked to his car he began to cry to himself, "What have I done? What have you done, you idiot?"

He slid into his expensive car that was doomed to be seized and drove off quickly, screaming obscenities at himself when he drove.

Elizabeth was always his angel. This event was the first time he truly clipped her wings.

Chapter 18

The Rogers Cellar Of Death and Prophecy

June 26th, 1984

Susan's breath was heavy as she stepped down into the darkness. She had no idea of what lie ahead. The stairway seemed to descend forever, but she realized it was only her imagination running away from her. She finally reached the bottom lit by lanterns, and let out a scream after seeing the terror facing her. The room was an old fruit cellar her grandfather had built under the house.

The size of the room was surprisingly expansive, and there was plenty of space to walk around, it could have easily held five or six people comfortably, without feeling crammed together.

The room was also lit by candles, placed all over the area; stacks of books were piled along a long blood-stained table, and in the center, lying atop the surface was a preserved corpse. The body was not clothed, skin had begun to peel from the arms and legs revealing muscle. The flesh had become a dull gray, but the identity, the face, was still covered in shadow.

Susan grabbed one of the candlesticks and attempted to slowly take a closer look. Suddenly, she felt like she was about to lose everything she ever consumed in her stomach, and her head became dizzy. She quickly recognized the face she had witnessed it in the pictures in the house, the body which belonged to her long dead father, Samuel.

Susan grew sick, spilling her bile, and as she was bent over, she realized there were strange markings all over the cement floor, she did not understand the symbols, but she knew they frightened her. Susan began to walk slowly toward the end of the illuminated room, and kicked something with her foot. She knelt down with the candle to inspect the object, feeling as if she was going to be sick again. A human skull.

Susan stood up, veered the candle flame to the right and left of her, and noticed there were remains strewn all over the hell pit. She began to tear up and spoke to herself quietly, "What have you done?"

Her silence became a war cry, "What have you done? Where is my boy?"

At that moment, she heard a raspy laugh in the shadows. "Mother, is that you?"

The laughter continued, when suddenly the flame on all of the candles jumped up, illuminating the entire room. Chained to a concrete slab was a decaying skeleton.

Next to the remains was another man, naked and chained by his arms and feet with rusty shackles, the victim was unconscious, but she noticed there were slices all over his arms and legs, as if he had been cut repeatedly in a violent interrogation.

Susan still heard the cackling and ran towards it. The voice of her mother cut through the darkness, her gray, decaying face and her milky white pupils looking directly at her now shaken daughter.

"Where is my baby? What is going on here?"

Helen's laughter stopped abruptly. She began to speak, her raspy voice echoing through the room, "Now you see. You see what I have to do, you see what I have done." Helen's hand pointed to the corpse of Samuel, and she spoke, "This is your father, the bastard, Samuel. This was his fate for what he did."

Susan asked, inquisitively and shaking, "What did he do?" She began to well up, "What did he do to deserve this?"

Helen spun Susan's body toward the table holding her father's remains and began to tell her tale. "One year after you were brought into this world, your father and I got into an argument. He was drinking heavily, I was sitting, holding you in my arms. The bastard always expected me to have dinner prepared." Helen then began to walk around the death table, looking down at her dead husband as she continued, "That same night, you had fallen ill, you were burning up, and I tended to your every need."

She began to feel tears flood her eyes, "Samuel, burst into the room, asking about his supper. I told him I had to take care of you, that it would have to wait." Helen once again stood in front of her daughter, and grit her now blackened teeth. "You could see the look on his face, change. It was so evil. He rushed toward me and pulled me up from the chair; I still had you cradled in my arms."

'She yelled, "I still had you in my arms!" Her voice began to break, "He pulled me toward him, and his fists balled up, and he struck me repeatedly. The pain was so bad that I dropped you."

Helen placed her hands on the sides of her face, "I dropped my feverish little baby, and he kicked me in the ribs as I was down. You were screaming. I crawled to you as he was still assaulting me."

Susan's mother never looked so emotionally broken in Susan's presence when she continued, "He pulled off his belt, and he raped me." Helen's voice bellowed, "He raped me, my own husband. You were lying on the floor and he didn't give a damn."

Her voice once again became calm, "Your father walked out of the room, and I was lying in so much agony."

Venom slithered through her words, "I vowed, he would never get away with what he had done. One thing you did not know was that I was raised on witchcraft. The Rogers bloodline have been practitioners for many years. We were always raised to do good, not to do harm."

She placed her hand on Susan's left cheek, "To show love, and bring peace, but I knew I was about to break that code." She again turned to the corpse, "Samuel was worth the risk, he had it coming. One night, as he was lying in his favorite chair, I stepped down into this room, and I felt a sudden presence reach directly into my mind. It instructed me to read an incantation, from this book."

Helen raised a decrepit hand and pointed to what seemed to be a leather book lying on the table, "The book was a tome revealing darker forms of magick. In fact, it was forbidden for anyone who had the book to use it, the book was passed down for the women in the family to make sure it was safe, to make sure it did not get into the wrong hands." Helen began to stroll around the table again, "I knew that I was doing wrong, but I planned to make him suffer."

She stopped to once again peer at the corpse. "I wanted him to bleed, to choke, to feel every single second of the pain I had felt before he died. I opened the book, and recited the words that the force I felt coursing inside of my head commanded me. My words brought back a lost soul, a woman seeking revenge, an all-powerful being." She walked back to face Susan who was stone-faced. "I begged her to give me the power to take Samuel's life. She advised me to repeat the words, again and again."

Helen began to grin, and her teeth looked cracked, "The windows rattled, the floorboards quaked, I felt her power inside of me, the heat from her presence. Suddenly, I heard screams of agonizing pain. I shot up the stairs to see what was happening." She turned to face her dead husband's body. "Your father had his hands wrapped around his throat, his filthy mouth wide open, gasping. His tongue had turned black, his eyes had sunk back into his head. And the blood, Susan, the blood."

Helen's wicked smile grew wider, "The blood seeped from his ears, his nostrils, it was quite a sight. He looked down at his hand, still gasping for air. I remember I began to laugh and dance around."

She looked at a now tearful Susan again, "Your father then fell to the floor, but he did not die right then. I watched him dying for about three months, he began to rot away. His insides had become liquid. I watched him decay, and I was happy with every moment. I could have watched him die forever."

Helen then laughed once again and continued, "I knew in my heart that ALL men, ALL men were bad! The female was truly the only sex that mattered. We are the child bearers, we are the life bringers. Men are the reason to all of our problem: they hunt, kill, they rape and destroy."

Susan swallowed, hard and calmly pleaded, "Where is my child, mother? Where do you have my baby?"

Her mother cut her off and continued. "The night Samuel died, I was graced with her power once again. She was so beautiful, her skin was alabaster. Her eyes white as the driven snow, her hair like black fire, the fires of hell itself."

Susan tried to wrap her mind around all of this, but she could not, all that she wanted was William, and did not care about anything else. She became angry, "Enough of this shit, Give me my boy, now!" Susan looked coldly into her mother's dead eyes, as Helen coldly warned her, "Susan Michelle, do not stop what I have to do, or you will be sorry."

Helen began to walk, and Susan stood very still. She could see her mother's hand rise and grip tiny feet. Dangling in front of her was Susan's bundle of joy, her reason for living. Around his mouth was a rag, the reason Susan could not hear his cries.

Helen revealed her other aged hand; it contained an item resembling a dagger. She placed it against the child's throat and Susan screamed, her face exploding in tears, "Mother! He did not hurt you, he is not like Bill, like Samuel. Please, give me my baby."

Helen replied with rage, "You will be strong, girl. You will let me finish telling you everything, or so help me, I will drain your little one now, do you understand? This is your heritage, your legacy, the understanding of yourself."

Helen laid the baby down on the table containing Samuel, and began to tell another story, "She came to me, the goddess. She told me I was chosen, that I was perfect. She told me she would guide me, in her vision, that she would become a part of me. This beautiful creature told me that she was a simple woman in life, and the pain of her death made her strong. She lived in the eighteenth century with a colony of women on secret land deep in the woods, somewhere around here. They were witches. These women believed in nature and beauty. She told me they had no men, that they did not believe in procreation. The women believed that if the Earth Mother wanted them to have a child, she would give them one. They were extremely capable and strong, and no one on the outside knew they even existed, not a soul, until the day of their discovery. A young man stumbled upon the site and ran to the town where the majority of the population was made up of dirty, horrible men. The boy addressed the group about the women in the woods, how beautiful they were, and how he saw them practicing sorcery, conjuring the devil." Susan attempted to slink toward her mother, but Helen placed the blade to the baby's throat again, and commanded, "Don't you move, you sneaky devil. Let me finish, I mean it."

Susan stopped in her tracks again, and her mother continuing regaling her, "The boy told the group that the women attempted to kidnap him, of course, the men believed this stupidity, and knew what they had to do.

They loaded up on weapons and ventured out to the secret reservation. The women did everything they
could to defend themselves, but the men butchered and raped them. They burned their homes to the ground, they kept one woman alive, because they had figured she was the leader because of her strong will. They dragged her back to town, naked and bleeding. The townsmen locked her up and abused her body repeatedly. She stood in front of the court, and did not receive a fair trial, the verdict was that she burn as an example to all of the women of the town. If they wanted to worship the devil, the same fate would fall upon any of them. They took the woman, tied her to a wooden post in the middle of the town square, tied her hands and her feet. She could not move a muscle, but she never showed fear."

Helen closed her eyes as if she felt the pain firsthand as she continued, "Her body was doused in flammable oils, and her hair was set ablaze. She began to burn quickly, and as she went up in flames, she told the on-looking men they would all pay, that their blood would spill into the ages. She told the women in the square, tears in their eyes, that one day, womanhood would feel her power, and then, there was nothing left of her."

Helen's eyes began to well up, "Her ashes blew into the air, carried by some supernatural wind."

Susan asked her mother in a demanding fashion, "So, what does this have to do with anything? I cannot stand here and listen to your ranting when you have my baby."

She took one step forward, "If you want me to truly understand, please give me my child." Helen began to look at Will's red, wet face. Susan saw her mother pick him up by his feet again, like strung up cattle, and she continued to attempt to be strong, while keeping her mother calm, "What does this story have to do with us? Help me to understand all of this."

Helen peered at Susan, her eyes a full white in the glow of the room changed to normal, "The day you left to be with Bill, the woman came to me again. She told me I would be the one, the one to pass on her legacy. She told me she would guide me, become a part of me. The visitor told me she had journeyed through heaven, through hell, and time itself to find me. She had been sleeping between spiritual planes, and only when I read the passage in the book so many years ago did she rise again."

Susan looked confused, and her head pounded, "I'm not getting this. What do you mean...she became you?"

Helen began to explain, "She entered my body, told me I could live forever through her. That I needed to aid her in her plan, the plan to destroy the men of this world. I agreed to the deal, but as time went on I realized I didn't have it in me. Because of my disobedience, the spirit caused my body to decay, slowly. I am dying now, girl."

Helen began to step toward Susan, still holding the baby by the feet. "She needs a new host, wants to become a part of you. She told me I could not teach you my secrets, if you did not kill. If you did not mirror her vengeance. She figured Bill would drive you to the brink, and then you would be strong enough to hold her within you."

Susan reacted with an aggressive tone in this sudden standoff, "So, you're possessed by a dead woman? And you killed men to sustain your life? You expect me to believe all of this? This is insane! Give my son, now! I don't want your life, and you can tell your spirit sister to fuck off!"

Susan rushed towards her mother, and Helen surprisingly stood still, pleading, "Please do not come any closer. She will force me to kill you, she's angry."

"Fuck her...and fuck you!" Susan clenched her teeth hard, and ran towards her mother with a war cry of sorts.

Helen's arms were powerful as she grabbed Susan and whipped her over the table.

Susan's head hit the concrete wall, and she could feel blood forming in her hair, and she heard a strange voice flow out of Helen's unmoving mouth, "You insignificant little girl. You dare doubt my power? I am the answer to all of your prayers. You know what it is like to be completely defeated by a man, as do I. The hatred of men molded me, the damage of the men from my time gave me my strength. I will show you this strength, you are young, you are truly strong, truly beautiful. You will be my next vessel. Together we shall bring along destruction, women will rule, will conquer all." Susan froze, and the voice continued, We shall raise your baby, together. He will be the only one to survive the holocaust. We will teach him our way. You will become me. We shall rule, together. You shall become a new Goddess!"

Chapter 19

Love Sets The Trap

September 22nd, 2014

Jason walked into the Blackbird Brew House right before ten a.m., and as he stepped in he looked to the back and saw Will, sitting down at the table where they first encountered each other. As Jason reached the table, Will outstretched his arms and said jokingly, "Look, it's our table. Isn't it romantic?"

Jason flashed him the finger and sat down. Will continued his humor, "So, what's up? Couldn't sleep last night? Maybe I should have been there to hold you." Will batted his eyelashes, and Jason finally let out a laugh. The waitress from the night he met Will came to the table, she was wearing a half shirt, and her now pink hair was twisted in pigtails on both sides of her head. She had a cup of black coffee and one cream in both hands.

"Hey there, Mr. Plain, I remembered." She smiled when Jason said coldly, "No thanks, I don't want coffee. But I'll let you know if something changes."

The waitress's smile disappeared, "Well, my name's Nikki, if you need anything else", she then walked to another table.

Will quickly looked at Jason, confused. "Are you telling yourself the truth about yourself? Are you proof positive you're not gay?"

Jason sucked his teeth, "What the hell are you talking about?"

Will tried to explain the obvious to him, "Did you happen to see that beautiful girl over there? Did you see her face? She likes you."

Jason shook his head, "Look, I'm not gay. You know what's wrong with me, I'm still in love, all right? Actually, that's what I called you about."

Jason looked at Will, and began to talk seriously, "I've been having these dreams. They involve this blonde woman."

Will continued with his jokes, "Now you're talking, tell me more."

Jason began to look aggravated, "Be serious, okay? This girl has a horrible face, she looks like a creature of some sort. This thing whispers to me silently, "You are perfect, you are the one."

Will said nothing and Jason continued, "It gets better. The woman starts caressing my body, and runs her fingers down to my, well, you know."

Will gasped. "She grabs your man meat, what else happens?"

Jason suddenly noticed Will's hesitation on the subject, "Are you getting offended by this story, I'm sorry."

Will became stone faced. "I just want to know what this has to do with anything."

Jason became perplexed, as Will acted very strange, almost standoffish, but he began speaking, "At the end of my dream, this woman becomes my ex-wife. She's...Elizabeth."

Will began to lurch forward, with signs of actual interest.

Jason continued, "This morning before I called you, I was in the bathroom, and I looked at my face in the mirror and I saw the creature again. I threw something into it, out of fear, and pieces of the glass cut into my forehead."

Will placed two fingers under his nose, resembling a therapist speaking to a patient, "So what exactly does that mean? Does that have some kind of meaning to you?" Jason explained further, "At one time, Elizabeth told me she was pregnant. Let's say, I didn't take it well. I had no idea what the future held so I threw something against the wall, and some of the pieces hit her in the same spot."

Jason stopped to take a breath, "I know it sounds ridiculous, but I see it as a sign. I feel that I will always be plagued by what I lost, unless I do something about it, Will."

Jason's eyes became very serious; he wanted Will to know he was not playing around, "I want you to give me the book you spoke of. I need to reach into Elizabeth, convince her into loving me again, somehow. If I do not try, I will never be the same. I need her love, please...help me."

Will stared Jason up and down, wanting him to fully

understand, "You wrote a book about the perils of witchcraft on the human mind. You don't understand this thing, at all. It's bigger than both of us, and if you mess up, the results can be catastrophic. It could change the outcome of your life. If you do not truly know about something, then by default, you really should not use it."

He rubbed his eyes, "You're my friend, I want to help you, but", Will then peered into Jason's sad eyes, "Ah, shit! I'll do it for you. I am going to tell you some things, and damn it, when that time comes, you better listen to every single word I have to say, are we agreed?"

Jason smirked and placed his hand out to shake Will's. "Agreed, and that is my solemn promise to you." Jason began to tear up, "Thank you so much."

Will touched his hand lightly, "It's okay. This is what's going to happen, I'm going to come to your apartment at ten o' clock. I will show you how to use the book, and then we'll go from there." Will narrowed his eyes. "Remember, you must listen to everything that comes out of my mouth; you must not screw this up."

Jason once again agreed to every word. He knew that soon he would have Elizabeth, and that was all he cared to know.

Chapter 20

The Rose Blackened

March 20th, 2006

Elizabeth had begun to feel the strain on her relationship after Jason's meltdown during her big news. She knew she still loved him, but she also realized that things between the two of them had changed, he had apologized to her immensely for his actions. There were tears, and flowers, everything that was part of the forgive me kit.

On this night, Elizabeth was in the bedroom brushing her luxurious hair, when Jason walked into the bedroom. He had been working on the computer downstairs, and had apparently had more than a few drinks.

Elizabeth looked radiant in a full satin nightgown, her growing belly fully visible. She was two months pregnant.

Jason stepped behind Elizabeth and kissed the pit of her neck, his breath smelling like happy hour. She closed her eyes, and did everything she could to hold her words. He had told her that he would slow down his drinking after the violent altercation. Jason was never a heavy drinker, but since he had started work on the new project, it had become more than a bit excessive. He told her it helped take the edge off, but she had started to notice that it was becoming a true issue. Jason asked her a question, slurring, "How are you doing, my beautiful, sweet woman?"

Elizabeth played along to prevent argument, "I'm doing okay. How's the book coming along?"

Jason stumbled over to the bed and flopped down. "I completed two chapters, I feel real good about this one."

He spoke with an intense sarcasm, and Elizabeth continued her nighttime routine at her cosmetics table, staring blankly into the mirror. Jason stared up at the ceiling. He began making noises with his mouth, "Yep, I am a genius. You're married to Hemingway, I have to say."

Jason began to laugh hysterically, and Elizabeth felt herself gritting her teeth, and instantly attempted to change the subject, "I think I felt the baby today, it was strange. But it's so beautiful, you know? I'm not really feeling too good right now, though. I have massive cramps in my stomach. It feels like the baby's firing off a cannon in there."

She laughed to herself, silently. Jason was still acting like a fool, and feeling sorry for himself, "So, I am going to call Lion Heart tomorrow, try to get an advance for the book. They aren't going to go for it, I suck and they know it."

Elizabeth turned to face Jason, her face showed nothing but anger, "Did you hear me, Jason? I was talking about the baby." He looked back at her, still lying on his back, his eyes appearing slanted, "Oh Liz, I heard what you said. But listen, the time for the baby will come soon. Now I have to think about this writing shit. It's not that I don't care, I'm going to love that kid to death."

He popped up, lying on his side, "Now, come on. Hop on the bed and give me a big kiss, and maybe,", he began to caress his chest, "We can get into a little something more?"

Elizabeth looked down at the floor and spoke under her breath, "Why, so I can get pregnant with yet another baby you don't give a damn about?" Jason lifted his head when he heard the comment and replied, unhappily, "What was that, Elizabeth? I don't give a damn about our baby? That is all I am worried about. If I don't finish the book, I have no idea what the future holds for us financially."

Elizabeth felt fired up. She knew her own truth, "You wrote a best-selling book, you were a very big deal. You made enough money to live off of for years. We're not living the big time anymore, but we will be okay, we will not lose everything."

Jason said nothing, and Elizabeth threw her hands up in the air, in defeat. "You know what? I do not know what to believe anymore, everything that comes out of your mouth lately is garbage. You say that you care about the baby, but you never ask me how I'm feeling. You work on this book like crazy, and that is all you do, and on top of all of it, you told me you would cut down on your drinking.

Everything you say to me is a lie."

Jason planted his wobbly feet onto the floor. His face had a very menacing look, his brow furrowed, and his mouth curled, "Okay, pretty princess Elizabeth goes to work at her little publishing job, brings a little money home, and now she's better than me. Well, let me tell you something, if it weren't for my book we would not be here now."

Elizabeth shot up from her chair, "You son of a bitch. How dare you say you did all of this. There is one thing you have to remember, I aided you in co-writing your real baby, and you never mentioned me. I did not say anything about it because I loved you enough to keep my mouth shut and let you live your dream. Now, I have a baby and this is my dream, to have a normal family life, with you. To be a loving wife, and a nurturing mother."

Jason stayed quiet, but his eyes said everything. Elizabeth continued her assault, "You know what else, Jason? You can talk about my job like it's worthless, but let me tell you something. My job has brought food to the table, and has taken care of us so much recently. That's more than your so-called riches have in a very long time. You are pathetic for throwing that in my face."

Then she said something that unraveled Jason at the seams, "Fuck you, Jason Cain." His eyes popped wide open, his curled hand went forward, and Elizabeth's head went back as his fist slammed into her left cheek. She fell to the ground like a bag of bricks, and she looked up, tears streaming from her face, her final words seemed to hit Jason in slow motion, "I...hate...you."

Jason looked at her, saying nothing. He was completely stunned. Ironically, Jason met his soul mate by hitting her, and ended the relationship with the same action. The love story of Jason and Elizabeth Cain had truly become tragic.

Chapter 21

The Shift Of Her Power

June 26th, 1984

Susan was lying on the floor, the cut on the back of her head stung her eyes, Helen's body now hung in mid-air. Her decaying form had become nothing but a puppet for the voice which continued to speak, "Do you want your mother to die? She disobeys my will; she is of no use to me."

Susan slowly rose to her feet, the pain making it difficult for her to stand, she pleaded, "Please, give me my mother and my son. Please? I will do anything you say. What do you want me to do?"

Helen's body once again reached the marked floor, her body still overtaken, "Complete your destiny, kill this man." Helen's body waltzed over to the chained man, whose face hung down toward the floor, she held her blade tight, and looked down at the prisoner, "Wake up. You pig. You disgrace. Come here, child, stand by my side."

Susan drug her feet, still holding her head, toward her "mother."

She saw the man's face in the candlelight. Her eyes became wide, and she felt a chill in her insides. The first thing she noticed was that the man's head had an infected wound where his ear should be. She placed her hand over her mouth, "Oh my god."

The voice boomed inside Helen, "You remember your husband, don't you? The pain he inflicted on you? He is just like all of them, he does not deserve to breathe our air."

Susan felt like she was going to be sick again, as Helen continued to coach her, "You punished him, you showed him your strength, but you did not complete your task. Your mother showed you the way, she tried to make you strong, and failed. She does not hold the power that you have." Susan attempted to grab for Helen's throat, and placed the dagger underneath her chin.

The voice laughed and became louder, "Ah, so much courage, I knew you are truly the one. You will only get one chance, you will kill this man. You will show me that you are truly worthy."

Susan held the blade closer, and the voice continued, with no signs of fear, "We shall become one. We will live forever, together. We will bring about their extinction. Pigs, worthless, like your husband. We shall sit on a golden throne, surrounded by a sea of their corpses. We shall raise your child, teach him the way of the true goddess. He will bring us the one to unleash our vengeance upon the world. He will be pardoned from the slaughter, your mother's pitiful life will be spared. Her skin will form, her sickness cured."

Susan continued to stand behind her, holding the knife, undecided, "What if I do not succumb to your will?" Helen pointed to the baby, still dangling like a fish on a hook in her closed fist, "If you do not, your child's blood will be spilled at your feet, and then you will watch your precious mother die."

Susan thought about the voice's vision, the things she would be accountable for, the absolute destruction of man, the taking of millions, possibly billions of lives. Then, she envisioned a world ruled by women in her head. She saw a beauty in it, a peaceful world. She saw blooming flowers and the end of destruction, the end of violence. She thought about all of it and surprisingly, it enticed her. Susan released her grip from the back of Helen's head, taking the blade from under her throat.

The voice seemed very pleased, "Kill him. Unleash your power!" Susan raised the dagger over Bill's head. He stared up and squealed when he saw pure murder in her vacant eyes.

"Do it," commanded the voice. Susan brought the blade downward. The first strike punched through the top of his cranium, and she slowly pulled the blade out with a squish, Bill's body flailed on the hard floor like a fish out of water. Susan then pierced his heart, and punctured his abdomen. She was stabbing wildly now. She slashed his right arm, his chest. Her face and clothes were covered in sticky blood. Susan laughed maniacally as she picked up Bill's head. She smiled from ear to ear as she looked directly into his dying face,

"Die, you fucking pig."

She screamed as she slammed the blade through his forehead, the blade protruding from the back of his skull, the power of the thrust so strong, it impaled his sticky head to the concrete wall.

Susan heaved, wiped the blood from her face, and then she giggled.

She looked upon Bill's lifeless body sitting in a giant ocean of red, and in her pants she felt a little wetness from the excitement of the experience.

The voice's laughter echoed, "Excellent, you have done it. You are truly the one, the one I desire."

Helen's body placed her hand on Susan's shoulder, "Now, it is time. Your destiny has come."

Susan pleaded to Helen's visitor, "I have done what you said; I have agreed to everything. Now please, let me have my child."

Helen nodded. "As you wish, my strong child, one more thing has to be completed. We must become one."

Susan stood still, took a deep breath and closed her eyes, Helen's mouth opened wide, a ball of what appeared to be flame shooting from her decayed form, bathing the room in an immense ball of light.

Helen dropped to the floor in a heap. The flame shot toward Susan who began to cry, her eyes opened wide; she saw the amazing light rocket toward her. The flame entered her corneas, and Susan let out an intense squeal as the flames continued to enter her frozen body. She fell back onto the cement, and the light in the room was once again normal.

The cellar was silent. Helen moaned and slowly rose to her feet. Her face had changed, her eyes were once again a beautiful emerald, her skin was smooth, and the flesh had ceased the decaying process.

Helen raised her hands to her eyes. She noticed she was normal, and began to cry. She yelled happily and looked to the floor to see little William, quiet and gagged. "Oh my god", she yelled as she knelt down to retrieve her grandson. She took the gag from his mouth, "Oh my god, poor baby."

His revived grandmother clutched him to her bosom, and

looked over to see her husband's corpse sprawled naked on a table, the skulls and bones on the dirty floor, and the man shackled sitting in his own blood. The sight made her feel as if she was going to pass out.

In an instant, she noticed her daughter's body on the floor, "Susan, my girl."

She bent down to check if her daughter was breathing, and Susan slowly opened her eyes. She lifted her head from the floor. Her hair was as yellow as the golden rays of the sun. The streaks of gray and silver had disappeared, her eyes had an intense shade of blue like the deepest ocean, and all of the cuts and scars from her extremely abusive existence were gone.

Susan was eighteen again; she was an innocent girl again. But underneath her new found beauty was something very sinister.

Helen handed the baby over to her daughter, Susan stood up, and held William in front of her eyes. She stared at her child's face and asked, "Sue, my little girl, are you feeling okay?"

Susan could faintly witness her reflection in her child's wet, crying eyes. A smile spread across her now ruby lips, "I feel beautiful, I am beautiful."

She walked past her mother, to stand above Bill's bloody corpse. Helen's daughter smiled devilishly as she looked upon him. The massive wounds still leaked red, sticky viscous.

The young mother placed her hand on the silver dagger handle in his head, and pulled it from the wall with ease. Bill's head went forward; blood dripped from the gash slowly.

Susan dragged the blade across her tongue, savoring her first kill, "So delicious."

Helen tiptoed over to Susan. She knew there was something different about her, powerful. She placed her hand on her daughter's shoulder, and Susan turned to face her, her eyes becoming a flaming light. Susan stared as if she was peering directly into Helen's soul. Her voice echoed, "I am not Susan, Susan is no more. I am Sara, Sara Rinehart. "

Helen gasped and began to walk backward, "Oh my god, the spirit. What have you done here, what have you done to my daughter?"

Susan/Sara looked down at the baby and began to rock him. He seemed extremely pleased to be in his mother's arms, "I have made her everything. Age cannot touch her, no one can harm her. I gave you the gift, and you failed me."

Helen had a sudden look of fear, "Sara, you placed the words in my brain. You forced me to bring you back." Susan's eyes became an illuminating white light, and her pupils rolled back.

Her now powerful voice shook the foundations of the room. "Silence! You pitiful old woman, I made a promise, to spare your life. You are only here because of her good nature, and are now nothing but a slave. And you will do everything I command of you...or else you will feel pain you can never imagine."

Helen bravely answered back, "What do you want from my girl? What do you want from my family? Tell me, demon!"

Susan smiled, "Hmm, demon you say? I am doing this for her! I do this for the Earth Mother! She once was a powerful being, but alas, the folly of man corroded her very mind, and she is becoming sick. The night before my execution she came to me in a dream. She showed me the future of the world, a world plagued by war. There was a massive depletion of her resources; destruction of trees, rivers, and oceans, the slow extinction of her beautiful creatures. I witnessed the outcome of her true children, the women. They had become jaded by their looks, many of them were only concerned of beauty, and the shape of their forms. They could not feel the growing scar of their mother. Men had created this deterrence as they continued to destroy and decay. In my travels, I saw a man, this man truly thought he came to believe the words of the mother, yet, he believed nothing. He only cared for the love of a woman, it was this reason that he was perfect, he was the one.

When I returned to my mind, the mother spoke the words for me, the words to scroll in the book that you possess. I took a blade and wrote every single sentence in my own blood, a contract. The mother told me of my death. She told me my sisters and I would be taken by the animal she meant to wipe out, that once I sacrificed my human shape I would become something much stronger. I would become a messenger of vengeance, and I would return when the keeper of the passage felt hatred in her own heart. She would call for me to aid her, and that woman was you. That same night, she left my mind, and I prayed in her name until the morn. The sun rose to its highest peak and our fate was upon us. Those horrible animals raped children, stabbed, tore into, and maimed them. I held my ground as they dragged me, naked and beaten from my burning home.

They gathered belongings, the piles of books were taken to the town, to be incinerated along with the bodies. The piles included the book, which contained the mother's legacy. The books were stacked in the town hall inside the judge's quarters. The judge was the father of a daughter who was fourteen years of age. Her name was Bethany, her last name also belongs to you." Helen gasped and her face froze in shock, "Oh my god, Bethany was our ancestor, she began our faith. I read about her in family journals."

Susan's hand stroked the baby's hair, as she continued her story. "She had the face of innocence, she was uncorrupted, and on the afternoon of my execution the girl broke into the judge's quarters and came upon the books. She was wide-eyed, instantly fascinated. She never touched my book, feared everything within, the way she felt inside as she gazed upon it. As months went by, she began to worship the Earth Mother. Bethany Rogers became a full-fledged practitioner of her power and philosophy. She aged, as all women do. She married, had three daughters of her own, and secretly carried on the tradition to her girls, safe from the eyes of her husband. She informed the girls to hold onto the book, to protect it from the wrong hands. As time melted away, every female in your bloodline held onto the book for safe keeping. The women of your family promoted peace and goodwill. Your mother also had these beliefs and brought you up in her way. Then, you gave birth to a daughter and you practiced the faith with only the intentions of good, until the evening your husband attacked you. Your beliefs grew darker, and there was nothing but evil in your heart. You wanted his pain, you wanted his suffering. These feelings burned in you as they burned in me. You called for my return, the writer of the book, I became you. As your daughter grew older, you kept the practice a secret from her. You never thought she was worthy. You conditioned her body and mind in your new belief system, that men were evil, and should be destroyed. You abused her, you made her bleed, attempted to place your anger in her. You planted the seed in her mind.

This rose blossomed when she began to defend herself, when she brutally attacked her husband. YOU began to murder innocents, stored them in this dank cellar, but then began to break from my control. You began to feel this was wrong, became weak, and I punished you for it. I made you wither, caused your flesh to decay, killing you slowly. After your daughter unleashed her strength, I knew she was the one I wanted. She resembled Bethany: her features, her innocence, and most important to me, her fire, that is why I chose her.

Without your ancestor, the Earth Mother's words would have been destroyed forever, and without your

daughter I would not have had the vessel to carry out these plans."

Helen felt her head become heavy; she felt her skin crawl. "What plans? What do you propose to do?"

"I will teach your grandchild the ways of the mother. I will tell him how he should be ashamed of his gender, how useless men truly are. He will hear how he should take his own life because he was born a man, and then, he will be informed that the only way to redeem himself is to seek out the man, the one I saw in my dimensional travels of time and space in my dream. This man will read the words of the mother thinking he will gain a love lost, and the words will strike the ear of every single woman in the world. They will be become connected to me, as I am now connected to your daughter. The women will then eradicate every male on her beautiful face, the planet. Think of it! A world controlled by women, the end of overpopulation. They will bring back resources, major war will cease…it will be glorious!"

Susan laughed when suddenly she was slashed across the face with something sharp. The wound opened, and then disappeared.

Helen looked on, shocked. Susan's eyes turned to face her, and her mother's face was now white as a sheet.

Susan's eyes shone red; her mouth became jagged. "What do you think you are doing?" Helen stumbled backwards, and her daughter's body followed her, slowly.

Helen raised the blade in front of her with both hands, "You do not know what you are doing! You are stopping procreation, you are murdering millions. Not every man is evil, you are wrong! There are loving, peaceful men in this world. You are just playing God."

The being in Susan grew enraged with the sheer power of Sara, "God? God is the reason we are in this mess. He made them in his own image. They fight and destroy in their Father's name, do not speak to me about GOD!"

Helen picked herself up as Susan growled, "Old woman, you are no longer of use to me. You plan to destroy everything. It is time to finish you!"

Susan's body flew full speed towards Helen, still clutching the baby, and grabbed her frightened mother by the throat.

Helen closed her eyes tight. Pain shot through every part of her body. Susan was like a locomotive. She slammed her mother's head into the concrete of the wall, and her vertebrae snapped like a twig.

Helen looked in the eyes of her daughter as her mouth became filled with jagged, razor sharp teeth. She opened her mouth to scream, but nothing came out. "It's a shame your grandchild should grow up not knowing his grandmother!", Susan's mouth opened as if she had unhinged her jaw, "Die, you weak woman!"

Her teeth clamped on Helen's face, chewing flesh from bone. Blood spattered her face, and the wall behind her. Susan continued to mangle flesh, and then with the power of something otherworldly, slammed her mother's head into the wall, causing it to explode in a shower of blood and brain matter.

Susan licked the blood from her lips, looking at her baby who was surprisingly still quiet.

She smiled, her face now normal. "I never cared for her anyway. Come, little one, there is no time like the present for you to begin learning."

Chapter 22

The Rose Disintegrated

August 12th, 2008

Elizabeth had finally given birth to her child, a baby boy. She decided to name him Matthew after her late father.

The baby was almost two years old and Jason was attempting to change, to become a better husband. He began to attend AA meetings after the incident which occurred in the bedroom.

He continued to find inspiration for his book, but nothing came to mind. In his own thoughts, he had typed five hundred and fifty pages of nonsense.

The thought of having a drink always tightened like a noose, and as he continued to sink into frustration, Elizabeth had never been more alive in her entire life. She loved her son, and would do anything for him. His mother worked at home so she would always be by his side. When he went down to sleep, she began reading her piles of manuscripts.

Jason and Elizabeth were disconnected, even though they kissed each other, and occasionally attempted to find time for romance. The two hardly spoke, and if they did it was usually concerning something lost in the house, or something extremely petty and unimportant. It was a cold environment, even with all of the baby toys and accessories strewn about, and it was Jason's final action on this day that would cut the artery of the love Elizabeth had for her one and only.

Jason was typing furiously when Elizabeth stepped over to him, their child in her arms. As he continued to look to the screen of the laptop, tapping the keys with two fingers, she placed the baby into the play pen next to his work station. Elizabeth huffed when she spoke, as if she were doing one hundred things at once, "Jason, can you look at me please?"

He abruptly stopped typing, took a deep breath and turned to face his wife looking upset. "What is it, dear? Did you not see me working over here? Was I not focused on attempting to make our lives better again?"

Elizabeth stared down at her husband and rolled her eyes. "Jason, I need to go out and pick up some things for the baby, we need formula, I need you to watch him. I'm sorry, but please, just continue to work and keep an eye on him. Put him in your lap, I'll be quick."

Jason shook his head and did not say a word, Elizabeth bent down to place a fast peck on his lips, thanked him, and headed towards the door. The room was silent, except for a ticking clock.

He blew out air and spun around to stare at his son, who was playing with a stuffed toy intently. Standing up from the computer chair, he picked up Matthew, and slunk back down to stare at his albatross on the bright screen, his still unfinished second manuscript.

He sat back down, placing his young son on his lap as he continued to jot down words. Matthew playfully tossed his favorite toy around, laughing and giggling, and his father's preoccupation allowed him to forget the unfinished glass of water sitting on his work table.

As Jason clicked and clacked like a man possessed, the heavy stuffed animal left his son's tiny hands and hit the glass, causing the liquid to cascade onto the floor, and flow onto the table surface heading toward the work he had completed. The screen fizzled and turned black. The little boy's lips began to tremble, and his father's facial expression changed from determined to pure anger. Jason attempted to click the on button, again and again, with no response.

Matthew began to wail, and Jason stared into the blackness. His work was nowhere to be seen, and the knowledge of this caused a hearty yell to escape his throat as his son continued to cry. Jason peered into his boy's eyes. His lip curled, and the venom of the moment escaped, "What the hell are you crying for? All my work gone, my livelihood, you little bastard."

His mind was so occupied with rage that he did not hear his wife walk through the door. He shot up, crying baby in arms, and he continued to express himself to the baby, "You did this; you ruined me."

Jason's lip curled, the same way it had when he struck Elizabeth, and without thought or sense, Jason snatched his child's hand and pulled. The boy screamed in pain, and Elizabeth was right behind her troubled husband.

She snatched her pride and joy, her child who was now wounded and afraid, and punched Jason directly in the nose causing him to topple backwards and fall back hard into the wet work station causing it to tip over, and just as he fell so did everything he held dear to his heart: his work, his love, and his life with Elizabeth.

Jason hit the floor hard, and pushed the broken table off of his chest, Elizabeth stood over him like a warrior preparing to kill her enemy. Tears filled her eyes, and she spoke the words that would always resonate in her husband's soul, "You fucking son of a bitch, you are so lucky I don't kill you."

Jason stood up at her beautiful eyes, filled with fire and hatred, and he trembled. Elizabeth leaned in closer, her every word clear and her teeth clenched, "Get your sorry ass up, and get the hell out of this house. If you are not out of here in twenty minutes, I will have every single squad car lined up out front to take your pitiful ass away."

He slowly stood up, holding his face, and the hatred emanating from his lovely wife rang very clear, "I want you out, I want a fucking divorce. I want you to sign the papers, and never see your ugliness again. And I want you to know, you will never see this little boy again."

Jason still held fingers to his broken nose and his eyes began to well, Elizabeth pointed to the front door, "Now, get some things together and get out of my life. You are truly the worst thing that has ever happened to me." The pain in his nose could not come close to the ache in his chest. It was as if someone had wrenched out his insides. Jason stepped away from Elizabeth still stone, clutching her child to her chest.

Nineteen minutes later, Jason, bags in hand entered the room where Elizabeth was lying on the couch, her child now quiet and cooing. He looked over at the woman who had changed his entire life, the one who had truly given him life and he sucked back tears as he spoke, "Elizabeth, I just want you to know that I am so very sorry. I obviously have extreme issues to deal with, and I know that I need to seek help. I am so very sorry, baby, for everything. I just want you to know that I will always love you."

Jason clicked the knob on the door, and Elizabeth's words were heard but not seen as his back was facing the door, "Jason, you will give me custody of our child. You will not see him, you will not have to tend to him, he is mine. As for me, I want you to know that I don't love you, Jason. I have not loved you for a very long time; I just want to let you know that."

When she said goodbye, it felt like he had been hit with a boulder, and he stepped through the door. As she heard his car engine start up, Elizabeth began to cry hysterically, clutching her son tight. This was the end for everything she and her husband had built, and this was truly the death knell for her life with the man who changed her life, and her thoughts on love.

Chapter 23

Her Soldier Who Could Never Be A Soldier

Many years had passed since Sara became one with Susan Rogers. William was just seven years old and already had a very horrific life. He had been abused by his father, and his grandmother had held him upside down with a blade to his throat. Most important of all, his mother had been possessed by a messenger demon who had a plan to kill all of the men of the world, and Will's progression into manhood was not an easy one. He was never aware his mother was not who she claimed to be, that there was something evil inside of her, what he did realize was that she had a pure hatred for men.

His mother told him on a daily basis that they were horrible creatures, and that he should be ashamed of being one himself. When William turned eight, his mother beat him for playing soldier in the backyard, she scolded him, "You want to be a filthy soldier? They are one of the reasons our Mother is dying, they destroy everything in their path, they use Her fertile land as a playground to kill each other! Disgusting filth! No feeling animals." William was beaten to the point of passing out; the skin on his body was red and very raw.

When William was thirteen, he was playing a game of touch football with some boys who lived in their small town.

Susan rushed toward him as his body was covered in dirt, pinched his ear hard with two fingers, and pulled him back to the house, and for this offense, he was whipped with a leather belt. He was punished so viciously that some of the skin tore from his upper body.

William always held in his screams, and his mother had always told him, "No matter what I do to you, no matter what I say, you must always hold your ground. You must always be strong. You are going to make the world right again, be strong."

She usually gave this speech before she was about to lace into him.

When William turned sixteen, he had a monster crush on a girl he attended drama with at his school, Curtis High, the same school his mother had attended. Young Will was never able to do anything considered masculine. He was never allowed to play sports; was not allowed to listen to aggressive music, and he was not allowed to have racy pictures of women in his room like most boys his age. In fact, he was conditioned to treat the female form with nothing but the utmost respect. William agreed to this demanding and solitary lifestyle because he truly loved his mother.

The girl in Will's drama class was named Stephanie Matthews. Stephanie had the most beautiful green eyes, her hair was dark brown, and William always focused on her lips. They were full and luscious, and always made him think nasty thoughts forbidden in the Rogers household. He had no idea what these thoughts were. His mother had never given him the sex talk; everything he heard about anything sexual was overheard during his friends' conversations and the language coming out of their mouths seemed foreign to him.

Stephanie invited William to spend some time together after school one afternoon, and they headed toward the wooded area behind his house. William knew that he was doing something that would break his mother's heart, but he also knew the tree-lined area was thick and deep enough to hide them both.

When they headed into the trees, they walked as far back as they could. William and Stephanie both sat down on a thick trunk that had fallen to the earth and talked. She opened her backpack and pulled a flask she had filled with different types of alcohol she had stolen from her father's liquor cabinet, she took a deep sip and passed the concoction to a flushed William, but he denied her.

Stephanie scoffed, "Why are you so uptight, are you Mormon or something?"

Will seemed to stare right to Stephanie's soul as he spoke. "That's not it at all. My mother is very strong, and she taught me to be like this."

Stephanie took another long sip, as he continued to speak, fear forming in his eyes, " She always told me men were pigs. That I should kill myself before I ever became like any of them. I respect women and I don't know what I'm doing out here with you, I'm very nervous."

In her mind, Stephanie knew that this guy was a bit more than strange, but his company was better than being with the normal guys; aggressive horny jocks that only thought with their dicks. William was different. He respected her, and she also felt safe with him. Stephanie went back into her bag, and pulled out a compact, while William stared deeply, a bulge began to pulse in the front of his jeans.

Stephanie placed the makeup back, and licked her lips, "So, Will? Have you ever kissed a girl before?"

He shook his head hard, Stephanie laughed and tossed her hair, "Do you maybe...want to kiss me?"

Stephanie grabbed his head with both hands, shoving her soft tongue deep into his throat. William slowly placed his left hand on her back when Stephanie took a hand from his face to pop open two buttons on her aqua blouse. She placed his trembling right hand on her exposed bra cup. He shuddered, and continued to lock lips with her. Suddenly, something in him snapped. He loved every single second that had passed, and began to feel less ashamed. Will placed his lips on Stephanie's swan-like neck, and he could taste her salty, sweet perspiration mixed with a faint fragrance.

She moaned deeply and crawled down to the fallen leaves, and William followed, planting his body on top of her. Stephanie began to fumble with the button on his jeans, finally popping them open, and pulled his pants and boxers down to his sneakers. Stephanie placed her hand on his swollen member and began to stroke.

William moaned silently when she placed those lips he always dreamed of on his throbbing penis, when suddenly, her quivering body hit something very hard.

She slowly opened her stinging eyes to witness a young blonde woman standing in front of her. Stephanie suddenly realized what had happened. This strange woman had grabbed her tight by the hair and flung her into the bark of a thick tree behind the two lovers. Her head ached, her back felt raw, and she could not stand. "Who the hell are you, are you his girlfriend or something, bitch?"

Susan stared at Stephanie on the ground, eyes narrowed. "I am his mother." Stephanie's eyes widened, no way was this possible. She began to speak sarcastically, "What the hell? Did you have him when you were five?"

Susan laughed, "No, but that is really quite humorous. A great sense of humor coming from a dirty corruptor!"

William hopped up quickly from the ground, pulled up his pants, and stood tall in front of his mother, "Mother, please. It's my fault, okay? Stop this!"

Susan grit her teeth as he continued, "I love you, and I'm sorry, I'm weak. I'm...weak." Susan's lips began to curl as she grabbed her pleading son by the throat and tossed him a few feet in front of her.

She then turned her attention back to the wounded and now startled girl by the tree, Stephanie felt sick creep up her throat; she was absolutely frightened now. Susan began to walk toward her, and the girl did get ill, all over the front of herself.

She began to cry as the blonde woman seemed to tower over her.

The usually tough teenager felt as if she was begging for her very existence, "Please don't hurt me. I'm sorry! I'm so sorry. If I say anything to my parents I will get in trouble anyway. I won't say anything, I swear. Please, let me go home."

A smile slid across Susan's face, as she grabbed the sobbing girl by her sore throat, a supreme fire burned in her eyes. "This is exactly what I speak of. You are weak. All of you younger women are weak! You give up when there is a threat to you. You urinate all over yourselves and cry, I am going to change all of that, do you understand? For Her, I am going to change the balance. We will rule someday, my girl." Her gaze froze Stephanie's entire body with her last words, "We...will....rule!"

Stephanie had no idea what the woman was speaking of, but she shook her head in agreement, and felt like she was going to have an attack. Susan lightly dropped her onto her quaking feet, "Now, GO!"

Susan slapped the quivering girl across her wet face causing her to turn and run full speed from the wood line.

Will knelt down on both knees as Susan turned around, stabbing into his soul with her gaze.

He began to plead, "Thank you, mother, thank you for not hurting her too bad. I am the one who was weak, I am the one who has hurt you." He began to slap himself hard on both sides of his face, "It's my fault. I am a man! I am a pig, I should burn, I should burn in hell."

He continued to slap himself, his cheeks raw, but still tearless, "Take me into the house, mother. I love you so very much. Do what you plan to do to me. I will take it, with all of your love and your strength."

Susan grinned and stepped over to her son. She lifted him off of the ground and they both headed out of the trees toward the house.

Only William knew what was ahead for his disobedience.

More time passed and William graduated from Curtis at the age of eighteen. He occasionally saw Stephanie, but she always turned her gaze, and walked away from him, quickly. In his last year at school, he had become disconnected from his small group of friends, and talked to no one. Will's hatred toward himself had grown to epic proportions due to the constant words by his mother that he was some kind of monster, and there were moments where he attempted to drag a blade across his wrists, but of course, never could achieve death.

Will knew cutting his life short was not his legacy. His matriarch had much bigger plans for him.

Finally, after graduation, his life came full circle. The boy's mother commanded him to follow her to the locked bedroom door, and just like his mother before him with Helen, he had always been forbidden to enter and he never tried. She opened the bedroom lock and he witnessed the forbidden room for the first time, there was nothing out of the ordinary.

It looked like nothing but a regular room, until Susan pushed the bed toward the back wall, facing the backyard window and Will noticed the hatch on the floor.

He always knew his mother was a practicing witch, but never in his wildest dreams would he think she had a secret room inside of a secret room. She opened the creaky door, and he saw the concrete stairs leading down into darkness.

Susan looked into her son's wide eyes, "Come with me." William felt his throat tighten and his stomach churn as they descended. His mother made it to the floor, and lit a row of candles, "Join me, my son." William touched down to the concrete floor. He noticed markings etched all over the stone, a wide table was covered in stacks of books and paper, but the room was clean of anything evil or sinister.

"Join me here", his mother's voice echoed. He stepped over to her slowly and she looked down on him and began to speak softly, but with authority. "Here it is, it has all come to this. It is now full circle, you will now begin to fulfill your destiny. Everything that I have taught you over the years has come to this moment, in the Mother's name."

Will hung his head to the floor, repeating the words, "In the Mother's name."

Susan continued, "My child, you are to go to Philadelphia and start a new life. You are to act normal, never let people in on the fact that you are different." She placed her hand under his chin, "That you are special."

Susan continued to look into his face, "Close your eyes, my son." He sealed his eyes tight as Susan placed a thumb on his forehead. William began to wince as she spoke, "I am now anointing you, with a vision, a vision of the man you are to seek out."

Will witnessed a picture forming in his thoughts, an image of a dark-haired, blue-eyed man, he had been crying and lifted a bottle to his lips. William shook as he asked, "Who is this, mother?"

Susan closed her eyes, "This is Jason Cain, he is the brokenhearted man we seek. Years from now, he will lose a love, and will do anything to bring her back to his loving arms." She began to smile. "He will tarnish the name of the Earth Mother and her children, this is why I chose him, to punish him! This man will be accountable for everything that is soon to occur." Will kept his eyes shut as he asked another question, "How do you know this man?" Susan placed her hand on her son's warm cheek, "I saw him, in a dream. The Mother came to me. showed him to me. She told me he was the one she wanted."

Will attempted to nod in understanding, his eyes fixated on

his mother as she began to explain her son's future orders. "You will follow this man, Jason Cain. You will watch his every move, you will become close to him, and when it is time you will have this man trust in you; he will confide in you. He will tell you of his lost beloved."

Susan then stepped to the table and slipped a violet satchel open to reveal a leather book. She caressed the material as she began to explain, "This is the book I have held in my possession for many years, this is your legacy. You will tell Jason Cain that he can cast a spell by reciting a series of words inside, you will tell him that the words will influence his love to come back to him, without consequence. When he reads the passage, the cleansing of the Mother shall be released."

Susan never revealed the truth about herself. She did not want William to know that Sara had been in the body of his true mother. She placed the book back into the bag and placed it into her son's waiting hands when he asked her, "What will the words do?"

Susan smiled, "The words will aid the women of the world, the Mother's children to witness their true power, and they will begin to make...changes."

Her son stared at her, concerned, "You don't plan on killing anyone, do you?"

Susan's face became stone as she spoke, "My boy, it is necessary for the balance of the planet, the Mother bids it. The men must die, it is written. You are a prophet, my son, you are carrying on the message of our beautiful and dying Mother. This is a gift to you. You are giving so many your gift."

William looked at his mother with the eyes of a frightened child. "That means they will kill me, doesn't it, I'm a martyr?"

Susan walked over to his back, wrapping her arms around him, "You will be pardoned. Your life will be spared. When the world is cleansed you will rule by my side. You will have millions of women throwing themselves at your feet, you will be the only man left."

Will swallowed hard, he remembered his time with the beautiful Stephanie, he envisioned being royalty, ruling by his mother's side. Susan's arms pulled him tighter, "Think of it, my son. No democracy, no sexism, no war. The destruction of the Mother will cease. Flowers will grow in places they have never blossomed before, many species will be safe from murderous hands; we will dance around the fire and worship Her, in peace, forever, in the Mother's name."

Will repeated, feeling closer to his mother than ever before, "In the Mother's name."

He grew quiet, and thought hard about everything he was told through the years, the mission now laid before him. Susan stepped to the front of him to face him, and her eyes never looked more inviting, Bill stared into her crystal pupils, "I will fulfill my destiny, in your love, and in your strength."

She gave a big smile. "Wonderful, my child, the Mother will be pleased."

Susan walked back to the table, picking up a long silver dagger and clutching it close to her chest, "Now, my son, please present your palm." William stepped over to his mother, and presented his right palm to her. She began to slice, slowly. He kept his eyes open and did not wince or make a sound. Ironically, he took the pain like a man.

Susan continued to slice as she spoke again. "Whenever you feel any doubt or confusion about what you are meant to do, look upon this. You are the true messenger of the Mother She will keep you under her arms as you live out your journey. The faith of the Mother forever binds our souls."

Dark blood dripped from Will's wounds to the floor below, as he held out his hand he saw the symbol, it resembled an eye.

The wound suddenly began to close, and the sticky blood seemed to absorb back into his hand, the symbol becoming nothing but a scar. "Thank you, mother, your love will keep me strong."

He wrapped his arms around Susan's small waist, and she did not tear away. The truth was, her bodily visitor came to feel real love for the human boy herself.

Susan then slightly shoved him away, "Now, go upstairs and pack as many belongings as you can. When you are packed go to the vehicle outside, open the compartment. Inside are all of the tools you will require to make a life for yourself."

Will nodded his head as his eyes began to feel wet.

His mother's voice became stern. "No tears, go and do what

you were placed on this Earth to do."

Will, with book in hand, bolted up the concrete stairs. As he reached the bedroom he stared down into the darkness, hoping to see her beauty one last time. He yelled down to her, "I will be strong for you, and I will complete Her legacy."

As the hatch door closed above, Susan's lips began to curl, her laughter growing louder as Will's footsteps grew quiet as he exited the secret bedroom and all of the mystery inside. It was time to complete her legacy: the devious plan to unleash Sara's true vengeance.

Chapter 24

The Words Spoken

September 22nd, 2014

After returning home, Jason ran through the apartment picking up empty liquor bottles. He checked in every single corner, dumping glass after glass into large garbage bags. In his mind, he thought that if Elizabeth were to come back, he would want to change his ways, and this meant he would have to cut all of his vices cold turkey.

He could not stop his heart from racing, and needed to calm his pulse rate. He discovered half of a joint in one of the ashtrays in his bedroom, pulled a lighter from his pocket, and began to puff, swearing that this was the last time that he would ever touch such a thing again.

Jason was going to be more attentive to Matthew, and he was going to be the father he never was. He was going to continue writing after all of these years and find a real job, he would be more caring and more understanding of Elizabeth's needs. Jason continued to smoke away, stood up from the bed he plopped down on and entered the bathroom.

He washed his face and stared back at himself in the medicine cabinet mirror. Jason smiled and spoke back to his reflection, "This is it. You are going to be happy again, be in her arms again."

Jason felt a tear slide down his cheek, "Everything's going to be okay, soon, very soon, Jason."

He pulled a hand towel from the rack and wiped his hands and teary face. Jason turned to leave when suddenly he felt a strong grip on his shoulder. He screamed and the force behind him pulled him backwards. His body was spun to face the mirror and he was now peering into white, dead eyes, the mouth was a huge smile, teeth sharp and jagged.

He never stopped screaming, when he yelled, "Who are you?" The razor mouth opened wide, resembling a shark, and Jason heard the creature silently utter one word, "Soon."

Jason screamed so hard that blood mixed with his saliva. He opened his eyes and the thing was gone as he peered back into the mirror. Jason spat his bloody mucous into the sink and looked down; he realized that he had been so terrified that he urinated all over the front of his blue jeans.

He silently scolded himself. "Oh, that's just fucking great." He looked at the pictures left on the other side of the mirror and began to speak to himself again. "Elizabeth, you have me all screwed up in the head. I am seeing things that aren't there, freaking out."

Jason then had a flash of realization. If Elizabeth were to come back to the apartment, the first thing she would see was her pictures covering everything. He pulled the photographs off of the medicine cabinet, and rushed out of the bathroom.

He began to peel every single picture from everything; Elizabeth in a gown, Elizabeth in a bikini, holding Matthew, kissing him deeply, they were all thrown into a black garbage bag.

The apartment was no longer a museum of obsession, and Jason changed his wet jeans and slipped on another.

He was way too alert to head back to the bathroom, especially to take a shower.

Time slowly ticked away, and he could not stop his heart from beating rapidly. Jason moved into the small living room and sat down hard on the sofa in the middle of the room.

Jason stared at the clock on the wall, it read 7:30. He muttered a curse word under his breath and flipped on the television. Flicking through every channel, he still could not find anything to occupy his mind, his eyes began to flutter, and finally closed. He fell asleep to Peter Griffin doing something really stupid on the screen, but he jumped from the couch when he heard a knock at the door.

Jason looked at the clock that read 10 o'clock, and a smile slid across his face, " It's time."

He resembled a child on Christmas morning, but he composed himself before he opened the door. The door opened and there Will stood, wearing a black sweater, dark jeans, and the combat boots he wore when they first encountered each other.

He noticed Will was carrying a purple velvet bag and attempted to make a joke, "Did you bring alcohol?" Will walked in, and chuckled, "This is what we need to cast the spell. It's all here."

As Will walked into the apartment, he investigated the room, and noticed the glass table in front of the couch.

Jason asked Will to sit and he sat down on a lounge chair on the left of the sofa. Will looked serious, "Tell me everything you remember about your lady, Elizabeth."

Jason cleared his throat and sat on the couch, never breaking Will's gaze, "Wow, where do I start? I met Lizzie-" Will interrupted him, "Jason, please, when you speak of her, address her by her full name, okay?"

Jason nodded and continued, "Okay, I met Elizabeth at a bookstore, actually, I ran into her. She asked me to stay and have coffee with her, I felt that I was in love from the very beginning." Will nodded his head, staying tight-lipped as he listened to Jason. "About seven months later, we moved in together. We lived in a very small apartment, I was a student and she worked as an intern at a publishing company. We both decided to write a book about the negative effects of witchcraft, and then we began our research."

Will stayed silent, and Jason continued to speak of his life with Elizabeth; the highs, the lows, their life after the book was released, their deep love, and their disconnection. He spoke about the birth of their son, and even the incidents of abuse.

Jason told his new friend absolutely everything and had almost completed the stormy tale, "Elizabeth sent divorce papers to my mail slot, I was living in this apartment. She moved out of our dream house, moved into a loft about five or six city blocks from here. I never got another job, lived off of the money I received from Cauldron. Elizabeth and I saw each other one more time, at the divorce hearing, she did not tell the court about the incident with our son, but she did ask for full custody. Of course, I didn't fight it. I wasn't ready to be a father anyway. But I do miss that little boy, I do, Will."

Jason placed his hands over his face and began to wail like

never before.

Will did not comfort him and began to speak, "Let me ask you one question, and look at me when I say this. Do you love Elizabeth, Jason?"

Jason raised his head, tears glistening on his face, when he spoke from the heart, "I have never loved anyone more in my entire existence. She is my world and I messed up. God, I love her so goddamn much, it hurts."

Will continued his direct eye contact and asked another question, "Jason Cain, would you do absolutely anything to get Elizabeth back?"

Jason did not hesitate, his voice very clear. "Yes, I would. I would travel through hell itself to win her back, and I'm already halfway there."

He wiped tears from his face, "I love her, Will, I do." Will closed his eyes, inside he cringed, his legacy was about to be fulfilled. He was going to unleash the vengeance of the Mother, and everything was going to change. He opened his eyes and began to speak again, "Jason, I am going to give you what you want, I am going to give you, Elizabeth."

Jason smiled and Will stood up, "It is time for me to prepare." He picked up the velvet bag he had placed on the side of the chair, opened the string, and pulled out a leather book.

He looked at the cover, caressing the rough material, "This is the book I spoke of, the book that contains the spell that will bring back your love."

Will stepped over to the table and began to pull out more items. He set up a candle for every year Jason and Elizabeth were together, "These candles represent every year you were in Elizabeth's presence."

Jason nodded, and Will pulled a lighter from the bag, lighting each one. "I need you to give me something that belonged to Elizabeth."

Jason began to think about what he could use and it hit him, "I have my wedding ring."

He was advised to retrieve it from the bedroom as Will continued to set up the table, and as he worked he continued to ponder what was about to occur.

Will began to feel ill. He made this broken man believe that he was a friend, and the man had confided on him, cried on his shoulder. Now, Jason was going to be responsible for mass genocide.

He shook his bad thoughts and stepped over to the light switch, clicking it off.

Seconds later, Jason walked into the candle-lit room and witnessed Will's handiwork firsthand. The candles burned in the blackness as he sat down next to Will. On the table was a silver cup, a dagger, a photo of Elizabeth which was on top of Jason's television set, and the leather-bound book that would make all of his dreams come to fruition.

Will addressed him, "Will you please sit down on the floor in front of the table?"

Jason did exactly what he was told and set his wedding band on top of the glass table top. He felt his stomach churn.

Will's eyes appeared red in the candlelight; he began to resemble something from another world. He spoke again, "Do you give yourself to the power of the Mother, with all of your faith and love?"

Jason answered, not knowing what he was saying, but he felt it, "Yes, I give all of me."

Will raised the silver cup over his head, "Oh Mother, we give ourselves to you; we believe in your power with our very souls. Here we stand, in your name, your humble servants. I give you an offering of our will to you, and to your love."

He placed the cup on the table and picked up the blade. Will made a small slice on one of his fingers and placed his hand over the chalice. Drops of red blood spilled slowly inside.

Jason's stomach flipped, but he did not say a word as Will continued to chant, "Oh Mother, our blood and our hearts are yours." He looked at Jason, who was sitting on the floor, startled.

Will commanded him, "Please hold out your hand." Jason hesitated, but did as he was instructed, Will sliced into his fingertip, and placed his hand over the cup as his friend winced. He opened his eyes to see Will smiling at him in the soft light. "Will you please hand me the photograph of yourself and your lost love?"

Jason handed Will the photo and he held the frame over his heart, "Mother, I give you Jason Aaron Cain and Elizabeth Mary Rinehart, these lovers are your humble servants, they will give you all of their love and strength."

Will picked up the lighter he had used to light the row of candles, took the photograph out of the frame, and lit the end of the picture. The paper burned quickly, and the ashes lifted into the air, spinning upward like a tornado, and Jason was absolutely amazed by what he had just witnessed.

Will continued, "Thank you, Mother for showing yourself to us, your unworthy and loving servants who stand before you." He stared down at Jason, a wicked smile plastered across his face. It was time to complete his destiny, the destiny placed upon him since that day in the cellar. "Now, Jason Aaron Cain, we can begin."

Miles away, in the dilapidated Rogers home in Indiana, Susan sat in the cellar, her body circled in candles. She wore a black cloak and nothing more. Her eyes were closed. 'Oh Mother, it is time to cleanse the world in the name of your majesty and beauty. Show them my strength."

Back at Jason's apartment, Will sat on the other side of the living room table. He looked at Jason, his face pale and sweaty, "This book that lies before you has been passed down to the women of my family for many a year, it is your key to winning the hand of Elizabeth once more."

He slowly opened the book, and the candles flickered. A strong wind howled outside of the living room window and Jason swallowed hard, his throat extremely dry. He could not bring himself to look down at what was contained inside.

Will spoke, "Jason, my friend, now is the time to regain happiness, all you have to do is speak the words in front of you. When you finish reading the words I will tell you to repeat yourself again, I will address you when it is time to stop."

Jason nodded and looked down onto the page. He noticed the ink was very strange, it did not resemble any he had seen before, and he began to feel his stomach flip once again. Will closed his eyes and grabbed onto Jason's trembling hand, "Whenever you feel you are ready, please begin the passage."

The wind continued to slam the tiny window as Jason took a deep breath and attempted to slow his pulse.

Will felt himself crack a smile as Jason began to read the words unknown to him,

The world will change…love will return.

Your true fire will once again burn.

I ask you for love…to return me once more…

I plead for your strength…I need it once more.

Jason began to read down the page and realized the rest of the words had nothing to do with his situation. He stopped and Will opened his eyes and looked at Jason concerned. "What's wrong? Why did you Stop? Keep going." Jason looked at the page once again, he looked back up at Will confused, "What does this have to do with bringing back Elizabeth?"

Will looked angry. "Jason, I promise you, after this, everything will change. I promise."

He immediately barked, "Do not screw me on this, I set all of this up for you. Now, come on, just trust me, and get back into character."

Jason swallowed again, and continued hesitantly, his voice shook.

Cleanse…everyone

Show me…the way

Give me…the power

I need to…feel you, oh Mother!

Jason continued and felt sick in his throat. He did not want to let down his friend after all he had done for him. He had practically begged Will to do this, and he had agreed, he did not have to do perform this act, and Jason remembered he warned him about participating. He read on,

Your love is necessary

To the balance…we seek

To show the world…

That we are not weak

I want your love…for you to…rule again

Will calmly instructed Jason to finish the last words of the passage. "You're doing good, really good. Now, finish the last

sentences and she is yours again."

Jason felt like he was going to pass out on the floor. The branches outside of the window smacked hard against the glass. The candles continued to flicker, and it felt like a cold chill entered the living room. Jason continued and he thought to himself deep down, "This shit had better work."

Will commanded him once again, "Jason, finish it!" His throat ran dry as he spoke the final words,

Give me...love...oh, Mother
Resurrect her soul...oh, Mother.

The branch outside of the window crashed into the glass. Jason jumped, but Will did not budge.

The candles flickered out and they both sat in total darkness, the wind howling hard outside of the now broken window.

Will spoke through the blackness, "Now, Jason, repeat the words until I tell you to stop."

Jason felt his heart seize, and he repeated the passage, the sick in his throat he swallowed down as he felt his esophagus burning. He continued to chant. The light bulb on the ceiling popped and Jason felt like he was going to pass out; scared to death.

The wind continued to howl. The two men were now surrounded by glass. Jason continued, sweat covering his face when suddenly Will asked him to stop. Will fumbled for the kitchen light switch and Jason could not move, he was frozen solid in fear.

Will knelt down and stared into his frightened eyes. He no longer looked demonic and serious, he was the friendly face Jason recognized once again. He spoke, in his normal tone. "That's all there is to it. Now all there is to do is wait for your sweet Elizabeth."

Jason broke from his cold shock and looked around the room. The wind had died down and the branch still hung inside the broken window, and he realized he was surrounded by shards of glass, big and small.

He began to interrogate Will. "Do you destroy everyone's homes when you help them out, or am I just the lucky one?"

Will began placing the items on the table back into the velvet bag. "You're just lucky, I guess. But look on the bright side, dramatic effects usually bring results."

Jason slowly stood and shook Will's hand, "Thanks so much. So, I have to ask, how do I know this worked?"

Will released Jason's clammy hand. His sudden expression placed a shiver in Jason's soul. "Oh, Jason, you'll know. You will know." His expression went back to normal quickly, "Listen, I have to go. I'll...uh...see you around."

Jason smiled as his new friend opened the door. "I'll give you a call and we will get together soon. Of course I would want you to meet her." Will suddenly peered down at the floor, he did not have a warm feeling. He had destroyed this man's life, and now he was leaving him with the pieces, "You see, that's funny you mention that, I have to go away for a while. It's just something I have to do, I'm not too sure when I will come back, and I'm not sure when we will see each other again."

Jason felt his heart drop. He had made a new ally in his lonely existence and now he was going away. He did not know if Elizabeth was going to return so the news crushed him even more, but he still attempted to keep his composure, "Oh, okay. I understand, Will Thompson. Well, it's been a real pleasure. I hope to see you again. But if I don't...good luck...with whatever you have to do."

Will nodded, "Thank you, man, I hope everything goes well with you too. I'll see you around."

He began to exit and turned to face Will outside in the hallway once more. "Be good to that lady of yours."

Jason smiled, "I know what I have lost, and I never will again. You didn't waste your time, Will, I promise you that."

Will waved and walked down the stairs, and as he was about to enter into the night, he felt tears roll down his face. He realized he was truly hurt by his deceit.

He had come to know the man in his vision, and also to enjoy his company.

In truth, Will never had a good friend and he found it difficult to place on Jason's shoulders. Will opened the front apartment door and looked out onto the dark street. He took a deep breath and stepped out into the night.

Will spoke silently to himself, tears cold on his face, "In the Mother's name, I've done it, in the Mother's name."

Chapter 25

A Picture Is Worth A Hundred Shards

September 23rd, 2014

Sara spoke from the pitch darkness, her face covered in shadow. "It is time for you to become strong, it is time for you to unleash her vengeance, my vengeance. Awaken, my child, cleanse the world, kill them. Kill the pigs. Kill them!"

The concealed face became revealed in her mind, her eyes glowing white, her flaming mane illuminating Everything. Suddenly, she saw a vision of a woman burning alive, men raping and butchering a colony of innocent women, their blood seeping slowly into the crying earth, their screams echoing into the air.

Elizabeth rose slowly from her pillow. She did not say a word, she did not scream and did not show any signs of distress as she placed her naked feet onto the floor and stood. The alarm clock on her night side table read 5:15 a.m. as she walked past a mirror in the black of night. Her raven hair had a fluid bounce, her face was pure and snow white like a china doll, and her lips were wet and full, as her cream nightgown wrapped around her upper torso revealing every contour. Although she had always beautiful, she had never looked better.

Elizabeth glided from the bedroom and headed for the kitchen located next to the large living room. She never turned on a light, walking through the dark like a feline, her vision was perfect, she could see everything.

As Elizabeth entered the kitchen, she opened a drawer and rummaged through the pile coming across a large butcher knife. She pulled it out of the drawer, slowly. She walked back to her bedroom and stopped abruptly when she passed the bedroom of her now eleven year old son. Matthew's door was open halfway, and she could hear his tiny snoring in stereo. At times like this, Elizabeth would open the door and peer in at her sleeping angel, but not this night. She spoke as she stared at the bedroom door, her voice low and eerie, "Pig."

Elizabeth went into her bedroom and sat down on the bed. A light from the window hit a wedding photograph she could never have the heart to get rid of on her bedroom night table. Jason's smiling face crossed her perfect vision.

Elizabeth, blade in hand, stepped over to the photograph, her face expressionless. She picked up the frame and threw it to the ground. The glass shattered on the floor as Elizabeth knelt down on her knees, shards cutting flesh, as she wildly stabbed at the picture. The glass continued to shred her bare knees, but she did not make a sound, she had become a woman possessed. The remains of the photo were on the floor as she rose to her feet, glass still sticking out of both of her knees. Her bare feet cracked the shards into smaller pieces as she walked out, leaving her son alone. In her mind, she knew where she was going, knew what she had to do. Elizabeth had to cleanse the world for the Mother, and she would begin with her ex-husband.

Chapter 26

Knock, Knock? Who's There?

September 23rd, 2014 8:15 A.M.

After Will had left the apartment, Jason could not sleep through the night. He stood up from his bed and began to sweep the glass on the floor, placed a new light bulb into the ceiling, and attempted to push the branch out of the broken window.

The branch would not budge, and Jason spent an hour slicing through the obstruction with a rusty saw, he duct-taped the hole, scratched the candle wax off of the table with a fingernail, and instantly went against his word picking up the half joint from the ashtray, puffing away as he flipped the channels on the television; filled talk shows, mediocre sitcoms, and infomercials.

Time ticked by quickly enough, and Jason thought to himself, "It's only a matter of time. I will know it worked soon enough." Jason continued to sprawl out on the couch. He stared at the open bedroom door and began to daydream.

Elizabeth stepped in, she was wearing a satin robe with matching high heels and stared at Jason seductively, running her hand through her dark, flowing hair. Jason's pants began to feel tight and he set his burning roach into the ashtray resting on the arm of the couch.

Elizabeth opened her ruby red lips, "I'm coming for you, Jason. Are you ready for me?"

Jason ran a hand down the front lining of his pants and began to speak to himself. "Please come to me."

Elizabeth stepped slowly towards him. Her prowess drove him wild, she placed a finger in her mouth and ran it down the inside of her robe. The seductive Elizabeth moaned and raised her head as she finally reached her pleasure. She stopped abruptly. "Today is the day, my love. We can finally be together, I cannot wait for you to taste me again. I'm coming." Elizabeth ran her fingers down the strings of her robe and released the tie. Her porcelain body stood in front of Jason, her beautiful breasts, her form glistening and inviting. She smiled playfully, "Are you coming? I'm coming too."

Jason still rested his head on the couch, his head turned upward as he pleasured himself. Suddenly, she stepped over the glass table and laid her body atop of his hips. Jason released himself, placing his hands onto her shoulders, and slipped the robe downward. Elizabeth laughed again and placed her soft tongue into his eager mouth.

Jason brought his hands downward and began lightly squeezing her naked buttocks.

Suddenly, Elizabeth bit Jason's lip and stopped embracing him. She looked into his eyes in the darkness, the television flickering in the background. She licked her soft lips and spoke, "Are you coming for me, my love?"

Jason peered into her gorgeous, sparkling eyes. "Yes, you know it." Elizabeth's mouth opened wide, her teeth had become jagged and razor sharp as she spoke once more, snarling and snapping. "Good, because I am coming...for you!" Her mouth opened wide as Jason screamed, she latched her jaws onto Jason's face as he yelled bloody murder. Her teeth began to bite down. Jason's flesh tore and ripped as he attempted to fight, but her mouth gripped his head tight, like an alligator with its prey. The creature who had once been his love bit down, his blood spurted all over the couch, and into its throat. Flesh flew in all directions of the living room. The room was now coated in pieces of skin, and red, sticky viscous. Elizabeth's face changed. Her messy face peered at the mangled stump which was originally Jason. She licked the blood from her lips and laughed silently, "I am coming for you too, Jason, I am coming for you."

Jason screamed and hopped up from the chair, "Oh my god! What the hell is this?" He raced to the bathroom, but stopped, remembering the image in the mirror. Then he placed his hands on his face and felt for everything, relieved to find everything intact. "Oh, Jesus, thank you."

He stared at the clock on the wall, it now read 8:30 a.m., and it caused him to wonder where Elizabeth was. Would she walk to him? Would she appear in a sudden mist? He sat down on the couch once again, when suddenly there was banging on his door.

The rapping curled his blood, it was not a friendly knock. Jason slowly stood, and walked toward the Banging. His heart crept into his throat as he walked. Was it Elizabeth trying to get his full attention? Could it be Will telling him that he was not leaving and he wanted to apologize for making him worry?

Jason looked into the peephole on the door and breathed a sigh of relief. It was his senior landlady, Mrs. Crawford, and Jennifer Sullivan, a young twenty-something college student who lived four doors down in 4-A. He began to turn the lock, wondering why they were at his door. Jason was paid up on his rent, and he promised the young girl he would keep his television down, and the volume was low. He opened the door fully, and the two women changed their expression. A fiery looked appeared in their dead eyes. He began to speak, "Hi ladies, can I help you? Mrs. Crawford, I am surprised to see you here, I'm paid up, and Jenny, my television's real low. So, what's going on?"

The older woman opened her mouth, speaking quietly. Suddenly, the young woman also spoke in the same quiet tone. Jason could not understand either one of them, "I'm sorry ladies. You're speaking too low. What are you saying?"

The babble from the two women grew louder, "For the Mother. Kill the pigs."

Jason began to feel upset; his heart raced, "What are you saying? Did you just call me a pig? Why are you bothering me with this?"

The chanting continued. "Look, I don't know what you're on, but no offense, get away from my door."

Their eyes turned egg white, and Jason's body became frozen as the chanting grew louder, "Kill the pig. For the Mother." Jason's eyes seemed to bulge out of his head as both women proceeded to attack him. He tried to slam the door shut, but failed.

The old woman blocked his attempt with a frail, wrinkled arm. Jason yelled as he attempted to block the women with the flimsy door, "Okay, Miss Crawford! I don't know what's going on here, but you need to back the fuck off, before I call the police!"

Outside, the young girl stepped backwards toward the other wall and ran full speed into his meager blockade. He flew back onto the carpet, and the two attackers stood leering at him. They continued their chanting, "Pig. For the Mother."

Jason crawled on his back as the two approached. Jenny stood over him and picked him up off of the floor with the strength of a body builder. Jenny then threw him through the glass table in front of the couch causing him to shut his eyes tight as the pain shot through his entire body.

Jason slowly stood as the old woman grabbed him by the head and tossed it hard into a wall, causing framed photographs to clatter to the floor. His head swam as he lay on the floor. The two women stood, continuing to chant, "For the Mother."

Jason felt as if he could not get up, but he knew if he did not fight back, he would not survive too much longer. Jason, his body screaming in pain, stood up, and stumbled to the kitchen, the two right behind him. He yelled as he picked up a shiny cleaver, "Listen, I don't know what is wrong with you, but please, do not make me do what I am about to do. Leave, now!"

Jason wondered why no one heard the commotion and called the police. Something was definitely wrong due to the fact that there were thirteen people on his floor alone. The two women stood, babbling continuously, "Kill the pig."

He began to realize he would have to do whatever it took to live, including murder the two women before him. He took a deep suck of air and ran toward the two women, cleaver tight in hand, raising it high into the air. Jason swung it down hard into the side of the young female's neck, making her expression resemble immovable rock as he saw that she did not scream.

Blood spurted from her neck where the blade still protruded. The wounded young neighbor picked up her head, and opened her red, sticky mouth, "For...the Mother."

Jason pulled the cleaver and slammed it into the top of the old woman's head, Mrs. Crawford dropped to her knees, her eyes fixated on Jason.

Jenny staggered on her legs, blood coating the carpet around her from her arterial spurt. The old woman began to speak as Jason stepped towards the front door, "Kill…the pig. Kill him."

His fear began turned to rage, "What do I have to do? Why won't you die?"

Jason's eyes saw daggers as he ran towards the woman and pulled the cleaver from flesh, swinging it into the air once again, bringing it down repeatedly and screaming violently. The woman's head split in two, blood and pieces of bone covering Jason's ghostly white face and everything in close proximity.

The old woman's eyes became brown once more as she flopped like a fish to the red carpet, Jason, beaten and bleeding, turned quick to see the young girl rushing towards him. Jason examined the room to discover the old saw he used to attempt to cut the tree branch, lying by the window.

Lunging toward the tool, with Jenny fixated on him; Jason stood up and ran a fist towards her waiting mouth. She stumbled as Jason bent over to grab the telephone cord, and wrapped it around his attacker's throat and pulled the cord tight. She fell hard to the carpet.

Jenny, gagging and spewing red, continued to sputter words from her now busted lip. "Kill. Kill…the pig."

Jason yelled, as he jumped on her back, "Shut the hell up!"

'He picked up the saw from his side and began to drag it across the back of her neck. The girl did not scream when Jason dragged the saw back and forth against her skin. Blood once again hit him in the face as he furiously pulled the teeth downward, Jenny still babbled even as he reached the base of her spinal cord, "For…the Mother."

His saw was too old to cut through to her bone, so he picked up the metal rotary phone that a man his age should never have possessed and began to beat the back of her skull until her head caved in towards the floor.

Brain matter seeped out of her ear holes, and her head seemed to explode. Jenny's body convulsed, and then suddenly, it stopped.

Jason tried to catch his breath. His head still rung from the contact with the wall and he attempted to stand, and fell atop Jenny's lifeless corpse.

He screamed, and tried once again, Jason reached for the arm of the couch, covered in blood, and tried to push himself upward. He slowly shuffled toward the bedroom and began to toss drawers around the room. He walked back into the massacre after finding a half empty bottle tucked behind the two drawers in his sock dresser, and even though he could not breathe, took a huge swig of the bottle, coughing.

Jason looked upon the mess covering the room, sealed his eyes from the nightmare before him, and spoke to himself, "Elizabeth, I know I said I wouldn't do this anymore, but this seems to be a very special occasion.

He dropped the bottle and groggily walked toward Jenny's body, to retrieve the phone. It was off of the receiver and stuffed inside the mush which had once been her skull.

"What the hell is going on here?", he said out loud. "What the hell did you do, Will?" Jason lunged down and pulled the phone from the young girl's battered remains, feeling himself holding back sick as he held it to his ear. The ear piece itself was covered in her material.

The phone rang twice, and Jason waited to explain to the operator that he was attacked by two women in his building and that he had mashed the young girl's head in, and repeatedly sliced the top of an old woman's neck with a sharp implement. He knew immediately that the story was not going to fly, that his life would no longer be lonely due to the many new friends he would make in prison.

Waiting for an answer, someone finally picked up the line, but no one spoke. Jason began to yell into the receiver, "Hello, operator? Is this 911? I was attacked...and had to defend myself...hello?"

Jason still did not hear any voices on the other end, but he suddenly heard screams in the background, the screaming and yelling of men.

"Hello? Is anyone there? I've been attacked! I had to kill two people, is anyone listening to me?"

He heard a voice through the thick static, "K—l." He attempted to understand, "I'm sorry, could you repeat yourself? I...couldn't hear you."

His heart pounded, and he could still hear screaming on the other end of the line. The voice spoke again, "Kill. Kill the pigs.

For...the Mother."

Jason yelled an obscenity and threw the phone against the wall. He then headed toward the front door, clicked the lock and bolted the flimsy chain. Now breathless, Jason placed his back against the door. Screams came from the hallway. "What is going on here? What the hell did we do?" Jason cried out, placing his hands over his face as he began to sob uncontrollably.

Chapter 27

And Now The News

September 17th, 2013 9:00 A.M.

Jason sat on the couch. His head still throbbed, and the bodies of the two women continued to stain the apartment. Even over his heavy breathing, he could still hear the cries of male tenants as the on button of the television lit up.

The stations had all been interrupted by breaking news and Jason clicked the button to Channel 3. On the screen, the usually grinning news anchor sat at the desk, his suit wrinkled and crusted in flecks of blood. His perfect hair was mussed, and he had a wild look in his eye.

He began to speak, his voice distressed. "This is a Special Report from the Channel 3 news desk…I'm Brian Cartwright."

He stopped the report to loosen his tie and pop two buttons on his shirt, then the anchor continued, "I do not know what to say about the cause of what is going on, what I will tell you is the situation is completely out of control."

The news anchor loudly cleared his throat. "Apparently, the women of the world, have begun to murder every man in their path."

Tears began to cover his face. "I regret this information. My…co-anchor….Lisa Carter…attacked me during our early morning newscast. I…had to…kill my anchor woman, my partner."

The man began to stammer, "I had to stab her to death with a ball point pen. She…she said over and over again…that she was…doing it for the Mother. We have no information on who the Mother is." He attempted to be strong as he addressed even more horrifying news, "Our friend and lead sports guy, Dick Cunningham, was killed during a brutal struggle for survival, when our weather girl, Pamela Winters...attacked him. He had to take her down...but was ambushed by three women on our production crew." The anchor placed his hands over his face as Jason watched the screen in horror. The man continued, "As I stated, the women of the world are attacking....and killing men. This is a global epidemic, stay locked away...defend yourself....as best as you can."

The now pale man paused, "I have just received word from our surviving male crew members locked in the control room...that we have breaking news from Baghdad. Our veteran correspondent is live via satellite...from atop a hotel rooftop. James, are you there?"

The satellite feed was scratchy, and Jason could hardly see the picture, when suddenly the waves became more clear. The anchor in the Middle East was wearing a Kevlar bulletproof vest and yelling from behind a cement wall, loudly, "This James Hunter reporting from outside Kuwait City! Strange occurrences are happening here...and I will now try to explain!"

In the background, shots from M-16's and assorted weapons could be heard close by. Jason leaned up and the anchor continued, "For the first time...the women have retaliated against the oppressive men of this region."

He swallowed, "They are now, butchering...the population of men...in this vicinity! The fighting has apparently...stopped abruptly. From what I hear...I don't believe this...United States soldiers positioned in the area., and even members of terror groups...including insurgents have banded together. They are attempting to fight off...large swarms of women!" The gunfire continued as he shouted, "I will repeat, U.S. soldiers...along with male Iraqi residences and members of terror groups have banded together to keep the women of this region...at bay! I am now going to attempt to peer over the wall and show you firsthand...what it's like down there."

The anchor slowly crept his head up over the foundation with a hand held camera in his hands, Jason felt leaned in close to the screen as he looked upon the carnage; it appeared that women were running, with weapons of all sorts in their hands including pitchforks, knives, and other sharp objects. A group of United States soldiers dressed in digital combat attire and Iraqi men were huddled in a tight formation firing wildly. Suddenly, a shot was fired into the anchor's direction, and nearly missed his face, he slunk back down the foundation of the roof, cursing, "Jesus Christ, I felt the heat on that one! We are receiving word that this same thing is happening in Asia, Australia, all of Europe it's happening everywhere! No man is safe. Are these the end times? We are not sure, but I will tell you this, fight with everything you have in you!"

The man began to unravel on the screen, " I will return to the airwaves...if I get anything new. Brian, back to you, and good luck, my friend."

The feed buzzed and fizzled out. Jason popped up and felt the blood rush from his head. "Oh shit, what did we do? Will, what have you made me do?", he muttered.

Jason picked up the television and threw it hard against the side of the wall near the kitchen.

He cursed the air. "Fuck!" The skin peeled from his knuckles and the pain began to get to him. With his hand throbbing, he attempted composure. "Okay, you survived this long. You have to keep your cool, you have to get out of here."

Suddenly, a thought entered his mind, the safety of his family. He rushed to the phone, still bloody on the carpet, and began to dial, while the screams in the hallway grew louder.

He dialed his brother after attempting to call him earlier., but there was no answer, Jason then began to dial Elizabeth's number, and the sound on the other end jangled his brain. Someone picked up. A little voice spoke, "Hello? Hello?"

It was the voice of Jason's estranged son, Matthew, he had not seen his little boy since he was still a baby, when he had done the unspeakable.

Jason attempted to clear his mind and speak to this boy who had no idea that his father was on the other end of the line. "Matt, I am a...a friend of your mom's." Jason felt saddened by his lie and continued to speak to the boy, "Where is your mom?"

The frightened child explained the situation and Jason could tell he was distressed. "Mom's not here, she left me alone. The door is open."

Jason gave his son commands to protect himself, "I need you

to go to the door...and shut it tight, okay? Did anyone get into the apartment?"

His son became silent, and Jason felt a rush of panic. "Matthew? Are you there?" His son spoke, "There's no one here," his son said, "I closed the door."

Jason sighed with relief, when suddenly he could hear a faint banging in the background of the conversation. His skin crawled.

Some women were beating on Elizabeth's door and muttering, Jason continued to aid his son, "I need you to go into a room and lock yourself in tight. Do...do you play baseball? Do you have a baseball bat?"

The boy answered, breathing heavily. "I play ball." Jason smiled, "Good. I want you to lock yourself in your mother's room. Do not even let anyone in, not even your mother, do you understand?"

Matthew agreed with everything the man on the other end of the phone was saying, and Jason continued to conceal his true identity. "I want you to know, I'm coming for you. I am going to do this, for you and your mother. Now, go to the room and stay there, okay?"

Matthew was about to hang up when Jason slipped in his frustration and fear, "I love you."

He threw the phone to the blood stained floor, and raised his trembling hands to his face. Jason's son was alive, and he now knew that he would fight through the hell now on Earth to reach him.

Chapter 28

Signs Of The Sara's Massacre: One Night Standoff

Michael Wilson and Jill Pepperidge
8:00 A.M.

Michael Wilson opened his eyes. His head felt as if it were going to split in half. He figured it must be due to all of the test tube shots he had ingested the night before. He had drunk so much that he forgot the woman lying next to him in his bed, and he was startled by her gorgeous face, eyes closed.

He could hear her low breathing, and at that moment the jigsaw puzzle of the night before came together. Michael's friends, Alex and Tim, had dragged him to a seedy nightclub called Sin, an extremely popular nightclub located about two city blocks from their school, The Academy Of Art and Design. The crew stepped into the club at twenty minutes before ten and the house was packed.

Michael noticed scores of men dancing with women, men grinding men, women making out with other women, and began to feel more than a little uneasy. Michael hit his friend Tim on the side, and yelled over the crowd and the thumping music, "Hey man, let's roll, huh? This is majorly crazy!"

Tim yelled back into his ear. "There's a reason we brought you here tonight, man!" Tim pointed a finger toward the four-sided bar in the center of the room and there she was. Michael's eyes began to sparkle and he whispered to himself, "Jill…Pepperidge." Jill was Michael's crush ever since he began Graphic Design classes almost a year and a half before this night. He had spoken to Jill once or twice, but he never had the chance to have a meaningful conversation with her, and here she was.

Jill was sitting with two of her Fashion Design girlfriends, and he thought she looked absolutely beautiful. Her small amount of make-up allowed her natural beauty to show through, her tight jeans and baby doll shirt accentuated her every contour. Jill was never flashy, she was always whoever she wanted herself to be, and that was exactly what her secret admirer fell for.

He smirked as he made his way through the crowd and toward his conquest. As he walked, he checked his breath and practiced what he was going to say. Michael was never flashy himself, and he truly hoped he was the kind of guy a girl of this caliber went for. Finally, he approached her, and surprisingly, she asked him to sit next to her. After a few hours of alcohol and incredible chat, it happened. Michael planted a kiss on his dream girl's lips for the first time, and as the bar closed, they walked out outside arm in arm. Jill whispered into Michael's ear, "Take me home with you." They hailed a cab back to the student housing apartment Michael resided in and embraced the entire ride back. Michael remembered the glorious night, and continued to stare upon his sleeping beauty. He looked underneath the covers and realized that they had certainly had sex, but he was so drunk the night before he could not recall any of it. Michael clenched his teeth in frustration, and reached for a pipe on the bed side table.

As he inhaled the smoke, he heard a sudden commotion from outside his bedroom window. "Damn, this city's fucked up." He laughed as he blew smoke throughout the room, he looked over at Jill again and squealed; she was wide awake. He peered directly into milky white eyes and threw himself hard onto the floor. His one night stand opened her mouth, "Kill...kill." Michael shot up from the floor and Jill, naked, lunged from the bed, and grabbed him by the face with both hands. Her perfectly manicured nails dug into his skin, her body straddled him on the floor and she was still moaning, "Pig. Kill."

Michael attempted to reach for something to keep her at bay, as Jill's nails sunk deeper into the flesh of his cheek. Finally, he found something, the neck of an electric guitar which had fallen off of its stand during the struggle. The pain in his face was excruciating as he looked into the face of his school crush who was now trying to kill him. Michael began to speak through the pain, "Jill, I am...really sorry for what I'm about to do. It's a shame...you were so damn pretty!" He swung the base of the guitar into the side of Jill's face with full force. Her supple body crumpled to the side of him.

With nail marks embedded in his skin, Michael shot up quickly, a warrior in boxer shorts. He looked upon Jill as she rolled on the floor, the side of her face caved in from the blow of the heavy instrument.

The still chanting naked young woman sat in a pool of blood and teeth, and Michael stood over her, the guitar neck clenched in sweaty palms. He thought of old action movie catch phrases, but only felt fear and pain, and as the woman he had fallen jumped up like a cat landing on its feet, face shattered, he knew what had to be done. Michael had no clue what was going on with the world, or if this was a nightmare, but tears welled in his red eyes as the instrument crashed into Jill's once perfect features, again and again.

Chapter 29

The Hallway To Hell

9:50 A.M.

Jason sat on the blood covered couch and wiped his eyes after his conversation with his son. He was disgusted with himself for having to lie to him about his identity, and he felt even worse when he attempted to contact his father and his older brother, Scott. Every single time he heard the phone ring he thought of the two of them, lying in a pile, and the tears fell from his eyes once again.

He shot up, holding his head in his hands and muttering to himself, "Come on, Jason, what the fuck are you going to do? I have to go…I have to go." He had no plan of escape and continued to contemplate his next move. In his imagination, he busted through the door like a comic book action hero, but in reality he was panicking. Jason knew he had had to make a move. He stepped over the mangled young woman, and headed to the small kitchen area which resembled a war zone.

Jason opened every single drawer searching for anything that he could use as a weapon. He rifled through spoons and forks and found two sharp butcher knives which belonged to a set he had received for his wedding to Elizabeth.

He knew the only thing that would be of any use to him in the apartment was embedded in the split skull of the senior landlady laid out on the floor. He placed the two knives into his belt loop, and attempted not to vomit as he stood over the body containing his treasure. The sickness crept in his throat as he pulled the handle, hearing the squishing sound as the cleaver pulled from the bone.

Jason headed toward the front door and heard absolutely nothing from the outside. Where he once heard screams and cries, there was now nothing but silence, Jason knew this was the opportune moment to head out into the hallway. He peered into the peep hole and saw no one, then he took a deep breath and clicked both of the locks on his door.

Jason bravely opened the door, stuck his head out slowly, and saw the carnage from the hour before. There was blood and matter splayed across the walls, bodies of men and women decorated the carpet, corpses were in front of open doors, and pieces and parts were strewn everywhere, Jason cupped his mouth as he held the cleaver tight in his white-knuckled fist and stepped over the mess leading to the staircase.

The hallway looked as if someone had thrown a grenade in the middle of the entire floor, but Jason continued to advance to the first stair, squinting his eyes to avoid the mess and speaking to himself, "Only three doors left. Three doors to pass, you're doing good."

With a tightness in his throat and a foul, sick feeling in his burning stomach, Jason finally reached the stairs. He stopped to take a breath, and not knowing what lay ahead on his usually simple descent, he slowly stepped onto the fourth carpeted block, when suddenly he saw them, and they spotted him.

Jason froze in his tracks as he witnessed three women heading up the stair. He raised the cleaver in fear as the first woman who looked to be in her mid-thirties peered at him with wide milky white eyes. She rushed up the stairs, and the African American woman and the second Caucasian woman followed behind her with a slower but predatory pace. Just as the first sprinting woman reached out for the statue-like man, Jason felt a grip pull him hard backwards.

The action was so instantaneous Jason felt as if he was finished, especially when the force of the unseen slammed his head hard into the floor above the stairwell. And as he groggily peered up at his assailant, he noticed a balding man in his late forties looking down at him. The man yelled out commands that Jason could understand, although the words were muffled from the pain in his head, "Get this guy the fuck in the apartment! We have two on the move, one down, let's go!" Jason closed his eyes as his body was dragged into the nearest apartment to the staircase, and the door slammed behind him.

Chapter 30

Signs Of The Mother's Massacre : All's Fair In Love…War…and Death

Jason's Older Brother, Scott and His Wife, Cara
September 17th, 2013 7:15 A.M.

A few hours before his younger brother had attempted to call with no result, military hero and all around nice guy, Scott Cain, was going through his very own personal torment and damnation, and the result was much worse for him than anything he had ever seen in combat. Scott had seen burnt bodies lying on roads, corpses of women stoned to death for so-called crimes, fellow brothers in arms gasping and coughing up blood bubbles before passing away before him, but nothing would prepare him for what had occurred earlier. Scott had kept in contact with his brother on the phone at least a few days a week after his divorce to Elizabeth and they even met for dinner and drinks a few times so that Scott could truly have a chance to console him. Although Scott loved the bright lights and constant entertainment of the city, he and his lovely wife, Cara, had always wanted the simple life, a life of tranquility and absolute quiet.

They chose a home in the suburbs over the hustle and bustle, and after returning back to the States, Cara a few months before her loving soldier, the two were wed in a small ceremony and a week after had moved into the two bedroom home they had always had their eyes on.

The street was quiet, the neighbors were courteous, and the only noise usually came from a few neighborhood kids listening to loud music or playing a sport of some type near their home. The house itself was very well kept; Scott cut the grass every single weekend and

Cara tended to her garden that she had built on the side of the house. She had also hung potted flowers and other forms of vegetation all around the covered porch where the two always held hands together, drinking a bit of wine now and again or coffee in the morning. The inside of the house had a massive living room that the two had turned into a den suitable for both parties. On one of the walls hung a massive flat screen television where the two watched sports of many kinds and their favorite shows.

The room was a little man, as well as a little woman, but everything in the room fit the pair nicely and agreeably. Next to the giant living room was a massive kitchen with nothing but the newest appliances; black marble floors, a high tech cappuccino machine, and their pots and pans hung nicely on a rack above the clean and beautiful counter top.

Since Scott and Cara met during their time in the military, their lives together were nothing but a dream come true, Cara was adored by Scott's family and friends, and the same applied to her family in the case of Scott Cain. As strong and as manly as Scott was, Cara's beauty and her ability to always make him feel special always astonished him and made his heart feel light.

He never had an issue being romantic or sappy in public, but Cara was just as much of the guy's girl when she needed to be, playing pool and drinking beer. On the morning the world became pure horror, the soldier, the fighter, the lover, and the loved had to do the unthinkable.

Scott woke up at six a.m. and turned off the alarm clock on his cell phone. He leaned up, stretched his arms and turned to see that his wife's beautiful face was not present. He figured to himself that she was already up and preparing for her morning shift at the city hospital approximately forty-five minutes away, the massive St. Augustine's. Scott, still in boxers, opened a door and threw on a pair of sweatpants. He got down on the carpet and performed his daily regimen of pushups and sit-ups which he did every morning to keep himself lean, and of course energize him for the day.

After working out, Scott pulled on a white cotton shirt and headed for the stairs. Walking into the hallway, he passed the second bedroom which was turned into an office for the couple, but it also held boxes and stacks of other things they were planning to store. As his first foot touched the Berber carpet of the stairwell leading to the downstairs portion of the house he heard a commotion, the sound of glass breaking and the silver of pots banging to the floor of the kitchen.

He stopped, stepped in a slow stealthy fashion to the bottom and slowly slid to one of the side walls facing away from the open kitchen. He slid from the wall to the couch and knelt down. The noises became louder as he picked up his head to look up, seeing Cara in a frenzy tossing everything in her path to the ground, Scott stood and headed in her direction, slowly. He placed his hands up to show he meant no harm and an expression of confusion showed in his features as he pleaded to his lovely and incredible wife, "It's me, Scott. Listen honey, I want to know why you are so upset, but we can talk about this. You know that we can talk about anything."

Cara threw the cappuccino maker down onto the floor and the hot mixture inside spilled onto the marble as the machine smashed to the ground. Cara screamed, and Scott thinking she had severely burned herself, and ran toward her. As he stepped close enough, he noticed that Cara was in her bra and underwear, and her bare feet were blistering and peeling in the brown steaming liquid coating the tiles. Scott screamed, "Oh my god...Cara!" Cara turned slowly, but she did not budge. Scott stopped dead in his tracks.

Her eyes had lost all of their majesty and were replaced with a sickly pale white coating. Everything in this amazing woman resembled death, and she was in no way the magnificent and breathtaking woman Scott had fallen for while lying in the military hospital. Cara's milky saucers bulged when she finally saw her husband, and her mouth opened wide, lips dry, and uttered one word, "Pig." Scott stepped two paces backward and attempted to ask his wife what she had said when she screamed into the darkly lit early morning shadows of the room, "Pig. Pig!"

Cara quickly grabbed a knife from the cutting board still on the counter and propped one blistered heel onto the top of the counter, bounding over to the other side. Scott stepped back three paces and once again pleaded to his wife, Cara, what are you doing baby? What is wrong with you? Let's get you help."

Cara snarled, fixating her white eyes on her trembling but

steadfast man. Scott placed his hands over his head as in defeat and asked her to place the knife on the carpet and talk. She looked down to the ground, leaning her head to the side as if she was thinking it through, but just as Scott thought the worst was over, he realizes that the worst had only begun. Cara, sweat forming in her short black hair, lifted her head once again and released three words that echoed throughout the room, "For the Mother." She then rushed toward Scott, and he stood in a defensive stance. As she rushed him, knife raised, Scott gripped her hand holding the blade and brought her soft but stiffened body toward him. Cara released the hand wielding the knife and turned to slash her husband's face with the blade, as she cut the skin, she knelt down to the floor in a warrior cat-like stance, the knife in the hand behind her. Scott's body became rigid and he spoke to his crazed animal-like wife, "Cara, you do not want to do this. What are you doing?" As he stepped toward her, she rushed him again, spinning quickly and slashing the top of his hand. She performed a spin move on the carpet driving her husband's tall, strong body into the floor.

She lunged on top of him as his head ached and licked her lips as her chant began again, "Pig. Piiiiiiig."

Scott's eyes began to well when he looked upon his crazed, rabid wife and realized that he must defend himself, at all costs. She raised the knife with another cry and Scott raised one foot kicking her square in her small chest and throwing her backward. She quickly shot up, but he was ready for her.

Nearly breathless, he tried to speak to her good nature once again, "You love me, I...love you. I can get you help. Please, baby." The talk did not work, and the small-framed former soldier ran forward tackling her husband as hard and strong as a defensive lineman. He fell hard as Cara, with sweat and red marks adorning her body, slashed wildly at her husband's white shirt, causing streaks of red to form.

Scott grabbed her by her throat and threw her hard against the floor. He did not release his grip while she snarled and snapped. There was no pain in her face, only rage and hatred. His grip grew tighter until he released her, stood up quick and walked away backward facing his wife lying on the floor, he gave in, "I cannot do this, baby doll. I won't, I am just going to go and get you some help."

Cara turned her head, her dead eyes ablaze with madness, and she got to her scarred heels once again.

One of the cups of her bra had slipped off and she looked as crazy as ever. She snarled like a frothing sick dog and ran towards her husband screaming her insane chant. With no thought, he pulled a fire poker from the unlit fireplace in their unisex den and slammed it hard into his wife's temple, screaming as he pushed the metal in deeper, and deeper. Cara continued to scream in rage, and Scott pulled the sharp end from her skull, dropping his love to the floor.

He looked down at her crying, "Why did you make me do this?" The wound in her forehead leaked onto the once perfect carpet, but she did not fall. Cara lifted her head once again, red spilling into her face, causing her teeth to look black in the shadows. She began to chant louder, lifeless eyes bulging, "Pig!"

She leaped again, and Scott closed his soaked eyes. In what seemed to be slow motion, he swung the metal poker causing the sharp end to smash the side of her head and embed itself. Scott watched in horror as her eyes once again showed beauty, wide and clear even through the blood on her face, and as she dropped to the floor for the final time, Scott recalled her tending to his wounds for the first time.

He then remembered slipping a platinum ring on her finger and kissing her deeply, and in his memories, they were now making love, hot and heavy, but with a passion that always overshadowed the need for simple sensation. As Scott watched the love of his life fall, he dropped the bloody poker onto the carpet next to him. His wife's head fell into the carpet, her body lifeless, resembling nothing but death. Scott dropped to his knees, defeated, even though he had won his own life.

Chapter 31

The Martyr, William Thompson

8:45 A.M.

Will Thompson peered out the window. His nerves shook, his heart beat rapidly. The screams in his hallway had vanished from his ears, and the chaos in his building had journeyed out into the open air. He wiped tears from his eyes for hours as the guilt slowly but surely tore into his soul. Will had a small studio apartment only a few blocks away from Jason Cain so he could survey his every movement as easily as possible.

The apartment was nothing fancy. It contained nothing but the essentials: a bed with sheets, a small bathroom, and a small kitchenette area with a stove and a microwave, and even though the place was not fancy, it wasn't a dump either. It was evident he had some money to play with: a new television, new computer, stereo with stacks of DVD's and Compact Discs lined neatly on racks.

He also had concert and film posters nicely framed on the walls, until now. He had tossed his belongings across the room, smashing CD cases against walls, tossing frames to the floor smashing the glass. Will yelled and paced like a hungry zoo animal, "Why did I do this? I...I unleashed hell on earth." He raised his fist in the air and began to curse, "Damn you, mother! Why did you make me do this?" He puffed on one cigarette after another, putting the burning embers out on the skin of his forearms to attempt to calm his nerves.

Will continued to yell, the sound echoing through the destroyed, tiny room, "I...am a bad person! I am terrible! I fucking caused...all of this! Oh my god, Jason....I deceived you." Will knelt down amongst the debris, and held his head, shaking his neck back and forth, "I put this on you. My bullshit legacy."

He picked up a shattered photo of Susan's sunny, smiling face and stared at it, longingly. His eyes grew wet once again, and he spoke to the cracked frame, "It was not right to do this. You were wrong to make me do this. You were…fucking wrong!"

With that, Will tossed the frame against the corner of one of the walls causing it to explode into fragmented pieces. He stood up, "You were so wrong. I…am a man; I should never have done this. I was raised on your bullshit promises. Your hatred! I have to stop you." Will stepped over to the cabinet lying on its side and pulled the velvet bag from the broken remnants. He held the book of evil in his hands, and stepped over to the kitchen area, floor covered in glass from broken dishes and cups. He opened the leather book to the first page.

Will opened a small drawer picking up a small can of lighter fluid with his right hand, and with his left he grabbed a book of matches. He then coated the page and his breathing became heavy as he struck a match against the flint. Will smirked, with a hint of lunacy and desperation, "I am going to stop this, do you hear me?" And right as he held the match to paper, Will was violently picked up by something unseen and slammed hard against the wall, the pain coursing through his spine causing him to scream out loud.

In an instant, the force began to close in on his throat, and as it tightened, Will could feel the oxygen in his brain drop. He could not breathe. As he was flung to the floor he attempted to catch his breath and heard the angry voice of his mother, "What are you trying to do, my child? Were you going to defy me? Were you going to defy your dear mother?" Will attempted to catch his breath, staggered on his feet and spoke back to the detached voice, "How could you do this? How could you make your own son do this? I did everything for you! I live my life in your ways, I lived my life…for you!"

The familiar voice spoke again, "You did what you are meant to do, you were placed on this Earth to bring about the legacy of the Mother." Will threw his arms in the air, "Do you really believe the Mother wanted to do this? She obviously wasn't thinking if she felt she had to resort to the slaughter of millions! The Earth mother doesn't murder, you were wrong about your beliefs!" Suddenly, invisible hands caressed Will's burning cheeks, the tone of the voice sounded lower, more nurturing. "My child, every time there is a natural disaster, waters rising from their banks covering entire towns, every single time a force from the sky destroys homes that man built, every time there is a human casualty resulting from the ultimate power of nature, THAT is the strength of the Mother. She is crying out, her majesty is being destroyed, she is being decimated by the hands of men. That is why we are doing Her work."

Will stepped backward as he felt his mother's sweet breath on his face, and he continued to plead, "That's exactly it! We are doing her work, her dirty work. Her hands are clean, ours are stained with blood. You made me deceive a good man."

The voice broke into uproarious laughter, "Good?!He is a good man? My child...he is not good!" Will cut her off. "He told me everything, he accidentally hurt his son, he did not treat his wife with dignity or respect in the end, why does this make him accountable? Why did you seek him out? Why did you make me destroy his life?" His eyes grew damp, "He trusted me, he confided in me...and you made me deceive an innocent man!" His mother's voice boomed yet again, "He is NOT innocent! He hurt her! He...HURT her! He had to be the one...he had to pay!" Will began spoke slowly, and more to himself, "I have to tell him, I have to tell him." He stood up to his mother's commanding tone, "I have to tell him everything, I am going to fix this, I am going to find him, and I will tell him everything."

The voice growled, and laughter once again reverberated off of the small apartment's walls, "You cannot stop me, and it is too late for him! She is on her way to kill him; she will finally receive her chance to murder the pig who ruined her life."

Will questioned the voice, his brow furrowed with confusion, "Who are you speaking about? His ex wife? Why do you care so much about them? Why are you being so evil?" The voice grew, and the ceiling shook, "Susan Rogers was always so beautiful, I knew this the first time I laid eyes on her, ever since she was a small child. I saw her...through her Mother's eyes. I trained her personally in the truth of the Mother. I knew that she was always the one, the perfect vessel for my power. And here I stay, in her form, waiting to stroll along the tall grass of newly cleansed Earth."

Will's voice boomed as he asked his questions, confused, "I...I do not understand, what are you trying to say? Are you trying to tell me you're hurt? Are you just attempting to stop me with more of your mystical bullshit? What are you trying to say to me?" The room became silent, and the voice spoke in a low tone, "What I am attempting to say is," Will felt the grip tight around his throat again when the voice became louder than ever, "I am NOT YOUR MOTHER!"

His eyes nearly popped from his skull when his mother's face appeared from out of nowhere, her teeth jagged and pointy, saliva dripping from her lips. She growled low and snapped. The force tossed Will off of his feet, still cutting off his air completely. Will gasped and attempted to release words from his blocked passage, the sentence raspy, "I...will...stop...you." His face changed hues, his eyes rolled back until the voice screamed, "No!" Will dropped to the carpet like a brick, and began choking for air, he coughed and hacked, "Why didn't you kill me?"

Susan's true voice broke through the evil, "I cannot, I cannot do it with my own hand. I raised you, I molded you, and I sent you off to fulfill your destiny. I...am Susan...I am your true mother." Will, still hacking, snapped back, "You are not my mother! You made me...a monster! You made me a murderer! I am going to stop this...and I am going to kill you if you hurt her...I promise you."

Susan's face reappeared and Will lunged, attempting to attack the vision with a closed fist. He fell hard and the voice bellowed, "Do not defy me child! You cannot stop me, your friend will soon succumb to her fury! She is on her way, she is going to kill him, very soon now! Soon, Elizabeth RINEHART will become one with ME...her TRUE blood!"

Will rushed toward the door, and unbolted the lock, "I am going to find Jason Cain, I will do everything in my power to stop you, you bitch!"

The voice threatened him. "Do not defy me or else. Do not go to his aid! If you do you will no longer be protected, you will suffer, do not step out of this room!" Will bolted through the door into the hallway, feeling nauseous from the paranormal choking, as well as the bodies lying on the floor: bloody, mashed, and beaten.

The voice echoed from out of nowhere, "You have incited this, you are now nothing but cattle for the slaughter! You have defied my power! You have defied your own Mother!" Will screamed at the top of his lungs as he slowly ascended the stairs, "Fuck you!"

He reached the door leading to the outside and saw his old beaten truck parked on the street. As he opened the bloody fingerprinted glass, he looked to the left and the right and walked briskly toward the vehicle.

Will suddenly heard a low growl and quickly turned his head to face the noise. He swallowed hard when he realized he stood in the vision of two women, their clothes soaked in blood. One of them, a blonde woman, held something dangling in her hand. Suddenly, it became quite clear as Will realized that she was gripping strands of brown hair on a severed, dripping head like a medieval mace prepared to attack.

He sprinted to the door of the truck and dropped his keys after fumbling for them in the pocket of his tight jeans. The keys fell underneath the chassis of the vehicle and Will slid down on his belly, with one of the women standing over him, only this time the chant was personalized, "Kill. Kill the...defiant child." He quickly turned, and dropped a solid kick to her nose, causing her to double back, and finally got his hand on the key ring underneath the truck.

Will shot up quickly, leapt on top of the wobbling woman, placed one of the sharp keys in between his knuckles and jammed the sharp, blunt key into the soft tight skin of her neck. He screamed as he jabbed continuously, "Fuck you!" He then slammed his body against the door of the truck and released the lock as fast as he could. Will jumped into the seat and turned the key in the ignition. The woman with the decapitated head climbed on the hood of the truck, and attempted to smash the glass of the windshield with her trophy.

The glass split down the center as she screamed, swinging wildly, "Kill the pig. Kill the pig." The head shattered on the final blow, causing brain fragment and fresh blood to smother the cracked glass.

Will pushed the pedal down and the motor revved as he slammed the skull shaped shifter into drive The woman fell off of the hood, and tumbled onto the pavement below, the right radials lugging over her abdomen.

As Will rolled forward, he stopped the truck to see the woman stagger to her feet in the rear view mirror. Her greasy gut was exposed and hanging outside of her body, but she did not scream.

Will put the shifter into reverse, whacked the woman in the chest and knocked her to the concrete once again, hitting the button for the windshield wipers to clear a pathway through the viscous mess. He pressed onward to fulfill his new destiny.

Will Thompson was going to do anything to stop the Mother's destruction. He was going to make things right, and he was going to find the man that he was raised to punish, the man he had befriended, Jason Cain.

THE BINDING BOOK TWO: WICKED WOMAN, WICKED WORLD

ROB DiLAURO

FEAR FRONT
PUBLISHING

CHAPTER ONE

Meeting the Neighbors
September 23, 2014
10:30 A.M.

Jason's eyes fluttered, opening slowly as the room he was lying in came into focus. His head ached something fierce as the reality of the situation became apparent.

At first, he thought that the most ridiculous idea in his head could be the most plausible: that the life he remembered never happened. The encounter with Elizabeth leading into years of courtship, the marriage that fell apart, and the time lost in a small apartment crying and drinking heavily, never occurred. More importantly, the incident that he had encountered in his apartment was nothing more than a horrible nightmare.

Jason lifted his aching head from the made bed and realized quickly that he was still in the hell he had created, and in moments, he recalled everything.

His mind began playing the entire story leading up to this room in fast forward; the visions of Will handing him the leather book, the vicious fight for his life with the old landlord and the young student, the phone call to his young son, and then being pulled backward, hitting the floor and being dragged on the rough carpet of the hallway witnessing a door close in front of him.

Now he was in this small bedroom with two end tables on each side of the bed that looked more expensive than anything in the room, a long dresser against the wall in front of him housing a small flat screen television, a rack that was filled to completion with different types of movies, and clothes piled into two laundry baskets by the only window in the room. And as Jason stumbled on the floor, he saw pictures of a balding man who appeared to be in his forties with a teenage boy hanging on the wall.

As he leaned in closer to examine the photo, it hit him like a jolt to his heart.

The man in the photos was the same man he witnessed yelling orders in the hallway. The same man who dropped him on his head, preventing him from completing his mission to step out into the city which was probably overrun with bloodthirsty women, chanting and frothing for violence.

Before he opened the door, framed by a long mirror, he stopped to stare at the man peering back at him.

Jason could see the cuts on his face, the caked, dried-up blood coating his body, and the massive amount on his clothes. His garments were ragged and torn, especially his jeans which had a massive rip revealing his knee which was quickly turning black and blue, the universal colors of pain.

Shaking his head, he finally turned the knob after examining himself, and walked slowly into the other room.

The size and style of the living room was a bit different than Jason's apartment. The couch in the room did not lean up against any of the walls, but was placed in the middle of the floor.

There was an assembled entertainment center which stood up against the wall that housed another closed door which appeared to lead to the bathroom. In front of the sectional was yet another self-constructed piece of furniture, this one being a black table which housed cabinets, and on the table surface were unfolded maps with an ashtray littered with cigarette butts.

Jason inspected the maps, realizing each one detailed a certain part of the city, and it became clear that whomever this place belonged to, they were extremely methodical as well as tactical.

Those two words in his pounding mind made him think instantly of his brother.

Jason pictured him with his wife Cara cutting down everything that lay in their path, back touching back in a formation of teamwork and he slightly smiled, until his anger kicked in once again.

Who pulled him off of his feet, and drug him into this apartment?

Jason had to find out the answer, and hopefully confront the middle aged man who had assaulted him. He stood for just a few moments, thinking of opening the front door leading to the hallway when suddenly his mystery man appeared.

The front door to the apartment swung open, and the man facing Jason was dressed in a white dress shirt and a wool p-coat. He also wore a pair of blue jeans that appeared to be loose and comfortable, the knees looking as if he had slid in crimson.

The man turned to yell out to people Jason could not see until the unseen crew carried another younger man into the apartment by his arms and legs and put him on the couch in the living room. The stranger was leaking blood from a wound near his abdomen.

Jason ignored the group, and rushed in the direction of the man in the jacket, his fist curled as he snapped in the man's face, "Why the fuck did you toss me around like that? What was the problem? You stopped me from saving my son!"

The man's face stretched and quickly expressed fury. He grabbed Jason by the collar of his bloody t-shirt, throwing him up against the wall and slightly spitting as he screamed in his flushed face, "You dare come at me after I risked my goddamn neck to make sure you were safe? Are you too stupid to realize that I was saving you?"

Jason looked into the stranger's hard eyes and the man pulled his collar harder, slamming his already aching head into the wall behind him again as he continued to yell, "You want to save your son? How about this? I lost mine!"

The man's hands let go of Jason and he began touching his face as he spoke, "I lost mine, goddamn it. I lost my boy."

He looked directly at Jason once again, "So don't come at me like you're going to do something. I saved your fucking life, okay?"

Jason peered down at the floor, suddenly feeling guilty for being so upset with the man, and the picture became clear of the woman two inches from his face, snapping ferociously with a knife in her hand when he was quickly pulled away from potential death.

He took a deep breath and placed his arm on the upset man's shoulder attempting to console him. As his hands covered his face he cried, a manly wail.

Jason began to speak, "I'm sorry. I know what you were trying to do, and you saved me. Thank you."

The man picked up his head to face him, and Jason gave condolences to the loss of his son.

The stranger placed his hand on Jason's shoulder, a faint grin on his face, "I really do thank you for that. The name is John...John Robertson."

John resembled a man who worked hard and had a life of playing even harder, an existence of hard days of labor, many drunken nights, as well as many moments filled with arguments, possible road rages, and nights spent with attractive younger women who found his rugged and strong looks attractive, even at his age. But then Jason thought his perception might be completely off. This man could have been a cop, a by the book officer with a perfect record of truth and justice.

Or he could have been an attorney, tossing papers as he ripped into the defense, his words ripping into the very fiber of the individual in his path.

Whoever this man was, Jason knew that he was brave in this newly formed world and may be a valuable ally to aid him in rescuing Matthew from his own peril.

Jason quickly noticed after quenching the fires of his altercation with John that the yelling and screaming of the man on the couch had stopped.

One of the men cried out, "He's gone...he's fucking gone!"

John stepped over to the two men crouching, and Jason stood closely behind him.

The men were silent, but Jason could see the African American man who was holding the dead body's hand was breathing heavily, and was crying silently.

The other member of the small crew kneeling in front of the couch stood up when John began to speak to him, "There was nothing we could have done...absolutely nothing."

John shook his head and pointed over to a dazed Jason behind him, "I know this is not the greatest time for introductions, but this poor soul is apparently Jason Cain. He also lives in this building."

The man who wore a baseball cap and a bloody concert t-shirt with jeans placed out his hand, "I'm Tim...Tim Palmer. Welcome to hell."

Tim smirked at Jason as if he was attempting to bring humor into the proceedings, but to no avail.

John lurched over the black man and placed his large hand on his shoulder, "Hey man, I am so sorry for your loss. I really want you to know that, but you did everything you could."

He attempted to lift the man, but he would not let go of the now ice-cold hand.

The deceased man was also African American, and from the look of the rags and extremely bloody towels wrapped tight around his abdomen, he had been stabbed with an object so deep that it punctured a vital organ and instantly caused him to bleed out.

John finally got the man to his feet and he was only a little taller than Jason, who was himself about five foot nine. The look on the man's face was anything but welcoming.

He seemed to growl under his breath and looked at Jason with rage in his face, although Jason had no idea why.

The man lunged forward, getting past John, and smashed Jason square in the cheek with a hard fist. He began yelling, "You son of a bitch! It's your goddamn fault, you motherfucker! John told me to drag your stupid ass in here, and I had to leave my cousin in the hallway to fend for himself!"

The ferocity of the man continued as he pointed to the body on the couch, "That's him, man. That's my cousin Ray, who's dead because I had to save your white ass! And I don't even know your ass!"

Jason placed a fist to his jaw staring directly at this man spitting in his direction. After all he had been through the entire day; the hits against the walls, the slashing, the scratches, and now the slapping, he finally snapped.

Jason ground his teeth and flew toward the man with a fist in the air. John quickly stepped in the middle like a referee during a heavyweight fight.

He shoved the two apart and shouted at both of them, his voice filled with superiority, "Goddamn it! Stop, the both of you!"

He turned his back to Jason to stare at the angered black man, using his name as he spoke, "Russell, it was not this guys fault. You thought your cousin was tough, and he was. But this is survival at its best, okay? You either have it, or you don't."

Russell peered at John, whose jaw clenched as he continued, "But it wasn't this guy who took him out, okay? You did a good thing. You did a really good thing."

Russell bowed his head as if to agree, but still stared coldly at Jason.

John walked toward the window, witnessed the absolute carnage still raging outside of the window, and began to speak to the group, "Listen. This is no game here. Things are out of fucking control, and I have no clue what the fuck is going on here."

John stared down at the carpet as he continued, "But, I do know this. We did this. Us men, always throwing around our weight, always dominating everything, but I never figured something like this would go down."

He turned to face the men in the room; Jason holding his face, Tim standing by Russell's cousin's body, and Russell himself staring down at the floor.

John sounded like a general in a high command, "We have to set our differences aside, gentlemen. It's us, against them. It's not black, or white, or green. It's not about color. It's not about race. It's about gender, the survival of the male species...at any cost. So we better find a way out of here and find some place safer. That is what we should be focusing on. Now, let's make a goddamn plan and drop these bitches into the holes they crawled out of."

No one in the group cheered in unison. In fact, the speech brought nothing but silence.

Jason knew that one way or another, with or without this new group, he was going to get to his son.

CHAPTER TWO

The Possessor and the Pawn
Fort Wayne, Indiana
September 23rd, 2014

The cellar was still lit with candles as the lithe, snow white body of Susan Rogers strode through the room underneath the family house, her bare feet caressing the marked stones of the floor shaded in darkness.

The fabric of her cloak waved away from her naked body, revealing her supple and still young form.

Susan had lived in the house alone ever since Will had left to pursue his legacy, the legacy that he had just recently turned away from, vowing revenge on the demon that overtook his mother.

Since the day of his departure his young mother, still overtaken by the evil entity of the long dead witch, Sara, spent most of her days in the cellar while the rest of the house practically fell apart around her.

The outside of the house had grown vines around the foundation, and the paint had almost completely chipped and dried off.

Susan never had any visitors, and any person who came near the home would have surely rushed away as fast as they could.

She had become a recluse before the spell was cast.

The spirit inside her ventured like a thief in the night, like a vampire, and preyed on the flesh and sinew of men.

With the power of the host controlling her, young Susan could vanish and appear anywhere. And through Susan, Sara would feed on the flesh and relish every single moment as the pieces sliding down her throat signified nothing but her pure hatred toward them.

The demon simply controlled everything. She wanted to feel them cower, to devour them as they screamed, and to ingest their very souls until they were nothing but useless gory scraps in her wake.

Not unlike her mother when controlled by Sara, Susan would sometimes attempt to show herself occasionally, crying over her son while Sara screamed inside of her head, "I have control of you, girl. There is no escaping me. You are weak...but I have all of the power. You have nothing."

Occasionally, Susan would scream back at her thoughts, "Let me go! I do not want this!"

When this occurred, Sara would put so much pressure on her mind until she bent to her will, becoming pure Sara once again.

As Susan's untouched porcelain body swayed in the darkness, a man cried out, muffled by a velvet cloth tied around his face.

The vibrant young girl smiled as she approached the man. His body was glistened in sweat, the fear was evident in his face even in the glint of candles.

She bent down and licked her lips as she removed the cloth from his face and the man screamed, "What are you doing, you bitch? What the fuck is going on? It's all of you! All of the women have gone insane! Please...let me go."

His eyes pleaded as Susan's smile grew bigger and the man's face, still filled with terror began to quickly flush with anger, "I said let me go...you fucking cunt!"

Susan stopped smiling and she stared down at the man who was chained to the wall. The voice and mannerisms of her body host reigned over her as she spoke, "Now, that is no way to talk to a lady. You have no manners. You kill and you maim...you rape! You are disgusting creatures."

The terrified man coughed, and spat in Susan's beautiful face, "Fuck you."

She wiped the slimy gob from her cheek as the grin reappeared, Sara still in control, "I find your foul words...," Susan's face distorted into the creature of Jason's dreams: the gnarled, sharp teeth, the fiery eyes as she finished her sentence, "Delicious!"

Susan's body bent down and her mouth latched onto the top of the man's skull, causing him to scream into the darkness.

The bones snapped, and the blood flowed onto the floor and into the man's face.

The sound of bone twisting and snapping sounded like a fallen tree, and the writhing of her meal suddenly stopped.

The creature possessing the beautiful young woman stopped feasting, and she fell to the ground near the body.

In her own voice, Susan yelled, and she spat the pieces of the man's skull and brain matter she had ingested onto the floor, causing her to vomit.

Her eyes turned back to the beautiful color she was born with and she yelled at the demon controlling her for many years, "Enough! Get out of me! I want this no more!"

The voice of Sara pierced Susan's mind, and she felt like her brain was going to split in half as the words were shrilly spoken inside of her head, "You pitiful little girl! Just like your dear mother, useless! You are so weak. I am done with this, I am finished with you!"

Susan felt her eyes burn and she screamed in shrill pain as the fire, the power that had entered her body escaped from her pupils as they did when it had invaded her.

The force that urged her son to hate who he was as a man, the force that had sent him out on a mission to release her evil spell had left her, causing her to fall to her knees, her mouth covered in blood.

The fire illuminated the room as it had the night it had entered, only this time a form appeared through the swirls of what appeared to be flames of hellfire, the form of a woman.

Susan stopped screaming and lifted her face to see the true image of the woman who had taken over her, the one who had made her perform her evil deeds and push her son into something she did not believe in.

The woman was a picture from her own time; her long black hair resembled the color of a crow's feathers as it flowed in waves as if on a wind.

Her eyes were as blue as a calm ocean, and her body was thin. The woman's legs were long, and as incredible as she was to Susan's widened eyes, this woman emanated nothing but pure evil.

She stood in front of Susan who was now pale; the white dress she wore was tight around her body.

Susan looked on as the woman knelt down, placed her slender hand under her trembling chin and lifted her up with force.

Susan began to cry as her eyes met the woman before her, and the woman finally spoke, "Susan Rogers. You disappoint me. I thought that you had true power. The grace, the beauty I thought you always were."

A grin swept across her face, "And you felt that you…and your pitiful mother were the keys to great power?"

She slipped her hand around Susan's throat pulling her forward, "You were only a pawn! Your mother, she called upon me, bringing me back from time and space, and damnation. Through your pitiful mother…I showed you your own power. But you were all weak!"

The lovely and frightening entity dropped Susan to the ground hard, and she attempted to slide away from the woman who glided toward her on bare, slender feet.

She stalked Susan, continuing to speak her true disdain for the Roger's clan, "It was all so beautiful! I used your entire family…like sheep! I used you all like…PIGS!"

Susan picked herself up from the floor, and with a sudden burst of power and rage ran toward the spectral woman, slapping her hard across the side of her cheek, "You fucking bitch! You told my son lies while I screamed as if for air, attempting to reach him, while you fed him bullshit!"

The woman laughed hard, as Susan's teeth grit, slightly chipping the enamel.

She balled her fist, and attempted to strike her, but the woman caught her attack in mid-air, snapping the bones in her fragile wrist.

Susan screamed as her arm was released, and the woman lunged for her face, laughing maniacally as she reached her target, "You thought that you were the one? You are nothing! Your mother, as well as your son, all of you are NOTHING!"

The nails of Sara's fingers dug deep into the flesh of Susan's face, causing her to howl, "Fuck…you!"

The woman's searing gaze once again planted fright on Susan's face, "I used you...to find her!"

The bones in Susan's face began to snap, and the screams of pain filled the room once again.

Her head began to cave under the powerful weight of Sara's fingertips embedded in her skin, squeezing into the muscles and bones of her jaw.

And as Susan spit out pieces of marrow and cracked teeth, the woman's eyes blazed.

Her mouth grew jagged, but her words were extremely clear, "There is no mother, there is only me, SARA RINEHART."

Susan's head smashed under the pressure like a watermelon hit with a cannon, the parts flying in all directions.

The laughter from Sara as she licked the blood from her fingertips echoed in Will Thompson's mind the same moment he was veering through the carnage all around him in the city.

The vision was extremely vivid, and he witnessed everything, including his mother's horrible death.

He screamed, shut his eyes tight, and pulled the wheel to the left, slamming the truck into a car which had already been tossed on its side. Sara was still laughing like a super villain of a comic book in his mind.

In the old cellar, the beautiful and wicked woman said words only she could hear, "I am coming for you, Elizabeth."

And in a moment's time, her body changed, forming a whirlwind of fire that shot through the small chamber door, through the house, and out of the window of the living room of the Roger's home, causing glass to explode from the sheer force of power.

In the cellar, Susan's lifeless body was lying on the floor.

She looked beautiful in her death, her torment over.

After everything that young Susan had been through; her life with her mother who was taken by evil, her life with Bill, and her many years possessed by the evil demon of a witch burned alive long before, she could finally rest.

The tragic and painful journey of Susan Rogers was finally over.

CHAPTER THREE

Ready for War
September 23rd, 2014
9:56 A.M.

Scott Cain did not leave the body of his wife for many hours.

The tears constantly fell as he knelt down next to her, holding her soft but cold hand in his, hoping and praying in his mind that she would revive.

He longed to see Cara's familiar smile once again planted across her face.

Scott also hoped that he was dead asleep and that he would soon arise from the worst nightmare he had ever had.

The once vibrant and fun loving Cara did not wake from her stillness and Scott never woke up in his bed, turning to see that Cara was lying next to him the entire time.

The only sound came from the screaming outside of the front window.

Scott continued to hold his dead wife's hand, staring into her eyes knowing that they would suddenly dilate, or that her smile, he was so fond of, would never return to her face.

Cara was truly his entire world and he knew he would have to press on, and that he would be lost without her.

As he continued to mourn, he heard a window in the room shatter behind him, the pieces of glass cascading onto the carpet inside of the house.

In seconds, a woman in her twenties Scott had occasionally seen around the neighborhood burst through.

The woman who spent her time jogging for exercise in the early morning was now attempting to get herself into the Cain home to attack a man she had never had any anger towards..

The brunette woman attempted to slide herself into the window as Scott shot up to fend her off.

He leaned over and picked up the metal fireplace poker, his body feeling shock for a moment when he held it in his hand.

The woman continued to squeeze her form into the giant hole she had made when Scott snapped back into reality, and rushed quickly toward the window.

Her body was halfway through when suddenly she stared up at Scott, snarling and chanting the same strange words Cara had when she became crazed, "Pig! Kill the piiiig!"

The young woman's eyes were gone; there was no color and they had a milky fog-like gloss.

He swung the poker at her face, smashing the bridge of her nose instantly.

Blood shot onto the carpet, but just like his wife she did not scream from pain.

The woman once again looked up at him and he swung, hitting her even harder in the back. His attacker continued to attempt to slide her body in slowly through the broken window, which still had giant shards blocking her way.

Scott yelled and raised the poker, bringing it down wildly.

He hit her, again and again, when suddenly she began sliding backwards.

Her stomach was now gliding against the shards.

Scott hit her with the poker again on the top of the head, but she continued, snarling and snapping.

Feeling as if he was losing his mind from the sight in front of him, Scott howled.

At that moment, a warrior, a soldier who had had enough gripped the woman by the hair and brought her neck down hard toward one of the giant pieces of glass blocking her entrance.

Scott screamed as his body slammed down to the floor, causing the shard to enter her throat and pop out of the top of her skull. Her movement stopped quickly, and just like that, the fight was over.

Scott stayed on the carpet as the woman's blood trickled like a waterfall above him He tried to catch his breath and began speaking to himself like he had gone mad, "What is going on here? What have we done?"

Scott wiped away some tears, and attempted to gain composure as he stood up.

He did not turn to see the woman impaled in his broken window, and walked straight past his sweet and beautiful wife in the middle of the room.

The former soldier headed up the staircase leading to their bedroom.

Scott Cain was gentle, and had nothing but love and respect in his heart for everyone he had come across.

The man was able to hold intelligent conversations, or he could be foolish and have a good time when the situation called for it.

Scott enjoyed life at every single turn, and he had seen so much death and bloodshed over his military career that he had reached a point where it did not affect him.

His experiences were always a mystery, and the only one he ever opened up to about his scars, his demons, was his wife who knew the perils and mental struggles of being a soldier herself.

In the situation facing him at this moment, Scott knew he had to be nothing but a man of action.

He opened the bedroom closet door, and pulled a metal box down from the top shelf along with small boxes of bullets for the weapons contained within.

Inside of the open box were two 9 mm. pistols and a .22 handgun revolver.

Scott enjoyed going to gun ranges and keeping his skills sharp now and again, but never thought that they would be put to the test in his own quiet, married life.

Shaken, he got down on his knees by the bed and pulled a rectangular military issue trunk from underneath.

From inside the box, Scott pulled out memories; two holster straps, a surplus belt with a side holster of its own. He also picked up a sheath which housed a machete used on many occasions during his career; to chop vines, find and kill potential food when the situation arose, and in some cases, fend off a human being.

Scott also collected a pair of black Government Issue combat boots, polished even though they were not worn for many years.

He slipped on a black shirt, a pair of black cargo pants with enough pockets to carry anything he needed; bullets, food, maps, and placed the holster straps over his shoulder, clicking them together.

The belt was in place, and the guns were placed in their proper homes; the 9 mm's were to the left and right, and the .22 was placed into the holster on the side of his hip on the belt, along with the machete cover to his left.

The bullet boxes he had placed into the pockets of his pants, and the guns were already loaded and prepared to fire.

Scott took a deep breath and exited the room he and his wife had slept in, laughed in, made passionate love in for many years, and headed down the staircase to the massacre below.

Cara was still on the carpet, and Scott kneeled down once again and placed his fingertips over her eyes, closing them for the last time.

Scott felt tears form, and he spoke softly to her lifeless body as if she was still responsive, "I will stop this, baby. Whatever happened, whoever did this, I will fight until my last, dying breath.

He caressed her face with the front of his hand, "I love you, baby. I will...always."

Scott stood, and slowly walked toward the window, inspecting the woman impaled on the glass as he moved forward.

Her eyes were slowly changing to color, and her pupils were once again green.

Scott jumped and breathed heavily. "You have to do this, be strong. You have to go, now," he pleaded to himself as he put his back against the wall by the window and peered outside.

He witnessed three women from the neighborhood stalking the outside yard. Each of them had once been friendly and courteous people.

After taking a deep breath, he exhaled and opened the door to the outside, pulling one of the 9mms from its holster as he approached the women, who were now snarling and filled with rage.

The first woman was frail and walked with a limp, and Scott knew her as little Mrs. Montgomery from across the street. She was the type of older woman to make cookies, drink lemonade on her porch on the weekends, and every time her grass became too tall he was always kind enough to give it a cut, and was rewarded with sandwiches.

Scott attempted not to think about the fact that this wonderful woman was the snarling beast snapping and lurching towards him.

He felt tears as he fired the 9mm at her face, striking the old woman in the cheek. She did not fall.

Just then he felt something sharp rake across his back, and he yelped in pain.

He turned around quickly and witnessed his neighbor from next door standing in front of him holding a small rake used for digging soil.

Scott never had a problem with this young woman, and on many occasions he and Cara had Amy the neighbor and her husband over for drinks.

He pulled back as she continued to swing the implement wildly, and fired a shot directly into her heart.

Just as his wife before her, the woman in the window, and the old lady moaning behind him, she did not go down.

His head was stunned by the sheer thought of it, and he quickly thought to himself, "Are these women undead like in an old Romero film?"

He did not take his watchful eyes off of the tattooed woman as he kicked Mrs. Montgomery right in her wrinkled face while she attempted to lunge behind him.

His younger neighbor shot forward like a ferocious tigress, and dropped on top of Scott as they hit the grass.

The woman's power was evident when she grabbed his head and slammed it hard into the ground repeatedly. The soft grass and the dirt beneath felt like a brick to the back of the head.

Amy snarled as she grabbed him by his throat, and Scott fumbled for the snap on the sheath containing the blade to his side as the strength of the woman grew.

Finally, Scott felt for the handle, pulled out the still sharp machete, and brought it forward into the wild woman's neck.

The blood sprayed like an old Kung-Fu film and the meat of the neck was severed causing her head to hold together although it hung to the opposite side.

Surprisingly, she began to slash at his face, taking away skin with her chipped, polished fingernails.

Scott gritted his teeth and brought the blade forward, causing the woman's head to fly from her neck onto the yard.

With pain in his head and face, Scott quickly hopped to his feet, swinging the blade into the senior woman's head, straight down the middle. The woman drop hard like a sack of rocks.

The last woman lunged as he shot her directly in her milky white eye with the 9mm, the bullet tearing a small hole in the back of her skull, dropping her as quickly as Mrs. Montgomery.

Scott knelt down for a moment, attempting to catch his breath and noticed the old woman's headless body still wriggling underneath him.

He sealed his eyes for a few seconds, and headed toward his car which was parked on the street, opened the door and placed the key in the ignition as he sat down in the leather seat.

In an instant, one of the young neighborhood girls ran toward the driver's side door attempting to get inside. She attempted to climb onto the hood and smash the window with her tiny fists.

Scott placed the car in drive and brought the vehicle forward, throwing the girl who lived across the street back onto the street in front of the car.

He felt nothing but queasiness in his stomach when he hit the gas, hitting the young girl with the metal of the bumper and slamming her hard into a car parked next to his.

Placing the car in reverse, Scott pulled the car into the street and began to drive.

Through the rearview mirror, he could see the young girl was standing, her intestines hanging from her tiny body like garland.

Scott felt as if he was going to be sick on himself, but instead turned the dial on the radio. There was no news, no sign of hope, only static.

He knew where he had to go, even though he was not certain of his brother's condition or if he was dead or alive.

Scott was going to find out what happened to Jason, and feared the city was going to resemble one of the war zones he faced years before.

As the car drove on; past the carnage, the flipped cars, the bodies of young and old lying on the ground, he muttered to himself, "Hell hath no fury. Hell truly hath no fury."

CHAPTER FOUR

Reunion of Evil
The Connection of Sara and Elizabeth Rinehart
September 23rd; 2014

The violence on the city streets was intense; women of all nations, all creeds, and all colors were smashing the front of shop windows, pulling men out of cars, out of their homes, and killing them on the streets like an angry mob.

Their chanting in unison sounded like the hissing of a basket of snakes, and the screams of men filled the air as a possessed Elizabeth walked forward.

Her bare feet touched the asphalt, and the blood caked on her soles had dried up.

Elizabeth's sleep clothes seemed to float on the light breeze, and her hair swayed beautifully to and fro.

She was a true goddess amongst all of the terrifying things happening around her.

Her eyes were the color of milk, and they never blinked.

Elizabeth did not chant. She did not snarl or growl as her body strolled forward in the middle of the street; she did not attempt to move when cars and trucks veered past.

And she did not see the sudden fiery mist flying toward her.

The speed of the fireball was intense, and funneled directly into Elizabeth's lifeless eyes until it was gone.

Sara was now a part of her. She was one with her true vessel, her ancestor.

Elizabeth dropped to her knees and screamed when she heard the voice of Sara in her mind, "Elizabeth Rinehart, my blood, my family. Now, we are truly one. I am you! It is time to show the world our true power! It is time to rid the world of everything! It is now time to kill the man, the man who harmed you, who raped your spirit as the pigs did with me. Now, my beautiful one, stand!"

Elizabeth's body shot up from the concrete, only this time, she had a slight grin.

She began to step forward on bare feet again, light and careful.

The sheer power of Sara seemed to vibrate her entire body, and suddenly Elizabeth, without moving her head to face her intended targets, raised her arms and waved her hands.

Men running in the streets instantly stopped as their bodies crisped and blackened in the thick flames Elizabeth was somehow throwing at them.

She never lost her step, and the voice of Sara laughed inside of her head.

Elizabeth waved her hands again when she witnessed a young man to her side being attacked by a woman who appeared to be Asian, and blew his body against the wall behind him.

The man's spine cracked and split from the sheer force.

All around her, men were being blown apart, set ablaze, and tossed into the air.

Elizabeth was now a supernatural being with unstoppable force, and she walked on, destroying everything in her path.

She was quickly becoming Sara, and the Rinehart women were finally reunited: murderous and strong.

CHAPTER FIVE

The Darkness Has The Answers
September 23, 2014

Nothing but blackness surrounded Will Thompson as he slowly stepped through the expanse surrounding him.

He had no indication of where he was, but something compelled him to move forward.

The ground underneath his feet was flat at first, as if he was stepping on nothing.

The area was a limbo, and also a mystery.

He stopped for a moment to put his hand in his left pocket, pulled out his cigarette lighter and clicked it twice before it flamed up. Will still saw nothing but pitch black in front of his eyes.

As he pressed on through the nothingness, the floor began to squish.

The sounds inspired sickness in Will's stomach as his boots made one small step after another.

The sound grew louder and seemed to echo in the black hell surrounding him.

He stopped his movement and lowered the tiny flame of the lighter to investigate, witnessing nothing but human body parts splayed everywhere.

As he continued walking, trying to illuminate the floor, he saw the parts: torsos splayed open, intestines stinking and steaming, human heads with looks of fear implanted in their faces, severed legs and arms all bunched together creating the putrid flesh carpet.

Will suddenly felt an acidic mess flowing through his esophagus, but nothing escaped.

The smell of the room as he tread further into the darkness.

The skin on his thumb started to burn as the lighter grew too hot, and he tossed the lighter to the fleshy earth.

The room was once again black as his boots squished, and the sounds became more terrifying when he could not see them with his own eyes.

Suddenly, echoes and voices filled the room. Male voices filled Will's ears and their words displayed nothing but pain and torment, "Why...did you do this? Why?"

Will's head began to swim and his teeth gritted hard when he yelled out to the detached voices. "I had no choice!"

As he felt as if he was about to lose his mind, falling victim to this unknown room, a soft voice filled the air, and at that moment the pitch darkness in front of him was illuminated with a faint candlelight.

The image of a young woman appeared-a delicate and beautiful young woman with blonde hair as bright as the sunlight.

Cradled in her arms was an older woman, her face timeless even though she appeared to be in her golden years.

As Will stepped forward, he knew he recognized her features, and a lump filled his throat as a childlike tone escaped his quivering lips. "Mom? Mother, is that really you?

He reached out to caress the skin on her soft cheek. It felt so real to his fingertips and to his senses.

Will's throat was tight, and tears filled his eyes, "Mother, are you really here? Are you...dead? Am I dead?"

The young woman smiled at him as he continued, his words quaking, "I saw you...die."

She put out her hand to touch his, and her voice was almost angelic in the hellish black tomb. "Yes, it's me. And this woman is your grandmother, Helen."

The woman huddled under Susan did not say a word, but Susan continued, "Yes, we are dead, in the earthly plane of existence. Our souls are meant to travel on, but we remain here. We will remain in this prison until she is stopped."

Will looked down at his mother confused as she attempted to explain life before he grew to fulfill the legacy brought upon him. "Your grandmother was killed by the demon inside me when you were just a baby. Your grandmother was tricked...into bringing the demon witch back to the world of man."

Tears fell from Susan's eyes, reflecting the candlelight as she peered down at her mother who remained silent, "The witch tricked the entire bloodline of our family. The first of our kin was compelled to hold onto the book we have possessed for many, many years, the book that has brought all of this...chaos and hate upon the world."

As Susan spoke, silently, Will touched her hair. The texture felt like comfort, it felt like home to him.

The lost son could not believe after what he witnessed in his mind that she was before him at this moment.

He started to question his young mother, innocence in his words, "Who is she? Who made you do such things? Who made me...do the horrible things I have done?"

Susan placed her hand gently in his, comforting him as she explained, "Her name...is Sara Rinehart."

Will ripped his hand from his mother's, placing it to his mouth in astonishment.

He could not say a word as she spoke. "When your grandfather hurt your grandmother...she somehow willed her soul back from the dimension we are now. We are between heaven and hell. We are nowhere...and we are everywhere. Helen asked for revenge against her husband, your abusive grandfather, and Sara aided her. In return, your grandmother had to allow Sara's evil spirit to inhabit her. Through your grandmother...she taught me HER way. She taught me how to grow up strong, to get rid of my fears, to feel my **change** as she called it. When I graduated I went out with a few friends, and I was assaulted by your father."

Will looked on in shock, the tears becoming heavier as Susan's speech continued, "Through him...I had you. And you made everything I went through worthwhile."

A smile slid across her face, a beam of joy, "You made my LIFE...worthwhile."

Will felt his own smile through the tears, but it was abruptly wiped clean when his mother explained life after his father did the unthinkable. "It was your grandmother who had forced me to move on, to live with your father, to feel a difference in myself. Your father, he was terrible my entire year I had to stay with him."

Will looked on, trying very hard to wrap his mind around all of his newfound answers, and Susan continued, "One day, I placed you in your room, and I felt it. I felt this force, this power enveloping my insides. I felt as if I wasn't truly me. I was something...someone else. And then I walked into our bedroom with your father...and I maimed him. I tore into him, and ripped through his flesh."

At this moment, Will could see his mother's smile through the darkness, "And, even though I felt as if free will was held captive, it felt so good! I absolutely loved every moment, every whimper, and every drop of blood."

Susan's son, still as a stone, trembled as she looked back towards his teary eyes, "I took you back to your grandmother...and she was old and weak. She was falling apart, quickly. She looked like something from a Grimm story and she took you. She stole you away into her dark secret room."

Will, still shaking, opened his mouth to ask yet another question, sounding like a wounded child, "Why? Why did you agree to take in Sara? What...drove you to agree to any of this? Did you agree to treat me like shit? Did you agree to teach me a bunch of garbage spouted from the tongue of some ancient bitch?"

Susan watched her son's eyes become wide, and she began to plead like a prisoner begging for life, "I had no choice! As your grandmother, she was going to kill you. She was going to spill your blood...in front of me. That is why I did what I had to do , I swear, to save you."

Susan looked down at the quiet woman again, her eyes staring back up at her with no motion, almost dead.

Susan's lip trembled, "And I felt the change. I felt that I was going to be something more than I ever was. It was selfish, it was a power trip."

She caressed the old woman's hair, silver and perfectly brushed, "I became Sara and I killed your grandmother. I felt that force again, and I was all-powerful. Her magick emanated from me, from my every pore. But I did attempt to fight her, to fight her power...to stop her. I was too weak."

Susan began to cry and her soppy eyes glinted in the candlelight as she stared at Will, "I am so sorry. I really didn't mean to do anything to you, to hurt you, to hurt anyone."

Will knelt down onto the stinking earth to wipe the tears dripping from his mother's cheeks. Her face grew serious with a heavy hint of fear. "She is pure evil, Will. You must stop her. Go and protect the man you were forced to deceive. You must save him. You must save them. You must save us. We are lost, the world is cannot become the same."

Susan glanced up at her son, causing him to jump back after witnessing her now cracked, wrinkled face, "She must be stopped, Will!"

Susan slipped away as the entrails and parts creating the carpet began to move, quiver like the tide of an ocean, causing Will to slip back into the pitch darkness of the room. The wails of pain were ringing in his ears once again.

As if waking up from a horrible dream, Will popped up from the steering wheel bent from the impact. He looked into the mirror above the dash which was cracked, and saw a huge gash on his forehead, along with a deep cut that looked as if he needed instant medical attention.

Finding a t-shirt he had used to wipe off gasoline cans, he wrapped the fabric around the wound, tying it in the back, and examined the wreckage in front of him; the folded dashboard panel, the severely cracked windshield, and the front bumper completely caved in toward the windshield.

Will held his head, and began to heave heavily. He thought of the death of his mother, and the horrible, dark place.

Was it a dream? Was it another plane of reality? Was it real?

Will believed anything could be possible, especially after what the world had become after the events of his fucking legacy.

As he closed his eyes to stop the spinning, Will heard a hard banging sound coming from both sides of the truck.

He turned to the driver's side door, and the image caused him to scoot to the middle of the truck.

Many women stood on either side of the truck, growling and screaming, chanting their cadence, "Piiiiig! Killll the piiig!"

Frozen in fear, he witnessed five women on the passenger door side, one practically behind the other, as well as four of the small group on the other side.

Lunging down underneath the seat, Will attempted to feel around with his hand until he finally clutched his prize: a heavy crowbar.

With all of the strength Will could possibly gather, he propped up on the middle of the seat, practically leaning back in midair, and kicked the windshield with his now dirty combat boots.

The pain in his brain made it difficult.

Kicking again and again, the windshield started to give way, and he finished the job with the bar causing the pane of glass to fall outward.

Taking a deep breath, he slid his battered body over the busted dash, panting and grunting until his stomach reached the hood of the heavily damaged vehicle.

The small group around him attempted to slash and swing at the now standing man with their knives and assorted implements.

Will took one of the psychotic women with ease, slamming the end of the bar directly into the top of her head, causing it to protrude from her chin.

As her head hit the hood, the now heroic-looking Will Thompson slammed his foot on the top of her head, and pulled the long bar out with a squish. She fell lifelessly onto the concrete.

The bar then swung into the forehead of another, causing the woman to drop her bloody knife and stagger backwards.

As he looked down, Will noticed he had cleared a small panel and quickly slid down the left side of the truck.

With feet on hard ground, the crowbar swung again and again, until four of Will's attackers were lying on the road, pools of blood surrounding their still shapes.

The fight caused the young man to pant and grunt, almost resembling the women he ferociously fought.

Slamming the bar hard into one of the jelly-like vanilla eyeballs of one of his assailants, Will quickly pulled his arm backward, tearing his weapon from the hole and forward where it made contact with one of the jaws, still chanting.

The Caucasian woman's jaw shifted to the right, after the snapping of bones caused her tongue to droop due to her busted features.

The second whack to the temple caused the bones in her skull to shatter, filling her brain with blood. She dropped to the earth.

With three females left, Will stepped backward, never taking his eyes off of his target.

He stared, eyes dilated, and rushed forward like a mythical hero, swinging the end of the metal to the side of one of the psychotic females temples. The blow caused the hook to hang above the ear, blood flowing slowly and then with a tiny spurt.

The body was thrown to the ground, and the crack of the crowbar made a hard sound when it exited bone. The sudden warrior swung again, connecting with the opposite side of the next woman's head, the temple exploding, leaving a small river of blood to her side as she fell.

With crimson, sticky mess all over the front of him and sprinkled on his hot, sweaty face.

Will growled like a dog, the whites of his eyes staring down his final victim.

She stared at him, foggy saucers dilating, her mouth curled in anger and rage.

The woman rushed forward and her intended target followed suit, slamming her to the ground with all of his might. Will brought the crowbar down onto her face repeatedly.

He was a wild man in the jungle atop his frightened prey as the bar hit again and again, sloppily.

The final woman's head smashed, a pumpkin dropped on the street.

Will's howls echoed all around him. The blood on his face resembled some kind of war paint as her name could suddenly be heard, "Sara, you fucking bitch! I am coming for you! I am coming for you!"

CHAPTER SIX

Nothing Sweet In The Union of Lost Love
September 17th, 2014
11:32 A.M.

In the silence of the apartment, the front door banged and creaked with the forces hitting the wood from the other side.

The number of women outside was undetermined, as all of the men in the living room remained quiet, cracking their knuckles or staring down at the carpet.

John had attempted to turn on the television and found nothing but static, fizzling and crackling on every single channel. The white noise rumble caused hairs to stand on everyone's arms.

Russell Williams sat on the end of the sectional couch where the blood of his nephew still stained underneath him. The man did not speak and he did look at anyone.

The body was now missing after John had aided Russell in picking up the tall teenager, dropping the body gently into the bathtub in the bathroom on the left of John's deceased son's room; the door was still wide open.

After the two left the body to once again enter the somber front room, Russell plopped down hard on the seat, and he seemed to become catatonic.

He did not move, and barely breathed.

With the body now tucked away, the living room turned into a funeral parlor as the door in the front continued to crash as unseen hands attempted to kick and bash the object.

John was the first of the group to make any movement as he stood and opened his mouth, "We cannot stay here for too much longer. We are absolutely fucked if we stay here. We have to figure out what we are going to do from here, but first I am going to go to that door and see what the hell we're dealing with.

Jason, sitting on the carpet, also got to his feet. "I will be right behind you."

He felt a kinship with this middle aged man and he could not explain the feeling. Perhaps it was his thirst for survival, or the same feeling of failing a child. Whatever the feeling was, he knew he would help this man through any event.

The two slowly walked toward the pounding wood, the heaviness splintering, the locks still steadily holding.

John looked at Jason, and turned the knob until there was enough of a gap to peer out into the hallway.

As soon as John poked his closely shaved head out like a rabbit popping out of a hole in a children's cartoon, he could see the back of one woman by the stairs, with another on the step behind her.

As he quickly craned his neck to the other side, he gazed upon three other women; the first in front of the pack caught his eyes, and leapt toward him.

In a flash, Jason grabbed John by the back of the shirt, and tugged him hard before the slashing, spitting lady could reach him.

The two men slammed the door, fastened the locks, and stared at each other, expressing the exact same thought, "Holy shit."

Jason and John headed back toward the others, alert but still extremely silent.

John took a deep breath, blew out and sat directly opposite Russell, who was still examining the floor; shoulders tense, hands clasped together.

He made the situation known, shaking his head, "Well, it's not good. We have five outside, and I couldn't tell you about the stairwell."

The door continued banging, as John placed his hand on Russell's shoulder and spoke to him with a calm tone, "I am sorry about your cousin, I really am."

Without picking up his head, the burly man shrugged his shoulders and slowly shook his head in acknowledgment, when suddenly he spoke, "Before this, I had my cousin move here from Florida. He was always a smart kid, but his neighborhood the way it was, he had to what he did to do to survive. The hard things. Selling drugs, getting into fights, all of that shit."

All of the men looked at him as he continued, "He got here two fucking days ago. Two days, and the world went to fucking hell. We had no clue what was going on, but we were both attacked on the street."

Russell slammed his balled fist into his other open hand. "And we fought our way back here. It was crazy. The women snapping like pit bulls in a dog fight, foaming out of the mouth."

His eyes touched the floor again, "Then we saw you, John. We all fought hard...together to get back here, and that little dude was right behind me."

Russell cracked a smile. "That little hard-headed motherfucker, Chris. He was a tough little kid, and he was right behind us the entire time."

Jason felt Russell look over at him momentarily when he mentioned the next incident. "Then, you told me to grab up this guy. As soon as I turned around, one of those bitches must have received the upper hand and gave him a shot right in the stomach lining with a blade. I turned around and he was lying on the carpet raspy, in a pool of his own blood."

Russell stared down at the floor yet again. "It was only a moment, an instant. That's all it fucking took. I turned around and this thing was laying on top him, smiling...calling me a goddamn pig. I smashed her with a bat, and she fell."

John latched onto his shoulder tighter, as Russell began to tear a little, "I should have been there, man. I should have fucking been there...to save him."

John kept his hand in place, and began staring at the carpet as well, "But, you did well." You did a good thing. You're a good man."

Tim sat against the wall by the window of the living room and began to speak to the room, mostly looking in Jason's direction, "I lived on the second floor with my girlfriend, her name was Julie. She was my world, and I absolutely loved her to death. We met on the internet, were together for eight months after we talked for three, and we just decided to move in together last week. I will not forget the joy on her face when she laid in bed next to me in our own place for the first time."

Tim began to feel wetness on his lashes as he continued. "She was glorious, so awesome. Everything was going amazingly when earlier this morning I woke up, and she was standing over me, acting like a Saint Bernard bit by a rabid bat or something. I had no clue what was going on, but she was snarling, and she kept saying something, over and over again."

He stared down at the floor, the tears dripping off of his nose, "That was when she attacked me. She continuously came after me, but I finally had to do what I had to do. There was no other choice. After that...I lost it."

Tim's eyes met Jason yet again, "I went to open my door and I was chased back into the room. I could not stop yelling. I felt like such a bitch, but I couldn't. Then, I heard a huge commotion outside and then the door busted wide open. I looked up as I lay next to my girl, and it was these two, John and Russell, and the big guy's cousin we just lost. They actually fought through these monsters...to help me."

He broke down, placing his face on his knees, when Jason continued the round robin discussion on loss, staring directly in the direction of the pounding door in front of him, "I know how you feel. I was absolutely in love with a woman, and we were divorced before these events occurred."

As Jason's abridged tale of love continued, he explained that he was meant to reconcile with his lost love on this day, leaving out the story of Will and the book of evil.

In his mind, Jason began thinking about Will and what he had incited him to do, and thought of how if he saw him again it would take absolute strength not to grab him by the throat and strangle him until there was no life.

Jason turned his head to John who was looking directly at him, "So John, what is your story if you don't mind me asking?"

John blew in a deep breath, twiddling his thumbs slowly, and began to speak, the authority and command in his voice now gone, "I was a divorce'. My wife had gained a massive addiction to painkillers. She became lazy, she didn't do anything but get high on the shit. One fine day she graduated to heroin, began dropping weight, losing her hair and her looks, and beating my son when I wasn't around."

John's thin brow began to furrow, "I did everything I could for that woman. And she didn't want to stop...the dragon had her by the neck and she began to resemble one of these...fucking things outside the door. I gained custody of our Dean, and we both moved here. It wasn't much, but we had each other."

John's head stared downward, his voice got lower, occasionally cracking, "I worked as head of security for that huge nightclub, you know Lumina? Anyway, I came back home, and something compelled me to check in on my son. He was safe and sound, but it was that fatherly instinct."

Jason's tears welled in his eyes, and he wiped them with the back of his hand, John continued, with the same tone, "The next morning we awoke at about six am...just like we both did every day. I was extremely exhausted but we still had breakfast together; eggs, juice, toast. I had my coffee as my son, my goofy son, talked about friends...and girls."

A small smile grew on John's rugged face, "He kept talking to me about this one girl all the time. God! He loved this little girl, Melody. Jesus Christ, he would not stop bringing her up."

John began to chuckle slightly. Jason peered at the carpet, shaking his head slightly, and once again lifted his head toward John, "My son is named Matthew. I made some massive mistakes in the past with my wife, and with him. I always wanted the opportunity to fix it all, to end all of the pain in their lives, and be the man they needed me to be. My son is in my wife's apartment...locked away alone...and I need to save him. This is the ultimate chance...to redeem myself."

Tears fell from his eyes, and John slowly nodded his head.

Jason began to wonder about the condition of his son. Was he safe?

Then he began to think of his beautiful ex-wife, Elizabeth. Was she walking around, aimless, chanting and cutting into every male she laid her now dead eyes on?

His thoughts were broken when John exhaled, making a pass at his face with his big hands as if he was giving in to common sense, "I will help you get to your son. I really don't know you and I have no idea why, maybe it is a lord I do not believe in at work. But maybe this will give me some peace with the loss of my own."

He stared at Jason, whose tears were very visible after his offer, "Someone in this group should be able to hold their child tight, and know they're okay."

The now splintering door with the noisy rattling chain caused Tim to break the momentarily silence, "Guys, this has been really wonderful, but we need to get the hell out of here, now. John has kept me alive this long, so damn it, I'm coming with you."

The chanting behind the door grew louder when the men planned their next move to come together in a flank, fighting their way to the door leading outside.

They performed an inventory of everything on their person as well as in the apartment that could be used as an arsenal; Jason with the crusted cleaver from his apartment as well as Tim with the baseball bat next to the growing chaos of the door and a few steak knives from John's tiny kitchen.

John opened kitchen drawers with loud clangs, finding a large carving knife and placed it in his belt loop.

Suddenly, he headed toward the open room of his son and stepped out with a long silver sheath with a shiny metal handle.

As he walked out, he spoke out loud to the group, "My son was into some crazy shit. He would watch "Lord Of the Rings" and "Game of Thrones", all of that stuff, he loved it. I remember he went to the Renaissance Faire somewhere outside of the city for a school trip, and he came back with this sword."

He began looking at the sheath, "He knew it was a replica but he loved it. He placed it over the door and everything. I broke his stones about it, but I always loved him for being him, for being true to himself."

John pulled the sheath from the blade, "In honor of my son, I will fight through the darkness and the dragons, so to speak. He would love that."

He giggled slightly, when Russell shot up from his spot on the couch, "No! Fuck no...I am not leaving my cousin, man! I will not leave him...that is not happening!"

John walked over to Russell, dropping the sword lightly to the carpet, and placed his hand on his arm, "You cannot stay here. I understand how you feel, believe me. When I had to leave Dean's body I wanted to kill myself. We were surrounded, and I couldn't get to him. I ran because my son would never forgive me if I gave up."

Russell's teeth grit, and he stared at John, a rigidness in his body language and words, "I will not leave my blood in a fucking bathtub...covered in a fucking bed sheet."

The banging and chanting grew, and the door began to snap and break when John peered into Russell's dark eyes, down into his very soul, "Look man, you do what you have to do. There is no time for planning, we need to get the fuck out of here. We have to act...now."

Just as Russell was about to respond, the door snapped inward, and the mysteries outside of the door poured in.

Psychotic women of all ages and races, one after the other, rushed through the door when John picked up his new weapon, yelling, "Okay...look alive! It's go time!"

Every man in the room placed one of their chosen tools in their shaking hands, while Russell walked past, going into the bathroom and shutting the door.

John was the first to make the first attack, slashing the weapon in the air, splitting the neck of a large Hispanic woman, causing blood to spurt onto the carpet below.

The woman, still standing, came toward John again, the knife in her hands now slashing at him wildly when Jason and Tim passed John heading toward the other women in the apartment.

Jason yelled and took his cleaver to the throat of a lightly colored female, causing her to instantly fall, the trachea in her throat now hanging from her neck.

John took another crack at his attacker, causing her head to fly off of her shoulders onto the seat of the couch. Her head hit the cushion , performed a strange bounce and dropped in front of John.

Tim was already close to the door, taking his chipping wooden bat directly to the face of the final woman who entered the apartment causing her milky white eyeball to pop out of her socket like a cork, still hanging from the vein.

John made quick work of the last woman when the sword in his hand connected with the top of her head in an upward motion, splitting the skull in half, and caused blood to run down her face, her milk eye turning green before she collapsed, wriggling on the ground like a fish out of water and then stopping.

One by one, the men flanked together in the hallway, John facing the staircase as Tom and Jason eye the other side of the hall. With no one in sight, the men broke from their position, John fighting with a black woman who looked to be in her fifties.

The woman was strong just like the others, but she was no match for the attack from John's sword, cutting into her throat causing a crimson spray.

After a second swing, Tim hit her hard with the baseball bat across the temple, her head snapping off of the root of her spine, and reflecting off of the wall causing a massive blood stain from the impact.

Covered in gore, John reached the staircase step leading down to the other floors, a woman standing between them.

He took the sharp knife from his belt, slashing the blade in front of her face causing her to stumble backward when John kicked her square in the chest causing her to fall.

The woman still hissing began rolling down the stairwell, when she slowly stood up, and gained her composure.

Jason nudged past John on the stairs and held his cleaver over his head, bringing it down into her head.

The woman grabbed him by his own head throwing him down to the carpeted steps.

As Jason tried to pull himself up quickly, John knocked the woman's head off with a swiftness ending the fight in the stairwell.

Attempting to catch their breath, the crew ran down to the first floor, their target-the smashed door- was now directly in their sight.

Tim and Jason headed to the door first, John right behind them.

As John rushed to the door, he did not notice the female security guard, her eyes wide and clear as she pulled her heavy flashlight over her head, stalking him.

The young woman began to drop her power on an unsuspecting John when the screwdriver in Russell's closed fist slammed down into her brain.

John spun around and witnessed his savior, the man from the apartment standing before him.

John flashed a quick smile as the men proceeded to exit into the street laden with bodies, raging fires, and smashed vehicles. The windows of building and shops were smashed, the doors kicked and busted in.

They instantly noticed the four women waiting for them, one wielding an axe, the others with different weapons in their hands.

The group charged the women, Jason right behind them, when suddenly he stopped.

The event in front of him began to feel like it was in slow motion, and the presence near him caused everything in his body to tingle.

As the rest fought, swinging and cutting, Jason slowly turned his head and saw the vision in front of his wet stinging eyes, Elizabeth.

Her eyes were as blue as he could remember; her lips were lush, and her skin resembled fine china.

The nightgown flowed ever so gently, causing the fabric to resemble many soft wings.

She was truly his angel, and she resembled one in every single way imaginable.

Jason dropped his hands and stared directly at her radiant visage, not saying a word.

Elizabeth, still standing very still, looked in his direction, raising her hands with a softness she spoke, "Come to me, Jason. Come to me, baby."

Jason glided forward, entranced by her every feature, as Elizabeth planted a grin on her sweet lips.

He continued to walk toward the goddess before him, her open arms, her heaving chest, when suddenly Tim tackled Jason pushing his body hard, allowing John to grab him and hide him behind the van the group now used as a shield.

With Tim exposed in the street, the men watched as the woman screamed loud, her harpy-like screech putting a skip in the beating of their hearts.

Elizabeth, looking extremely upset lifted her hand causing the tall, lanky Tim to rise into the air and hover over the street.

With Tim suspended before her, the lovely woman opened her mouth and Jason instantly felt the hairs standing at attention on his neck, "You…filthy…PIG! He is mine!"

There was another wave of her hand, and the suspended man began to scream, as if being taken apart piece by piece.

With slight movements of her wrist, Tom bellowed louder and louder as the skin on his arms and legs began to peel back, muscles and bone exposed.

The flesh on his face began to sizzle, causing the eyeballs to cook in his skull. The screams from the man caused Russell to vomit onto the street.

The men could see the woman waving her hand to and fro which was somehow tearing their teammate apart; his abdomen exposed, his gut spooling out and unraveling.

And just like that, the man who was now nothing but a liquid mess splat hard onto the concrete; his liquid parts hitting everything in their path.

Jason attempted to run to his beautiful wife when John grabbed him, spinning his face to his, "What are you doing, man? We have to go the other way! We cannot get fucking past her!"

Jason clammed up in front of John, as Elizabeth once again moved her hands in a circular motion, and the van in front of the three flew up into the air, exposing them.

"Shit! We have to go…we have to go now!" screamed John as the van lifted higher.

The large vehicle slammed into the building in front of them as they ran.

Elizabeth picked up everything in her path, swirled them around in a tornado and tossed them like projectiles.

The rest of the group began to run hard, vehicles, hydrants, trash cans, and bodies slammed the earth all around them.

The group rushed away as Elizabeth stepped slowly behind them, her screams shattered glass in the buildings around her, the debris cascading around her bare feet.

As the meteor of objects still continued to fly nearly hitting the men on every single step of their feet, the group somehow made it to the next street.

Jason continued to run when John turned to yell to him, "We have three city blocks, and a right to go! This is not going to be easy!" With battery acid in their ligaments, the newly formed team continued to run as Jason attempted to get a grip on his now swirling mind, **"What have you done, Will? You made me do this. You made me bring on this hell, didn't you?"**

Meanwhile, on the next street, the silky soft form of the all-powerful Elizabeth stopped.

She stared forward, scowling as she focused on the debris in front of her, "Go get him, my love. Go to get our son."

A smile broke on her face, and laughter filled the smoke covered air as Elizabeth changed shape, turning into a fiery mist and shot into the air as a massive ball of fire and death.

CHAPTER SEVEN

The Bridge of Fears
September 23rd, 2014

Scott drove towards the highways to the city for a little under an hour, passing chaos and potential death at every single turn.

After Scott Cain left his home and the body of his loving wife behind, he drove his vehicle onto the usually quiet streets, witnessing the bodies mutilated and still on the concrete.

Smashed cars were piled everywhere as if everyone had crashed into each other and then left the scene of their accidents, glass and metal strewn across the streets.

Scott had seen much in his life, but nothing of this magnitude.

As tough of a man as he was, it took everything in him to stop to have a very deep cry.

First, he had to kill his beloved, shoot and decapitate his friendly neighbors, and now the unknown lay ahead of him.

He felt a shiver in his body as he drove on through the hell surrounding him.

On his journey, the small family car was attacked many times and Scott had to fire his weapon out of the windows and swerve through stacks of debris.

Turning left off of his street, Scott was attacked by a young girl who had to be at least five years old and a woman that appeared to be in her twenties.

The woman and the little girl banged hard on the car, the woman almost smashing the back window with her fist while the child chanted with a tiny lisp, her words sounding like "kiw da pig". instead of the well worded hateful phrase Scott heard many times on this day of the damned.

As the car drove past a playground which was two blocks from his home, he witnessed two little girls bashing a little boy's head open with rocks as his body wriggled.

Scott rolled down his window as fast as he could and vomited onto the street below.

Many minutes had passed since the soldier left his small suburban community and reached the larger roads heading toward the highway, the scene was no different.

Destruction and vicious murder were imprinted everywhere he looked, and there were automobiles lining the streets, causing obstructions and inciting Scott to drive slow and past them like a driver's license test.

Passing the cars, he saw the bodies lying in some of the seats, their bodies flopped out of open car doors or appearing to sleep on steering wheels.

Some of the car seats held little bodies; one in particular made Scott's strong stomach spit bile out of his window yet again.

Store doors were smashed, and the bodies of many men, young and old, lined the streets. Around the doors, on the grass now black with their blood, everywhere his eyes looked upon, he saw corpses.

The car finally reached the entrance to the highway and he was attacked again.

Scott pushed his foot to the pedal as hard as he could to break away from the mob of females lining the streets. The same pile up of vehicles and bodies obstructed his ability to drive fast, and as he finally was able to pick up speed, the women ran behind him, seeming indestructible and not losing their wind.

The car was dented with balled fists, scratched with tools of every kind, and the only sound Scott heard was the chanting, the sick vicious chanting as he drove by slowly.

He checked the radio when he was about to reach the bridge taking him to his destination, the city where his brother was either dead or fighting for his very life with every breath.

Of course, Scott hoped for the latter.

Every time he turned the dial, the radio crackled and no one spoke, not a reporter, a drive time deejay, not a single soul.

The bridge was a huge mess as Scott drove onto the shoulder leading to the entrance; the typical car pileup was much larger than anything he had seen on his journey; bodies lying in seats, as well as on the ground, including one in particular that had a tire jack sticking out of his back.

The pileup was not easy to get through, and it took precise driving to swerve past the mess including a few close calls where Scott had hoped he would not have to desert the car, having to head to the city on foot.

The drive was slow, and the terror in his eyes was very visible as he continued on. And as he finally reached the middle of the bridge he could see the landscape of the city from his front window.

It was evident that the nightmare was far from over.

There were no chanting psychotic women on the bridge, and the thought floating around in his mind was that they all headed to the city, their snarling group, hands on weapons of many kinds marching forward to continue their slaughter.

The lined roads on the high bridge cleared, and he finally put his foot on the accelerator, blowing past the destruction on every side of him.

Scott thought of the whereabouts of Jason, was he dead or was he alive fighting for his life with every single breath, and he thought of the perils that faced him as he drove into the heavily populated death trap.

The older brother's running thoughts stopped suddenly when he noticed an object hurtling toward him, something that appeared to be a large comet created by what appeared to be flames.

He hit the brakes hard, and attempted to swerve out of the way, but the flying fireball smashed through his front window, causing it to explode all over the dashboard, Scott covering his face as he was assaulted with the shards.

He could not feel heat off of the ball of death, but could feel its massive speed as it crashed into the back window, the glass cascading all over the back seat and the trunk of the car.

Scott wiped glass off of his clothes and he was shouting obscenity which was extremely rare for the career soldier since his discharge.

He did not turn his head, but instead peered into the rear view mirror without rolling down his now cracked window that revealed a woman in what appeared to be a nightgown standing behind the smashed vehicle.

Scott instantly pulled the car into reverse, and the learned instinct of survival kicked in hard.

The tires screeched as the car headed backwards, the soldier gunning the gas, his eyes not leaving the rearview.

Momentarily, the brakes slammed and the car stopped hard.

The car door slowly opened, and Scott grabbed the now replenished 9mm from his holster.

Lowering the gun to his side, without his finger leaving the trigger, he stepped slowly toward the woman, his former sister-in-law, Elizabeth Rinehart.

Elizabeth was as beautiful as ever to him, her skin was like a china doll, her hair flowed and appeared black as midnight.

As he approached, he attempted to speak to her as if he was small talking with her during a meal, "Hey Elizabeth, it's been a long time."

Elizabeth had a scowl across her face, her blue ocean eyes never leaving him.

Scott continued, never allowing his finger to leave his weapon, "So, what are you doing here? How did you get here?"

The scowl turned into a grin, and Scott could hear a slight chuckle exit her throat, her mouth still closed.

He stepped backward, his sidearm still by his hip, "Why don't we just get in my car, and we can talk all about this. Perhaps…we can both see how Jason is doing. Come on, let's get out of here."

As Scott stepped forward with his right foot in front of the other, Elizabeth's blue pools suddenly changed.

Her eyes seemed to turn to embers and her hand lifted from her side, causing Scott to feel as if he was being lifted off of the road into the air.

As his feet left the ground, the soldier pulled the gun from his side and squeezed two shots toward his brother's former wife's face, but the bullets seemed to burn away before they made contact.

Scott's eyes grew wide as Elizabeth grinned once again as he began to yell, "What have you done? Is all of this your doing?"

Elizabeth's teeth seemed to grit, as her fist closed tight, the sudden pain causing the 9mm to drop from her once brother-in-law's hand onto the ground below.

The pain became excruciating, and his insides felt as if they were being folded, the bones making small snapping and popping sounds.

Scott's lungs tightened and his entire upper body ached as every breath of air seemed to leave.

Elizabeth's anger turned into sudden bursts of laughter watching the man writhe a few feet above her.

The tall soldier choked and gasped, when suddenly her slender hand was waved in front of her, throwing Scott by the large concrete wall of the bridge.

He attempted to catch his air again, coughing flecks of blood in front of his crumpled form.

As air settled slowly back into his lungs, he began to scream, "Who...who are you? Why did you take my wife from me?"

Once again, his usual demeanor of courtesy and respect left as he uttered his next sentence, "Answer me!"

Elizabeth began to laugh once again, only this time the inflection of her words were truly not her own.

Something seemed to flow through her, "Tell me, Soldier, how would you enjoy joining your sweet, sweet Cara?"

With one weak, trembling arm, Scott attempted to pick himself up, with nothing but bravery in his words, his eyes looking coldly in her direction, "Do...what you are going to do to me."

On weak legs, the large muscular man, still heaving, lunged for his gun when Elizabeth screamed and was waving her slender hand in his direction.

Scott's body lifted again, only this time he was tossed to his side onto the concrete like a rag doll.

Elizabeth's gaze as he looked up at her resembled nothing but death and destruction as her fist balled again, caving in Scott's large throat, the air escaping quickly.

With all of the strength he had left, he pleaded, in a manly tone, "Do...it!"

The woman stepped closer to his slowly fading eyes, her voice boomed, a voice of history, a voice of a different time, "Oh, strong man, you cower in front of a woman."

The unseen grip was finally released, and Scott fought for the air in his lungs, coughing up gobs of blood and spit, the pain inside of his body intense.

The voice inside of his beautiful former sister-in-law, the woman he had loved like his own family for many years continued, "I am going to kill you, all of the remaining Cain brethren, in due time. I know that your father is already gone."

Scott's lip trembled as she continued, her words emanating joy, "I watched him die in my mind...horribly! I see you all! I see you all die...and it brings me much jubilation!"

Still on the ground, Scott, still gasping attempted to speak, "Why...did you do this? Why would you do such horrible things?"

Elizabeth chuckled lightly, lifting the large former combat soldier as if he was a sheet of paper on the wind with the wave of her hand, bringing him directly in front of her.

His eyes felt as if they were going to explode when her face began to distort, her eyes began to change and her teeth became jagged, her hiss placed a quiver in his body from head to foot. "Power!"

Her face became normal again as Scott was dropped hard to the road, hearing a voice piercing his brain, "You better not miss the family reunion. Your brother has gone to save his boy. Better hurry! Come to reunite, and then die!"

Scott screamed, the pain in his chest excruciating, but he knew where he had to go, and he knew that his brother was alive.

Scott Cain had to get to the city, and he had to get there quick.

The Cain and Rinehart family reunion would soon be underway.

CHAPTER EIGHT

The Hot Seat
September 23, 2014

Jason and his group continued to rush through the streets after their encounter with Elizabeth.

Everyone was hurt and extremely tired, especially John who was now limping badly from the shrapnel imbedded in his leg from all of the falling debris.

Jason was breathing heavily, but kept up with the two other men.

Russell was sweating heavily but did not miss a step, convincing Jason that in some point in this man's life he had to have been a great athlete, perhaps seeing much glory in his high school years running for touchdowns or perhaps slam dunking a ball causing glass to shatter onto the court.

At any rate, Russell was an extremely strong man as well as a valuable ally to have in this hellish new world.

John was weakened, but it appeared that he would fight until his dying breath, holding the blade to his side, resembling a modern day knight holding in his shouts of pain as he continued on the perilous road.

As John reached the middle of the street, the group encountered chanting women on both sides of the street, sprawled out over a gurgling man, his chest spread wide open as he was repeatedly struck and stabbed with what appeared to be rusty shears.

The woman over top of him was large, and it was extremely apparent that when the world was normal she did not count carbohydrates or exercise for many years.

In this instance, the woman was feral and powerful as she leaped from the dying man, rushing toward John with all of her bulk and fury.

John stood strong, and Jason right beside him pulled out the two knives he had stuffed in his belt.

Across the street was a bashed green vehicle which had appeared to hit another car after something had veered in front of it, the driver at the wheel obviously unable to escape the accident.

As Jason and John fought the woman, Jason witnessed Russell rush across the road toward the car, the screams of a scared individual echoing through the air after a young black woman smashed the driver side window, two of her minions on the other side shoving and beating the metal of the car.

Jason composed himself, getting his head back into the matter at hand when John raised his son's sword, chopping into the neck of the heavy set woman, causing a fluid spray from her artery.

As she stumbled, Jason stepped around her, attacking a thinner woman with the two knives now clutched in his sweaty palms.

The woman seemed to hiss as Jason bounded toward her, her hands stretched out attempting to slash at him with pink fingernails.

Across the street, the tough Russell pulled out a screwdriver which was hanging out of his pocket, held the handle tight and drilled the instrument directly into the back of the woman's skull.

The squish could be heard as she spun around to face him, Russell yelled for the first time as her milky white eyes peered at him, her chanting resembling the sounds of a reptile, "Piiiiiig! Piiiig!"

He placed his hand behind her head, and twisted the handle of the tool, causing the woman to spill in front of him, the younger man in the beat automobile screaming like a wounded child.

Russell stood firm as the one of the other women who was absolutely beautiful, her cocoa skin glistening as she slid over the car, the other woman circling around the hunk of metal causing Russell to spin around to face her, taking his eye off of the black goddess now behind him.

On the other side of the road, John had knocked the head clean off of the obese lady, her head in the middle of the black tar of the street.

Jason was still fending off the thinner woman, her swiftness and agility becoming a bit of an issue for the man who had never had to fight for his existence before.

The woman slashed at Jason's face until he finally received the upper hand as he kicked her in the chest. Her head dropped down.

As she picked her head up, growling and screaming like a banshee, Jason stuck the sharp blades into both sides of her neck, his attack in an upward fashion allowing the blades to touch and causing the blood to stay in the woman's body until he yanked the knives from her.

Russell had one of the women down, her head spilling blood on the side of the car as he turned to fend off the female who had the looks of a supermodel.

The young man inside of the car continued to moan and yell as he saw Russell toss the young woman over his back, turning to pull one of the knives from John's apartment and drilling the top of her skull.

The guy in the car started to heave as the huge man poked his head in the broken window to attempt to speak to him, "It's safe now. We have to go."

The man seemed to be in his early twenties. He was a pale white kid, but the loss of color in his face made him resemble a ghost, and he began to hyperventilate as Russell's reassurance turned quickly to anger.

He placed his upper body into the broken glass of the car sliding the kicking man out of the available opening.

As he pulled, he also yelled, "Get the fuck out here! It's safe! I have you!"

John and Jason looked on at the spectacle, the man was now out on the street, and his body was in a heap as Russell seemed to speak to him, now bending over him.

The man nodded his head back and forth, tears streaming from his eyes as the man leaning over him appeared to be assuring him that everything was okay.

In a few moments, the man got to his feet, and Russell guided him to the rest of the group.

The stranger was covered in flecks of blood and his sweatshirt was extremely dirty and crumpled, some of the fabric unwinding and coming apart.

Jason placed one of his knives back to his side, and placed his hand out to the shaken man in front of him. He spoke, "Hey, I'm Jason…this is John, and you've met your hero, Russell. What's your name, kid?"

The man did not look at him, but held out his hand, which was shaking intensely, "I'm Michael…Michael Wilson."

Michael began to tear, and his trembling hand left Jason's when suddenly Russell pushed Jason hard to the wall behind him, his teeth were grit and his fist was clenched as John jumped in front of the oncoming brawl, "Russ? What the fuck are you doing, brother! I told you…this shit was not going to go down, didn't I!"

Russell shoved John hard, causing him to stumble, and began yelling, "Fuck you, John! You saw it yourself! That woman, he knew who she was!"

He began pointing his big finger directly at Jason, "This motherfucker knows something! He probably made all of this shit happen!"

Russell grabbed at Jason again, screaming, "Who is she man? Who was the woman! Why did you lose your shit when you saw her?"

His fist was held high in the air again, "Tell us, before I knock you the fuck out!"

Jason pushed his attacker backward, and looked into the fatigued faces of everyone circling around him.

He began to spill everything he knew about the situation, "It was…my wife. It was my ex-wife, Elizabeth."

John looked on surprised, his words were calm but his voice quaked, "Did…you have something to do with this? Please tell me this shit has nothing to do with you?"

Jason began to look down at the ground when Russell piped in, "Don't look at the ground, you son of a bitch. Tell us what you know."

Jason looked at his new friend, his knee now on the ground, the novelty sword to his side.

His voice quivered, "I don't know if I have anything to do with this. I mean, I don't think I do."

Russell shoved Jason again, "Hey, stop back pedaling. Tell us what you know!'

Jason noticed John get to his feet slowly as he continues to speak, swallowing hard. "I was just trying to bring her back. I was in a coffee shop. This guy in black, he came up to me, his name is Will."

He sat down and asked me about our lives, our troubles, everything. He asked me about my book...and why I wrote negatively about witchcraft when he was a practicing witch himself."

At that moment, the young man began pointing and it appeared that a thought had entered his brain causing him to shout out, "I knew it! I knew I recognized this guy. This guy's the writer, Jason Cain! Yeah, that's his name. He wrote that book about witches. It was about...witches being fucked up or something!"

Russell turned to face Jason who was now losing color in his cheeks, "Is this what this is about? You pissed off some fucking witches with your nonsense?"

Jason slid down the wall, his breath heavy as he watched everyone lunge over him. He was now on the hot seat, and he feared for his life not from the women but from the now angry men that agreed to aid him in helping him get to his son.

John leaned over wincing, and pulled his sword from the concrete, his face fixed into anger, "You better tell us what book, my friend. Who the fuck are you?"

Jason placed his hands over his face, took a deep breath and began spilling his guts, "I am a writer of a book...called Cauldron Of Lies. I wrote it with my ex-wife, and I said some very bad things about a group I had no business saying anything about. They did nothing to hurt me, and I wrote that garbage to be a success, to attempt to make a buck. I met this man, and this guy told me I could bring my wife back to me through a spell in a book passed down through his family."

The men's brows furrowed as Jason continued his story. "He told me that these words would bring her back without consequence, and I agreed."

Jason held back instant tears. "Will Thompson came to my place, and he handed me the book, after a pretty intense ritual. It felt wrong from the beginning, but I continued. The words, they looked funny to me. They looked sinister. Will assured me that nothing would happen, that I should continue reading, so I did. I woke up and I was attacked by my landlord and a woman who lives a few doors down from me...but she never came."

His voice began to shake and become louder, "But I have no fucking idea what any of this has to do with me wanting to bring my wife back! As I said, I have no idea what the fuck is going on here! I know as much as all of you."

Michael ran toward Jason attempting to kick him with his sneakers, causing John to grab him from behind. The young man yelled, "It's your fault! You made me kill Jill! You made me kill my classmates! You fuck! It was you!"

John, with all of his strength, tossed Michael to the ground, gained composure and brought order back to the group. "Everybody needs to calm the fuck down! Russell, back off...I've got this."

He bent over Jason, now holding his head in his hands, his voice calm but stern. "Jason, I confided in you...I trusted in you, and I followed you to help you gain something I lost."

John placed his hand under Jason's chin, pulling him up to view his now wet face, the wetness glistening in the manly cracks of his skin. "Did you have anything to do with the death of my son?"

Jason remained still and silent, when Russell opened his mouth, "You know the motherfucker does, John. Why are we allowing him to breathe another moment?"

With that, Jason growled and bounded to his feet, swung his fist wildly and connected with Russell's cheek.

The large man fell to his knees, and Jason began kicking him in his exposed rib. "It wasn't me! I was attacked too! In my own home, I was attacked! I am not a witch, you prick!"

Jason began heaving and spitting as John pulled him away from Russell's hunched over form, and Jason turned to face him, his face red but his words relaxed, "I think it was the man I spoke of…the man who incited me to do this. The words made no sense to me, but they do now. It was him, it was Will Thompson."

John stepped in front of Russell, grabbed his large hand and pulled him up, speaking as he looked at his anger, "Russ, I believe him. I do."

Russell nodded his head in disagreement, as John began speaking to the man he truly wanted to beat senseless, "Let's continue to get your son. Take us to him."

His voice began to shake, and his eyes dilated, "Let's hope and pray that this piece of shit turns up. If he does, he's a dead man."

Jason nodded and Russell walked past him, glaring and holding his rib.

John pulled Michael from the ground, causing him to pull away and curse him, "Get the fuck off of me, asshole!"

The group now beat and extremely tired, with the student in tow, headed toward the next street, noticing the many dangers that lay ahead.

As Jason stepped forward, holding in tears and rage, he thought about how close he had come to his own death, and his fury for Will Thompson grew at every step the now larger crew took.

In their heads they all hoped that the woman with the power to destroy everything in her path was far behind them.

CHAPTER NINE

A Little Happiness in Hell
September 23, 2014

After his encounter with Elizabeth on the bridge, the soldier known as Scott Cain ached throughout his body, his throat had become extremely sore, two of his ribs were in searing pain and every muscle ached.

The man who had encountered many harsh conditions for many months, had been shot at over hundreds of times, and had been wounded by the bullet that brought him into the medical camp where he had met his true love felt like half of the man everyone portrayed him as.

Scott Cain did not feel like a warrior; he did not feel the strength he usually had in life, simply defeated.

The sheer power of Elizabeth's force had destroyed his body in many ways, and his mind was worse for wear.

Scott had done everything he could to not break down. He tried breathing techniques, but they made him feel as he would double over, and he hard to take his mind off of the death of Cara, the things he was told about his father by Elizabeth, her smile huge as she relished her every word, and of course, the whereabouts of his only brother.

As he drove, sitting in tiny pieces of glass on his driver's seat, the fatigued and wounded man did think of one woman: his ex-sister in law, Elizabeth Rinehart.

His mind burned with the thought of her, her beautiful form grinning as he was crushed by unseen magick, her laughter as she kneeled over his broken body.

Scott pondered how long she had had these powers. Was she something from another world, or possibly a demon from Hell?

He wondered if she had been the evil he encountered when she was with Jason.

Also, was it her plan all along to undo the world itself, causing the women to become her mindless slaves?

Of course, Scott had no answers.

As the dented and smashed vehicle left the destruction of the bridge to reach the road heading into the large city, Scott took a very deep breath, hit the gas pedal down to the floor.

There were many obstacles in his way just as there were on every street and major highway he had travelled, but he had managed to find large enough gaps to swerve past them.

The streets around him were littered with upturned cars, glass was sprinkled everywhere threatening a flat tire every second, the dead were mangled and beaten; every face was turned into a story of terror and bloodcurdling fear as they were stomped, kicked, maimed, or brutally taken apart by women, their seemingly blind eyes shimmering above them as they spat out one word sentences of hatred.

The car continued its speed, and on many occasions Scott ran into groups of women who attempted to leap onto the car or cause it to flip over.

He had placed his weapon along with several boxes of bullets on the passenger side seat.

Scott pointed the 9mm out of the broken glass like an action hero, squeezing the trigger, bullets ripping into many parts of the hordes, but only knocking them backward slightly.

The women continued to stand, chanting and snarling as the tires of the car sped past them.

When Scott reached the street of Jason's apartment, the tires screeched to a halt, and he stepped out into the open air for the first time in the dangerous city.

Keeping the door open, Scott surveyed the area and only one sentence entered his brain, **"What the fuck happened here?"**

The street looked as if it had been hit by an atomic bomb, and even through all of the chaos he had already faced, there was never as much destruction in his way as what was now before him.

Everywhere the former soldier's eyes wandered he saw an object blocking the path of his vehicle: cars upturned and smashed, metal mailboxes bent and broken beyond repair, pieces of human remains spattered on the black asphalt as if they had been dropped from extreme heights, and the corpses of women littering the street as if a major battle for survival had happened.

As Scott stepped slowly past the splattered remains, he looked forward so he would not focus on the gruesome scenes around him.

He walked past the mangled metal, and realized that the force of whatever had occurred had put holes in the street where the cars had been thrown.

Scott had seen much in his life, but he had never seen anything of this magnitude.

Finally reaching the front of the apartment, Scott had stopped dead in his tracks, his eyes widened as he peered upon the husk of what used to be a man. The skin appeared to be stripped from the bone and the form was folded over like a guest room mattress placed in a closet for storage.

He heaved, and the violence in front of him caused Scott to vomit lightly on the street, the pain in his body surging as he wiped his mouth with his sleeve.

All around the steps of the apartment which were caked in blood were the bodies of women, and the scenario of whatever had occurred danced in the older brother's brain.

But the biggest question Scott asked himself was quite simple: **had his brother escaped?**

He swallowed hard as he stepped lightly onto the concrete stairs toward the busted front door.

The inside hallway was darkly lit, and one bulb flickered on and off as Scott continued on.

The body of a young woman in a security outfit stained the carpet of the first floor. Scott spoke to himself as he continued to investigate, **"I wonder who got out, and how many occupants did this?"**

The next obstacle was the staircase leading to the three floors of the building, and as his stained boots hit the carpeted steps he saw even more of the picture unfold.

On the stairs leading to the second floor was a scene just as gruesome, the bodies of females folded over the stairs as if they were struck hard and then toppled from the gap of the metal rung on the top floor, causing their bodies to plummet, hitting steps on the way down.

Scott continued to the third floor where the situation was just as horrific.

Next to the steps was an open door. The wood had been battered and the metal hinges were bent inward.

He peered inside to see that there were bodies staining the carpeting with pools of red.

The darkness in the long hallway could not hide the images in front of Scott, as he held the gun tightly in his hands, finger directly on the trigger.

The walls were painted in blood, and there were many corpses and parts around his feet.

His eyes began to well as he looked down on the crimson stained floor, fingers and pieces of brain stuck into the rug fabric as blood pooled and dried causing his boots to stick in certain places.

Scott spoke to himself yet again, "Please...please don't be Jason, Please, don't be Jason."

He continued to examine the fallen, and recognized no one.

Breathing a sigh of relief, Scott knew that his brother was not among the cadavers before him.

Finally, he reached Jason's apartment door which had been left halfway open.

Scott slowly pushed the door inward and dropped his hands to his sides when he saw the massacre that had taken place.

His words to himself grew louder, filling the room, "What the fuck happened here?"

On the carpet were the bodies of two women, and one of them Scott had recognized as the surprisingly gentle and kind landlord of the building. She no longer resembled herself, only meat caked into the apartment floor.

Beside her was a young woman, her face completely caved in as if the skull was smashed like an egg thrown against a wall.

Scott placed his hands over his mouth, and once again felt a wave of nausea as he continued toward the back room. His brother was missing.

He checked the bathroom only to find that the bathroom mirror had been broken and never replaced.

Scott turned around to once again enter the living room, the table had been obliterated, shards and pieces were all over the floor. The television had been destroyed, its remnants could be seen everywhere.

He walked out of the door and back into the hallway which resembled a painting from "Dante's Inferno" depicting one of the many levels of Hell.

Scott's footsteps were quicker than before, and in an instant he reached the other open door on the other side of the hall.

Having no inkling of who the apartment belonged to, or if they were still present, he stepped inside slowly.

The bodies of the women were beginning to collect a faint odor of death as his boots stepped over them, his eyes darting to the left and right rapidly.

It was evident to the career soldier that the events he had seen before had stemmed from this very place as he examined the two small bedrooms finding no one.

The closed door beckoned to him, and Scott slowly opened the door, gun drawn.

It was the bathroom of the apartment, and as tiny as the space was, it was evident that it was taken care of.

Toiletries neatly lined the back of the sink, and the mirror was spotless. A fuzzy blue toilet cover encased the toilet seat, and two towels of the same color hung neatly from the towel rack, almost uniform.

The shower curtain was closed, but a small trail of blood led Scott to believe something might be behind it.

Placing his tense finger on the trigger, Scott pushed the curtain open to find what appeared to be a body wrapped in heavy garbage bags. His eyes widened and Scott quickly dropped to his knees.

The tears in his eyes began to flow once more and his words became rapid and nonsensical, "Oh no...fuck...shit...no no."

He had no idea who the body belonged to, but his racing thoughts prompted him to think it might just be his younger brother.

The pain grew and his ribs ached as Scott began hyperventilating, the tears still continuing to fall.

Feeling as if his heart had become too heavy to hold in his body, he ripped open the bag which had covered the victim and opened his eyes before the reveal to look upon the face of a young black male.

The look on the dead boy's face was peaceful and still, his eyes were closed, never again having to see the damnation enveloping the planet.

Scott fell to the tile by the shower, and began to cry hysterically, the gruff manly cry of a wounded warrior.

Stopping the tears, he propped himself up on top of the toilet seat and began his slow breathing, the pain surging through his broken ribs.

He winced and stood up, heading out of the bathroom door into the living room.

Scott investigated the area around him, witnessing nothing but the stains which had once been women, women who once had lives, jobs, and possibly husbands and children.

The thought of Cara seeped into his mind, and he did everything he could to not break down.

And then, he found the cure for his emotional strife.

As Scott looked upon the couch, he saw a piece of newspaper, crumpled but open to read.

When Scott stepped closer he saw the strange writing, writing that could be seen up close, writing that was written in some kind of browning, dried blood.

The smile growing on his face was immense as his eyes darted across the script before him:

Scott,
Went to get son
Jason

Jason was not a psychic or a mystic of any kind, but the thought of his older brother being a brave man who would in most cases come for his sibling gave him the idea to give the sign of his life a chance.

He never knew that Scott would come to the city to protect him, or if his former combat heavy brother was even alive, but something in his heart told him that his brother would come for him.

The letter that he had left to chance had actually been found.

Scott dropped the paper to the carpet and bolted out of the broken door.

He stomped quickly down the stairs until he reached the first floor.

As he stepped toward the busted door leading back into the devil's playground, he raised his 9mm and slowly poked out his head to survey the street.

Heading towards the apartment was a small group of women, one behind the other, snapping and snarling.

Scott took a deep breath and rushed right out in front of them, gun drawn to fire.

Like a professional quarterback, Scott weaved his way through the horde, squeezing off shots as he zigged and zagged.

One of the women had fallen to the street hard, but the others continued to attempt to grab him and kill him.

He rushed past the now chanting crew, and continued to run hard toward his open car door.

Finally reaching it, he slammed the door hard, placed the key in the ignition and gunned the engine.

The car spun into reverse, and the smile that Scott had acquired had never left.

The tires spun out and the smashed vehicle hit the next street, the street that Jason and the group had taken after their encounter of raining blood and steel.

Scott did not know that he was on the trail of his younger brother, but he was aware that he was still alive at the time the letter was written.

He did not know what lay ahead; the perils he would now face.

All Scott Cain knew was that for a brief moment, the wounded and mentally beaten soldier forced to come out could have a little piece of happiness in the hell surrounding him.

CHAPTER TEN

Out of The Frying Pan, Now A Pariah
1:06 P.M.

The group had reached the middle of the next two blocks after a little under an hour, the street to the left after they had grilled Jason was surprisingly quiet.

Bodies littered the streets, but there was only one woman strolling around. John took quick care of her, lopping her head clean off as she turned to face the group.

Her lips were curled in a snarl, but looked very sad as she stepped toward the men dragging her sneakers along the sidewalk.

John almost felt bad inside taking this lone female's life, and when her body flopped in front of him he walked backward two paces, sank to his knees, and wept silently.

The events of the day had been setting in, but the sympathy John had was counteracted by the rage he felt in his heart after the death of his only son.

Jason had stepped toward John, kneeling down to place a hand on his back, he spoke quietly, "I know that this is a lot to take in...its killing me too. These women, they're wives, sisters, and children. We have been killing them all, and for what?"

John wiped his falling tears, and slowly began to stand.

He turned to face Jason, his jaw clenched before his mouth opened, "I have no clue why any of this is going on...but I will tell you this. We find this son of a bitch you told us about, he's going to rue the day he dropped into this world, make no mistake about that."

Jason nodded in agreement, and the two headed forward, prompting Michael and Russell to follow on behind them.

Russell continued to glare at Jason's back as he walked, which became evident to Michael who asked him, "So, what is it with the two of you?"

Russell, continuing to walk, turned to look at him. "What do you mean? I just don't trust him, that's all. Now, if you could please keep all questions to yourself."

Michael shut his mouth, strolling a little past Russell, who was now at his own pace behind the other three.

As they reached the next large block, they made a left and the situation was no different. Carnage from the day's events were seen everywhere: bashed cars, broken windows and doors, and the corpses of men which seemed to line every street like flowers growing from fresh earth.

The group stopped to survey the situation, and Michael began to speak, his demeanor less timid, "You know, I don't know if you guys have noticed...but it seems as if the women are thinning out."

John clenched his jaw, and began to nod his head, "You know what? I did notice that. It's as if they are going somewhere, or being lead somewhere, like puppets...no control over themselves."

He finally turned to face the young man, placing a hand on his shoulder. "That was a great observation, though. You're obviously a pretty smart guy." John smiled, "You're going to be useful, I can see that."

Michael grinned when John began to walk again, Jason by his side, and Russell stepping behind as usual, pouting inside like a child jealous of a younger sibling.

As they continued in their formation, John not facing Michael asked him a question, "So, Mike, what brought you out to where we found you?"

Russell broke in, "Don't you mean where I found him, and saved his hide because he was too damn scared to get out and defend himself?"

John stopped, turning to face Russell, he grinned slightly, "I am so sorry. Okay? I would like to know how you got to where...Russell found you."

John winked at Russell and turned his foot to continue his limping walk, and Michael who was directly behind him, began to tell his story. "I just remember, her. There was this girl, and we went to school together, her name was Jill. I went to this club with two friends of mine, and we saw her. She was at the bar, and she was so beautiful."

Michael began to smile a little, "I went up to her, it was the first time I had ever really spoken to her. It was incredible, and I remember we had so much in common...just all of the tedious bullshit that makes people connected: movies, sports, and of course music. We drank a lot...and everything was pretty fuzzy from that point on."

The young student began scratching his head, "Imagine it. You finally have a moment with a woman you have admired for a very long time, adored and loved from afar without her knowing. And then one fateful night...you get to be with that woman intimately. And you drank so much, you don't remember shit."

He began to walk with his head down toward the sidewalk, "I'm an idiot, what can I say? So how did I smash my car and find you wonderful gentlemen? Well, I woke up, and I looked over, and there was Jill. Thing is she wasn't Jill. She was looking at me with these eyes that were foggy. They were misty somehow, and she attacked me, plain and simple."

Michael felt tears as he continued to spin his story, "I had to...kill her. I killed her, all beautiful and naked. I smashed her face in."

John stopped and faced Michael who was now weeping slightly, and placed his hand on the side of his arm, the sad young man began to speak again, "So, I sat there...and I looked at her for a bit. And I heard the commotion outside of my room. I had no clue what the fuck was going on, so I put on some clothes and I grabbed an ice pick which I had lying around. I'm a student, you need lots of ice, you know?"

John chuckled and began to walk again as Michael continued, "I stepped out into the hall which was part of the co-ed dorm I stayed in. It was usually awesome, but at this point, it was a death trap. There were these three girls, and they were acting just like Jill had been, snarling like dogs and calling out their favorite barnyard animal. I had no clue why they were chanting, why they were saying pig. These girls who were usually so cool, these girls who were always so much fun, they came after me. I defended myself...but I hesitated and they got me on the ground a few times. I scrambled to get back on my feet. They were piling on me and I had to do something."

Jason without stopping asked him, "What did you do?"

Michael quickly answered his question, "I dropped them. I fucking killed my friends. I remember I attempted to stab the one girl, but she did not scream. She didn't cry, and just kept coming. So I did something that I saw from the movies. I attempted to destroy the brain…and it worked."

He began to chuckle, but tears still fell onto his nose, "I couldn't believe it. Something we witnessed from a movie worked like a charm. I mean these girls weren't eating flesh, but they certainly had zombie traits. And their eyes were white, like "The Evil Dead" or something."

He wiped the tears from his face, "Anyway, I rushed for the stairs when I saw this guy, and his door was open. He was bleeding out, and asked me…he begged me…to kill him."

John still walking broke in, "Jesus Christ, that's horrible."

Michael thanked him for his sympathetic ear and continued, "I got outside, there were women everywhere. They were chanting like crazy, and they were violent, ripping people apart. First thing I noticed was that there were no men who acted like this, it was very fucking strange. I headed toward my car. I was sneaky and I reached it fast without having to kill anyone. I reached the driver's side door and I jumped in, it was smooth sailing until I reached the street you found me on. There were just too many of them, twenty or so. I panicked, and I did not slow down. And that was it, car crashed, me freaking out, and you now you three. Hopefully that tale was interesting enough for you."

John chuckled but felt a bit of empathy as he spoke, "I am really sorry that you had to go through that, man. I don't know what I would do if I knew my son was going through some shit like that, alone. I'll tell you what though? We have all gotten together to help this guy here, to get his son, and then the plan is to hightail it the hell out of here, so you are welcome to stay with us."

Michael thanked John, and the walk grew quiet.

As John limped forward, he had noticed that the herds were thinning, and he began to ask himself where they could have gone and why.

After a few minutes of silence, Michael spoke up, "So, can I ask you guys a question? I just wanted to know why you never hotwired a car, or at least tried to. I mean, wouldn't this trip had been easier?"

John began to explain how they had no time, when Russell began to giggle, his manly voice cutting all conversation.

He boomed, "So what are you trying to say there, young man? Are you trying to say that because there is a black man amongst us, I would know how to steal a ride?"

The group halted, and Michael began stretching his face in confusion, "What man? Uh no."

Russell stepped toward him, causing him to shake a little, "No, I think that is exactly what you were trying to say."

Jason walked forward, "Are you fucking kidding me? C'mon, we are not the enemy here, we are in this together."

Russell, still staring at Michael, pointed his finger in Jason's direction, "Shut up! You will if you know what's good for you."

John sighed deep, and walked behind Russell speaking quietly, "Russ, you need to stop this. I told you this shit wasn't going to happen.

The large black man spun around, a look of pure anger. "Oh yeah, you know what, John? I'm getting real tired of your shit, too. You think that because you have some kind of leadership you can boss me around. Well, that is not the fucking case."

John clenched his jaw, stepping forward to touch chests with the large man, "Fuck you, man. I'm no leader, I just have sense to not act like an asshole when I know that I need people in my life to survive whatever the hell this is."

Russell smirked, pushing John a little with his body, "Yeah, what are you going to do?"

John smirked back, clenching the fist not holding his sword when suddenly the screams of a man cut the air.

Jason turned away from the confrontation to focus on the sound, and he called to the others, speaking quietly, "Knock it off, do you hear that?"

Russell and John broke their gaze on each other and John stepped toward Jason, he asked him, "What is it? What do you hear?"

Jason remained quiet, and then suddenly the voice ahead of them began yelling a name, "Sara! Sara!"

Jason ears pricked up, he knew right away that the tone had a familiarity, a voice he had heard not that long ago.

He began to run without the rest of the group, prompting the rest to become immensely curious and quickly follow.

Jason suddenly stopped, and the group could now finally see what they had heard, a man was in the middle of ten women. His face could not be seen but he appeared to be swinging a tire jack, hitting them directly in the face attempting to fend them off.

As one of the army dropped to the ground, Jason noticed the mystery man through the opening, Will Thompson, the modern day pariah.

Will was covered in blood, his usually neat hair was messy, and sweat coated his face as he swung the metal, breathing heavily.

Jason targeted in on him, but Will did not notice him as he fought hard.

Jason pulled his knives from his sides and rushed the women, their backs toward him as Will swung.

Jason stabbed away, slamming his knife into one of the women's heads causing her to fall quickly like the others as if a link had been severed.

John handed Michael a knife from his pocket and joined in, swinging his sword with all of his might, taking off a redheaded females arm, causing her to spin around and face him.

The second slash cut into her skull, causing blood to spray onto his face and neck.

Seeing that there was no room for them to fight, Russell and Michael stood behind as Jason and John continued to cut and swing.

Finally, the last woman fell, and John to stopped to take a breath.

Jason, on the other hand, never let his eyes leave his so-called friend.

Will was breathing hard, and his eyes were closed, when he instantly opened them to see the man before him.

He stopped breathing, and the look on Jason's face made him swallow deeply.

Jason looked at Will, grinning, and then he yelled, "This is him...Will Thompson!"

Jason turned to face everyone, "This is the guy!"

Will tried to speak, and Jason brought up his fist, punching him directly in the lips.

The rest of the group was behind him, and the look of vengeance was painted all over their faces.

Jason stepped to the side and addressed the group, "This is the guy I spoke of! The man who incited me to read from that goddamn book, this is the one!"

Jason stepped behind them, his face showed no concern for Will's inevitable punishment as he only said one sentence, "Do what you will."

John grabbed the man off of the concrete and punched him hard once again, laughing as he kept him on his feet.

He spoke to him, pushing his face in close, "This is only the beginning boy, believe me."

He punched Will in the stomach hard and motioned to Russell who was beating his fists together.

John pulled his grip from the bleeding man's shoulders, causing him to slide down the wall.

Russell took a running start and kicked him hard with his large foot, dropping Will on his stomach.

Michael attempted to get his licks in, but Russell placed out his other arm to stop him.

Will, in excruciating pain, was on his feet staring into Russell's angry brown eyes, his voice made him shake, "We got you now, motherfucker. You want to act like a witch, we are going to treat you like one."

And with that Russell head butted Will's skull, his body dropped hard, face hitting the concrete.

Will was now in the clutches of the man he deceived, and a group of men that believed he was the true maker of the end.

He knew that that was not too far from the truth.

Will Thompson was only performing the tasks he thought his mother had placed upon him, but the old adage did not ring in the ears of the men surrounding him.

They were definitely dying to kill the messenger.

CHAPTER ELEVEN

In The Dark Again

Will's eyes opened to nothing but darkness. His eyes began to focus and he realized that he had been thrust back into the same empty plane, his mother and grandmother's purgatory.

He stepped forward, his boots once again creating squishing noises as he stepped on the strewn out parts, only this time Will Thompson was unaffected.

He was not haunted by the moans and shrieks of male voices echoing in the blackened cavern.

As he continued to walk in a faster pace, the disgusting sounds under his boot heels, Will cried out, "Where are you!"

As he ran forward into the abyss, Will recognized a faint light in front of him, and began walking faster, the light growing as he approached the faint candlelight in the distance.

The light illuminated a young woman that Will knew to be his mother. Susan was still cradling his grandmother like a figure in mythology doomed to an eternity in the same place.

Will stopped in front of his mother, causing Susan to look up, her eyes instantly wet with tears.

Her voice quaked, "Will...I didn't think I would see you again."

The young woman laid her mother's head to the living earth gently, and stood up to look upon her boy, Will clenched his teeth hard.

Susan laid her hand lightly on her son's defined jaw, when suddenly Will gripped her hand in his own and knocked it away.

There was pure anger in his words, "Do not touch me. You have no right to touch me...ever."

Susan's eyes grew wide, and her son gripped her hand again, he seethed as he spoke, "You have done this to me. It was you...who agreed to Sara's demands. You allowed her to become a part of you." She began to cry, and her voice still shook. "I...I had no choice! She had become a part of your grandmother, she was killing her slowly, and then she was going to kill you in front of me."

Will's brow furrowed, "Don't! Do not try to make this all right." His grip on her hand gained more pressure. "You made me do this, and you raised me to kill people, to hurt like it was okay, like it was common."

Susan began pleading, "I had no choice. It was Sara...it was all her. I would never do anything to hurt you, ever. I had no choice."

With those words, Will brought his hand back and slapped his mother's face, he also began to yell, "Stop! It was all bullshit! My entire life was a lie!"

His face was almost red. "I never did the things that little boys were supposed to do like play in the dirt....pretend to be a fireman...I was told it was all wrong."

Susan still held her face, a look of pure disbelief as Will continued. "I lived my entire life under a power that you agreed to. I never kissed a girl, without fear. I never had sex with a woman as a man because of some stupid fucking Earth Mother!"

Susan caressed the sting in her cheek as she tried to calm him. "Please do not blaspheme....the Mother is real! The Mother is strong! Sara is the deceiver, she is the one who brought on this darkness, not the Mother."

Her son's voice began to gain a sense of calm, but his anger remained intact, "You left it up to me. I was your messenger."

He grabbed both of Susan's hands and placed them on his chest. "Now I am in pain! The men...the men know the truth....and they are going to kill me."

Susan took a step back when Will released her shaking hands, her tears flowed, "I am...so sorry. My love and the Mother will protect you. You must keep faith in her power, in the power of our family.

Will dropped his head for a moment, and then looked directly at Susan's damp eyes, "Fuck the Mother...and fuck you."

Susan stumbled, and fell to the putrid ground. She looked up and her shock was evident across her entire face. She lowered her head, and began to sob quietly. "I am so sorry, baby."

Will began to feel a touch of guilt after his last words, stepped over to his mother and placed a hand on her shoulder, speaking with peace in his voice. "Mother, I need to know everything about Sara Rinehart. You must know something, she was a part of you. You have to tell me, there has to be some way to stop her."

His mother eyes were still damp when she attempted to explain, "When Sara was part of me I could free myself from her every now and again. She was too strong so it did not last for long. I attempted many times to learn more. I had hoped that I would see a way to break free."

Susan waved her hand around the room, "This place is where she dwelled. I did witness this wretched place."

She stood slowly, "This was her purgatory once, and now she has set me in her Hell. Your grandmother and I are now suffering...in death."

Will shook his head, "So, you know nothing? We have no way to stop her?"

His arms began to wave around in frustration. "I need to know who our enemy is. If we don't figure out something....then humanity is lost. Her army will roam the planet until everything is gone."

He held his hand over his face, and looked up, suddenly jumping backwards.

Susan turned her head to see what had startled him.

Both Will and Susan looked upon a miracle. A once catatonic Helen stood to her feet, her body still, her eyes open wide.

Susan smiled seeing her mother break from her frozen state.

Helen began to speak slowly, almost robotic, as if she was in a trance, "I have all of the answers you seek. I saw her entire existence in my thoughts....I saw everything."

Helen eyes began to glow, like the headlights on a car, causing Susan to latch onto her son's arm.

Her mother's arms rose slowly into the air, and she closed her eyes.

A mist circled the room, and the pitch black hell disappeared.
Will and Susan saw an image swirling around them, a quaint house and a girl sitting in the grass speaking to an angry faced man.
He appeared to be in his late forties, possibly older.
His face was weathered, and his blue eyes looked directly at the young girl's face as she looked at him intently.
The girl appeared to be at least fifteen, and she was a wearing a dark colored working dress with a white cotton wrap tied around her waist.
Helen's voice could still be heard, still robotic as she explained the story unfolding in real time before Will and Susan's very eyes, "This young woman is our enemy, Sara Rinehart."
Will looked on, and he had a look of shock on his face.
He was about to see the life of the woman who deceived his entire family play before him, and he was hoping that the answer to her end would be revealed.

CHAPTER TWELVE

Child of Light, Lady of Darkness:
The Life and Death of Sara Rinehart

AMERICAN COLONIES
1775 TO 1799

As Will continued to watch the scene unfold, his grandmother continued, her words still resembling that of a tour guide, "Sara Colleen Rinehart came to the Americas when she was six years old. Her extremely Catholic family consisted of her mother, Margaret, and her father, Collin. Her father grew up with five brothers and absolutely no sisters, so ever since Sara was a small child he neglected her due to the fact that she was not a boy. She was always raised to believe in the word of the Lord, and if she ever broke any laws of the Bible, she was swiftly and severely punished. Sara was always a sweet girl, but extremely rebellious. Due to her father's swift hand of justice, the young girl was always digging ditches, peeling potatoes, or Collin would just beat her to the point of fainting. At times, he would force her into a large closet he had originally used for storage, but was soon utilized as a room for his daughter to sit in for punishment. The space was always dark, and she had once sat for days before she was forgiven. Her father had only opened the door to slide plates of food onto the wood floor, forcing his own flesh and blood to eat like a canine."

Will and Susan heard a young girl sobbing in the darkness, and the sound was clear as day.

Suddenly, the scenery changed, and Will was inside a small classroom, sitting behind small polished wooden desks were children: four boys and three girl, including Sara.

All of the girls were in day dresses of many colors and of the time, and the male students wore waist coats and breeches, their shoes were black or brown with buckles.

The teacher, also adorned in a beautiful day dress which had a mint green tone, wrote on a long chalkboard as she spoke on the story of Macbeth.

Susan was sitting behind a desk in the middle of the classroom, a look on her face revealing a pure disinterest in her teacher's speech, and probably everything else in her life.

Sara was a beautiful girl. Her hair was jet black and could be seen underneath a bonnet adorned atop of her head, with a face that should have driven all of the young lads absolutely crazy, but she never received any attention.

The voice of Helen was heard again, "Sara never desired to be around them, to be wooed. She always felt different; something in her desired something more. Sara was always starving for a new knowledge, she never believed in the words of the church or of her parents. The young girl always felt as if her family's forced teachings were tearing something from her being, from her very soul. She never had anything to cling to, a part of her that truly made her happy: a confidant, a friend that she could spend time with, having the chance to forget the pain in her life."

The picture in the mist changed, and Will and Susan were in a bedroom lit by only one candle.

Sara was sitting in up in her bed, her eyes wet as she stared at something intently in her hands.

The tour guide Helen explained what was before their eyes, "This is one of the many occasions young Sara had actually contemplated ending her life, but she was constantly afraid that her already lost soul would end up in the damned hellfire her father and mother always spoke of. She did not want to continue her own existence in this world, but she was also frightened of death and its many mysteries as well. There seemed to be no way out for her, and there was nothing that she had discovered to make her heart feel something, anything"

Sara tossed the object onto her wood floor. It clattered and she placed her head on her knees and sobbed uncontrollably.

Will attempted to step further into the picture, and noticed quickly that the object was a straight face razor.

He felt a lump in his throat and the mist around him swirled, until he stood on the side of a sacristy where the priest was giving a sermon to a packed room.

There were many families from town sitting on pews, women and female children in dresses. The majority of women had their hair tied back, the dresses and ribbons were very colorful.

The men and boys were dressed in lace shirts and vests that were black or brown, and were not as vibrant with bright color as the females.

The families sat on long wooden pews, Will witnessed the Rinehart family in one of the front seats, Margaret listened to the word of the Lord intently, and their daughter seemed to be holding in her sheer disdain.

Sara's father began a prayer and the congregation kneeled.

Everyone repeated the words in unison, all except for Sara.

Will had seen the young girl crane her head and begin to stare at a girl who appeared to be her age.

The girl's hair was a fiery color of red, her gorgeous Sunday dress was blue and white, and her lanky father was praying with the rest of the group.

She looked back at Sara, although she did not notice after her mother had quickly smacked her in the back of the head for staring.

Helen began to speak, "One Sunday, during her family's Sunday ritual of church, Sara feasted her eyes on the one thing that had somehow made her feel any breath in her body, any life at all in her young heart, a young female who had moved into the town only just a few weeks before. The girl was Patience McKinney, and she moved into her grandmother's old home with her father John who was a doctor, as well as with her mother, Patricia, who never attended the church gatherings or town meetings. There were already rumors spreading about the McKinney clan, especially the women. Maggie McKinney who was the grandmother of Patience, as well as the mother to her father was also shrouded in mystery. Everyone felt there was something off about their new neighbors of Scotch Irish descent."

The scene changed, enveloping the entire dark stinking room, and Will and his mother were suddenly on green fresh grass outside of what appeared to be the school Sara attended.

The walls were made of red brick, and the windows were outlined with a painted white wood that matched the dynamic of colors.

The pathway leading from the door to the street was lined with cobblestones, and surrounding the walls of the brick were flowers of many colors and species which were all potted by Sara's teacher, Mrs. Joanne Williams.

Will looked at the white door fly open, the children he had seen in Sara's class were rushing toward the road.

Another minute passed and the door opened wide again, and walking out into the open air, her hair in a bonnet, her dress made of a white lace was the girl from the church scene, Patience McKinney.

Patience was holding a brown satchel containing her math and history books, and she was not paying attention when she started walking down the path.

Halfway down the path, her white shoe caught one of the protruding stones and she tumbled forward.

At what appeared to be the same moment, Sara had stepped out of the door and instantly dropped her satchel to the ground. Her face was frozen in shock as she saw the girl she had eyed in church hovering right above the path as if being held up by an unseen force.

Sara attempted to hold in her gasp, but it had escaped, causing Patience to fall to the ground hard, hitting her chin slightly and hurting her knee.

The girl brushed the slight bit of dirt from her dress and looked up at the frightened girl before her.

Patience suddenly looked concerned, and as she stepped toward Sara, the black haired girl stepped back, shock still evident in her eyes.

As Patience approached her, Sara's body began to shake violently and the strange girl put out her hand, speaking very calmly, "Listen to me. I do not know everything you just saw before you, but please, do not be afraid."

Sara pulled back when the girl slightly touched her arm. Her voice was still calm and assuring, "I am not going to hurt you....I am not anything that you are probably conjuring in your thoughts."

Sara peered directly into the girl's almost emerald eyes, and the sparkle in her corneas instantly calmed her like a tranquilizer. Her body stopped shaking, and Patience slowly placed out her hand again, her touch was soft.

She continued to plead her case, "I am not a devil. I saw you in the town church as I was sitting there with my father. I saw you, and you peered back at me."

Sara shook her head and the fiery haired girl introduced herself, "My name is Patience, Patience McKinney. My family and I just ventured here, to live in my grandmother's old house."

Sara recognized a small brogue in the girl's words.

Her skin was smooth, and her cheeks and nose had a light freckling.

The girl's hair was in fact red, almost the color of a fresh strawberry.

Her hair was rolled into a bun, except for two curls that hung down in the front of her ears.

Sara finally spoke, "My name is Sara, Sara Colleen Rinehart."

Patience shook her hand which had been already placed in hers slightly and let go. "Pleased to meet your acquaintance, Sara Colleen Rinehart. I told you I was not going to hurt you."

Will witnessed Patience had turned on her heel and headed down the path to retrieve her satchel of books laid out on the stones.

She faced Sara and smiled, "Well Sara, do not be a stranger. I will see you in class tomorrow. Goodbye for now."

The new girl strolled away, and Sara watched her every movement.

Will heard Helen speak as he looked on. "Sara Rinehart was frightened, but there was something about young Patience that gave her mind calm. She felt compelled to yell out her name."

Will watched Sara begin to run and yell at the girl who was halfway down the dirt road.

A carriage had passed her, the hooves of the horse blocking out her cries, she continued, "Patience...please wait!"

Patience stopped walking and asked Sara who was breathing hard, "Yes, what can I do for you?"

Sara looked down at the rocks and dirt by her feet, and lifted her head again to inspect the girl's map of freckles. She caught her breath and spoke, "I saw you float like a ghost on the wind...I saw it all."

Patience felt a frog in her throat as Sara continued, "I have to know....how you attempted that. How did you stop yourself from falling to the ground?"

She looked into Sara's soft eyes. She said nothing to the inquisitive girl, but all of her words could be witnessed in her quivering lip.

She was frightened, frightened that she would be discovered.

Patience was worried that she would be drowned, or burned at the stake.

She turned and began to rush away, holding her satchel by her chest, "I am sorry, Sara...I cannot reveal that to you. It is just not a possibility."

Sara rushed behind her, grabbed her shoulder and turned her toward her now wet face. "I know that we have just met, but you have to understand...I am lost. I sense nothing but a dark path in my existence, and I seek answers. If you have anything that you can help me with, some kind of joy that I could never see in myself. Or even the Almighty, the lord and savior that is crammed down our gullets, I would be eternally grateful to you."

Patience look puzzled. She was stunned by the young girl's honesty.

Sara continued her plea, "I promise you, I will not reveal anything to anyone, for any reason...ever."

The young girl licked her lips and attempted to break a smile. Her voice cracked, "I...I do not know if I should. I am sworn to the utmost and ultimate secrecy."

She looked into Sara's eyes once again, and to her they resembled that of some kind of some small animal lost in the forest.

Patience put her satchel over her shoulder, and placed her hand on Sara's outer arm, she sighed. "You are the most honest young girl I think I have ever witnessed."

She cracked a tiny smile, and pulled Sara forward, "Come with me, please."

The two girls walked on the side of the road as carriages drove past them, the men driving, bidding the young girls, "Good day."

Sara asked Patience where they were heading, only to have the red headed girl say, "Follow me. No questions until we reach our destination."

The girls stepped on the road for what seemed to be hours, but the journey to the McKinney home only took twenty minutes.

The house was on a small road outside of the town which was finely crafted, and had two doors, the main entrance faced the south and there were two windows on the side of the house that the girls passed with red trim work.

In the back was a fantastic rose garden, the petals wide and in their final stage of growth.

The grass in the back of the house was short with a mild scattering of weeds in certain spots.

Sara grabbed the girl's hand as she began to pull her into a heavily tree lined area, her grip was tight and she swallowed hard.

Sara began to ask questions, "What are you? Are you...a human being? Are you like the rest of us, the same organs, and the same blood?"

Patience chuckled and responded, "Of course I am a human being, and do not worry, Sara Rinehart. All of your questions will be answered very shortly."

The two girls headed deeper into the wooded area when they suddenly came to a clearing.

The area had short grass, even though it was lined with trees and large brush.

Sara could see flowers of all kinds lined everywhere, the sun and the shadows of the branches hitting them so majestically, shadowing and lighting every petal.

On the ground were stones lined in what appeared to be formations as if they were placed together in some type of ritual.

Patience released Sara's hand when they came to a large boulder in the front of them. Sara was puzzled, and began to lightly scratch her head, "What are we doing here? It is....just a stone."

She smiled and turned to look at Sara, "That is the problem with our world, we only see what we would like to see when the answer is always right directly in front of you. I am about to show you, are you prepared?"

Sara began breathing heavy, and she felt like she was going to faint on the grass beneath her feet.

Patience took her by the hand, her smile warm. "Please do not be afraid, Sara. I am intending to bring you joy, to help you feel the love that you have been lacking. All you have to do...is trust in me."

She grabbed Sara's hand tighter, "Do you trust me, Sara?"

Sara peered directly into her inviting eyes and once again felt calm, at peace.

She shook her head lightly and answered, "Yes, I certainly do."

Patience let go of her hand. Her body moved back and she once again looked at Sara who began stepping backward as well, "Sara, do not be frightened by my movements."

Patience sealed her eyes and raised her arms in the air slowly, she was chanting something very lightly, but Sara only caught three words, "For the Mother."

The large, heavy stone in front of them began to quake and shift slightly; the girl's arms were raised even higher, and stretched out above her head.

The boulder began to shift even more, shaking dirt and kicking brown powder into the air.

Sara looked on, her legs shook slightly and she muttered under her breath, "Holy Mary...Mother of God."

The rock shifted to the right of its original spot and stopped instantly when Patience opened her eyes.

Right in front of her was an opening on the ground where the boulder once rested.

Patience walked over to the secret opening, bent down and placed her body onto what appeared to be a ladder.

She looked at Sara. "Please do not be afraid...come with me."

As Patience stood in front of her, Sara caught the breath she was holding in. "How on earth did you do that? What are you?"

Before she climbed down she explained, "The only way to describe what you just saw is that the stones, the rocks are a part of Her, and in turn, they are a part of me as well as my dear mother."

She began to climb down and Sara stepped to the opening, her heart pumped wildly, her fear broken by her new friend's echoing voice. "Sara...come down, please. I have many things to show you!"

Sara did not have an inkling of what Patience truly was.

She thought to herself that this girl could be a bloodthirsty creature spoken about in old lore, but something about her drew Sara's pain and anguish away, and for the moments she spent with this new stranger, this beautiful stranger, she felt free.

She stepped down slowly into the darkness, climbing down into whatever had awaited her.

As she reached the bottom she could see the illumination of candlelight, and as she turned she was in a room. The walls seemed to be held up with heavy wood logs which prevented the dirt from collapsing.

The room was small but deep; there were tables as well as bookshelves that were rotted and appeared to be in this secret underground room for many years.

Bathed in the candlelight in the very back of the room was Patience, her green eyes shining in the flickering flame.

She waved to Sara. "Please, come sit with me."

Sara slowly stepped over and sat in the empty wooden chair as Patience lit two more candles, and placed them around the floor so that they can see each other in the dark.

She sat back down, lifted her dress slightly, and crossed her leg properly. As she reached out for Sara's quivering hand, she spoke, "What I am about to tell you shall never escape your lips, are we understood?"

Sara looked into her green eyes and shook her head in agreement. Patience continued, "If what I was about to relay to you were ever to hit the ears of the townsmen, my mother and I, my family...could be in much danger, or even face impending death, do you understand this?"

Sara shook her head again and smiled even though she felt a mild queasiness.

Patience began to explain. "This room was built many years ago, and my grandmother who once lived in the home that we reside in utilized this place to hide a family secret, the secret of the women in our line...we are witches."

She could feel Sara recoil slightly, and she spoke calmly, "No, no please, Sara. Witchcraft is not terrible...we are not bad people. Nay, we are children...children of water, earth, and sky, nothing more."

Sara inhaled deeply and stood up from her chair. She bent over to pick up one of the candles she stepped lightly to one of the wooden shelves, she spoke. "This place is where you practice?"

The shelf where Sara stood had small stacks of books, and she held the candle to her face shining minimal light on the spines.

Patience stepped behind her. "These books were all written by my grandmother, these are her spells, her life, as well as her love and devotion to the Mother."

Sara ran her fingers across the leather books. She began to speak with a calm in her words, "Do you know why I came to you? Why I had requested that you show me your secrets? I felt this light in you, this pure happiness, even when I witnessed you in church. Your light...the light inside of you invited me, I cannot explain the feeling. It beckoned me to you, but I did not have the strength to confront you...not right away. But the light finally allowed me to come to you as if it...as if **you** were calling to me."

She turned to face Patience, and with a candle in one hand, Sara placed the tips of her fingers to her cheek, the light and shadow making her look like an eternally beautiful being from some other time.

Sara closed her eyes, "I would like you to show me your way...to show me the love that you possess. Show me how to feel something, for the first time ever. Let me feel the love of this Mother you hold so dear."

The young witch's smile could be seen in the light, she placed her fingertips on Sara's cheek mirroring her movement. "Sara Rinehart, now is your time to feel your true power, your femininity, and your strength, just as my mother has taught me. I will teach you all that you need to know about the magick and majesty of the earth. I will show you Her love."

As time drew on, Patience did as she had promised, and she was a true sage, a teacher.

Will witnessed the two girls in the same clearing. Patience was holding a seed in the palm of her hand, her eyes were closed and she chanted something quietly as Sara looked on.

The seed began to shake as her words continued, "Come, oh loving Mother. Bloom in the comfort of your love and power."

The seed broke open, forming petals instantly. It had grown into a gorgeous wildflower and Sara clapped as Patience stood up, holding the sides of her dress and bowing playfully, pretending to be a gentleman. "Thank you so very much, ladies and gentlemen."

Days had passed, weeks changed into months, and Sara's training continued.

Patience told Sara everything that she needed to know, and she met with her every single day after school.

They headed to the clearing and read spells together, practiced, and prayed hand in hand in the name of the Mother.

Sara felt a hole in her heart becoming filled each second she spent with her new found friend.

She did everything that she could to keep her secret from her father and mother, and any material she had kept in her home involving her teachings were placed underneath two broken floor boards beside her bed.

Life became a pure joy for Sara, and every time she woke she knew that she would look upon Patience, her features in front of her causing her heart to race.

Patience McKinney was a true sister, as well as a kindred spirit.

Everything that Sara once felt, her pain and her loneliness was gone.

And nothing in her was aware that her good feelings, as well as her entire life were about to change, bringing her closer to the darkness she would feel growing inside her until her death.

On one of the afternoons Sara was spending time with Patience, her mother was doing her daily chores while her father read a book in his favorite wooden chair.

She had stepped into her daughter's room to sweep the floor, and stopped abruptly when the heavy bristles knocked a piece of wood by Sara's bed loose.

Margaret knelt down to put it back into place, when she noticed there was something tucked away underneath the floor.

She was puzzled, and placed her hand inside finding a small book.

Sara's mother was shaken to the core when she opened the pages as it contained a listing of spells, prayers to the Mother Earth, and all of Sara's experiences.

Margaret began to cry, but her sadness turned to sudden rage when she had seen a name. The name of her devout daughter's corrupter, Patience McKinney.

She rushed into the den and immediately relayed the information to her husband, and they immediately concocted a plan to keep their reveal a secret from their daughter, to make her feel like her secrets were still safe.

Collin then opened the door, and jumped on his horse which was tied to a post in the front of the house and headed into town during a council meeting.

Sara's father stood in front of the group in the small hall, spitting fire and hate for the McKinney family in front of the wood podium.

He told the people that the McKinney women were the whores of Satan himself, and he felt slight tears as he mentioned that his daughter's soul was taken by a demon child, and that she now too was in leagues with evil unknown.

The town heard all of this and had quickly come to a vote, they decided that they would arrest the McKinney females, and the price would be death.

The next day had approached, and it was business as usual for the two young girls, only this time the clouds covered overhead as the rain poured hard.

Sara and Patience did not run, instead they danced, their hair and dresses soaked, laughing playfully.

The young teacher looked at Sara, water dripping down her face, "My sister, I have taught you many secrets, you are full of the

Mother's love. You feel her now, in every part of your soul, just as the women in my family have felt her love."

Patience caressed Sara's face, her fingers wet, "And I love you, Sara Rinehart. You are a part of me just as I am now a part of you."

She leaned in and kissed Sara sweetly on her lips, but she did not pull away.

At this moment, she felt nothing but love swell in her heart, the blackness she had felt before had left her soul.

Sara was truly in love with the powers of the Earth, as well as her sister in mysticism.

The girls stopped embracing, and they both smiled and giggled.

Suddenly, Patience grabbed Sara's hand and smiled. "Sara, please show me everything you have learned, all of the power that you now embrace. Let us stop this beautiful rain, together. It is only water, after all. Water is part of her cycle and our practices."

The two girls shut their eyes tight and began to chant in unison,

Oh, brother rain...you give us life
you take away the dry earth's strife.
You come down heavy...you come down slow
your love is grand...but you must go."

At that moment, the sky began to open up and the rain stopped falling.

The young witches still soaked to the bone hugged hard, and Patience yelled, "We did it, Sister!"

Sara smiled at her deeply when suddenly they heard a scream, and faint voices in the distance.

The girls grew very quiet, and the voice yelled out again.

Patience and Sara knew right away that it was the screams of her mother.

She gripped Sara's shoulders, "My goddess, Sara, we have to go. We have to flee...now!"

Patience ran forward toward the large boulder when Sara gripped her arm, "Please wait! Is there something that we can do?"

Patience was now in a panic, and her eyes began to well up, "I have to go...I have to go right now, please!"

Sara looked right into her Sister's crying eyes, "I am coming with you, wherever you go. I am coming with you. Please...do not leave me."

Patience embraced Sara and grabbed her hand. "We have to go."

The girls began to rush toward the brush behind the boulder, when they were suddenly stopped by four townsmen holding rifles in front of them.

Startled, they turned to run toward the woods, and were once again stopped dead in their tracks, five of the townsmen had circled around the clearing, three were holding rifles and the other men, looking to be younger than the rest, were holding what appeared to be clubs in their hands.

Sara's face turned to rage when she looked upon the ringleader, her father Collin, who was holding onto a woman, her head was down and was covered with a sack.

Her father's voice boomed, "Miss Patience McKinney, do not move, devil! Sara, release her hand and come toward me, child!"

Sara did not move, and he spoke again, "Sara Rinehart, I am your father, and I order you to step away from the child!"

Sara looked at her friend, her hair and clothes still damp. "I am not leaving you, what happens to you happens to me."

Patience gripped her hand tighter, and Collin's voice grew louder, "Lady McKinney, I order you to release my daughter, or by order of the town council I will have you watch me slice the throat of your bitch mother!"

He pulled the bag from Patricia's face, her eye was swollen and there was blood spilling slowly from her mouth as if she was beaten, or worse.

The mob began to step forward and Patience released Sara's hand before got down on her knees.

One of the men grabbed Sara's hand, and she was too shocked to fight back.

She looked down at her sister, her knees on the wet grass, and began to tear when three men surrounded her.

Patience placed her hands behind her back, and two of the men pulled her up to her feet.

She stood proud and strong showing no sign of fear. "You have no worries, gentlemen. I will not retaliate, that is not my way. I am a child of love and beauty; I am a child of the Mother."

She looked at Sara as she finished her last sentence, "Do what you will...I surrender unconditionally, and I forgive you."

Collin stepped forward, along with the young townsmen with clubs; he shouted command, "To the stone with her!"

Sara could not believe what she was witnessing and she ran toward her father who tossed a beaten Patricia to the grass and slapped his daughter with a closed hand.

Sara fell to the ground hard, when the large man grabbed her by the hair as she screamed, "Do not do this, father! She is not a demon...you are doing wrong!"

Collin ignored his daughter and made another command, "Take the mother to the tree!"

Sara screamed and her father cupped her mouth with his big hand as tears squirted from her eyes. Two men picked up Mrs. McKinney and brought her toward one of the larger trees as her daughter looked on.

Collin still held onto his daughter's wet hair and spun her in his direction; his eyes seemed to burn. "Sara, you are a disgrace to the family name, to this town, and to God. You are in leagues with the devil, and for that you will be forced to witness his wives suffer."

Sara spat in her father's face, "Go to hell, father!"

Collin laughed heartily and pulled his daughter to the front of the stone throwing her to the ground.

Patience McKinney's hands were still behind her back and her face did not reveal her fear.

Sara's father began to speak again, the voice of a preacher, "Patricia and Patience McKinney, you are guilty, guilty of performing the devil's work...**you** are guilty!"

He rushed toward Patience and hit her hard with a closed fist, dropping her to the grass in front of a tearful Sara, he continued, "And you, you little whore, you take my God fearing daughter, and you make her one of your own."

One of the men picked up Patience, who had shaken the pain from her mind and stared directly into Sara's father's eyes. He smiled, "And for that you will suffer the most."

She smiled back, her lip cut. "And once I do, I will be in absolute bliss. I will become one with the Earth and its cycle; the plants, the trees, my soul will be connected with the creatures, great and small. That is the finish to this body, as well as this life."

Collin grit his teeth, stepped over to his daughter and pulled her up by her hair again, he roared out the women's sentence, "McKinney women, by order of the townspeople...you both are sentenced to death!"

One of the men in front of her mother pulled a bag from his shoulder, and placed it on the ground pulling out a rope already tied in a noose.

Sara cried for her father to stop, but it only caused her hair to get pulled tighter.

Patience, still standing strong, had a single tear fall from her eye when Collin snapped his stubby finger, and two men dropped their rifles to throw the rope up and over a heavy trunk of the old tree Patricia now stood by.

The rope was placed over her neck, the slipknot pulled tight as her legs shook slightly, but her face showed the same calm of her daughter.

Sara's father stepped over after tossing his daughter to the ground again. "Patricia McKinney, do you have anything to say before your sentence is passed?"

Patricia only said three words, "For the Mother."

Collin Rinehart laughed and turned his back after commanding, "String the bitch up!"

Sara cried as two of the men pulled the other side of the heavy rope causing Dorothy's mother's feet to leave the ground, gagging and spitting until her legs stopped kicking, and her body swung in the breeze.

Sara was gripped under the arm and tossed on the ground in front of the large stone.

Patience looked upon Sara. Her eyes were wet.

Collin stepped behind his daughter, the two younger men holding clubs to the side of him, he looked at the once again strong young woman. "Patience McKinney, your sentence is next. Do you have anything to say before judgment is passed?"

She wiped her tear with the back of one hand and repeated her mother's words, "For the Mother."

Collin Rinehart asked one of the men to grab Patience and place her head on the stone beside her.

Sara cried out, and he looked down at his daughter, "And for your unbearable treason to the Almighty and his word, my daughter, you will watch every moment of her pain, and you will feel the blood cleanse the evil from you."

He peered at her teacher, head now against the large stone, "We anoint you of your wickedness. Your blood will be that of the Lamb now."

Collin clapped his hands together and the men with the heavy clubs stepped forward. He commanded, "It is time, give the demon child to the Lord."

One of the sandy haired men was beating the club against his fist and Patience looked at Sara, her eyes no longer wet. Sara cried out, "I am so sorry...I love you."

Patience smiled and spoke, "Be strong, my Sister. Keep what you have learned in your heart, and I will always be there."

Collin Rinehart yelled, "Shut her wretched mouth, now!"

The two men raised their sticks and brought them down hard on the side of her face, her head was smashed after the second blow, and her blood spilled down the stone and splashed Sara's face, intermingling with her tears.

They hit her again and her skull cracked wide, revealing bone, and her body instantly stopped wriggling.

The blood continued to flow down the stone, and her body dropped to the grass, staining the ground.

Sara cried heavily and her body dropped to the sharp grass, her face streaming with the blood of her sister.

Her back heaved as she sobbed, and her father towered over her quivering heap, he was smiling. "Do you have anything to say now, daughter?"

Sara was silent, and her body was still over the grass.

Collin Rinehart and his henchmen looked at each other as the air suddenly became chilly and the wind blew hard around them.

The mob began to look frightened when the flowers around the open circle grew black as midnight, and the petals circled around their bodies.

The trees rustled and the sky above turned dark, as Sara began to heave in front of her father causing him to jump back.

She raised her head. Her face was still coated in her Sister's blood, a pure fire was present in her now crimson colored eyes.

She screamed loudly, a banshee scream that caused the group to shiver and hold their weapons at the ready.

Sara stood perfectly still, her teeth were grit together and her wet hair blew in the cold wind.

One of the young men with clubs rushed toward when in an instant Sara lifted her hand, and the men could hear pieces of tree snapping and breaking.

Her young attacker was tossed high into the air when Sara brought her hand toward the trees. Sharp sticks impaled the man's body, the others screamed as he gurgled, his flesh torn open as his entire body was impaled and violently thrown to the ground.

One of the other men fired their rifle. The circular bullet headed toward Sara who raised her hand once again, pushing it forward and causing to bullet to fly back toward the man at heavy speed, hitting his chest like a cannon causing his insides to spray onto the grass.

Sara smiled slightly, lifted her hands again, and the heavy rock formations on the ground around her lifted up into the air, and were tossed at the rest of the men. Their heads and bodies were hit hard breaking bones instantly.

Her father looked on in amazement as his daughter began to step forward, seething,

One of the other men fired as well, and Sara moved her right hand upward, lifting the man into the air.

She closed her fist and her victim began to scream as his bones snapped. They poked out of his skin and blood shot out in spurts.

Sara sealed her hand tight and the man's head caved in, his skull creaked and cracked, and his brain squeezed out of the wounds. The lifeless body was tossed hard in Collin's direction.

There were bodies lined in the open circle, broken, their eyes lifeless and Sara began to walk once forward once again.

Collin tried to run when he was swept up, his large body slammed hard in front of the stone where her Sister was murdered for her beliefs.

Sara spoke, a hiss in her words. "You have taken my heart...my love. You will pay! All of you pigs...all of you men who create destruction and death...will pay!

The trees around Sara began to burn, the flames surrounded the circle. Her father now had his knees on the ground, he was begging his daughter for forgiveness. "Sara, what are you doing my child? Find your faith in Him! Find our Lord, and end this suffering!"

Sara raised her hands up into the air; the wind knocked her father to the ground.

She waved her hands towards the burning trees and sharp branches flew forward hitting Collin all over his entire body like sharp knives.

Sara waved her hand forward and the wind blew her father onto his back, when suddenly pieces of tree impaled his hands on both sides of him, causing him to resemble the crucifixion of the Lord he had forced on his daughter for so many years.

He cried out, the pain excruciating, "You demon, your soul will never reach the Heavens, child! And no matter what you exact on me...I will reach the Kingdom while you suffer in a dark and putrid hell!"

Sara smiled and lifted her hand. "I will bask in eternity by my Mother's side...the Mother of this Earth. This is something you would never understand, so your death is your own doing, you pig."

With that, the boulder where Patience was clubbed to death shook and rose from the ground, causing flecks of dirt to hit Collin's face.

The boulder now hovered over Sara's father's head as if being lifted by an invisible giant, he yelled out, "Suffer forever, you bitch devil of mine!"

Sara smiled once again, "Father, say hello to your God for me."

The boulder dropped hard on top of her father creating a squishing and cracking sound.

Sara looked on for a moment, and walked over to the lifeless body of her friend, her Sister, and her love.

The cold wind began to cease as she knelt down to pick up her friend's shattered skull, the blood dripping and staining her hands.

Sara sobbed silently as she spoke, "I love you, my Sister. I will have no fear...I vow this to you."

She kissed what was left of her forehead, "Be in peace with our beloved Mother."

Sara clenched her jaw hard. "I will make her pain...her suffering known. She will receive her vengeance, through me. This is my promise, with all of my love and trust."

In the dark room, Helen opened her eyes, and the scene disappeared.

With a buzzing in his head, Will spoke, "Jesus Christ, so that is what made her all messed up? I think I get it now. I felt her pain, her anguish, and I almost feel sorry for her. So how did our family come into play? Why does she hate us so much?"

Susan stood close to her son, her tears were gone but her cheek was still red from when her son struck her, "Yes, why did she choose us to bring on her horror?"

Helen waved her family over, her face still looking forward, illuminated by candlelight.

Susan and her son stepped in front of her, and Helen closed her eyes once again.

Will looked over at his mother.

Suddenly they were whisked into yet another time in Sara's life, Helen spoke once again. "After Sara had vowed her hatred toward men in the name of the Mother she disappeared into the woods, never to seen by anyone in the town ever again. Margaret Rinehart passed away five years after the body of her husband was discovered. She never remarried, and she constantly thought of the whereabouts of her only daughter. Sara traveled alone for many years and she continued to practice the magick that she had learned from her Sister. The lonely woman showed love to every animal she had feasted upon, every deer she had killed with the wave of her hand, every fish that she had lifted from the water. Sara walked through many different areas, and she slept amongst the trees and plants, her love for the Mother unbroken, even though her heart grew darker and her soul grew colder. The girl who was now in her twenty-fifth year had no love for man, they were nothing to her and she promised every single day to destroy them all. Sara felt in her blackened heart that women were the true seed, the bringers of life, as well as the daughters of the Earth."

Helen lightly waved her hand, and Will and his mother saw a village, a village filled with nothing but women, young and old. The village was hidden in the trees, built on a massive field where every female had a home of their own. They built every single foundation, laid every single brick.

The Rogers saw everything in vivid detail; clothes hanging on lines, food being prepared, as children plucked feathers from the latest hunt. Little girls played while women sat in circles reading books.

Sara had formed her own little world hidden from the communities nearby.

Throughout her travels, Sara had waltzed into the small towns, speaking to women in secret about the power of the Mother and how they should shed their allegiance to men becoming strong once again.

Sara was very convincing and manipulative with her words, and many women with husbands, even some with male children left their homes and followed her.

She also took in women who were cast from their homes: outcasts, a few adulterers that were banished, and mostly intelligent women of all ages who desired another way.

Sara did in fact teach these females the ways of the Mother, her majesty as well as her love.

Although she always preached the Mother, her intentions were very dark in nature.

She became a dictator, shouting her word on how the men of the world were bad, how they all should suffer for their wars, for the raping of the land, and for the persecution of the female species: beating them, making them cook their meals, and bow to their every whim and sexual hunger.

The village was quickly persuaded, and after a few months, they believed in Sara's every word.

They stole away into the night in groups kidnapping male children, sometimes men straight from their beds and brought them to the village.

The scene was always horrifying, little boys stuffed into sacks and men waking from sleep or unconsciousness to see a sea of female forms in front of them, all chanting in unison.

Will and Susan witnessed one of these moments in front of their eyes.

The female villagers were chanting, "Kill the pig...kill the pig!"

In the back of an old cart was a frightened older man from one of the towns, he was grabbed by the legs and tossed to the hard ground.

Sara walked over; her body adorned in a red cloak and waved her followers away.

She smiled, and waved her hand in front of him causing his body to lift toward her, and his wide eyes met hers as she grinned. "Do not cry, you destructor...you deceiver. You rape our Mother and now you must pay, in her name.

The man pleaded, sounding almost childlike until he began smiling, fear still in his eyes, "Go to hell, you demon!"

Sara smiled back, her lips opened, "You first, good sir."

She yelled out to her followers, "Take him to the altar!"

Two of the women grabbed the man and carried him, Sara and the rest of the group behind them.

They walked over to a pile of stones on the ground which had signified the object that her love was killed upon, and threw the old man down hard.

He was gagged as Sara stepped over on bare feet and towered over the man, her naked body underneath her cloak bathed in moonlight.

Torches burned around them, and the light eerily illuminated the chanting mob.

Sara raised her hand into the air, "Oh Mother, we give you this man who has helped reap your soil with the blood of many, a man who abuses your true children, forcing them to be their unthinking and unfeeling monsters. Oh, Mother, I give this man to you, his pain, his flesh, and his blood. I give you the dirty soul of this swine in the name of you, our precious Mother."

The women chanted, "In the Mother's name."

Sara knelt down over the man and she was handed a silver dagger by one of the group.

She raised it high as the followers chanted, "Pig...pig...pig!"

Sara raised the blade and brought it down into the victim's chest, he screamed and blood swirled and gurgled in his throat.

He tried to speak, "You will not get away with this, you will be found out soon enough! And all of your concubines will rot in damnation!"

The group laughed hard and Sara had a look of pure satisfaction, "I believe that is going to be the last squeal you make."

She brought the dagger down again and again, laughing maniacally as she sliced into the man's face, and cut off pieces and threw it to the cloaked women and children surrounding her.

She ripped the flesh of his arm with her teeth, relishing the torrent of blood in her throat, and the man underneath her stopped moving.

The women laughed as Sara stood up and ordered her congregation to drag the body to a fire that was already burning.

Sara spoke to them, "We dine on his flesh as they have feasted on her creatures, with no remorse and no regret!"

The women placed the body on a pole, tied the hands, feet, and the waist with rope, and two women picked up the pole and laid it atop the flames.

As the flesh bubbled and cooked, the women danced around the fire. The body giving a putrid almost chicken-like smell.

After the body was cooked to a crisp, the women tore into the man, tossing pieces of him to hungry onlookers.

The charred corpse was then taken from the spit, his ribcage torn into to retrieve the heart that Sara consumed, licking her lips as she dined. The man whom Sara and her group had sacrificed was absolutely right. The cult would be discovered, and that night happened to be the very same.

The senior captive had a teenage grandson who was in his home at the time he was kidnapped.

The boy followed the cart of the women on horseback and was led right to their hidden village.

He watched as his grandfather was brutally killed just like many before him and headed back to town waking everyone as he yelled out, "There are devil's in our midst...they gave my grandfather to the devil!"

That same evening, Sara had a vision of her own death, of Jason Cain, and of her only living female ancestor left on earth in the year two thousand and fourteen: Elizabeth.

She envisioned Elizabeth's love for the man, and she had seen her devotion as well as her inevitable heartbreak and pain.

She witnessed the women of her village attacked, beaten to death and shot, and she had seen the man who had made this assault possible: the honorable Judge Walton Rogers.

Sara took this as a true sign and began to form a plan.

She used the power of the Mother which had been tarnished by her own hatred to create a spell in one of her empty leather bound books. She sliced her finger and dripped blood into an inkwell.

Using a quill pen she began to scrawl quickly.

Sara had thought to herself that if she was going to die, she would return once again, that she would be the strongest when she was one with her only remaining female ancestor.

The woman would feel a connection, a compulsion to a man that she would meet unexpectedly, and through his deceit and abuse, she would become strong and the man whom she once loved would be at his weakest.

She had also plotted to use the family of her captor to make her evil plans come to fruition.

Once her words were spoken aloud by the man with the broken heart, she would have her followers again, the women of the world would be connected to her, every woman willing to viciously kill, with no thought and no mercy.

The women would become stronger through her, unstoppable until the link in their mind was severed.

The next morning, as the sun was high in the sky, her visions did come to fruition.

Her followers were attacked, they were beaten and some were shot immediately.

Young children were stabbed to death as their mothers looked on.

Sara did not leave her home even when she heard the screams of her Sisters.

She sat on the floor, naked, and waited.

The men finally discovered her and automatically pinned her as the head of the coven.

Sara was tied to the back of a large horse and dragged through the streets of the town, the rocks scraping and tearing at her skin as the animal was forced to trot at a medium pace.

In the town, she was tossed into a dank cell located inside of the courthouse and waited patiently for her inevitable fate.

She did not pray to the Mother and she did not shed any tears.

The day turned into night, and Sara was pulled up to her feet and taken out to the town square where onlookers of all ages, male and female, and even children, looked at a bloody and beaten Sara who was now wrapped in a dress which was tight-fitting across her entire body.

A burly man was piling up pieces of wood, and Sara's body was slathered in flammable oils and shoved forward, the onlookers tossing rocks and vegetables as she walked by them, smiling.

Children yelled out their hateful words, and men spat on her, but Sara did not make a sound.

The man who was piling the wood took a torch and lit the fire, the embers cracked and the orange glow grew high.

The young woman stood still and strong as another man stepped in front of her, his face covered in sweat from the high flames behind him.

The man was the one in Sara's vision, and he was wearing a black vest and carrying a bible.

This was the Rogers' family ancestor. He was a stern man, a gray beard on his plump face.

The judge was absolutely justified in his actions against Sara and her village, albeit, they were extremely violent.

The judge began to speak, "Sara Colleen Rinehart, you are guilty of kidnapping, cannibalism, and murder! Not to mention worshipping the devil and cavorting with demons. Do you have anything to say for yourself?"

Sara, sweating as the flames grew around her laughed as she was tied to a post planted in the wood and packed with dirt so it would not fall, her skin began to bubble and she laughed as she spoke.

Her face was melting slowly like a wax candle, "You men...you pigs bask in your disgusting existence while it lasts, because one day you will all pay! Your blood will spill, and your bodies will be piled high to form my tower where I will rule on high!

Sara's skin continued to melt and slough off, and her bones turned to ash until there was nothing left.

Her ashes twisted in the wind in an upward spiral.

All of the books and tomes in her village were retrieved earlier on, and the bodies of the women were thrown into a pile and set on fire; women stacked on top of children, their smell filling the air as they disintegrated.

The books collected were thrown on a cart and taken to the courthouse waiting to be destroyed until Judge Rogers' precocious daughter found the book containing Sara's vengeance.

As the young girl grew, she passed the book on to her children, and the book was protected by every female in the Rogers bloodline.

A still Helen slowly opened her eyes once again, and the images in front of Will and Susan stopped like the end of a film.

He began talking after he shook the pain in his mind, "Let me guess Grandma Helen brought her back with her own hatred, I get it."

He began to pace. "That was a hell of a history lesson, I feel like I know her so much better now. In the meantime, the world is shit and continues to get much fucking worse!"

Susan stepped over to her son, the same pain rushing through her head as if she had a hangover, "I am sorry, I do not have the answers for you. I have always practiced in the good of the Mother, until I was deceived by Sara, enticed by her evil masked in some kind of sick goodness."

Will looked at his mother, "There has to be something that we can do...that I can do. You do not have any answers for me?"

Susan shook her head no, when suddenly Helen's eyes were normal and she began to step forward, acting like herself once again. In the hellish dankness, she spoke in a voice that young Susan quickly recognized. "I have the answer. Through the power of the Mother, you need to bring back the only thing that she ever loved to break the chain of her darkness."

Will stepped over to his grandmother, "Bring back...her only love? How do you expect me to do that?"

Helen stretched out her arms, "Come to me, Will. I have a gift for you, a gift of love...her love."

He did as he was instructed and walked to his grandmother who wrapped her arms around him causing his body to convulse.

Susan held her hands together as if she was praying, and Helen whispered something in her grandson's ear

Will dropped backward and his mother caught him before he fell to the stinking ground, she asked, "Is he okay?"

Helen looked at her daughter's concerned eyes. "Yes, for now. But he will make a great sacrifice to attempt to save his friend, and the world. The Mother is angry, Sara has misused her love for too long, and she must be stopped!"

Will's body began to dissipate from Susan's arms as if he was being erased.

He opened his eye, and his head once again swam with pain as he looked into the faces of the men who had beaten him, the men who had desired his blood.

Will had the answer to stop the powerful force known as Sara at the moment of his highly inevitable death.

The thought left his aching mind when Russell's hand gave him another devastating blow to the face.

CHAPTER THIRTEEN

Reduced to Nothing

After the final blow from Russell's large balled fist, Will's head was blank. There were no thoughts swimming in his mind, and he could not feel his body.

The youngest of the group, Michael, was told to pick the man up off of the ground, his face practically nothing but cuts and swelling, and his left eye was completely sealed shut.

After their small battle with the group of women to get to a cornered Will, everyone felt fatigued and their throats were dry.

The wounds on their bodies felt like needles dug into the skin, especially the slices on John's lower legs and ankle causing him to limp even worse than before.

As the group headed forward past the bloodstained sidewalks, the bodies were about them like grotesque art, splayed open and bleeding out.

Jason recognized the street sign in front of him, and it was clear to him immediately that the tired group, along with their bruised and bloodied guest who was being held up by the youngest member of the small survival party, stumbling as he tried his hardest to keep Will's quivering body upright, that they had only one more city block to go until they reached his son.

Jason had known where Elizabeth and Matthew were the entire time of the divorce. She did not hide that fact from him, but the court decree stated that Jason Cain would never be allowed to step foot around the vicinity of her place of residence.

This was Elizabeth's way to keep Jason out of a cell for what he had done, and to keep his existence hidden from her young son as agreed after the incident that split them apart.

In the middle of the street the group had stopped and Michael laid Will's battered form onto one of the building's steps.

John was kneeling, tending to the wounds on his leg with a half empty water bottle he found in the mess of the street. Jason took a deep breath and smiled down at him, a pure expression of relief on his face.

John continued to pour water on the cuts in his leg and laughed slightly, he looked up at Jason but his look was uncertain; it was a smile mixed with anger.

His trust for Jason during the journey had slowly faltered, and after thinking about every little detail that caused the events before him if he could have any trust at all in this man.

As John looked up at him, his smile never left, but his brow furrowed, "That's...that's real good, man."

He attempted to stand, his leg still a bit wobbly, and picked his weapon up off of the street.

While John had tended to his wounds Russell had lifted Will from the stairs, holding his limp body with the greatest of ease, and glared at Michael who had a difficult time and shook his head in disbelief.

As Will was held in front of the large man, his arms around his waist, he began to gurgle, blood trickling out of the side of his mouth as he tried to speak, the words sounding like nonsense.

Russell chuckled to himself, and craned his head down to Will's ringing ears; he began to taunt him, "What was that? Are you trying to say something?"

He squeezed his body hard toward his chest, his grip tighter around his waist causing Will to heave slightly. He still felt every bit of pain, even though he could not respond.

Russell continued to toy with him, "What did you say?"

Will still tried to speak; the blood dripping from his mouth onto his ripped black shirt. Russell laughed louder and yelled to John to get his attention, "Hey, John! I think our guy here has something to say."

John continued to peer at Jason, his stare ice cold and then he turned on his foot and limped in front of Will, who was still being squeezed by John's re-appointed right hand man.

He placed his hand under Will's jaw, squeezing hard so that blood and spit spilled out of both sides of his lips, and he grit his teeth as he spoke, "What do you have to fucking say, huh?"

John's grip on his face grew tighter, and his thumbnail pressed hard against the flesh of Will's cheek. He continued to bare his hatred for the man, "You bring this on us, bring on this mess, making women crazy as bat shit. You have a hand in killing my son, and now you want to be chatty?"

Jason was now in front of John, watching his every movement, sensing the sheer pain Will had to be feeling at that moment, and began to feel a tinge of guilt.

Jason knew that the man had everything to do with what was occurring; every single moment of pain, every fight that he had encountered, and the many times he had to kill these demons he had wrought upon the world.

He realized that Will Thompson had tricked him, enticed him to be a pawn in his family's endgame, and he promised him the world, forcing him to help bring the world to its knees.

But even through all of the deception and lies, he remembered that the man he saw before him, being tossed around like a rag doll, being spat on, kicked and humiliated was once his friend.

And no matter how angry he was, how hard he wanted to hit him himself, Jason did not want to see Will beaten to death, or worse. He continued to watch John leer into Will's dead eye, his saliva flying in his direction as he spoke, his words venomous.

And just at that very moment, John railed his fist into his stomach.

Will began wheezing, and his body fell backward, but Russell held him up before he fell backward.

Michael was sitting on the step next to Will's bloodstains before he was lifted and yelled in John's direction, "Hey man! I know that carrying this ass the rest of the way is going to be my job. What the hell? The guy's already heavy enough without that shit!"

John turned to look at him quickly, his finger pointed in his direction, "You should just shut your fucking mouth! You will do as we tell you to do, and we will do what we want to do, okay?"

It was evident that John Robertson was snapping, eroding after everything he had been through, and that he had nothing but violence as well as vengeance on the brain.

He attempted to lift his arm and strike Will again, but this time he was stopped.

Jason caught onto his arm in mid-swing before he could throw the punch causing John to spin around immediately to face him, shoving him hard with both hands, and furious as he yelled, "Did you just put your hands on me, my friend?"

Jason stepped backward, but remained strong as he looked at John's fiery eyes, "Look, we have our man, but you do not have to beat him to death. Have we lost our sense of humanity, our moral center, ourselves? All I am asking is that you lay off of him a bit, he's damn near dead already. You did enough, John."

John began to laugh, and Russell chimed in, the cackling of the men in unison made Jason want to scream.

John stopped and looked at Jason, a shit eating grin on his face, "What is going on here? Are you beginning to feel a little something for your friend here? That's cute. Feeling for the witch boy, huh?"

The older man stepped forward and grabbed Jason by the front of his ragged stained. Jason did everything he could to push him off.

John smiled, "Let's get the rules of the road straight here. You didn't lose your boy, we are going to get yours. If he's still alive, that is."

Jason pulled back, and John released him, dropping him hard to the sidewalk.

Jason began yelling, "Get the fuck off of me! What the hell is wrong with you?"

John held his bloodstained sword into the air, "You know what my problem is? I am not so sure, at all, that I trust you."

He pointed at Will, now being held up by Michael, who was having a difficult time, "You were in leagues with this piece of garbage, weren't you?"

Jason continued to yell, "I was not in leagues with anyone...I was tricked!"

John began to step forward, sword clutched tightly in his now white knuckled hand. "Nonetheless, you would have done anything to bring your piece of ass back, even sorcery, right? Did you know the consequences, did you even think of what they could possibly be?"

Jason stepped back, and his legs began to quake slightly, "No, I did not. But, I didn't even know if it would work!"

John laughed hard again and Russell followed, and then the oldest of the group dropped the blade to his side. "Let me tell you something about your friend over there. None of us give a shit about him. And if I didn't have other great plans for him, we would kill him right here in front of you, and drop him in the street like food for the goddamn vultures."

Jason noticed John step backward as he fumbled for something near his belt loop, he grinned at Jason as he spoke, "This man is bait now, that's all. We are going to use him to attract these gals out here, and more importantly, your beautiful wife...who threw a fucking car at me!"

His voice grew deeper and louder. "We are going to get your son, you are going to hunt around the apartment quickly for some fucking car keys, and if her ride's intact, we are going to get in said vehicle, and try to get the fuck out of this hell!"

Jason noticed that John had pulled a knife from his loop as he continued to explain his plan. "And that's that. As far as you are concerned, you can cooperate and come with us, or you can stay right here and die alongside your boy. You can feel the pain that I felt for a simple decision...it's your choice."

John pointed the blade of the knife at Jason, "But you are not running shit here. And as far as your buddy...this is what I think of him!"

He turned on his foot and shoved the blade into Will's shoulder, causing him to become truly animated for the first time since his incredible beating,

He yelled out, blood staining his mouth as John slowly slid the blade out of the wound. He looked back and stared at Jason, "So, what's it going to be, Shakespeare? Does he die right here, or do you stick with the plan?"

Jason looked at Will, blood leaking slowly from the new shoulder wound, his face mashed.

He clenched his jaw. "Yes, we are going to stick with your plan."

John smiled slightly, "That's a really good choice."

At that instant, Jason noticed Will peer over at him with one open, bloodshot eye, and he felt a pain shoot through his chest.

He then looked at Michael who had a look of pure shock painted on his face.

Jason did not have any upper hand in this situation, he could not run, and he could not attempt to escape the group to reach his son without them potentially trying anything crazy.

John stepped forward, limping slightly and asked Russell to take a now hunched over Will from Michael.

He then licked the blade of his knife and placed it back into the loop, and with a look of content in his eyes he looked at Jason, "Now, let's go get that son of yours."

CHAPTER FOURTEEN

The Lesson and The Answer

After Will Thompson was attacked by John's blade, the group ventured onto the following street.

Michael was standing right behind John and next to Russell who was dragging the shell of Will Thompson behind him; his arms around his neck, his feet dragging against the sidewalk with the large man's movement.

Jason stood in front of the rest, and constantly felt John's stare even with his back turned.

There were absolutely no women on the street. There were no potential attacks, and no wild chanting could be heard.

Jason pondered the whereabouts of his family; his father and his brother, but Matthew entered his mind more than the rest.

Was he safe, and if so where was he?

He hoped for the best, and that his young boy would actually listen to a supposed stranger when he instructs him to hide in a room. The suddenly tearful, estranged father continued to walk without anyone seeing his wet eyes, and he quickly wiped the salty discharge with the back of his hand.

He began to think of his game plan, that once he reached his son he would do everything that he could to let him know who he truly was, that he was his father, and that he was eternally sorry for what he had done to him in the past.

And of course, for not being sound enough to be in his life.

Jason began to think of himself, sitting alone in his apartment chopping up lines of cocaine from a baggie, and then washing the drips from his throat with alcohol of many flavors and colors.

His swimming head of regret was interrupted when he came upon a bastion of hope, a sign for Elizabeth's street, the word **CRAVEN** in white against the green metal of the sign.

He stopped for a moment, and was suddenly Robin Hood when he finally touched down upon England, kissing the soft earth before him with joy in his heart.

Jason was a sailor who had finally reached the land his crew had

mapped out for months, and he was going to be the hero he always wanted to be to his child after his many mistakes in his marriage, as well as life.

The image of holding his son tight was so much to bare that he stopped dead in his tracks. The moment was crushed when John nudged him hard in the back with the handle of his sword, he barked, "What are you waiting on? Let's hustle."

Jason peered at John's face after he had craned his head and darted his eyes over his shoulder, his growing hatred for the man he had an instant kinship with was growing, and enveloping everything that was decent in him.

He was beginning to picture smashing the middle aged man's face into oblivion. The crew hit the last street of their instant journey, and the streets were no different from the rest they had travelled.

They were littered with broken metal, and hulks of what used to be vehicles were planted in different areas around them. Their faces had a look of hopelessness, and there were parts laid about.

Michael stepped next to Russell, and the man was still dragging an

unconscious Will behind him, slowly. The sound of the toes of his boots scraped along as Russell trolled on, even breaking a slight sweat from the weight of the body, but he never complained about his weight.

The most fearful of the group surveyed the damage around them as they walked, and the rest of the men halted when Jason witnessed three women ahead of them.

Two of the women, one tall and blonde and the other medium sized with short hair, were lurching around as if they were waiting for a victim. They chanted uncontrollably as the third female, seemed to be hunched over someone, stabbing wildly.

There was nothing but silence from the body, and no one knew if the man who appeared to have darker hair, was dead or alive.

Michael swallowed hard and began to scratch his head, the fear was already evident in his dry eyes, "Hey guys...there is only three. You know, don't you think it strange that all of the women in this entire city are dwindling in their ranks?"

His sea of questions continued, "And where are all of the men in this giant fucking city? You cannot believe we are the only ones alive, do you?"

John was prepared to fight, sword at the ready, "Nah, they were just smart and left on the first thing smokin' before it all went down."

Michael was about to ask more questions but John had cut him off immediately. You are so full of questions, but I have a question I need answered myself."

He wiped a bead of sweat from his nose and turned around to face him, "When we get out of this shithole, we have no idea how far this curse goes. So I need to know, will you fight alongside us? Will you be a complete part of our little team here?"

Michael stepped back; a look of puzzlement was on his face as he replied, "Wait...what?"

John lurched forward getting closer to the young man's face, "I mean, it's time for you to finally go to work...grab your shit."

The timid young man could not speak, and John gripped him by his shirt pulling him forward. "I said...get your knife at the ready! You are going to help me kill these lovelies over there, let's go."

Jason who was still in front had noticed the two women flailing around had spotted them. He placed his hands on his cleaver, dried blood on the hilt, ready to take on the threat until John limped in front of his advance, "Oh no! I don't need you trying to take me out when I'm not looking, witch lover! Russ, make sure our man here stays put."

John began to tread forward, his stride hard as Michael followed behind him, his hand holding the knife was shaking violently.

The middle aged security guard raised his sword as Michael clenched his jaw until it hurt, tears welling in his eyes.

The two women seemed to be waiting for them to approach. Their milky white eyes fixated on their every move, saliva dripping from their lips as they hissed their sentence like cobras, "Piiiiigs...piiiigs....kill the pigs!"

Michael felt as if he was about to urinate all over the front of himself, when John held the sword at his chest, "You know what honey, you say the sexiest things!"

He swung the sword toward the average looking woman, but she was quick and jumped backward before the blade cut touched her.

The woman had a large piece of glass in her cut and bleeding hand. She swung the shard catching John's arm, causing him to wince, but hold steady as she began hissing again, "Piiiig...piiiig...for the Mother....for the Mother."

Michael finally had gained enough nerve to rush his target, he swung his knife wildly, and the woman slashed his left cheek with her fingernails causing him to stumble backward onto the concrete. He shook the pain as John fought next to him, still watching his every move.

Michael began to panic when the woman kicked him hard dropping him to the sidewalk, where he stumbled and tripped on the curb.

The tall woman slashed at him again and again, and the young man who knew nothing about combat but the occasional video game began to panic, cursing loudly. "Oh shit! John, please help me, John!"

John looked on at the now hyperventilating boy, his attacker already on the ground, her arm was half hanging from the bone, and was shooting blood in spurts.

Her throat was cut, a big gaping hole revealing the arteries and sinew inside.

Michael was on the sidewalk once again kicking wildly to fight off the slashing beast in front of him, and John began to smile, not because he was happy, but because the thought of his son entered his mind.

He thought of how his son would have fought no matter what the cost, just as he had tried to before his death.

CHAPTER FIFTEEN

Death of a Son, Murder of the Soul
The Death of Dean Roberson
September 23, 2014
Morning, 7:20 A.M.

John and his son were in the middle of a street, their car bashed as they quickly ran out of the open doors. Dean threw his school bag on the ground, gripped two sharp pencils and cupped them hard in his fist. John lunged for a glass beer bottle on the street and smashed it against one of the city's metal trashcans, breaking the bottle in half.

He looked at his son who had sucked back tears as he spoke to him, both hands on each side of his face. "We are going to fight. Together, we will be okay...you will be okay!"

Dean looked into his eyes, "Dad, what is going on here? What is this?"

John let go of his son, and began watching the movements of the women advancing them, his jaw clenched. "We will get out this, just stick by me...I will not let anything hurt you."

Three women advanced, and John held the only thing he had to defend himself at the ready, his son stood right by him and the three snarling women rushed the two simultaneously.

John kicked one of the women, a short black woman hard, and his son caught a dark haired woman in the eye with one of the pencils. She did not make a sound as she rushed toward him again.

His father gripped his son by the shoulder and they started to run. He stopped hard when he saw twenty women coming directly for their location, some of them breaking off and brutally attacking other men in their path.

John grabbed his son's hand but as he turned it was the same: a group of women all with different weapons, ten or more headed right for them.

Before the Robertsons had hit the fire hydrant folding the front of the car, John had tried to reach for the glove compartment to get at the licensed gun he sometimes held in a holster on the job, but the window was shattered.

Two women tried hard to get to the man and his son, cutting the flesh on their arms and hands as they reached into the car, forcing them to slide out of the passenger side door, fists at the ready.

John needed to get to his side arm, it was the only way to escape.

He did not take his eyes off of the large group, separating but still approaching as he spoke to his frightened but ready son. "Listen, I want you to stick by me. We are going to the car now, I need to get my gun. Stay by my back."

The family ran to the car, and as John reached the driver side door, he punched a woman hard and pushed her out of the way, Dean stood behind him and tried very hard to hold the groups off with kicks and punches. His father had taught him how to fight earlier on in his life, and to fend off the potential pitfalls of an urban public school system.

John opened the door to the car and slid onto the seat, when all of a sudden he heard a scream, the scream of his only son which had now enveloped his ear drums.

He looked up to see him being thrown to the ground, a woman who appeared to be in her sixties had a fire ax over her head, and her foot was placed on his son's back.

John screamed out, and slid around to the compartment, which was jammed after the accident.

He pounded the lid hard with his fist, but heard the sound that made his heart shatter: the sound of an ax hitting concrete.

John's world stopped, and he tried to break out of the driver side door when all of a sudden it was surrounded on the one side.

He held back tears as he opened the passenger side door, hitting a Latino woman in the chest causing her body to double over and fall to the ground.

John kicked her hard on the top of the head, and ran toward a fence that was free from this new enemy.

As he climbed, he looked beyond the women now in a huge mass, and saw the lifeless body of his son whose head was being held in the hands of the senior who had killed him so violently.

John screamed until blood was in his throat, and climbed the other side of the fence.

He was lost as he continued to run, his heart feeling as if it were going to explode from his adrenaline, as well as emotional shock.

In the reality once again surrounding John's eyes, Michael still fumbled with the woman shouting for his assistance to aid him in his fight.

With pain in his head from the memory, John planted his foot hard onto the woman's chest below him, still snarling and snapping, and slammed the blade of the sword into her forehead.

Michael stabbed the oncoming female with the large kitchen knife but she still came at him. John sighed, "Jesus Christ, kid", and jumped into action.

The young man screamed when the woman spit and snarled, his blade now protruding from her chest.

He sealed his eyes when suddenly her onslaught stopped.

Michael opened his eyes slowly to see that her head had been severed, sliced clean from her body.

He stood slowly, cuts on his face and arms, and bent down to pull his knife from the still woman.

As soon as he stopped paying attention to John, he kicked Michael in the side of the head, and he fell over the body on the street before him.

John roared, threw his sword to the ground, and jumped on Michael's chest, his hard movement had almost knocked the wind from him.

Jason and Russell watched from a distance as the young boy's head was slammed against the street over and over. John yelled, "You little son of a bitch, what the fuck was that display? I wanted to treat you like my son, but you aren't my son. You're a coward...and he was not a fucking chicken shit coward like you!"

Russell sighed and lightly dropped Will to the concrete. He ran toward the beating as he told Jason to stay put.

As the group was preoccupied, Jason knelt down by Will. His body looked as if it had beaten with baseball bats, and his right arm was broken as well.

His face was battered to the point that he was almost unrecognizable, and his breathing was raspy. Jason looked into Will's good eye, his pupil still dilated.

Will tried to speak, his words were garbled.

Jason placed his ear over his mouth, blood dribbled slowly down his cheek as he tried to speak again.

He held his ear closer. The words although broken finally made sense, "I am...I am so sorry. I was...I was...tricked...just like you."

Jason began to tear as Will continued, his words still separated, "I know...I know...how to stop her."

Jason looked confused, and he tried very hard to hear what his beaten friend had to say. He could barely make out his speech, but it sounded like some type of spell.

Jason had already been deceived by Will's witchcraft, but he felt like he had no other choice, and he attempted to remember the words Will was now repeating in his ear. Jason looked at him, his chest was heaving slightly. "I do not understand...what the hell do you want me to do?"

Will still spoke in a broken, raspy tone, "You...you must...say them, to...to bring back...your love...you must...you must bring back hers."

Jason nodded his head, not certain what Will was speaking of, but he did not have time to think too hard after he was kicked in the side by Russell as he attempted to stand.

John laughed slightly and began to taunt Jason, who was now on the side of Will. "Well, I guess you had a nice conversation over here."

He limped closer to Jason who was now upright, but still sitting, "What did your boyfriend say?"

Jason tried to stand as the stained blade of John's sword was under his throat, his voice grew menacing, "You can tell all of us...or I can just cut your fucking head from your useless body."

Jason stood up slowly, coughing before he answered, "All he told me was he's sorry. He is sorry, and he means that for everyone."

John looked down at Will's broken form, "Is that so? Not as sorry as you're going to be. Russ, hate to do it, but please pick him up."

Jason, still in pain, looked at Michael; he had cuts on the back of his Head, and his face was red and covered in tears. He stared back at Jason, with a look of helplessness.

Russell picked up Will from the sidewalk and John looked at Jason, "Okay, so where is this place?"

Without saying anything, Jason pointed to a building in the distance on the left of the street before them.

He could feel his heart beat hard and fast, it was evident that he was now a prisoner of some sort, unable to escape the clutches of John and his right hand, Russell. But soon he would be holding his son, and then he would make his move.

As the men proceeded to approach Elizabeth's building, Scott Cain's already beaten car laid on its side as he fired shots into the massive army of women behind him, as they seemed to march behind what appeared to be his former sister-in-law.

The pain in his sides was intense as he attempted to run from the group and hopefully toward his brother.

The woman in the nightgown chuckled as her army followed suit. She hissed, "Run as hard you can. For the end of your entire bloodline is at hand. It's only a matter of time now!"

Suddenly, Elizabeth stopped and the group stopped behind her, still hissing and chanting in unison.

In her mind, she witnessed Jason was close to his son's location.

She screamed, and formed into the fireball which now shot toward Scott causing him to scream, but it did not burn as it seemed to go through him.

He felt the icy intent of the woman, and her voice as it enveloped his mind. "Come to him! Come to be with your kin...come to die!"

Scott ducked into an alley on the left of him, as the army of women continued to walk in formation toward their destination. Sara was the supernatural magnet drawing them all toward the street Elizabeth and her son resided. She was drawing them to the final confrontation, as well as the fates of the players in her game.

Sara Rinehart was truly a wicked woman, basking on the playground of her now wicked world.

TO BE CONCLUDED IN THE EPIC
CONCLUSION
OF

"THE BINDING"
BOOK THREE

COMING IN EARLY 2015

ABOUT THE AUTHOR

Rob has been in the horror industry for six years. He began as a columnist for Horrornews.net, and began acquiring his own celebrity interviews and attempting to build a name, as well as a following. From there he started a horror podcast with best friend Amy Lynes, which quickly became a worldwide heard radio show. In his five years, Rob has written a screenplay for "The Binding" which was shopped throughout the entertainment industry with Executive Producer Sandra Araya, wife of SLAYER's Tom Araya in tow, and has written and directed two short horror films. He continues to show his love and entertain horror fans throughout the world, and was former Lead Genre Columnist/Interviewer with first monthly column for websites Metal Onslaught Magazine and Tom Holland's Terrortime. He currently resides in Georgia with his sinister and lovely half, Melody, and his first son, Gabriel Vincent DiLauro, whose middle name is in honor of the legendary horror actor, Vincent Price. He is the President of Fear Front Publishing, is a staff member for Rue Morgue Magazine and Horror Freak News, and is slated to write an autobiography with one of the most important female icons in the genre.

THE BINDING BOOK THREE: LOVE AND DEATH

ROB DiLAURO

MESSAGE FROM THE AUTHOR

Here we are, the end of the road. I cannot believe that after thirteen years of having these characters in my head and countless attempts to get the story to the masses with a few slips and fails here and there, I have finally closed this chapter in my imagination. And not only did I get the chance to complete the story, I actually had the chance to show horror fans that this is a story that can satisfy. It is not your typical slasher, it is horror on a greater scale, and I am so honored and taken aback by the love and attention you have all given this tale. I feel very fortunate and relieved. The saga of Sara Rinehart took three books to delve into, but here we are at the conclusion, and I really hope that you all enjoy it. I hope that you feel I gave the story the ending that it deserves, and have given the characters that I truly love so much their due, which I feel in my heart I have. The only way to find out is to open up the book and read on, and know that you all have me under your spell. I love you all, and thank you so very much for all of the continued love and support in my career and life. What's next for "The Binding"? Well, if all goes right with the balance, I could hopefully get a feature film off of the ground when it comes to the material you have in your possession, but only time will tell. May the "Mother" give me strength in that journey.

Enjoy the conclusion of "The Binding", and may the legacy of Sara always reign somewhere on your shelves.

Blessed Be,
Rob DiLauro

Love and death are two uninvited guests, when they will come no one knows but both do the same work, one takes heart and the other takes its beats

-Nishan Panwar

Love and death are the two great hinges on which all human sympathies turn

-B.R. Hayden

Love is stronger than death even though it cannot stop death from happening. But no matter how hard death tries it cannot separate people from love. It cannot take away our memories either. In the end, love is stronger than death

-William Penn

The best and most beautiful things in the world cannot be seen, not touched, but are felt in the heart

-Helen Keller

CHAPTER ONE
Breaking Point

After many grueling and blood-soaked hours enduring the violence of the city streets, Jason and his disturbed and exhausted crew had reached the street that Elizabeth and their son Matthew had relocated to sometime after their divorce.

During the preceding years before, Elizabeth had sold their beautiful suburban home and had moved back to the city where her status at Lionheart Press continued to grow. She was working many long hours but was always able to provide for her one and only child. She did not keep the identity of her location a secret from her ex-husband because she knew that a restraining order on Jason was never a necessity; she knew in her heart of hearts that he would do the right thing and stay away.

On a few occasions, Jason would run into Elizabeth and his young son, but he would never approach them. He would watch from afar as Elizabeth smiled as she held Matthew's hand, looking beautiful as she seemed to glide on air, enjoying every moment of her life without him. Elizabeth was happy and content, and he knew that she was always the strong one of the faded relationship, and there was nothing left of him in her thoughts. He was nothing but a bad dream.

As Jason stood in front of Elizabeth's apartment building, it looked ominous in its beauty within the chaos and gore surrounding his group.

The complex was large and it had been strictly for business professionals. It had four steps from the street leading to a walkway in which another pair of steps awaited to reach the front door. The windows of the structure were large and were adorned with beautiful silk curtains, and it was evident that the building owner had spared no expense to continuously keep the building pristine and up to code.

Jason swallowed hard as he witnessed the bodies splayed out on the small lawn, their insides spilling to their sides. The once breathtaking stained windows on the first floor were cracked, and some were slightly shattered, and even as he knew he was about to enter another house of horror, Jason felt in his heart that this building could be the gateway to heaven, leading him to his prize: his estranged son.

Russell was still behind Jason, carrying a beaten Will Thompson who was muttering words that could not be deciphered. As Jason looked to his left, he rested his eyes on John Robertson, saying nothing as he turned to look at the women still around their location.

Jason took a quick glance behind him, trying to utilize his peripheral vision to look back at Will, but Russell quickly caught his gaze causing him to turn his head quickly.

John raised his son's collectible sword turned true weapon when he witnessed two possessed females. Blood slightly coated their clothes, and the lighter-skinned female had blood on her lips and face as if she had dined on something messy.

He quickly turned to the young college student they had discovered in his wrecked car, and instantly made a snide remark, "Hey, you want a second crack at becoming a man?"

John chortled slightly until Michael said something under his breath that hit the older man's ears instantly, "Fuck you." The lost and slowly eroding father rubbed his left hand over his shaved head in frustration and turned to face the youthful but nervous grin of the young man. His face was serious.

"You know, if I didn't feel like I needed you with us, I would cut your jugular and toss you to these
slags."

Michael swallowed hard as John spoke again glaring coldly, "Learn some fucking respect." Russell snickered as Michael became quiet and looked down at the street.

As the women moved forward and were about to lunge for the wounded, self-appointed leader of the group, John limped forward and made the first move. The woman started to hiss. One of the females slashed at John with a kitchen knife. Her slice missed his arm. Although in slight pain, he suddenly thrust his blade, and slashed the possessed, snarling female in her abdomen. She didn't make a sound as a warm pool formed where the blade made its cut.

The young female stared at John with dead, milky eyes and he heard one word escape her lips like air leaving a flat tire, "Piiiiiiig."

As fast as he could, John reached for her long, mud-colored hair and spun his body around to her back, wrapping his thick forearm around her throat. Slightly growling, John turned the female, who was snapping like a trapped animal, toward his small team and began to shout as his eyes focused on each member, the erosion of his mind evident, "It's time! Time to teach these ladies that we cannot be fucked with!"

His grip became tighter as he continued to further lose his mind in front of the men, and although the woman resembled nothing but a monster, Jason felt a twinge in his stomach while he watched John humiliate the wild creature. The woman had once been a person with a life, a job, and possibly a family only mere days before.

Jason and the rest of the group continued to look on as John violently threw the young woman to the ground, and even as her head slightly bounced on the concrete, she continued to growl and snarl.

As John was about to attack the woman below him, the older woman of the duo ran forward. John swung his long blade with perfect accuracy. Red blood shot across his face as the massive cut in her neck spurted in his direction, and he swung again. Only this time, the power of his thrust knocked her head clean from her shoulders.

Jason now watched the man he met in his apartment building unravel even more, as John stood over his prey still lying on the ground. She attempted to stand but he kicked her hard in the chest, his voice nothing but commanding as he pointed in her direction, "You, stay down, bitch."

The possessed female attempted to slash wildly at his leg until John kicked her in the face with the toe of his boot and clamped his foot on her wrist. The weight of his body made bones snap, and he once again spoke coldly as he looked into her vacant eyes, "When are you going to learn, that you are inferior to us?"

John twisted his foot which was still on her wrist again as he continued, "No matter what you do… How powerful you become… We will always remain the winners because, quite simply, men have always been the alphas, and women are plain shit."

After his comment, John raised his sword over the woman's face and brought it down hard. Her cranium split, the sound of bone and soft flesh broke apart. Jason and Michael both felt sick churning in their stomach, and had to hold back.

The group looked on as John continued to bring the blade of the sword down repeatedly, creating chunks of meat and blood. He screamed into the air as the woman's head looked more disgusting with every hit.

. After his barrage, he dropped the blade once belonging to his son on the street, and with his back heaving, turned to face the group once again. John spoke loud, as if he wanted the world to hear his inner anguish, "You...killed my boy! You took the only person I ever loved... And you are all going to pay!"

The older, beaten father continued his rant. Jason stepped forward and, with no caution, placed a comforting hand on John's shoulder. With a growl, the man who Jason had instantly trusted became his enemy once more. As quick as the former writer tried to make peace with the man who had him in a hostage situation, John returned the favor by hitting Jason's right cheek with a closed fist.

Jason's head went back and his mind reeled as he quickly looked upon the once kind soul who was seething as if he had now completely lost his grip on sanity. John slightly gritted his teeth as he spoke,

"Listen, and listen real good. If you dare touch me again... I will split your fucking head where you stand. Do we understand each other?" His eyes seemed to blaze as Jason nodded his head in agreement, completely amazed at how quickly this new world had broken John Robertson.

John gripped a now wincing Jason by the shirt collar and shoved him forward.

"Now...MOVE!" he commanded. "Let's go get your kid and those damn keys!"

Jason looked back at John who spoke again, "You better pray that we can get out of here... Or I may just lose my kind streak and kill the both of you."

Jason scowled as the wounded man carrying his filthy weapon waved the rest of the group forward. The small group stopped at the steps of Elizabeth's building. The building was silent and resembled a combat zone with bodies strewn about the walkway, their innards spilling down into bloody pools staining the concrete of the stairwell.

Jason finally focused, and he began to think of a plan to escape the situation with the son he had not looked upon since he was an infant.

He shot a quick glance at Will who looked at his face with one open eye, and the garbled words he whispered in Jason's ear echoed in the estranged father's mind.

.

CHAPTER TWO
Hell is Like Home

In the darkness of the unknown surrounding her, Susan sat silently by the side of her mother, Helen.

They both rested on the unseen floor of the plane which had become their prison. Slight candlelight revealed their faces in the black abyss, as screams of pain circled around them, causing the hairs on the back of their necks to stand at attention, and their bodies to shiver.

Susan remained silent and began to ponder all of the wrongs she had done. Her unholy union with pure evil, and her final interaction with Will, the pain she had caused him and the pawn he had become in the twisted game of the witch who had possessed her for so many years.

She sniffled as tears finally fell from her eyes.

Susan wiped the wetness from her face and began to speak, her voice shaken, "We

deserve this… You and I deserve all of this." Helen looked down at the ground below her, and sighed as she replied, "The fault is mine, and mine alone. I brought that woman back to life…I'm meant to be cursed, even in death."

Helen lifted her head and looked at her daughter who was still shaken and continued, her voice calm,

"Susan, you did exactly what you had to do, nothing more."

Her daughter's eyes began to focus as her mother's sudden confession hit her ears, "I could have done the right thing… I could have left your father. I did not have to exact revenge on him." Susan felt more tears and wiped them back as her mother's words echoed in the blackness as the candle flame bathed her face. "Hurting your father seemed like the solution, and I felt like I needed her… Her power. I was so wrong, my girl. I have been wrong… I have wronged you my entire life."

The silver-haired woman looked downward again as her daughter continued to look upon

her. Her lip curled as Helen spoke with sheer honesty and pure apology, "Susan, I will never forgive myself."

Tears welled in her blue eyes as Susan took a deep breath and spoke coldly. "I also took up life with a horrible man, and I did help bring this horror upon the world in my selfishness and greed."

She slightly sucked her teeth, and took a deep breath as she continued, "I guess, we are both purely evil."

Susan began to stand and looked down at her mother who was still sitting, "I helped bring this bitch back... And we are both at fault for bringing on this destruction. We were fueled by greed, mother!"

She brushed a hand through her yellow hair and sighed deeply, "And if all of the horrible shit we participated in was not bad enough... We used our own children."

Helen's head quickly shot upward to look at her daughter's cold stare which looked slightly menacing in the flicker of the light. She felt her soul being torn to shreds as Susan's voice grew louder, "You thought you were helping me... But you used me. I was not even raised by you, I was raised by some horrifying puppet that was being controlled... Which just sounds fucking ridiculous coming from my own mouth!"

Helen quickly stood and stepped in front of Susan who was now vibrating. She tried to console her and spoke in a soothing tone, "You are absolutely right about me... About everything. I am a disgraceful woman, a disgrace to my family and to the women in our bloodline who once swore to protect the world from such demons." She gingerly placed her hand on Susan's shoulders as her eyes started to feel wet. "You are not at fault for anything. You did what you had to do... What you were forced to do."

Susan lifted her head and looked directly into her mother's eyes as she continued to reassure her. "You're a good woman, and an even greater mother! You only did what you had to do to save your family... To save your child. Please do not ever forget that."

Susan was silent and her body quaked, when suddenly she yelled in her mother's tearful face, "You would not know anything about being a good woman... Get the fuck away from me!"

The young Rogers placed her hands on her mother's chest, attempting to shove her. She screamed as she witnessed the pain Samuel had inflicted on the night she was ill as a child, the images of her father's violence shot into her mind, and her body could feel every blow, and the inevitable sensation of being violated.

Helen remained still as her daughter witnessed everything her father had inflicted on Helen as her younger self lay on the carpet wailing. She quickly pulled her hands away, and her small frame felt like it had been hit with electricity, her mind feeling as if she had just awoken from a nightmare.

Helen stepped forward and spoke, "I will never forgive myself for what I have done... But you and I have lived through the same pain... We are one and the same, you and I." Susan quickly snapped back at Helen,

"You forced me to live that life... You and that monster! That thing raised me, and I granted her the power to raise my own son! We belong here, mother... We are damned!"

With that, Susan turned and began to run into the darkness as her mother cried out for her.

She ran as if she would eventually find a way out of the hell she was in. Her mother's pleas were drowned out within the cries of the souls of Sara's victims. Their voices slithered in Susan's ears as her feet began to feel the quicksand, the sticky feeling underneath, "You did this... You killed us all."

Susan stopped and the voices continued to taunt her already fragile psyche. "Save us... Please... Save us." She swallowed hard and cried out when she finally stopped running into nowhere, "I don't know how to save you... Leave me alone! Please!"

Feeling tormented, she fell to the ground beneath her, and as her hands touched the

surface she grew sick from the texture. Susan quickly shot up as another lost soul spoke, the voice becoming an echo, "Patience."

A confused look crossed her face, but her expression could not be seen in the

pitch dark of the cavern. The voices began to say the word in unison, "Patience."

Susan grew annoyed and screamed out as if she was losing her mind. "What do you mean, patience for what?"

She grew even angrier as the voices continued to haunt her, "Answer me… Goddamn you!" The voices grew silent and a shiver shot through her spine. She was alone in the midnight blackness, possibly lost forever.

As she stood silent, her breath heavy, the unknown room around her grew cold and Susan felt as if there was something near her, something very close.

Her body sensed danger, and she quickly turned and screamed when the room Came

into view by a sudden, eerie illumination; the walls were adorned with screaming human faces. Susan looked down and grew sick when she realized the floors were a hellish carpet of human parts, and as she lifted her head, she felt as if her spirit had suddenly left her body as her saucer-like eyes focused on the leering face of her dead husband.

The corpse of Bill Thompson stepped forward. He looked monstrous, the meat of his bottom lip was missing along with his anatomy as his nude form stood in front of her.

His body was covered in bloody puncture wounds which were painted in dry, sticky blood. He spoke, his words hellish to his former wife's ears as they became garbled due to the loss of half of his face,

"Welcome to your hell, you stupid cunt." Susan could not speak and spun around, turning her bare heel to run, but her body would not move.

The grotesque, cold hands of her terrible past gripped her by the face and pulled Susan closer as she cried out.

Suddenly, she was directly in front of her monstrous husband as he attempted to smile, ooze and blood dripping from his teeth as he spoke, "Reunited, my precious little wife… Together in the hell surrounding us."

Bill pulled Susan closer and his eyes appeared to grow black in shade as he continued, her body frozen from the sight of him, "I'm going to love ripping you apart… Over and over again."

He gripped Susan by the throat. She gasped for air as his grip grew tighter, his prey attempted to break free but his hold was solid, until suddenly she lifted her hand and jammed her fingers in a huge gash in Bill's head. He instantly cried out and released his hold.

Susan fell to the soft, fleshy ground and Bill towered over her. Before he could attack her again, he began to scream and fell to his knees. His victim's eyes grew wide when she witnessed her savior: her mother.

Susan was finally able to stand, and Helen was slapped hard by Bill who quickly rose to his cadaverous feet and gripped the silver-haired woman by her own throat with both of his massive hands. Her daughter cried out and rushed to rescue her once abusive mother when Susan's sweat-covered hair was pulled hard from behind.

Unable to see her attacker, she screamed as her body brushed up against something sticky and slimy. The smell that hit her nostrils was horrid. Her back was still turned as a gravelly voice began to speak,

"How you've grown, sugar."

As her mother was still being attacked, Susan reluctantly turned around. Her lips quivered as she faintly recognized the skinless, rotted face from the photographs throughout the house, and her stomach began to churn as she realized she stood in front of the decaying body of her father, Samuel.

Susan's voice quaked as one single word spilled from her lips, "Daddy?"

The corpse which was once her father, a man who she had never met in life, smiled slightly, and as she felt herself welling up, Samuel slapped her hard across the face and grabbed her by her slick hair once again, his skin sloughing off and becoming part of the putrid floor as he used all of his strength.

He eyed his daughter up and down, his pupils lifeless. Suddenly, with no effort at all, his daughter pulled back to break his grip causing his hand to snap off of the bone, and Susan fell backwards onto the stinking earth below. As she looked up, her father towered over her, his deathly stink filling her nostrils as he spoke again, "I'm going to going to give you and your mother the tenderness you deserve. It's going to be so sweet."

Samuel bent down to grab Susan again, the muscles in his knees quivering and slipping away from the bone when suddenly the long-deceased father was blown back by an unseen force and fell to his knees, the sound of the ligaments resembling the snapping of small twigs.

Susan was completely still. She breathed heavily when she saw what appeared to be large vines wrapping around his throat and rotten torso, causing him to gurgle as they became tighter. Samuel spit bile over the front of his body, the ooze dribbling down his chin as he appeared to gasp for breath.

She quickly turned her head and became aware in seconds that her former husband was in the same grisly position, the vines appearing to sprout thorns which tore into his jugular, the thick greenery snaking around his form like a hungry reptile.

Helen quickly rushed to her daughter and held her tight as they both displayed nothing but fear in their eyes, as the evils from their similar pasts gasped, until suddenly with a quick action, the thick cords tore the men apart and the segments of their bodies flew in different directions.

Susan and her mother were silent and held onto each other as the voices in the cavern once again whispered the word from before, "Patience." The two women quickly turned their heads as the hellish room bathed in a much brighter ball of light, and a young girl in a dark dress stepped toward them. Her hair was crimson and her face slightly freckled around the nose and slender cheeks.

Susan swallowed hard as the stranger opened her mouth to speak, her voice displaying power even through her child-like features, "Rogers clan, please do not be afraid. I have come to take you from this hell." She reached out her hand to help them from the ground, and spoke again in a serious tone, the voice of a leader, "You have been summoned by the "Mother" to aid me in ending the evil of Sara Rinehart."

CHAPTER THREE
Friend or Foe

As Jason slowly walked toward the front door of Elizabeth's building, he felt his body grow tense and thoughts of his son suddenly entered his brain.

He began thinking of how awful he felt inside of his very soul the moment he had hurt Matthew, the rage that brewed inside him as he cried, driving away from the house he and his then wife had built together for the last time. Jason had hoped that after years of being away from his young son that he would find him safe and alive, and pictured the moment that he would hold him tight and look into his eyes as he revealed the truth about his identity.

Many thoughts had swirled endlessly, when all of a sudden he was shoved hard in the back by Russell's large hand, and the reality of the moment and life in a violent hell once again came into focus.

Russell and Jason reached the entrance, and Jason looked back at the man who loathed him. Russell glared back at him and slowly pulled what appeared to be a butcher knife from his belt loop. Jason followed suit and gripped the handle of the cleaver he had retrieved from his apartment, and slowly opened the door which was open halfway.

As he was about to step into the unknown, Russell shoved him once again, causing Jason to slightly grind his teeth.

The two sudden foes entered a large sit-in area with two fancy couches facing each other on either side of a large throw rug. A table made of glass sat in the center which held a fine vase of assorted and expensive flowers, Jason's eyes darted to the right and he looked upon what appeared to be a glass-encased kiosk which housed a small office for the on-duty security guard. The building was beautiful and was tailored for individuals with expensive tastes. It was protected every hour of the day, with two guards managing all floors in the evenings. But Jason and his large, appointed partner witnessed a different view of the room, the aftermath of another violent attack, with one of the couches flipped on its side and the center table was smashed, the expensive carpet was littered with the corpse of a man in a dress shirt, and as Russell stepped closer, it appeared that glass pieces from the smashed remnants of the table were used to slice the victim's throat. A massive puddle of blood had formed around the body intermingling with the flowers from the vase, a funeral fit for no man.

The carpet was stained red in spots and the kiosk glass was shattered, the body of the uniformed guard impaled on the large sheet which had turned into a guillotine for his insides. The skinny guard's head was smashed open to the skull as his sticky blood seemed to stain the wall where his torso dangled.

Jason's stomach felt uneasy. Russell snickered and began to speak, "Why do you think we continue to survive?" Jason clenched his jaw and replied, "Perhaps we are doomed to live in this hell for being a few of the biggest assholes on the planet." The built man quickly grew silent and began to laugh sarcastically before he pushed Jason again, "You can shut up now if you have any idea what's good for you, and point us in the direction of that kid of yours."

The intelligent writer thought hard about the information located in the many documents he had received from court during and after the court proceedings, when suddenly the numbers hit him like bricks, "He is on the fifth floor...the fifth!"

Russell craned his head to the left to peer at the elevator doors stained with dark red, opened halfway due to the opening being blocked by another brutally murdered corpse, the victim's legs sticking out of the shaft, the expensive dress shoes of the man touching the carpet.

He walked over to the elevator and knelt down to grab the feet of the body. As he pulled, it was revealed that the torso was cut off from the waist. Jason felt sick churn once again as the large black man tossed the legs onto the carpet and smiled snidely in his direction, a smirk on his face as he spoke, "Problem solved... So get your punk ass in here."

Jason entered the elevator and Russell clicked the button which read 5 with his thumb. The metal box began to whir as they headed upward. Russell pat Jason on the shoulder with one big hand as he spoke again, "I wouldn't look down if I were you." After the comment , he pointed to the floor and Jason was subconsciously compelled to look down at the other half of the body. He quickly shot his eyes forward, attempting to keep his composure as he allowed one word to escape his quivering lips, "Jesus." Russell peered at the side of Jason's face and answered with a sly tone, "I don't think Jesus is listening to anything we have to say, shithead. "

As the elevator finally stopped, the duo readied themselves as the door slowly slid open. Jason held his weapon in front of himself as he focused on what appeared to be a long, fancy hallway. The hallway was also destroyed by the chaos, certain apartment doors appeared to open, and just as he had witnessed in his own building, the walls and floors were caked in gore.

He swallowed hard and placed his foot off of the elevator first ,with Russell right behind him.

The hallway appeared as if it had sections, different apartment doors to the left and right of the central, carpeted area the two stood on. As Jason turned his head, he witnessed a plate on the wall which had the inscription FLOOR 5 501-525.

He began to think hard on the court letters that littered his kitchen table before the tense and grueling month of hearings, but the harder his mind worked, the less he moved , inciting Russell to quickly grow aggravated and shove him with force as he barked, "Hey, quit daydreaming. Which fucking door is it?"

The number finally hit the writer's brain like a flash, and he yelled the information out loud, "Five eighteen! She's…in five eighteen."

Jason quickly spun around to face Russell who looked him directly in the eye and spoke coldly, "You better be sure."

With those words, he shoved Jason again, and his large hand was surprisingly deflected. Jason grit his teeth hard as he spoke, "I have been putting up with your shit this entire time for something I had nothing to do with."

The large man clenched his jaw as the shorter and smaller-framed Jason continued, "I know that you have an issue with me, but I did not kill your young cousin, and I'm sorry for your loss." Jason stepped closer. A fire seemed to rage in his stare, "I'm through dealing with your taunts and machismo bullshit… It ends now."

Russell snickered and held in his anger as Jason slowly turned his head to face the hallway

and addressed the situation, "As I said, the door we are looking for is five eighteen. We will retrieve my son… You can get your keys, and hopefully we can part our separate ways."

Jason moved forward, past the apartment doors as their numbers climbed. Russell spoke as he walked to the right of him, "About what you said, about us parting our separate ways. You know John will never let that happen, you're *his* bitch now."

He laughed as Jason suddenly stopped dead in his tracks by an apartment door reading 508, after he heard a strange noise coming from the left corridor. The two men lifted their weapons as hissing switched to chanting. Russell and Jason held fast as two women stepped from the left into the hallway, staring them down with cold, dead eyes. The women hissed before they ran toward them.

Russell moved one of his feet forward, holding the knife tight in his fist as he knelt down to grip what appeared to be a thick screwdriver from the side of his ankle, and tucked in his sock. The woman to the right reached the pair first, and slashed at Jason wildly causing him to swing the cleaver forward, missing her with his attack when Russell's strength pushed his body hard against the door to his left, quickly dropping his stunned body to the floor.

After pushing Jason, Russell moved forward. His movements were quick as the dark-haired female attacked again, her slice missing him by an inch . He quickly brought the blade of his knife forward, instantly connecting with her throat. Blood spilled but she did not fall, nor did sounds of pain escape her lips.

Her dark brow furrowed as she attacked again, causing Russell to swing again, this time

reaching the skin of her face . With full force, he slammed the tip of the large screwdriver into the top of her skull with his other, closed fist, causing her to drop instantly.

The second woman who was a few inches shorter, and had olive-colored skin, attacked with speed in her step, although the powerhouse of a human being made quick work of her. He stabbed her deep in the chest, pulling the blade and sliding it deep into her temple with ease. The shorter woman fell and red dribbled onto the carpet below her.

Jason slowly rose to his feet as Russell was catching his breath. He looked at his attacker's

heaving back with large eyes. As Russell knelt down to pull the thick screwdriver from the dead woman's skull, he turned to Jason and smiled slightly, "You got in the way... Total accident."

Jason clenched his jaw again as the black man rose to his feet, and although furious, he tried to stay on the path of the mission. The two finally reached the end of the hall where they saw another gold-plated sign reading 513-518. Jason rubbed the back of his head and spoke without looking at Russell,

"We're close now."

He nodded and they both walked forward into the same grim scene of bloody flooring. As they stepped lightly on the long white carpet, Jason's heart felt like it had dropped as they finally reached the door reading 518. He had reached his son after everything he had been through, but felt defeated when he noticed the front door was battered and slightly open.

The excited father quickly rushed in. His heart felt tight as his quivering pupils glanced around the living room, which was in a complete state of disarray. Elizabeth's expensive table was flipped, pieces of china were smashed and on the carpet. The room looked as if it had been raided but Jason knew what had really occurred.

He swallowed hard and his head began to spin as he surveyed the room. Russell rummaged through certain areas, scrambling to find Elizabeth's car keys.

As he dumped her possessions onto the floor, Jason paced around the nice-sized living area and checked each door. He stepped into the kitchen and noticed one of the drawers was wide open. As

he entered the hallway once again, he pushed open another white door and saw that it belonged to his ex-wife. The room itself was clean except for an unmade bed, the covers flopped over, and a scene that made Jason feel ill—a photograph of his wedding ripped and strewn around. Pieces of glass, and flecks of blood decorated the lightly colored carpet.

He felt dizzy and rushed back into the hallway. After a few seconds, he gained his composure and checked the other doors until he stopped at one that was locked when he tried the knob. Jason knocked hard and called his son's name, "Hey, Matthew… It's your mother's friend. I came for you as I promised." He felt his eyes begin to well, as he knocked again and received no answer, his voice grew louder, "Matthew…please… Open the door, son."

Russell stopped his search and looked over at his enraged enemy as he began kicking the wood of the door until it splintered and flew wide open. Jason's jaw dropped slightly as he peered into the room of his son; the bed was unmade, and aside from a few toys on the carpet, the room itself was untouched and revealed no signs of a struggle. He walked over to a closet door and dropped to his knees when he realized that his young son was nowhere inside the room. He spoke to himself, "Where the hell are you, Matt? Where the fuck are you?"

Jason raised his hands to his face to wipe tears and then slowly stood, his knees buckling underneath him. He exited the room, holding his head downward as he once again entered the hallway. He finally reached Russell, who was standing by the front door, swinging a thick key ring around his finger as he spoke, "I found what we were looking for, but apparently, you didn't."

The now enraged father broke from his emotional pain and snapped back, "What is wrong with you? Don't you have the ability to show any compassion… My son is missing!"

Russell sniffed and stepped forward. Venom dripped from his words as he spoke. "Well, this is a matter of eye for an eye, wouldn't you say?"

Jason looked puzzled as the man continued, "I'm supposed to feel sorry for you after losing a family member myself, because I chose to help you?"

Jason snapped again, "That's right, you CHOSE to help me! Look, I feel really bad about what happened, but in situations like these…there are casualties. We are all victims in this new environment, and even if I have the possible solution, none of you will listen to anything that may… Fix all of this shit!"

Russell walked toward Jason slowly. "Did you really think that you were going to leave this place?"

His words caused Jason to step back as the man's massive chest stopped in front of him. Jason gulped and stared up at the giant. "What the hell are you saying?"

Jason continued to lurch backward, and Russell cracked his knuckles.

"What are you going to do, kill me?" Jason asked, his voice laced with sarcasm. " We need the entire group to survive. John would not condone this action."

Russell laughed as he replied. "John? What do you think I am, the old man's house boy? I listen to and follow his every word?" He sneered as he continued, "I am my own man. I follow no one but myself... And you are not leaving this building."

After hearing his sudden death sentence, Jason took a deep breath and tried to run from his impending beating, but Russell grabbed him by the back of his collar and threw him to the carpet. Jason pleaded as Russell towered over him. He pulled the bloody knife from his belt, and knelt down prepared to stab the smaller father in the chest.

Jason kicked him hard in the left knee, and Russell dropped backward as the now squirrely estranged father quickly shot up to his feet, taking the cleaver from his loop and holding it in front of him. His brow was sweating as he spoke, "It does not have to be this way! I know you don't care for me, but we're better off together. It's better for the group, and you know this!"

Russell stood slowly, wincing as he looked Jason in the eyes. "I do know a few things, you're right. I know that we're in this shit because of you... And that's all I need to know!" He lunged toward his weaker opponent and slammed his first hard into his cheek, causing Jason's already buzzing head to snap back. With nothing but reflex, he brought the cleaver down into the meat of Russell's arm. He screamed and tore the blade out, tossing it to the carpet.

Russell held onto his now gushing wound and slowed his attack due to his pain, as Jason tried to reach out again, "It doesn't have to be this way, think this through."

Russell grinned, "This is your last day on this maddened planet... This is happening, motherfucker."

Jason tried hard to hold his ground as Russell tackled him hard and dropped him to the carpet, placing his large hands on his throat.

As the air started to leave him, Jason pinpointed the open wound in Russell's shoulder, and with all of his available strength, he reached for his own knife on his belt as his vision slowly faded. His hand finally reached the kitchen tool and as Russell was occupied with rage, the once timid man used all of his force to push his body upward. He stuck the blade deep in Russell's chest cavity.

The giant's grip left Jason's throat and he was able to regain his breath as he struggled to stand on his wobbly legs in slow motion. Jason turned the tables on Russell who was in shock, and after all of the pushing and ridicule, Jason had finally stood up for himself and fought for his own life.

He looked down at Russell with contempt as he spoke, "I didn't want this! Even if you don't believe me... I didn't want any of this!"

Russell glanced at Jason as his mouth began to gurgle blood bubbles, "Fuck you... Let's finish this." Jason shook his head, but Russell's shouting grew louder, "Just do it, asshole! I... I guess I deserve this, and I'm ready."

Jason looked down at his attacker and began to kneel. As he reached his knees, his eyes staring directly at the large man, he spoke calmly, "No, Russell. None of us deserved any of this."

After his final words to the man, Jason placed his hands on the handle and pushed it deeper into Russell's frame until his head hit the floor, and the life instantly left the powerful specimen of a man.

Jason stood still. He thought of how his life had changed, how he went from a man with love in his heart for a woman, to a successful writer who transitioned to a broken man and at this very moment a killer. Although feeling slightly relieved that he had survived, he also felt ill.

He knew that it was only John Robertson to contend with now, and he would have to muster up the courage to face him. He also knew the answer to stop Sara's end game.

As he bent down to steal the keys from Russell's pocket, he stood up and headed toward the door, knowing he had to tell John Robertson that his right hand had died in a fight with possessed women in the building, and hope against all odds that he believed his words.

Jason turned to face the lifeless body of the man who had lost his cousin, the man Jason had murdered. He sighed, tossed the keys to the carpet, and closed the door behind him.

CHAPTER FOUR
Patience is a Virtue

Susan's breath was heavy and she clung tight to her mother as they gazed upon the young girl who resembled nothing but a powerful goddess before them.

The fabric of her dark dress clung to her frame. Her fiery red hair fell everywhere as she proceeded to step forward, the balls of her feet touching the putrid earth where the mother and daughter huddled together. The mysterious woman who had saved their lives stood in front of them, and without a sound held out her hand. Her eyes seemed to sparkle as she spoke in a soothing tone with a slight brogue, "Please, Helen and Susan Rogers, do not be frightened by me. I have come here for you... To save you from this hell you now reside in."

As they continued to look up at the powerful young woman who stood before them, Helen and Susan reluctantly released their grip from each other. Susan took a deep breath and held out her still shaking hand to be lifted to her feet. As she finally stood, she looked into the eyes of their savior . The girl appeared to be in her mid-teens, although her eyes had nothing but a gleam of pure intelligence, power, and class, a woman wise beyond her years.

Susan turned to help her mother off of the flesh-carpeted ground, and Helen stared at the girl as her daughter peered over at the scattered parts of her once abusive husband, the man who once took over every aspect of her existence, destroyed everything that she was and took away her light. Tears of joy filled her eyes. She spun around to face the girl again, still in awe of her power as she finally opened her mouth, "Who... Who are you?"

The girl stepped back and smiled at the Rogers family before she answered, her words showing her strength, "I am Patience McKinney, and I was once the teacher of the woman who betrayed the both of you... I was her sister in the arts of nature. The rage and evil that rests in Sara was the result of my death... This caused her heart to turn to nothing but blackness. In a way, I am her maker."

Susan stared at Patience, and began to piece the story together. The images she had witnessed of a young Sara's life once again grew clear. She gasped as she replied, "I know who you are! You were Sara's only love... We... We saw you die. So why are you here... How are you here?"

Patience swallowed hard, and quickly lifted her head to look directly at Helen and Susan. Her eyes appeared glowed as green as emeralds as she spoke, her words nothing but commanding,

"I have been appointed by the one humanity called the Earth Mother to come for you, to enter this plane and retrieve the mother and daughter who will aid me in silencing the terror of Sara Rinehart."

Helen grew puzzled by the young woman's words. "Why....why us? We couldn't stop her before, and she took both of our lives with ease... We couldn't stand up to someone with her power.

We are not soldiers... We were practitioners... Nothing more."

Patience looked into the older mother's brown eyes, and a voice which was not her own seemed to emanate from her throat as she replied. It was the voice of a god, the words of a supreme being, "My child, you are mistaken. You and your daughter possess great power. You always kept your secrets from your child, attempted to hide the legacy of the women of your family and the beliefs which were set upon you. You cannot hide from destiny, Helen Rogers. You and your daughter are the continued strand to a powerful bloodline. A family sworn to protect the earth and all of its majesty. Together you are all-powerful. Matriarch and offspring, sworn to fight together and bring love back to the planet, ending this evil before it blackens everything I have helped the gods create...YOU are my army!"

Patience grew silent and Helen looked to her left to catch her daughter's eyes. Her lips quaked as she gave a slight smile, and a shrug of her shoulders. Patience planted a hand on both of their shoulders, her voice once again her own, "I am the key, the Mother's charge to bringing the earth back to harmony, and together we are a weapon to destroy Sara once and for all. I am her teacher, but I am also the answer to her dark heart's silence."

Helen and Susan reached out for each other's hands. The younger Rogers nodded her head in understanding. Patience smiled and Helen began to question her, "You came here to take us away from this place... What is this? Where are we?"

The young girl's eyes met Helen's as she explained the origins of their prison. "This is a plane beyond what you know as Heaven or Hell. It's beyond the stars and the world you know as Earth. You are now in a dimension where Gaia had attempted to lock Sara away after her death. It was once a place of beauty and light, a level of existence built to show her the goodness of life, a place to show her the right path. Her dark and broken heart would not allow this to transpire, though, and her emotions turned this once glorious world into what you see before you. Sara could not escape the cries of pain in her mind, so they manifested and became part of her reality. The battered soul of my sister held nothing but vengeance and blood in her thoughts, the hatred she had felt since her childhood turned real, and this became Sara's own personal purgatory where she was tormented by her victims. As time went on, the trapped soul of Sara Rinehart ruled this realm, feeling comforted in the violence and suffering around her, biding her time to return to the world, to exact her plans of ultimate power."

Susan shook her head and scoffed before she replied, "So that is why she locked our souls away in this place, for both of us to blacken in our own torment and bad memories?"

Patience nodded at her. Her glowing eyes beamed as she answered, "She sent you here because she knew that you and your mother were a risk. Sara knows that our bodies are just vessels for our true power. That is what souls are, power! Souls have the ability to travel through space and time, to transcend anything the body we were given can do. We can be connected with the lords of this earth, realize that the

God we praised in life does exist, although there are many other forces at work; warriors and majesties, practitioners such as ourselves appointed to protect the people, the many beautiful creatures of the planet, and some who were meant to keep the balance of other worlds. The other side of life is more massive and important than you can possibly comprehend, and Sara understood that if you were shown the truth, you could become a weapon to destroy her plot of world domination."

Helen peered at her with a wild but attentive gaze as Patience continued, "My sisters, you are here because she wanted to veil your now open eyes from the truth, that you are truly the soldiers of the Earth Mother herself, and I am Her vessel to stop the greatest evil Her planet has ever known. I am the one to bring back Sara's humanity, if only for a moment, and destroy her."

Helen nodded and Patience stepped turned towards them, her words calm and reassuring, "Do not be afraid of me. Please, kneel before me."

Susan swallowed hard and slowly dropped to her knees. Helen was slightly hesitant but followed suit as Patience stood before them and lowered her fingers to touch the foreheads of mother and daughter. Their bodies vibrated as the powerful soldier of the Earth Mother's eyes shown bright green, and her voice boomed, "Now my children, take on Her love... Her true power... Become Her soldiers!"

Susan and Helen shook even harder as Patience continued her ritual, "You have been decreed the protectors of the planet Earth and its people, men and women alike."

The young woman looked down at the two women who lifted their heads to reveal their eyes. They flashed with a green hue as bright as the grass Susan once sat on after school, the air around her soothing as she escaped from her once mysterious and abusive mother, who now kneeled before her; her other half, and the woman who would die for her all over again.

The sickening and dark caverns bathed in light as the voices uttered the young witch's first name, "Patience... Patience." The powerful youth yelled , her fingers now pressed hard against the foreheads of Susan and Helen, "Now, my sisters, we are united... We are ONE!!!"

The floors began to change; the entrails and assorted human parts turned into moss. Wild grasses sprouted about the trio, and the tormented faces implanted in the walls seemed to sigh in relief as the world around the women grew lush and beautiful. With that, Patience released their hands, and the eyes of the Rogers women once again turned to normal.

Susan was the first to gaze at the new world around her, and she looked down to witness her wardrobe had changed. Susan was now wearing the same beautiful fabric as Patience, and her skin appeared to have grown strands of vegetation which pulsated with life. The Rogers women were truly one with nature and the majesty of the Earth Mother. She slightly shoved her mother who quickly opened her eyes. Helen's grin was bright, as she looked upon the change of the dark caverns and her clothing and melding of flesh and nature as well. The flowers in her view waved in the wind of the now fragrant air, the skies as blue as deep oceans, and insects buzzed around the three women.

Patience helped them up to their feet, and Susan and Helen stared in awe at the beauty of the changed world.

Patience looked stern. "My sister, your son who is now in much pain has told the writer Jason Cain how to summon us. Now we bide our time until we are called."

Patience smiled, and for the first time, looked like a happy young girl. "Until that time, enjoy the pleasures of this realm, in the Mother's name, in the name of your Queen."

Susan and Helen smiled and nodded to their sister, knowing in their hearts that another encounter with pure evil and death would soon be upon them.

CHAPTER FIVE
Calling Out The Evil

Jason's body felt broken as he stepped past the corpses of the two women Russell had taken out swiftly. He reached the elevator and pushed the button with a trembling finger.

As the blood-streaked doors opened, the beaten father stepped inside without a sound, and as the shaft closed, the man who once harmed his wife and son fell onto his knees. Tears spilled from his already puffy eyes.

He felt his heart breaking as he thought of the many situations that could cause his young son to vanish, and all of them made his stomach burn and his head swim.

He sighed deeply and quickly wiped the tears away. He stood up and started to think of a story to tell the leader of his captors concerning Russell's death.

He finally reached the first floor. As his feet touched down on the bloodstained carpet, a familiar voice pierced his ears from outside. John Robertson yelled at the top of his lungs, "Come, come for your boy, you devil! We have him and we're going to slit his throat in front of you! Come for your spawn!"

Jason's eyes grew wide. He charged to the front door to reach the outside, and as he turned the knob he saw the scene in front of him. Will sat on his knees in the middle of the street as a pumped up John towered behind him, crying out, "Come for him, you bitch! You murdered my boy… And now I am going to murder yours! You will both die by my hand, you demonic whore!"

John kicked Will Thompson hard in the center of his back causing him to fall to the concrete and split his chin. His body was already shattered and abused when he was picked up by tufts of his hair and pulled back up to his feet.

Suddenly, John had Will by the back of his neck when he turned to order Michael to grab the young witch. The art student looked at Will's battered face and only one eye open, glaring at him. Michael instantly shook his head. His voice quaked as he responded, "I... I don't think so, John. You are going to have to do whatever it is you are going to do on your own."

John quickly whipped his head around to face him, his grip not leaving Will's neck, as he beamed in Michael's direction, "What the fuck did you just say to me, boy?"

The youngest member of the group stood his ground. He stared the older, violent man down and repeated his words, "I said... Whatever you are going to do... You are going to do on your own. I will have no part in this craziness!"

John snickered and tossed his victim onto the street. The side of Will's face to hit the street hard.

As John was focused on the young boy, Jason tried to creep over to Will who lay behind him. A small puddle of blood had formed underneath his face.

Jason knew that he would have a difficult time taking on the older man, who gripped his son's sword tight in his fist, but after having the upper hand on the gigantic Russell, he knew that he had to save Will before he was killed in cold blood. Jason also began to feel for the youngest member of the group,

Michael, who had become nothing but a punching bag, a thing to abuse. The once timid writer had had enough.

Jason gripped his stained, dulling knife from his side pocket and reached John's back. John was still screaming at Michael, and just as he was about to strike, the moment was broken by a familiar voice in the distance, "Jason!"

Jason was the first to turn when he heard the voice of his brother. As he spun his head quickly to face him, John's vision also followed suit, and he saw that the man from his apartment was attempting to kill him.

Jason was distracted, his eyes teary as he looked upon Scott, giving John the opportunity to slam a hard fist into the back of his already aching skull, forcing Scott to raise his gun. Scott pointed the gun in the direction of his younger brother's attacker. His words of warning were stern, "Hey! Step away from that man or I will blow a hole through you!"

As Jason reeled from the hit, John slightly raised his sword and Scott stepped forward, his sights still pointed at the man who now yelled in his direction, "Fuck you, man! Who the hell are you?"

Jason's older brother kept approaching, and as John lifted his sword a few inches more,

Scott warned him once again, "I'm that man's brother, a former member of the Unites States military, and I assure you I'm a crack shot, and you are right in my sight."

John began to chortle, and just as Scott tightened his squeeze on the hammer of his gun, the wind blew hard about the group and the sky grew dark. Pieces of debris were pushed forward, and as Scott stood firm, holding his position on John, the two of them and Jason turned to face the left side of the street as they felt what appeared to be a sudden heat in the Fall air. Their skin glowed warm as the wind grew stronger.

Jason did everything he could to shake off the pain of John's punch. His eyes grew wide and filled with tears as he caught a glimpse of the terror coming toward the small skirmish; the lithe form of Elizabeth strolled forward with a massive group of possessed, snarling women marching behind her. Her slender fingers held the small hand of a young boy walking next to her, the hand of Matthew Cain.

Jason wanted to scream, and John and Scott lowered their weapons as they grew mesmerized by the army coming toward them. Scott swallowed hard.

Elizabeth's cobalt blue eyes darted from man to man. Her lips curled into an evil grin and revealed the demon inside of her.

She spoke, her voice instantly placing fear into everyone as the words escaped the beautiful woman's throat, "Welcome to your end, Cain siblings… It's time for you to die in the name of the Rinehart clan."

John took a deep breath, and quickly knelt down to lift Will's unconscious body off of the ground again. He placed the blade of the sword firmly on his throat and cried out to Elizabeth, "Hey, bitch! I have your messenger boy, and just like my child… You're going to watch him die!"

The entity disguised as Elizabeth turned to face the man. Her grin turned into a sly smile as his ranting continued, "You killed my boy... And now I'm going to send yours to the next world!"

CHAPTER SIX
The Chaotic Calm Before Her Storm

Elizabeth's hand wrapped around Matthew's throat and Jason finally screamed out,

"Elizabeth! Let him go... He's our son!"

She smiled wickedly, and the voice inside of her began to take charge, "He is not my child... He is a pig just like the rest of you, and he is your offspring. He dies because of your mistakes!"

Jason put his hands up into the air and attempted to plead to the witch possessing his ex-wife, "I know... I made mistakes, you're right!"

Elizabeth growled and her cold eyes fixated on Jason as he continued, his voice calm, "I know who you are, Sara Rinehart, and I know why you used me... I hurt her. I bruised a beautiful woman in your bloodline, physically and emotionally, and I cannot tell you how sorry I am."

Elizabeth's hand gripped onto the boy's throat even tighter. Matthew wept. The voice hissed as Jason took another step toward her, "Halt your steps or you will witness this child's death!"

Jason stopped in front of her and she stared him down, her words even stronger, "Elizabeth is not just a member of our bloodline, she is the strongest link... She is everything! There's a reason that she is the only woman alive in our family... It's because she has purpose...a vessel of true power to bring balance back to this disgusting planet, where men disappear and the women thrive! This is the true way of things."

John still held the blade to Will's throat and Scott watched as his brother spoke to the being that had once been his sister in law, the weapon now to his side as he looked on in confusion.

Jason stood still and continued to hold a conversation with the demon known as Sara Rinehart. She glared at him, and her left hand gripped the young boy tighter. Her right hand rose up, and with an unseen force, the witch inside of his beautiful former love growled and pushed the palm of her hand forward, throwing Jason's body to the street.

His back hit the street hard and his cries of pain echoed all around. Scott immediately raised his weapon in Elizabeth's direction and the evil voice inside of her laughed.

"Stop right there!" he yelled. "I mean it... Don't you move or I will put one in your head!"

Elizabeth's cold eyes fixated on the stronger, older brother as she spit venomous words again.

"You obviously have a terrible memory, soldier. Your silly weapons will not work. Or should I make you squeal like your father before he died once again?"

Scott gritted his teeth, and with all of the anger boiling inside of him, he squeezed the trigger. The bullet flew in the direction of Elizabeth's forehead, only to sizzle and melt before the shot reached her.

Her soft lips curled into a smile again, and with the wave of her right hand, she threw Scott backward with a massive force. He fell on his bruised rib and cried out in pain as Sara laughed inside of her vessel.

As the Cain brothers were incapacitated, John called out to Elizabeth. With the sword still in front of Will's throat, he made a small slit to grab her attention as he spoke, "You smell that? That's the blood of your little messenger here. First he dies... And then you!"

Elizabeth moved forward, her bare feet treading lightly on the pavement as the older man gripped the blade tighter.

Her eyes grew wide as she looked upon the adult face of the young boy she had trained since childhood, but her reply showed no remorse, "Go on then, kill the little deceiver... He is traitorous and just as filthy as all of you."

As her hand lifted Matthew to her chest, Michael made an attempt to save Will from John's grasp—he picked up a piece of broken glass and inched toward his back.

John and Sara continued to throw threats at each other. Michael raised his arm, and pierced John in his side with the glass. The shot of pain forced him to drop Will onto his stomach but as he cried out, John slammed his elbow into Michael's face. The young student dropped to his knees.

With severe pain shooting through his body, Jason crawled over to his brother who was still on the ground holding his side. He lifted him up by his back from behind, and gave him a slight embrace, holding him tight as he spoke, "Are you all right, Scott? You came here into the city for me, didn't you?"

Scott nodded his head and answered, "I lost Cara, and I refused to lose my little brother."

Jason smiled sadly, and tears filled his eyes as he thought of his brother's loss, but the sense of his sacrifice warmed his heart. He pulled his brother tighter causing him to wince, and spoke, "I love you, brother. You were always there for me, even when I didn't deserve it."

Scott chuckled and replied sarcastically, "You're a pain in the ass... But you're family. Now come on, help me up."

Jason tried very hard to lift his brother to his feet, and the two injured brothers looked upon the scene around them; John Robertson held the wound on his side, and young Michael now possessed his son's sword. The student looked like a pauper discovering he is king in a fairytale story.

Just as quick as Jason could feel relief from having the upper hand on the man who had turned crazed, the witch inside of Elizabeth spoke again. Her eyes flashed white and she gave a snarl before Sara sounded her battle cry, "My sisters, now is the time to show your true force... Kill them all! Rip them apart... KILL, my sisters... KILL THE PIGS!!"

Her grip on Matthew was still tight as more than a dozen of the women in the formation moved forward. Elizabeth smiled as they made their approach. The Cain brothers stood near each other and pulled out what weapons they had available.

Scott quickly opened his pockets, and with a shaky hand pulled a bullet box from one of his compartments. He loaded the chamber quickly as Jason once again took hold of the messy cleaver housed in the back of his dark jeans.

Michael, still reeling from John's elbow, sauntered to their side, the heavy blade dragging to his side, and all three turned their heads to notice Will still unconscious on the street. Confusion startled them as they realized John was nowhere to be seen.

Jason questioned his whereabouts for only a moment until he looked forward again and witnessed the small horde pacing toward them, hissing as they stepped closer.

The women were all seething, their eyes misty white. Scott spoke once he finally had his gun loaded and at the ready, "Well, my brother, looks like we're both in the shit now... But with you by my side, it's a good day to die."

Jason turned his head to the side of his brother's face and smiled. He looked behind him, at

Michael, repeating John's same words to him in a calmer and uplifting fashion, "Hey Mike, today it's time to see if you are a man."

Michael grinned, holding the sword higher at his side. "You just get the grog at the tavern ready, because I have just leveled up to Frodo status."

Jason peered quickly at Michael's weapon of choice and cracked a joke to boost the young student's morale, "We will get you to back to the Shire yet, young Baggins."

Scott broke the humor and addressed his brother and the young student, ordering them to line up. Michael stepped to his right, and his younger brother to his left.

Five women rushed the men first, and Scott fired a bullet into the skull of one of the blonde-haired females who appeared to be in her forties, dropping her to the ground instantly. He yelled, "Oh, it's on boys!"

Michael took a step forward and violently swung the heavy sword into the neck of a light-skinned woman. The blade sliced into her skin, but she did not go down.

Scott fired a bullet into the side of her head, dropping her to her knees. With all of his strength

Michael lifted John's blade and brought it downon top of her head.

Jason swung his cleaver into the face of an older woman who had been able to dig her nails into his face. He kicked her hard in the chest causing her to double backwards, and as fast as he could, he lunged forward, slashing into the side of the woman's throat, hacking until blood spurted from her wounds and her body dropped to the ground. Scott fired two more bullets, and stepped back to reload as Michael continued to swing the heavy instrument at a Hispanic woman, her body fully exposed as she did not have any clothing.

She came at him with a steak knife, but he swung the sword from his right, lopping off the female's head, her lumpy body quickly falling to the street.

Elizabeth growled as she looked upon the barbaric fighting, and as Scott and Michael fought on, Jason stood at his brother's side and spoke silently, "I'm going to end this."

Scott fired another bullet, his expression showing confusion as he answered back, "What… What are you talking about?" And with that, Jason dropped his cleaver to the street, and slid out of the line toward Will, inciting his brother to cry out as he fired another bullet into the side of an oncoming woman's face, "JASON!"

With whatever stealth he could muster, Jason arched his back and crawled over to Will like a military medic. He dropped to his knees and tried to lift Will's face off of the street.

Elizabeth focused her attention on her soldiers who were being knocked out one by one by Jason's older brother and the student. She growled.

Jason continued to try to revive Will, but turned when he heard someone yell out behind him. John grabbed Michael by the throat and tossed him to the street; Scott had no choice but to continue firing as the young man was beaten by the older security guard's fist.

Jason gritted his teeth and spoke to Will who was moaning slightly, "Will, it's Jason… Jason Cain."

Will moaned again and spoke, his words broken from the extreme pain in his face, "Jason? I'm… I'm sorry."

Jason tried to keep Will conscious as he continued, "I need you to tell me how to stop this. I need the answer you spoke of earlier, Will."

Will kept repeating himself, blood spilling from his lips, "I'm sorry, Jason." Jason sighed and turned to Scott who was still fighting, and then looked to the front where Elizabeth was still clutching a now crying Matthew.

Jason clenched his jaw. Even after everything, he swallowed his pride and anger. "Listen. I know why you did what you did… You had to. Now you can do the right thing, and fix this."

Will mumbled and Jason continued to speak, "You and I can end all of this chaos… You just have to give me the answer."

Jason examined the beaten man; his swollen eye, the busted lip, the blood spilling from his mouth, and Jason actually felt more than just a twinge of remorse for the broken shell who he recalled as nothing but vibrant and youthful.

As Will lifted two trembling fingers, Jason recalled their conversations. Even as it had all turned out to be part of a game, he always felt better and much more sane and happy around the man. In his heart, he had absolutely forgiven the dangerous mistakes of Will Thompson.

Will's fingertips touched the forehead of the former writer. Jason began to convulse as images swam through his head of Sara Rinehart's life; he saw her emotionally abusive childhood, her encounter with Patience outside of the school, he saw her live and he saw the woman perish.

As the story unfolded in Jason's brain, his mind fixated on a time in Sara's life that would hopefully stop her genocidal agenda: the time that Sara had written a spell that would bring Patience back, years after she had watched her get murdered by her father and his mob.

April 17th, 1799

There were many times that Sara had stepped away from her village and communed with nature, but her black heart would never allow her to keep the love of the scenery around her, the majesty of the Mother.

Sara had so much vengeance and hatred surging through her that even the woods, the beauty of the trees waving in the wind, and the flowers growing about her feet, did not manage to bring her any happiness.

She began to question life many years after watching Patience get killed, and Sara repeatedly asked the Mother Earth, and even the God she was once forced to believe in, the answer she so desperately required. Sometimes she would say the question aloud, "With so much glorious creations surrounding us, why is there so much hatred and sadness?"

She never received her answers, and her growing hatred fixated on the one sex that had enacted the atrocities on her sister: men.

On the calm spring morning of April 17th, Sara slipped away from her village. She had placed a leather book into a bag along with a knife, as well as a writing implement, and then took to the deep woods. She walked for nearly an hour until she stopped at the edge of a lake and finally sat down. The ripples and sounds of the water actually calmed her. The soothing noises connected her with Mother Nature, until her mind began racing, and just as it had after her sister's death, she saw the brutality and the pained look on

Patience McKinney's face over and over again.

Sara cried hysterically and reached for the satchel at her side, and plucked out the items inside.

She placed the book into her lap, and dipped her aching feet into the water below, the ripples feeling soothing as Sara placed the book into her lap. She opened one of the tattered pages, the musty smell of the paper permeating her nostrils.

Sara had become very acute at creating spells that were successful, and had a firm grasp on everything Patience had taught her, including many things that she learned after her death.

She picked up the knife with her left hand, placing the quill onto one of the open pages. With one tiny slice, Sara dragged the blade onto the tip of her finger until blood dripped from the wound.

As she wiped tears from her eyes, Sara placed the tip of the quill on her finger and began to write.

She scrawled many words, the rusty smell of her blood intermingling with the pages, and began to speak aloud, "Oh Mother, if You have any love in Your twisted heart, You are going to give her back to me. You will give me my sister before I burn this entire world down to its very foundations, this I vow."

Sara continued to write with her own fluid for many moments, and after she was finished, she dropped the quill to her side and took a deep sigh as she licked the red from her fingertip. "You will aid me in resurrecting my only love; she will come back to me.

The young witch closed the book with her resurrection spell. Her feet made splashing sounds as they left the water, while she got up.

Sara placed the book into the satchel and walked back toward to the village of her own making, and as time went on and her soul grew darker, Sara grew fearful of attempting to resurrect Patience because she knew that her heart was pure, and she would never condone the horror her sister in magic was waging on the townspeople about her village.

The book with the ability to revive an old love remained closed until the night she quickly jotted down her own revival, the spell that would bring her back to the present to become one with her only remaining female ancestor, tricking a man that had wounded Elizabeth into bringing her back to her full power, and making the women of the world her new army against the barbaric creatures that took her only love, had killed everyone in her village as they burnt it down. Any goodness within the pages remained a mystery until Helen connected with Sara, and though her own ability to truly meld with her host was unknown, she envisioned all, including her ultimate secret; the passage to bring Patience McKinney back.

Will released his fingertips from Jason's forehead and looked up at his friend who was still reeling from the visions shot into his mind. He peered down at his messenger and spoke, "I have the answer… The words on the page…I saw them clear as day. I know what I must do now."

Will gasped and tried to say something Jason remembered from one of their first encounters,

"Sometimes… You have to believe in things that do not seem like they could be real."

Jason nodded his head, and Will coughed, blood covering his lower lip. He laughed as he spoke, "Crazy shit, huh?"

Jason lifted Will's body, trying to move him away from the fighting occurring throughout the street, and within seconds he was stabbed through the shoulder by a hard thrust of metal. He quickly pulled the blade out, dumped Will on the street again, and cried out in pain. Jason spun around to see the glowering face of John Robertson.

Scott was now on his knees assisting Michael after his intense surprise beating as Elizabeth glowered at John. Her eyes blazed with rage, her lip curled and she cried out, "Kill the pig, my sisters!" Elizabeth's hand pointed toward the older man, and John quickly readied his sword as five more women approached him from Sara's flank.

Jason slipped away from the attack holding his shoulder but quickly fell to the pavement. The snarling group reached John. He swung his sword into the face of one of the red-haired women, kicking another in the chest before he swung again.

Scott finally craned his head and focused on his brother who was lying on the street. His jaw dropped and he looked down at Michael speaking apologetically, "I am really sorry about this, but I'm going to help you up."

Michael grunted as Scott lifted the student. Then Scott dragged him toward Jason who was still lying in the middle of the street. Michael was lightly planted down onto the curb and Scott rushed to his brother's side. He knelt down and pressed on Jason's wound, as blood gushed from the latter's shoulder. "Are you okay?" Scott asked. "Oh man…I'm so sorry."

"I… I'm fine." Jason looked up at his borther. "Scott, I'm fine. I know how to stop this…I have the answer."

Scott lifted his brow and just as he was going to ask Jason what he was referring to, the soldier was kicked hard in the side of the head. He dropped down next to his brother.

John Roberson was covered in the blood of the women who had attacked him. He towered over the Cain brothers, the hilt of the sword tight in his fist, his gaze reflected nothing but the madness his mind had acquired after the death of his son.

"You son of a bitch, I am going to kill you myself," Jason snapped at him.

"It's called an eye for an eye, Jason Cain."

Elizabeth darted her eyes in the direction of the angered man. Her face turned into a scowl and she screamed aloud, her voice echoing throughout the street, "They are mine! The Cain family is mine!" She lifted her hand, no longer gripping the youngest Cain, and held it in John's direction. Her eyes exploded with fire as he raised the sword over his head, about to swing down on her prey.

The enraged voice in Elizabeth screamed again and clamped her fist shut, and at that exact moment John felt his skin grow hot. He screamed out as his hand began to sizzle, and he cried out in pain as his face bubbled, the agony causing him to finally release the grip on the weapon and drop it to the ground.

Scott grabbed his brother and dragged him away from the scene as John continued to scream, the skin on his hands boiling hot as his body melted like ice cream on a hot Summer afternoon.

Jason and Scott both looked on as the man who once said he would aid Jason in finding Matthew, cried out in agony, the skin sloughing off of his face, his muscle turning to mush and falling onto the street in piles.

The sight in front of Jason sickened him. Not because John's death was grotesque, but because he knew that before the events that occurred John was a kind man who loved his only son. He had been a father and a hard worker, a provider, and the world surrounding him turned him into something he never could be, a monster.

Jason continued to look on as Elizabeth opened her fists and waved her palm in John's direction again. The fabric of his clothes fused to his skin as he continued to scream, the Cain brothers kept watching in horror as John eroded, his chest heaving until the cavity blew outward causing a shower of entrails and blood to spray onto the pavement.

Michael held his face and watched his brutal attacker turn into a puddle in front of him. He felt ill, swallowed hard, and then blurted out a cold sentence, "Sayonara, you motherfucker."

Jason turned his head to face him and scowled. The young man looked confused and did not say another word.

Jason, still holding his wound, turned his head to the left to face Scott. Trying to be reassuring, even though he felt in his soul he may die for his next action, he said, "Scott, it's time for me to end this. You have to understand that even if I do not make it, I have to do the right thing... For the first time in my life."

Scott held his ribs and furrowed his brow. He looked at his brother and felt himself tearing up, as he replied, "What are you going to do? How are you going to stop this? I lost Cara and Dad's gone... I cannot lose you."

With excruciating pain in his shoulder from the now gushing wound, Jason embraced his brother . He whispered to him, "Just know I love you. You are, and have always been, the greatest brother a piece of shit like me could ever deserve."

Jason winked, and slowly rose to his feet. Scott felt his insides shake but he did not try to stop his only brother as he watched him step forward to face Elizabeth who was caressing Matthew's hair. Tears smiled from the little boy's eyes, while the woman smiled wickedly.

She turned her head to face Jason. The latter spoke calmly, still clutching his wound, his hand covered in blood, "Sara... Sara Rinehart. I have some things to say to you... Before you kill us all."

Scott pulled Michael up to his feet and hid behind a smashed car nearby as Jason tried to seek the evil witch's counsel. Elizabeth smiled as he continued to speak, "I have felt loss, and I know you have as well. I have seen your past, and I am really sorry for what the world has done to you."

Her eyes grew dark and she gripped Matthew by the throat again as the voice escaped her lips, "What do you know about loss? You know nothing! Nothing about true pain, nothing about pure suffering!" Elizabeth waved her hand in Jason's direction once again, tossing him backward onto the street as she finished her sentence, "But you will. You will feel pain like you could never imagine as I spill the blood of your entire bloodline in front of you, before I rip out your insides."

Scott and Michael looked on as Jason used all of his might to stand to his feet again. He slowly walked toward his ex-wife turned powerful vessel, and struggled to keep calm as he spoke. "I know how you felt when you lost your only love, it feels terrible... You feel lost and alone... You feel weak."

The evil voice pouring from Elizabeth was released once again. She laughed before she gave her reply,

"What are you speaking of, pig? You know nothing of my past...

And I have no weakness. I am this world's salvation... The end of man and the birth of true harmony."

Jason stood in front of his beautiful love. His stomach was now in knots, but he stood his ground.

Elizabeth raised her hand again in Jason's direction which in his racing mind felt like the barrel of a gun, his impending doom staring directly at him as he blurted out two words, "Patience McKinney!"

Scott made a dash from behind the car and ran to Will. He pulled the injured man from the street, and with pain in his own body lifted Will, and dragged him over to the rest of the battered crew.

Jason continued to have his verbal standoff with Sara. She looked puzzled, and her jaw shook lightly as she answered him, "I do not know what you speak of! I have no weaknesses...I cannot be stopped!" Jason swallowed hard and chanted the words he had seen Sara jot down in her leather-bound collection of spells by the riverbed. He could envision every single word in his mind just as he had seen it before, "The fire inside me is deep The loss of your heart makes me weak."

Elizabeth released her hand from the young boy, planting his feet back down to the ground. Her lips shook for a moment, and in seconds her eyes had turned red as flames, she lifted both of her hands and was about to kill Jason when all of a sudden Sara felt the grip on her ancestor slightly weakening.

Jason continued to recite the spell aloud,

"I summon Her power so that my soul may stop weeping, by waking her from eternal sleeping."

Tears rolled down Elizabeth's cheeks, and the powerful witch inside her forced her vessel to throw her hands forward. The voice inside her screamed, "Silence, you pig!"

A massive ball of fire rushed toward Jason, and Scott's eyes grew wide as he feared he was about to witness his brother be incinerated. Jason saw the mighty inferno heading toward him and sealed his eyes.

Elizabeth's lips turned into a huge smile. She was ready for victory... Then, all of a sudden the flames appeared to be deflected, the fire Sara had thrown dissipated as Jason opened his eyes and took a deep breath before he mustered the courage to continue the passage,

"I beg thee, Mother for her touch once again, to feel the warmth of my true friend."

Elizabeth looked confused, and with Matthew crying in front of her, she threw her right hand forward again. Her invisible punch came toward Jason but he was not knocked down to the street. It seemed that Sara was powerless to stop him, and the witch inside Elizabeth caused her to scream as the words once again escaped him,

"I wish for my heart to stop bleeding, to feel her warmth all around me."

Elizabeth raged from the force of the powerful woman inside of her. Her mouth was agape as the former husband finished the spell, his voice growing increasingly louder.

"I call upon the powers of nature...to resurrect this wondrous creature."

Elizabeth swallowed hard as he dropped the final words he had read in the book,

"Mother, bring her black from black seas of the dead...MY SISTER, PATIENCE MCKINNEY!!"

The woman possessing his wife started to scream. The ear-piercing sound escaped his wife's throat, and Jason spoke, "I know that the Mother is angry... She did not want any of this. You used the Goddess and the creator of all life on this planet in your sick, twisted fucking game, and now my dear

Sara, you must pay for what you have done here!"

Elizabeth's mouth changed, grew distorted, her jaw extended and filled with sharp teeth as Jason still stood in front of her. His body was hurt but he stood strong as Scott continued to watch from the side of the street. Michael was holding Will's head up with his own body behind the shattered red car.

Elizabeth had changed into the creature Jason had seen the mirror before Sara's apocalypse. She then quickly shifted back to the normal face of her ancestor. Her hold was slowly breaking; Jason was getting to Sara and her true human form was beginning to be revealed.

Elizabeth's left hand grabbed Matthew by the back of the shirt as he tried to run from her, and her right hand rose into the air toward Jason, when all of a sudden her concentration was broken by the instant darkening of the daylight skies. The wind blew intensely as small pieces of paper and other pieces of trash on the street whipped around.

Jason and the rest of the group looked upward, afraid of what might come next. Jason did not move from his stance, his hand once again pressed onto the wound in his shoulder.

The sky continued to blacken and the wind still blew hard as Elizabeth's hand gripped the young boy in front of her tighter. The women behind her snarled as they sniffed the air like dogs.

Her eyes stared Jason up and down as he stood his ground in front of her. Her lip curled and she growled as he slightly smiled and spoke, "You're going down, Sara."

The voice inside of Elizabeth laughed and her eyeballs grew as wide as saucers when she fixated on a trio of women walking on the street behind Jason. Her eyes quickly filled with tears when she recognized the face from her past, and the witch inhabiting her broke from her hold after hearing the sweet brogue she had heard long ago, "Sara Rinehart! By decree of the Earth Mother Herself…I am here to end this evil once and for all!"

CHAPTER SEVEN
Love Kills

Elizabeth's eyes grew wet as Patience moved forward, her black fabric draped around her body, her strawberry red hair was everywhere, and her eyes fixated on the woman possessed by her former sister.

Susan and Helen followed her every move, adorned in the same uniform, their stride was in sync with each other, resembling a team as they walked toward Elizabeth who held her own son in her tight grip Tears still streamed down his face.

On the side of the street covered in bodies and other mess, Will, being held up by Michael recognized his family, and with blood lightly spilling from his mouth, he attempted to speak, "Mother? How is that possible?"

Elizabeth's hands released the young boy who hysterically rushed toward Jason. The writer quickly picked his son up and allowed the trio of women to step in front of him.

The voice inside Elizabeth started to shake, "My sister... Is it really you?"

Patience and her small group stopped in front of her, and the large group of women turned into cornered animals behind her.

Patience conversed with Sara, as Susan and Helen remained quiet, "Sara, I have come to stop you. This is not the way. I did not teach you the magic of nature and light to utilize it for your own agenda, and the Mother we worshipped and loved is very angry."

Patience put one foot forward as she continued, Susan and Helen following her every move, "It is time for you to return to Her and face your imprisonment!"

The voice of the host in Elizabeth's body cracked. "Patience... I did this for you! Everything I have done has been for YOU, and for all those women who have suffered under the hand of men for so many years. I received a vision from the Mother herself; She told me to return and exact Her vengeance, to return to this time to show that my family could endure, that we could return Her true balance by destroying the one thing that constantly destroyed Her majesty, and is the bane of the true beauty of this earth!" Elizabeth's eyes burned, "THIS is Her legacy... THIS is mine!!"

She slightly growled as Patience moved toward her, and looked deep into her eyes, her words soft,

"My Sister, this was all of your doing... It was YOUR heartache and pain after my demise that brought on all of this darkness. It corroded your mind! You turned something splendid and beautiful into something horrifying. You did not exact vengeance for me, I would never want this... The Mother would never want this, and you are wrong!"

Susan and Helen stepped backward, as did Patience. She glared at the vessel of Sara, "I am sorry, my sister Sara, I love you, but it's time for your maddening reign of power to end."

Elizabeth lowered her head and was silent for a moment before she laughed maniacally. The three women held fast and the group on the side of the street looked on as Elizabeth's hand was drawn forward. The three dug their heels into the street as they took the powerful brunt of her force.

Sara's voice cried out, "You think that you can stop me, my sister! I AM A GODDESS OF DEATH!"

Elizabeth sounded the call to her army, "My sisters!" Her hand pointed to Jason and the rest of the group, "KILL THE PIIIIGS!!!"

With her order, a massive group of women headed toward the men. Michael quickly lifted Will to his feet, and Jason and Scott also stood up quickly.

Michael, holding an unconscious Will, was the first to speak, "Umm...okay... What the fuck do we do?"

Jason shoved little Matthew behind the group, and the frightened men stood frozen as they waited for death.

Susan craned her head at the horde walking toward them, and then gazed upon her battered son. Her jaw clenched and her feet took two steps backwards before she cried out, "NOOOOOO!!!"

Susan's eyes changed color. They became as green as emeralds, and her hands rose over her head as Helen and Patience stepped to the side as the pavement of the street suddenly cracked and broke. Just like the power Patience had displayed in the dark realm, large thorny vines sprouted from the large cracks and flew straight toward Elizabeth's neck, the tendrils wrapping around her throat and instantly becoming tight.

Sara's voice laughed as the thick, dark green vines seemed to melt and burn away quickly.

Susan gritted her teeth as Elizabeth glared in her direction. She threw her hand forward forming a fireball which hit Susan directly in the chest and knocked her hard into the street.

Will's voice from the sideline displayed panic, "MOTHER!"

Helen broke from her stance and ran to her daughter's side, turning quickly to hold both of her hands in Elizabeth's direction causing a hale-like gust which knocked her off of her feet, blowing the rest of the women to the street. The supernatural army snapped and growled as they slowly rose to stand.

Elizabeth sprung up quickly, lifting her hand to Helen who had lifted hers toward the sky. Patience also lifted her hands above her head causing the street to crack yet again. The vines shot forward and around Elizabeth's body and neck.

The roots snapped and grew tighter, and for the first time Elizabeth's voice was her own. She instantly gagged and the witch's sounds inside of her intermingled with her own pain. Jason cried out, "Please, stop! You are going to kill her!"

Scott tried to hold his brother back, and Jason pushed him off hard as Patience turned her freckle-painted face to speak to him, "Jason Cain... She must be stopped at any cost!"

Scott held Jason back as he tried to pull away from him. Patience stood in front of Elizabeth who was still gasping and as the vein-like vines wrapped tighter around her throat, she spoke softly, "Show yourself to me, my sister. Reveal yourself to my love... Please, give in!"

Elizabeth's neck creaked as if her neck was being broken, when in seconds she released a banshee-like scream and her eyes shone bright white.

Fiery embers formed in Elizabeth's throat and as Patience stepped back, a massive ball sprung forth from her throat.

The body of Elizabeth flopped to the street, the vines finally releasing their intense grip.

Jason and the group look amazed as they gazed upon a woman who appeared to be in her twenties on the pavement, her hair raven black and her skin white as snowfall.

The girl was draped in a filthy white dress and when she looked up at the trio in front of her, her eyes resembled the true torment and horror swirling inside of her. Sara Rinehart was finally revealed.

She cackled as the three soldiers of the Earth Mother surrounded her from afar. Patience kneeled down and lifted her head, speaking with love in her words, "I taught you to do right, Sara… To harness the light and Her energy."

Sara's face glowered as the young girl tried to get through to her, "You abused life, the life of these women and the balance. You must stop this."

Patience released Sara's face from her grasp and Sara stared down at the street. Her laughter was silent but grew louder. The Rogers women held fast as Patience continued to use her soft and sweet brogue,

"Sara, my love, please come with us. Be free from your pain and witness goodness once again."

Sara began to heave and her laughter increased in volume. As she lifted her head Jason's heart jumped into his throat when he once again witnessed the beast from his nightmares, her teeth gnarled and broken, her voice turning into a hiss, "You dare challenge my power, you little whelp!"

The group looked up at the sky as it turned as black as midnight. Scott and Michael hid behind the car as Jason held his son tight to his body, the wound in his shoulder still bleeding out.

Sara's laughter echoed and she quickly sprung to her feet. The creature she had turned into was gone and her eyes had turned black.

Patience walked backward on the balls of her feet. Her pleas to her old friend grew louder, "I urge you to please come with us!"

Sara's laugh turned into a battle cry as both of her hands were raised, lifting Patience off of her feet and into the air.

Susan and Helen watched the strong youth who had saved them hover above, her skin cracking like glass. Patience winced as she was being broken in half by Sara's power.

Sara's intense hold was fixated on Patience, and there was no remorse in her face as she yelled out, her body still crumbling.

Jason glanced over and saw Elizabeth slowly stand, still groggy from the exorcism of her ancestor. She knelt down and lifted a piece of a broken street sign, then ran full speed toward Sara who was still focused on Patience. The rusted point cleaved Sara's chest and Patience dropped to the ground as Sara screamed.

The witch quickly spun around to face Elizabeth. She gripped her by the throat and tossed her to the pavement.

Sara launched forward as Jason's love stood firm, gravel and slight blood forming on her knees. T spoke, her voice holding a tone of humanity, "You miserable little woman... You cannot kill your destiny."

Elizabeth stared her down with tears in her eyes and replied, "I know who you are."

She balled her fist as Sara taunted her, her words coming to a hiss, "I am your hatred.... Your power... And your salvation."

Jason looked on in fear as Elizabeth stood in front of Sara. He released his hand from his wound and knelt down to talk to his son. Matthew still had tears in his eyes which his long lost father wiped away with his fingertips, "Matt... I am so sorry for not being there for you." Tears fell from his eyes as he finished his sentence, "Just know... That your daddy loves you."

He kissed the stunned little boy on the forehead, and reached for John's sword by Michael's side. Scott gripped his other shoulder and turned to face him, "Jason, what the hell are you doing?!"

Jason wiped his own tears away and smiled, "For the first time in my miserable life, my brother... The right thing."

He held onto the sword tight, "Take care of my son, okay?"

Jason's eyes beamed at Michael who was still seated with Will on the curb, "You did good out there, kid. Whatever you do, you take care of him."

Michael nodded and Jason raced toward Sara as she lifted her hand toward Elizabeth causing her body to lift, and with a swift thrust the blade came down on Sara's hand, lopping the appendage clean off of her wrist.

Elizabeth landed and Sara cried out, her screams breaking glass on cars and windows throughout the street. The survivors ducked for cover, and Scott hovered over Matthew using his upper body to shield him.

After a sharp bellow, Sara turned, and with her other hand tossed Jason on his back, the ground doing damage to his body on impact.

Sara's eyes were cold as he struggled to his feet, her words even colder, "You filthy beast! I wanted to use her to kill you for what you had done to her." Sara turned to face Elizabeth again, "But now I am going to force you to watch her die!!"

She placed her bleeding stump into her armpit and held her other hand in Elizabeth's direction, but as she was about to crush her body, Jason ran forward and cleaved her deep through the chest again with the souvenir turned weapon. The soul warriors of Patience and the Rogers women and the group of Scott noticed Sara spin around, and with the wave of a hand and a loud scream, she brought her body forward with intensity, and a ball of fire slammed into Jason's torso hard, knocking him over as a sharp cry spilled from his lungs.

He tried to get to his wobbly feet, and as he reached Sara, she smiled as a hole seemed to sizzle

through the fabric near his heart. Like a ton of bricks, he fell back down onto the cold pavement.

Elizabeth and Scott screamed, and Patience sounded her call to arms, "Now!"

The three women raised their hands in unison. The street below splitand cracked as if a giant was escaping from the earth.

As the Rogers and Sara's former sister chanted, massive vines with large razor thorns sailed from the enormous cracks and wrapped around Sara's arms and neck.

The sharp points sliced into her skin. She dropped to her knees as the grip became a vise. Patience and the Rogers women stepped closer as Elizabeth ran to Jason, who was still on the street clutching his chest.

Matthew watched his mother rush to the side of the man who had revealed he was his father, and nudged away from his uncle. Scott cried out, "Matthew!"

The young boy jumped into his mother's arms as Scott's concentration was broken by Will. The young man chuckled, coughing as he spoke weakly, "He finally received what he wanted... All he had to do was enter Hell to get it."

Scott lowered his head to look down at the wounded man dressed in black, not knowing that he was the lost soul who had tricked his brother into bringing about the madness surrounding him.

With tears in his eyes, he turned to see his nephew and his former sister in law by his wounded brother's side. He did not interfere with the horrible reunion, Elizabeth now clutching the burning hole in his chest with both of her palms as Jason moaned and shut his eyes from the intense pain.

The three newly formed sisters were towering over Sara who was drawn and quartered by the vines, Patience knelt down with tears in her eyes and caressed Sara's cheek as her long lost friend spoke, "It was supposed to belong to me... To us! We could have had paradise, the true children of the Earth."

Patience smiled slightly, but her eyes looked stern, "You made one fatal mistake... We are ALL Her children."

Sara sneered as the vegetation continued to slice into her body and tighten around her. Patience stood up and her new team towered over the wounded witch. Patience spoke softly and invitingly, "It's time for this to end, Sara... In the Mother's name."

Dark blood spilled from Sara's mouth as she replied, "Not even your love will stop me, Patience. My heart is cold... And even if you stop me now... I shall return."

Patience looked her directly in the eyes and one final sentence escaped her, "My love for you will always make sure that you do not."

Sara smirked. With the wave of all their hands, the protectors for Mother Earth snapped the vines as tight as a noose. The sharp thorns quickly decapitated the centuries old witch and her head hit the street, her dark hair cascading over her face.

The trio stepped back as a huge ball of fire swirled from the spot where Sara's body fell, and shot toward the sky which raged with fire, the clouds turning orange until the world turned to day once again.

The reign of Sara Rinehart was over as fast as it had come.

Patience smiled at Susan and Helen and slowly turned her head to Jason and his family on the street. The leader of the three felt her heart about to break as she witnessed the man who had risked his life to protect his former wife and estranged son finally with his family once again, and slowly fading away.

CHAPTER EIGHT
Writing the Final Chapter

Patience stood where Sara's body had disappeared and remained silent. Tears formed in her eyes but the powerful young girl remained strong. Susan took a deep breath and was the first to break the quiet, "Is this truly over?"

Patience finally turned to face her, the look on her face expressionless, "Evil like hers can never be contained."

Patience looked down at the pavement as she continued to explain, "Sara had the best of intentions in her own mind, but her goodness was always veiled by her vanity and hate. I know that she only held a candle for me, but her flame grew into a fire that could not be extinguished, and her pain would never die."

Patience McKinney's eyes met Susan's again. "But I still love her, as the Mother also holds her in Her heart."

She placed a hand on Susan and Helen's shoulders, "I'm so sorry that you were used in such a way, but know that your torment is over." She smiled, "You will bask in the light and tender love of the Mother, and be by Her side forever."

Susan nodded in agreement and Patience turned towards Michael, who was trying to lift Will with his weight. She spoke again, "Susan, before we depart, go to your child. Tell him that you love him. Show him that you are proud of him, and that he does not have to suffer anymore."

Susan nodded, and turned to walk toward her son. Her bare feet moved slowly as she glanced at the injuries to her son's face, the swollen eye and the blood dribbling from his lips.

Her heart sank from the image in front of her, and as Patience continued to look straight ahead, the women who were possessed by Sara's supernatural link began to slowly come to.

One of the women examined the mess around her and panicked

when she caught a glimpse of her blood-stained fingers. Another woman in the line held her hands to her face and began crying hysterically. Patience sighed as the streets became occupied by people slowly regaining their sanity, and with questions filling the air. An African-American woman began crying out and asked the other women around her, "Why the hell are we here? Why is there blood on my clothes?" A petite, short-haired woman noticed the bloody and violent mess all over the street, the bodies in piles, and vomited

Patience slowly walked over to the women. Her face was stoic as her eyes met everyone that she passed, and as she was grabbed and asked questions by every female, she lightly placed one of her hands on each forehead and spoke silently, "The power of the Mother is with you; She is there through your heartache and terrible times ahead. Live in peace and in Her love. She will give you strength and aid you in the darkness you will encounter."

As her hands touched their heads, every woman she cleansed could see everything that had occurred; the voice of Sara who lived in their minds as they roamed aimlessly, snarling and killing, and many witnessed themselves inflicting harm and even death to individuals they loved. This incited certain women to immediately fall to their knees and break down.

Half of the victims began comforting each other, they cried or remained silent, everyone had their own different reaction to the horrors of Sara Rinehart.

Patience walked away from the massive crowd, and once again turned around, her final words reassuring,

"My sisters, protect each other, be strong with each other and with Her." She smiled, turned, and walked away.

Scott shook violently as he crawled over to his brother on the street who was being comforted by Elizabeth and their son. She was holding her ex-husband's hand tight.

Susan stood in front of Will and her eyes immediately became wet as she lightly caressed his shattered jaw. He winced as he finally opened his eye and saw his mother standing in front of him. He spoke, his words broken, "I… I thought you were dead."

Susan used her left hand to wipe the tears from her eyes. She chuckled with sadness and slight confusion in her words, "I guess I am, but because of you, I'm free."

Will looked perplexed, "What do you mean... Free?"

Susan caressed his face as she attempted to answer, "Through it all, you believed. Now we can move on from our hell... And so can you."

Will's working eye widened and Susan leaned over to kiss him on the forehead, her blue eyes staring directly at his face once again, "I want you to live, to be free of all of this. Be the great man I know that you have become. Find love, or whatever you choose to do in life... For the first time."

Will nodded and Susan leaned down to kiss him on his cut forehead again as he uttered something that hit her ear clearly, "I am going to miss you, Mom."

Dampness spilled from Susan's eyes as she whispered in reply, "I will always be with you, baby."

Will tried to smile behind his cut lip as Susan faced Michael who was holding up her son. She smiled at him.

"Thank you, for being there for him, and for fighting for his life. Thank you for believing in his goodness."

She touched Michael's shoulder lightly, "Please, continue to do that for me... His mother."

Michael nodded and Susan smiled again before she walked away.

Elizabeth was now bent over Jason, her tears falling as she pressed her hands over the wound that was quickly bleeding out. Scott was holding his brother's head as Matthew cried hysterically.

Jason gasped and Elizabeth spoke, trying hard to maintain composure, "You are going to be okay... Please... Please do not leave us."

Jason grabbed her hand and blinked his eyes, and in a raspy voice he answered, "I... I did this."

Elizabeth wiped the tears from her eyes. Jason continued as her face turned from sadness to shock, "I... I was alone... Lost without you. I believed in things I should never have gotten involved in... I was tricked. All I wanted was to have you back."

She grew silent and finally reacted, "You... You did this?" Jason nodded. The color drained from his face, and his grip on Elizabeth's hand grew tighter, "I was never a good person... I never was. I do know this, I learned to truly love you... And realized that I love our child even more."

His shaking hand rose and touched her soft cheek. Elizabeth did not move.

Jason tried to smile as he stared deep into her eyes, "I came here... For him. It's the only thing in my life I have ever done right."

Jason craned his head to look upon his son and reached out for his little hand. Matthew turned to face him as he finally revealed the truth, "Matthew... I was never your mother's friend... I am your father...And I will and always have loved you."

For a few seconds, the child said nothing, looking as if he was trying to register the new information, but then he did something that made Jason's dying heart feel alive for that brief moment. His son leaned down, laid his head on his father's chest and began to cry out, "Daddy!"

Jason placed his hand on the top of his son's head and caressed his hair. He looked up at his brother whose eyes were red and addressed his love for him, "Scott. Thank you for truly being the greatest brother a man could ever ask for."

Scott nodded and replied sadly, "Of course, Jay. I was always there to protect you."

Jason's eyes began to flutter, and his voice grew more silent, "You don't have to... Anymore." The color left Jason completely as Elizabeth gripped her only love's hand tighter, and before his eyes rolled back he had one last sentence, "I love you all."

Elizabeth slowly craned her head and lightly kissed his lips. With nothing but honesty in her words she whispered in his ear, "I love you, too."

Jason Cain, the man who had made many mistakes in his life and lost his family for his actions many years ago, had finally gained redemption as a caring man who would risk his life for his only love, and was finally seen as a loving father.

The final chapter in the troubled writer's life had ended with the only conclusion he had ever desired.

CHAPTER NINE
Mother of the World

Elizabeth released Jason's hand and clutched her son to her chest. Her eyes were now on

Scott who was wiping away tears. She spoke softly, "I... I am so sorry, Scott."

Scott's voice cracked as he answered, "Maybe, it's time for us to reconnect. What do you say?"

Elizabeth nodded and held Matthew close, when all of a sudden there was a light tap on her shoulder. She quickly turned her head to see the young redhead woman standing behind her. Elizabeth quietly told her son to go with his uncle and stood to face her. She looked down at the young girl who was only a bit shorter, "Who are you?"

Patience looked serious, "My name is Patience McKinney, and I knew the woman who caused all of this, your ancestor, Sara. She returned to take you for her own. It was the only way that she could gain her full power."

Elizabeth wiped more tears away and gritted her teeth, "Am I supposed to feel guilty that my family did this? Am I supposed to feel... Evil?"

Patience grinned, "No, you are supposed to take care of them, the world."

Elizabeth's face was plastered in confusion, and the young girl placed her fingertips on her forehead. Her true purpose and the future was placed into her mind causing her to fall to her knees.

Patience spoke softly as Elizabeth breathed heavily in front of her, "I know that you are an incredible mother and a nurturer. It's time to for you to spread goodness, end all of the suffering that will manifest after these events."

Patience lifted her head so that Elizabeth's eyes met hers, "Your bloodline is not cursed; you are blessed. You were destined to take on this act of love and charity."

Patience stepped back, as Elizabeth looked at her with bloodshot eyes. Her lips shook as the young girl spoke again, "Show them your strength, my sister."

Elizabeth was still perplexed, but she nodded as Patience walked over to Helen and Susan. Susan blew a kiss in her son's direction before the trio was bathed in a ball of light and disappeared.

Elizabeth stayed on her knees for a few moments and finally stood up to see Scott and her son still sitting with the body of her first and only husband. She then turned her head to bear witness to the women who were all in a state of loss and hysterics.

The confused mother took a deep breath of air, and her feet gracefully stepped on the pavement toward the massive throng of females in pain.

Elizabeth took no time to become what she was destined to be. She had always been a loving and caring mother, but it was time for her to become a matriarch to a wounded and sad world.

As Elizabeth began comforting the women around her, embracing them as they cried on her shoulder, Scott finally stood to his boots. His mind raced as he placed the pieces together in his mind.

He turned to Michael, who was standing with Will in his arms in front of him, and began glaring at the beaten face of the man in his thirties, his jaw clenched tight.

Scott thought of Cara and looked down at his brother's blood coating his hands. Finally, it became clear to the former soldier that Will Thompson was the one who had forced his brother to bring about the slaughter, as well as the death of his wife.

He reached for the 9 mm at his side, and the blood in his body started to boil.

Scott's trembling hand reached the holster. His brain, and everything within him was prepared to pull the trigger, when all of a sudden he heard a familiar voice echo in his mind, that of his slain wife, "Scott!"

He felt as if he was losing himself in the middle of the street when a warm hand on his shoulder quickly cooled him down. Her light touch and her words hit his ear as if she was right behind him, "It's time to find your own peace, it's time for us to grow as a world and end this bloodshed together."

Scott cried, and her voice filled his thoughts, easing his inner pain as she finished her sentence, "It can begin with you. Show him forgiveness, allow him to keep his life... He never desired any of this, my love."

The soldier released the handle of the gun and dropped his arms to his side. He felt the sweet kiss of Cara on his neck and she finally said goodbye, "I will always love you... Do not allow my death to consume you."

As her words left him, the large warrior stood still for a moment and suddenly passed out, falling hard to The ground below.

Michael dragged Will over to the massive man whose eyes were still open, and knelt down with his appointed new friend's limp body in front of him. Scott looked at a concerned but battered Will before he closed his eyes, and the son of Susan Rogers had no inkling of how close he had just come to losing his life, after surviving a lifetime of Sara's torment, as well as the agenda he was forced to bring to fruition.

CHAPTER TEN
Everyone Will Remember

Two weeks had passed and people around the world had banded together to start massive cleanups, dumping bodies into large trucks as renovation began on roads and buildings, and cars and other debris were taken away to be destroyed.

A large percentage of the women in Sara's supernatural hold transitioned as best as they could. Many could not cope with they had done, and a few were so racked with guilt that they fell into dark depressions, even took their own lives or attempted suicide.

Elizabeth had begun her own relief efforts to assist in the healing process for the grieving and the hurt in the United States and across the globe. She also had a difficult time facing her own demons, and at times would be plagued with the voice of Sara echoing through her thoughts in the middle of the night, interrupting her peaceful dreaming.

Elizabeth had nightmares that were extremely vivid, one in particular where she planted her feet on the floor and entered the dark kitchen, pulling a sharp knife from the drawer, and just as she had on the night of her possession, the loving mother stopped in front of her son Matthew's door. Only this time, she opened the door wide and held the knife over his sleeping form.

She woke up screaming before she could witness the violence of her actions, running to Matthew's bedroom and holding him tight.

She also started to tell her son stories of his father, and she never spoke ill of Jason. In the eyes of his son, he was portrayed as a good man. Although there were issues, he had dealt with the pain of life in his own way, the right way. Elizabeth addressed her son that he should never feel any animosity toward his father, and that both of his parents had always loved him.

The newly appointed healer spoke in front of large groups in regards to change and the true answers for equality, and addressed the people of the supernatural and other forces at work. She spoke thoroughly after the events of Sara's return that the unknown did in fact exist.

Elizabeth also spoke in front of the United Nations, and her words were strong as she stood on the podium, looking regal in her fine grey suit, her eyes fixated on the men and women in the crowd, "We have all learned to believe... To believe in the unknown. We have all been privy to the events that shape not only the future of our lives, but events that have made what we thought imaginary real. There are evils lurking that we were not aware of, evils which have become true horror that we now face, and the torment and pain of what we have done."

Elizabeth took a pause and wiped a tear away. "But we can survive this, together. If we have learned anything from these events, we should realize that we are ALL children of the Earth, and we can make it a better world. We can learn to display true love and compassion to each other, help each other, and more importantly, guide each and every single person affected, and pull them from the darkness. Together, we can all see the light of humanity, and the higher powers that guide us."

Many in the crowd were tearful and clapped hard, and it became very evident that just as her uncle had stated on the night Jason proposed, the world had truly seen the true power of Elizabeth Rinehart, and would remember her forever.

CHAPTER ELEVEN
Becoming a Man by Letting Go

After the horrible happenings of the evil witch's apocalypse, Michael still continued to take care of Will Thompson, and made sure that he received the assistance that he required.

On the day that Sara was eliminated, Scott and the young student walked for blocks, both of the men dragging the unconscious messenger, and found a working car which the former soldier had hot-wired quickly.

Michael sat in the back seat next to Will, and as he peered out of the cracked window, he felt tears straming down his face as he witnessed the carnage, and realized that he had finally grown strong. He had learned to be a true man, and not only stood up to John Robertson, but saved the life of a man he felt deserved to survive.

The car finally reached a small hospital outside of the city. The parking area was filled with techs lifting bodies, dead and alive alike. The emergency room was filled with injured people, the scene resembling a true warzone.

Will and Michael were placed on a gurney, and Will Thompson had to endure extensive surgeries and reconstructions through many months. He even had to go through rehabilitation, Michael occasionally visiting with him.

The young student who had once wanted to see him dead, grew to become a true ally and even moved Will in with him.

After Will was released, Michael drove him to his small apartment he had found during his new roommate's rehabilitation.

Both men had a difficult time getting back to a normal life, and Will had extreme nightmares. His screams often urged Michael to rush into the room in the dead of night.

As time went on, Will appeared to be getting back to himself, but on one late afternoon as he stepped into the shared bathroom, he brushed his teeth and looked directly into the mirror and saw a young dark-haired woman staring back in his direction, her teeth gnarled and jagged. The vision frightened Will so horribly that he smashed the mirror and fell to the floor crying in pain, the torment of the once vibrant man being far from over.

Two years had finally passed, and Will revisited the newly renovated city of Philadelphia, stepping into the place where he met the broken writer, "The Blackbird Brew House". The place looked exactly how he had remembered it, and as he turned his head to take a look at the table where it had all started, Will's face cracked a slight smile when he saw another familiar face from his past—the grown-up face of Stephanie Chamberlain.

Will hobbled slowly to her table, using the cane that had to accompany him, since he suffered the damage John and the group had inflicted, and looked at his high school crush.

Stephanie appeared to be a different woman, more mature as she read the paper and drank a cup of coffee with the voluptuous lips he recalled kissing behind his childhood home.

Stephanie sipped her coffee slowly and peered up. Her eyes reflected fear at first, but as she continued to peer into Will's eyes, her face softened and she spoke, "Will? Oh my god, Will Thompson... Won't you sit down, please?"

He placed his cane to the side of the chair and sat down slowly. Both of them were silent before Will sighed and finally spoke about the past, "I just... I never had the opportunity to apologize for what happened that day in the woods, and I'm so sorry."

Stephanie shook her head, listening to his words as he continued, "I lost my mother. You know, the one who pinned you to a tree?" He sighed, "Let's just say... That wasn't her."

Stephanie held out her hand and touched the top of Will's. She began to cry, her voice soft, "I lost my father... And my brother. My mother murdered them, and I awoke in a house that did not belong to us... I did some... Really horrible things."

Will nodded and she released her hand as he replied, "I'm so sorry to hear that, Steph, I really truly am."

Stephanie wiped away her tears, and looked serious, "But

even though I always thought you were strange, and a little psychotic, after that day… I cannot judge you. In fact, I have always liked you." She smiled nervously, "There was just something about you."

Will smiled back, and his scarred lips answered, "I always liked you too… And I am so happy to see you, and know that you survived."

Will excused himself from the table, picked up his cane and turned his back on Stephanie as she watched him walk away.

Suddenly, Will stopped in the middle of the floor. He thought back on his life, how he never truly received a chance to be a man. He began to ponder the many things he had missed out on, and it became clear what he had to do.

Will turned around and paced himself as he stepped back toward the table. He quickly opened his mouth as he once again witnessed her deep expression and soft lips, "I don't have anything going on tonight… Do you possibly… Want to sit with me for a while?"

Stephanie was silent for a moment and finally flashed the memorable smile Will remembered from high school, "I would actually like that very much."

Will sat down, and he and his first love from his teenage years sat and talked. For the first time in his life Will Thompson was finally a free man, and he could let go of all of the pain he had been tormented with for years.

CHAPTER TWELVE
Soldiering On

Scott also had a very difficult time coping with everything that had occurred, especially the loss of his brother and wife.

After he had dropped off Will and Michael, he had disregarded his own wounds and drove a few hours to the home of his mother and father. As he walked through their quiet abode with all items intact, he finally entered the bedroom and dropped hard to the carpet when he found the slain bodies of both of his parents.

His father looked as if he had suffered deep wounds to the throat and had killed his wife with a letter opener, which still protruded from her skull.

Scott cried deeply for a few minutes and finally stood up. His body ached as he reached the hallway and stopped when he found a photo of the family; Jason and Elizabeth smiling, and Cara and himself next to their mother and father beaming with nothing but pride and love for each other.

Scott tried to smile and pulled the picture from the hanger on the wall. He turned to look at the exterior of the home one last time and walked back to the car he had found.

As the wounded soldier drove onto the street of his own home, there was commotion everywhere as bodies were packed in trucks, city officials, law enforcement, and neighbors alike were scattered everywhere, starting a cleanup effort of their very own.

Scott exited the vehicle and walked toward the front door which was still ajar. As he reached the floor where his wife's body stained the carpet, he threw his body on top of hers, and placed his head on her cold chest, crying as he spoke to her as if she still breathed, "I promise you, no matter how hard… I will get through this. I promise you, Cara."

After lying next to his first and only love for an hour, he stood up slowly. His boots reached the messy kitchen to rummage the cabinets for dark garbage bags. His soles left the sticky tile and reached Cara resting on the once clean carpet, he slipped her lifeless body into the plastic and lifted her off of the ground.

The serious and strong Scott Cain walked out of the front door, and quickly pinpointed a truck picking up piles of the dead. He took a deep breath and with his mind racing and eyes wet, he lightly placed Cara Cain on the pile. He stood in front of her for a few moments, and finally spoke out loud, "Peace be with you, my love. Peace be with us all."

Years later, Scott Cain spent his time helping with relief efforts and even rejoined the military, this time the National Guard. He did everything that he could to hide the demons swarming inside of him, and repeatedly had brutal nightmares of Sara.

Scott also spent many hours with his newly formed family of Elizabeth and Matthew, and watched his nephew grow up to be a well-educated, though tormented, young man.

Elizabeth's dark times also remained, and she not only continued to assist the grieving. She also began to take up the mantle of her husband and wrote books. Her first book was called ALL HER CHILDREN: HOW TO FIND THE LIGHT IN THE DARKNESS. The positive and inspiring novel was a massive hit and Elizabeth won many high honor awards for all of her work throughout the world.

The inscription in the published book even read, *In Memory of Jason Cain: My Life and My Pain, My Love and My Healing.*

Scott and Elizabeth never married again, and realized that they were satisfied with being a small family and being with each other, just as Jason had desired.

Even through their bleakest times, the players in Sara's evil and twisted game, came into their own and continued to find themselves after being broken for so long.

CHAPTER THIRTEEN
Pain Never Truly Dies

Matthew Cain's transition into adulthood was not an easy one.

As a child he began screaming in the middle of the night, the shrill noise waking up his mother and forcing her to burst into his room, holding him as he practically hyperventilated.

Elizabeth sought counsel for her son, and he began sleeping by her side at night, afraid to be on his own.

As hard as Elizabeth tried, Matthew grew to become distant, and had to take prescriptions for his mental stability. His highly concerned mother did everything she could to keep his mind strong, including constant contact, and spending much time with doctors and therapists.

Across the world, life was very dark for many years, but it was never mentioned in the Cain household when matriarch and child moved out of the city into a new home.

Matthew reached his teens, and his mother insisted that he begin travelling with her, to witness her relief efforts. She also thought that doing good for other people would make her son feel love and kindness in his heart.

As she had predicted, Matthew began to heal from helping and doing deeds that benefitted others, and just like Elizabeth herself, Matthew started his own campaigns and groups to assist the grieving. He also started to jot down his own thoughts and write memoirs.

At eighteen, Matthew attended college for human relations, and when he graduated at age twenty-one, his beautiful silver-haired mother clapped proudly as her child beat the odds of life and succeeded.

He began working for a world organization, and started up the ranks as an intern which lead to him becoming an ambassador, leading groups of men and women who travelled around the planet helping the less fortunate, providing relief food and water to areas that needed the support.

Matthew Cain was located in Africa when he truly fixated his heart on Tara Phillips, a beautiful woman in his group who had journeyed far and wide, spreading hope and constant support.

The twenty-one year old leader smiled at his teammate who was only a few years younger as she wore a brown muscle shirt carrying bales of water, her brunette hair soaked with sweat.

The two spoke at length, and had wonderful conversations, and as they worked in a town outside of Egypt, they locked lips for the first time.

Matthew quickly became head over heels for the girl, and their fling was bumped up to relationship status quickly.

When the couple was stateside, they spent a lot of time together, having dinners with Elizabeth and seeing each other on many dates including restaurants, movies, and cutting loose at clubs and local bars.

But it was on a sticky evening in August, a month and half after they officially began dating that Matthew turned to Tara in his smaller living room and uttered three words strongly, "I love you."

The young woman touched his lightly bearded face and embraced him with extreme passion. The two lovers locked lips, and as pieces of clothing were thrown to the floor, they finally slammed down hard on Matthew's bed and rolled around, their hearts and pulses quickening.

Matthew began kissing her neck as Tara moaned softly. She straddled her lover, slipping herself into position for him to penetrate her. She began to writhe, and as Tara licked her lips, the young woman's angelic features now faced the ceiling above.

Matthew Cain fondled her breasts, thrusting slowly, and he had no clue that something similar to his past was occurring.

A massive and intense pain shot through Tara's brain instantly, and she witnessed many images of a young blonde woman in what appeared to be a dank cellar. She was adorned with a cloak and she opened a ratty leather book, cutting her finger and writing with her own life fluid, a spell that no one was aware of, in the book of spells that had started to fall apart through years of decay.

It was a spell that Sara had written through Susan's hand in the case of possibly being defeated: a backup plan.

Tara continued to moan. Her lover was unaware of what was to come, as she heard a voice in her mind,

"Time for you to take her firstborn... Betrayal will be felt as her heart is taken away!"

With that, Tara looked down at Matthew Cain. Her eyes were dead white and swirling with the same supernatural mist Matthew had witnessed on the street the day Sara Rinehart had taken over.

The only son of Elizabeth Rinehart looked back at the once beautiful relief worker who had captured his love, and a lump filled his throat as she growled and screamed familiar words, "Kill the pig!"

In a distant plane, once beautiful and lush, moaning human faces planted into the fixtures of the dark cavern chanted their sorrow, and on a floor made of human remains stood a throne created by jagged human bone and purified flesh. Sitting on the horrifying seat, bathing in little candlelight rested a dark-haired woman, and as she heard the cries of her ancestor's only son, a sly smile slid across her slender face.

Her legacy was thwarted, but she had made sure that Elizabeth would pay for her deceit, and knew exactly where to strike: her heart. Just as she and Jason had fallen in love quickly, the evil woman would take the life of her son when he felt the same, powerful feelings capture his own soul. Sara realized that it was the greatest revenge if all failed, and she foresaw her ancestor's love for her child before he was born. It became clear that his demise would be the ultimate weapon, her twisted final joke on the goodness that would eventually fill Elizabeth's soul once again over time.

As Patience McKinney had stated on the street after her battle to contain Sara many years before, "Pain never truly dies."

THE END

ABOUT THE AUTHOR

Rob has been in the horror industry for five years. He began as a columnist for Horrornews.net, and began acquiring his own celebrity interviews and attempting to build a name, as well as a following.

From there he started a horror podcast with best friend Amy Lynes, which quickly became a worldwide heard radio show. In his five years, Rob has written a screenplay for "The Binding" which is now being shopped throughout the entertainment industry with Executive Producer Sandra Araya, wife of SLAYER's Tom Araya in tow, has written and directed two short horror films, and he is currently working on his second story and third horror story, werewolf novel BAIT. He continues to show his love and entertain horror fans throughout the world, and is now Lead Genre Columnist/Interviewer with first monthly column, "House of Blood, Scars, and Sinister Stars" for up and coming music magazine, "Metal Onslaught".

Rob currently resides in Georgia with his sinister and lovely half, Melody, as well as her incredible anime loving daughter, Brianna, and his new and first son, Gabriel Vincent DiLauro, whose middle name is in honor of the legendary horror actor, Vincent Price.

CHECK OUT OUR OTHER TERRIFYING JOURNEYS WITH FEAR FRONT PUBLISHING'S TITLES AVAILABLE NOW